01013

FLINT'S GIFT

**By Richard S. Wheeler
from Tom Doherty Associates**

SKYE'S WEST
Sun River
Bannack
The Far Tribes
Yellowstone
Bitterroot
Sundance
Wind River
Santa Fe
Rendezvous*

Badlands
Cashbox
Fool's Coach
Goldfield
Montana Hitch
Second Lives
Sierra
Where the River Runs

SAM FLINT
Flint's Gift
Flint's Truth*
Flint's Honor*

*forthcoming

RICHARD S. WHEELER

FLINT'S
GIFT

Richard S Wheeler

FORGE
®

A TOM DOHERTY ASSOCIATES BOOK / NEW YORK

FLINT'S GIFT

This book is printed on acid-free paper.

A Forge Book
Published by Tom Doherty Associates, Inc.
175 Fifth Avenue
New York, NY 10010

Forge® is a registered trademark of
Tom Doherty Associates, Inc.

Library of Congress Cataloging-in-Publication Data

Wheeler, Richard S.
  Flint's gift / Richard S. Wheeler. — 1st ed.
    p. cm.
  "A Tom Doherty Associates book."
  ISBN 0-312-86366-7 (acid-free paper)
  I. Title.
  PS3573.H4345F57 1997
  813'.54—DC21   97-11938
                      CIP

First Edition: September 1997

Printed in the United States of America

0 9 8 7 6 5 4 3 2 1

Conquering, holding, daring, venturing as we go the unknown ways, Pioneers! O pioneers!

—Walt Whitman
Pioneers! O Pioneers!

FLINT'S
GIFT

1

A white-clad lady was coming. Sam Flint steered Grant and Sherman, his big mules, off the two-rut road and halted them. He would let the approaching spring wagon by.

He reproached the lazy mules for quitting before they had pulled his wagon entirely off the trail. "Git," he growled, snapping the lines over their croups. They took a calculated three steps and quit. It was enough.

He waited in the breezy morning of a glorious April day as she steered her big, rawboned dray horse toward him. He meant to visit with her a little; getting to know his new neighbors was not a bad idea.

She wore a snowy dress and a wide-brimmed straw hat that shaded her face. He fancied that she was pretty, but the deep shadow kept him from knowing. A mysterious lady, he thought. Beside her sat a skinny boy of nine or ten, who eyed him solemnly from squinty eyes. Married. Flint sighed. She veered slightly to pass, and he knew she didn't intend to stop, not even in this sweet, ascending morning. Her wagon box contained sacks of potatoes, flour, sugar, coffee beans, and other items, no doubt purchased at Payday.

"Ma'am," he said, "how far to Payday?"

Reluctantly, she tugged her horse to a stop directly across from him and studied him as if he were a Virginia smoked ham. She didn't smile. She didn't seem frightened. She simply gazed at him, taking him in, the way one would any stranger.

"Seven miles," she said in a melodic voice. "It's a lovely drive through birdsong. The whole trip, you'll hear birds singing their hearts out."

"Is this the Garden of Eden, ma'am?"

She didn't reply at first. Her gaze settled on the wagon sheet, which concealed his printing press and other equipment. "Yes, it is," she said, and slapped the lines over the croup of her dray. Her wagon creaked forward.

"But we haven't seen the serpent," she added as she passed him by.

In that kaleidoscopic moment, Sam Flint fell in love. He didn't mean to. It was a ridiculous thing to do, and she was plainly married. She wore an unadorned gold ring. He knew she was the most beauteous lady he had ever seen, with great, warm-brown eyes as friendly as guardian angels', and a generous mouth that suggested courage, and a flawless golden complexion that peeked out from under the puff-sleeved and blousy dress. Her hair, what little of it wasn't jailed by that glorious hat, glinted a rich auburn in the fresh, fragrant morning.

He turned to watch her as she drove away. The boy stared back. The woman sat ramrod straight. She was slender; Flint's two big hands would have compassed her waist.

He sighed. They all belonged to someone. Love had passed him by. No, that wasn't honest. He had passed love by. He had had his chance, long ago, right after the war that had left him so restless and torn.

He listened to the creak of her wagon dwindle into the bird-song. He listened to the world, and heard the faint rustle of young grasses teased by zephyrs and the laughter of the Tonto River. She was as gorgeous as this country, and as complex. He had never been in more soul-heartening country, and it was fitting that he should find a soul-satisfying woman in it. He was venturing through a twisting valley, with the great escarpment of the Mogollon Rim on his right. Long, grassy ravines toothed the rim, each issuing a rivulet, each girded by black ponderosa-clad slopes that surrendered to the emerald grasses of the bottoms. Now and then the fragrance of pine, pummeled from above by the strident sun, engulfed him, along with subtler scents from juniper and sage and the still-wet earth.

He gulped a vast lungful of the ambrosial air and continued toward Payday, his mind focused on the woman without a name who had transfixed him. He concentrated on her voice, as low and soft as a cello, and then upon her doe's brown eyes, and then upon the mystery of her words, and then upon the swan line of her neck, and the place at its base where her creamy flesh vanished into the blousy white dress. She was his age, and she heard birdsong.

He was almost engaged in adulterous fantasies. He turned his thoughts sternly away, into the joyous morning. That had been the only incongruent quality. Nature laughed this morning, but the woman had an aura of sadness.

He would make Payday by late afternoon. Curiosity seized him. Would it be as much a demi-paradise as Abel Greene and Basil Cutlip had suggested? Until the letter from these Payday businessmen, Sam Flint had never been invited to start a news-paper in a town. Their long missive had certainly been persua-sive. Payday, they explained, was the brand-new Tonto County seat, with a population of a thousand. It was situated on Alpine Creek in some of the sweetest ranching and farming country in the Southwest, with hip-high grama grasses, great pine forests, and a climate so temperate that a man could hardly experience discomfort, summer or winter.

Everything was ripe for a paper, they said. There would be the usual courthouse and county printing business. Merchants would be eager for a medium in which to advertise. The town was booming; settlers arrived every week, guaranteeing a shining future. There were six stores going up on Prescott Street even as they wrote. What's more, the Merchants' Committee, which Greene headed, would guarantee at least four pages of advertising per weekly issue. So come to Payday and prosper!

Flint had pondered it and bought it. He reckoned that a place like that ought to afford an editor a good living and an even better life. So he sent Greene and Cutlip his acceptance, sold his old rag to one Jasper Bulwinkle, an itinerant printer armed with a jug and a type stick, harnessed up Grant and Sherman, and headed west. He did that every little while, moved when the itch to see new country bested him. He always meant to put down roots and take life seriously, but his unruly soul vetoed the plan.

He harbored a few reservations about all this. The Payday businessmen did not inquire into his character or politics, a great oddity given the passions that ran strong in small towns. He'd been in Republican burgs and Democrat strongholds. He'd been in Confederate hotbeds and rock-ribbed Yankee towns. He had fought Mr. Lincoln's war long ago, and never concealed it from anyone. His little paper in Confederate Hotchkiss, Texas, had lasted two issues. Maybe Payday would prove to be another burg populated by bitter Southerners, and he would be booted out of this Eden just as fast. He was used to that. As long as they let him pack up his Cleveland flatbed press, his fonts and caseboxes, his barrels of powdered ink and his stacks of newsprint, he could start somewhere else, either as a job printer or a newspaper editor, or both.

He could not banish the lady from his mind. He would start

up a flinty little weekly in Payday if only to see her again, and pine away his life in Arizona Territory for someone he could never possess. It was as if he had been flattened by a roundhouse punch. As if the Almighty had knocked him senseless. His payday would be to set eyes upon her again. He hoped passionately that she was a widow. Or even a divorced woman. But that was all foolishness. He was coming to Payday for an overdue payday, that and the salubrious climate; nothing more. And he was an honorable man, not given to stealing wives.

But the image wouldn't go away. He knew he was in bad trouble, about to get himself horsewhipped, or hanged.

The road abandoned the Tonto River and wound its way up a wide valley watered by Alpine Creek. He passed surly longhorns chewing their cud in hip-high grasses, and the log-built headquarters for a ranching outfit he took to be the D-Cross from a brand burned into a gatepost. The whole valley glowed golden in the spring sun, a place so perfect for livestock that God must have invented it for that purpose.

To the south rose the dry, chaparral-covered Sierra Anchas, and beyond that, rough, thorny, fierce desert. That was desperate country; here was Eden, and he had already found its Eve. It occurred to him that maybe he would be the serpent.

The heat rose around noon, and he rested his faithful plodders in a live-oak grove beside the purling creek while he downed some jerky and hardtack. He had never been much for cooking, and made do with familiar army rations out of some sort of masochism. Surely this was milk-and-honey country, steak-and-yeasty-bread country, apple-cider country, not a land of toothbuster biscuits and leathery beef. He intended to indulge his appetites in Payday: fresh, moist bread with slabs of butter on it; fine standing rib roasts; new red potatoes—all slaked with a lusty ale or beer kept cool in a springhouse.

Sherman attacked the grasses, while Grant sawed his neck on

an oak, his only known stab at eccentricity. Sam Flint stared at puffballs in a bold blue heaven and contemplated the mystery of womanhood and the deeper mystery of a man's wild desire that could override even decency and propriety.

Two hours later, he rode into Payday, observing his new home keenly. The air was so clean and sweet that everything looked like it had been chiseled from ice. A sleepy town, he thought as he approached the town square, where a crude log courthouse squatted amidst huge cottonwoods. He surveyed the empty reaches of its two main streets, Basin and Prescott, according to the signs posted at the courthouse square, where they formed a T. Basin stretched east and west from the courthouse; Prescott stretched south. He spotted only two broncos, each anchored to a hitchrail and drowsing hipshot in the sun. Buildings with false fronts and galleries over the sidewalks fronted both sides of Prescott Street.

He discovered Abel Greene's Drygoods and Sundries Emporium first off, next to the Nye and Gulick Hardware Store, which was across from Short's Bakery. Farther south, a large mercantile bore the name of Cobb. He spotted the Tonto Basin Drayage Company, Wiley's Feed Store, Adolph Zeppel Fruits and Vegetables, and the Cochise Café.

Payday seemed a comfortable, serene place, well situated on sunny flats, well watered, well supplied with firewood. Its buildings were typical of frontier construction, either log or board-and-batten. At the southernmost reach of the town stood the Cook Brothers Livery Barn, so Flint steered his knotheads there, where he deposited them and the wagon for the time being, turning them over to a skinny, lantern-jawed hostler.

"For one day?" asked the wizened fellow.

"We'll see," Flint replied. "I'll put up the mules for one night—for now."

"Suit yourself," the hostler replied testily. "You can harness in the morning. I don't do it, except for an extry four bits. I don't much like mules. I got nothing but mule toothmarks on my hide."

"These are gentlemanly mules, Sherman and Grant by name."

The hostler stared sourly, spat, and led them away.

The gob of spit in the straw at his boots confirmed the Georgia drawl.

2

Flint stood in the rutted street near the courthouse, absorbing Payday. He wanted to get a feel for the place before he hunted up Abel Greene and Basil Cutlip. He understood what had drawn settlers here; he had never seen a place so beautiful, so promising. Even the soft, dry air eddying lazily through town brought its own comforts, and a hint of mountain or desert or stream.

The raw courthouse had a just-built look. Greene had said that Payday was a new county seat. The front half of the building appeared to be an administrative office; a middle area probably was a courtroom. A sign directed one to the sheriff's office at the rear.

Sam Flint was not immune to the glories of nature, or to the aesthetics of this place snugged smugly below the Mogollon Rim. Nor was he immune to the potential for wealth here: the verdant grasses and rushing creeks that made the country perfect for stock-raising; the potential for minerals in the convoluted, dry mountains to the south; the abundance of water, always precious in the West, and its promise of truck gardens and crop-farming.

Settlers had drifted here, felt their hearts leap, and had stayed, some upon self-sufficient ranches, others in this little town. He meandered its broad, unnamed side streets, often in the shade of arching cottonwoods that long antedated Payday's population. Most of the log business buildings now boasted board-and-batten false fronts that made them look nobler than the low structures snaking back from the street. Many of the private homes were log, too, though the newer ones were whitewashed plank cottages, often with gingerbread trim to announce the arrival of civilization in the Tonto Basin. In the transparent air and under the kiss of the benevolent sun, they glowed cheerfully.

They sat on generous lots, many with carriage barns, most with wells, all with privies located at the rear property line. A few had log springhouses or earthen root cellars. In the amiable streets, catching the serene mood of Payday, Flint saw rather few people for a town of a thousand, and those mostly ragamuffins at play.

Were these educated people? Would they buy and read a weekly paper? He could not bear to condescend to readers. He had grown up the son of an academy headmaster; he was fluent in Latin and had mastered Classical Civilization and Literature. There were places all over the West that were too primitive, too mind-numbing, too devoid of amenities, for his tastes. And other places that would resist his paper right off. He would find out soon whether this town, like the hostler, was Confederate. He wouldn't last a month in a town full of Southerners.

As he ambled through Payday, feeling the velvety, sweet air of the Tonto Basin temper the sun, something began to trouble him, and he finally realized what it was: Payday could not possibly contain a thousand people. Four or five hundred at the maximum. Maybe enough for a small paper, with the county legal notices supplying the bulk of his revenue, but not enough for a living.

And there was something else: half a dozen empty stores. One abandoned log building announced itself as a bakery. He peered through a tiny glass window upon the gloom within. Another had been a smithy. Another large frame building with a gallery in front had a single tenant—the law office of a man named Culbertson—in one corner, but the other suites, two upstairs and one down, looked empty. He found an abandoned café with a forlorn "Home Cooking" sign wobbling in the eddying zephyrs.

Things obviously were not as the merchants' letter had described them. Well, if Payday wasn't the town he had been led to believe it was, he would harness up Grant and Sherman in the morning. He sighed. Greene and Cutlip were probably just eager promoters and businessmen, booming Payday, making things sound a lot better than they were. It was an ordinary human failing. But a newspaper was particularly vulnerable, and some towns simply weren't suitable.

His tour had awakened him to certain realities, and he now took a keener and more critical view of Prescott Street. The place had no hotel. He had seen a forlorn rooming house, though. The lack of a hotel meant that few people traveled to Payday, and he could well understand why: the place was fifty miles from any important road. Tucson lay far to the south in desert country. Prescott was the closest town, but no one went to Prescott by way of Payday.

If this was Eden, it was also the end of the world. He began to stroll around town looking for a stage station, and found none. Neither Butterfield nor Wells Fargo came here. He could not find a freighting yard or a forwarding company, except for the local drayage firm. Who wagoned supplies to Payday, and where did they switch teams? A schedule nailed to the front of the Tonto Basin Drayage Company yielded the information that a weekly mudwagon headed for Prescott, and another to the Fort Apache Reservation to the east. Obviously, few came to Payday, and few left.

As the afternoon lengthened, the town began to quicken. Four saloons lay at the eastern extremity, saddle horses slouched at their hitchrails. Two of the saloons had no visible names. The other two suggested a ranching clientele: the Salvation, and the Drover's Rest. A merchant in a white apron stood in the double doors of his grocery, surveying the silent street. A woman in a dark skirt, puffy white blouse, and straw hat hurried somewhere. Two men in their shirtsleeves and waistcoats stood talking under a gallery. The Cochise Café, obviously the gathering place for town people who didn't visit saloons, looked to be prosperous and busy.

Not a thousand people. Greene and Cutlip hadn't been square. It was time to look the men up. Payday was nothing but a sleepy little hamlet far off the trail, without enough commerce or civilization to support a newspaper—especially the kind of paper that Sam Flint liked to write.

He had passed Greene's drygoods emporium, with its gilded sign, several times, but had avoided going in. Not just yet. But now he walked up a block, studied the building, and entered into a pungently fragrant interior, passing shelves of ready-made shirts and pants, bolts of denim and calico, and racks of dresses mass-produced with Singer's stitching machine.

At the rear of the store, he confronted a burly, bald fellow with the devil's own eyes. The man had half a left arm.

"A present from the Army of Northern Virginia, canister right into my trench," Greene said. "Who are you?"

"Sam Flint. I was with the Ohio Volunteers," Flint replied, surveying the man who'd co-signed the letter inviting him to Payday.

Greene was big, faintly truculent, and on the prod. "You're taller than I thought; your nose isn't as red, and the last thing I expected is a tweed jacket with elbow patches."

"That sums me up as well as anything, Mr. Greene."

"Take a building and start publishing," Greene said. "There's a few."

"We'll talk first."

A bonneted customer interrupted. Much to Sam Flint's astonishment, Abel Greene hefted a bolt of muslin, unrolled it one-handed, measured it one-handed, cut a piece for the lady, and poked the bolt under his shortened arm while he folded up the fabric.

"It's forty a yard, Catherine."

"Put it on account."

Greene hesitated for a moment.

"I'll send a good steer," she said and walked out.

Greene tucked the bolt away and turned to Flint. "That's our problem. We need a paper. Not much cash in town. We need new blood."

"And I'll be paid in heifers I can't eat or pasture," Flint said. "This town doesn't have a thousand people."

Greene stared. Odd how big Greene looked. The man filled space, and Flint had an itch to step backward.

"Six hundred. There's three hundred more in the county, on the ranches. And we're buying a hundred subscriptions you'll send all over the Southwest. That's a thousand."

"We?"

"Town Merchants' Committee."

Flint pondered that. "You fought for the Union."

"I did. We're about half Union, half Reb here. It makes bad blood out on the ranches, but not in town. The saloons are segregated. You wouldn't want to hoist a beer in the Drover's Rest."

"What about the two without a sign?"

"Union saloons north side, Reb south side. They're likely to horsewhip a man if he walks into the wrong place."

"You're losing people. I walked Payday. Some county printing, legal notices—not enough to keep me aloft."

Greene shrugged. "Things'll change in a year or two. You're just getting in ahead of the crowd."

"Or three or five? This isn't what I was led to believe, Greene."

Greene didn't retreat an inch. "Temporary. If you want to turn tail, go ahead. Who wants a yellow newspaper anyway? Stick with the place and you'll make it."

The truculence rode in his tone again. He was dodging the question of misrepresentation. Sam Flint had driven four hundred miles on wilderness roads, in danger from renegade Apaches and bandits, on the strength of Greene's invitation.

"What connects this town to anything? One stage a week to Prescott? One wagon a week to Fort Apache?"

Greene seemed to deflate a little. "That's the nub of it. We've got the best ranching country in the Republic—water, grass, shelter. We grow beef like it was weeds, and there's no place to sell it. Some ranchers sell to the reservations. Some sell a few to Fort Whipple over to Prescott. We'll get a railroad in a few years— Santa Fe'll come through north of here. Closest railroad is the Southern Pacific. They're building east across the bottom of the Territory. California's a big market for beef, but we've got to drive to Yuma, down the Gila River to the rails. That's the problem. It costs too much, and it's full of renegade Apaches."

"So I'm here five years early. Is that it?"

Big Abel Greene wiped his bald head with his good hand and leaned over his plank counter. "You haven't got eyes that see a thing, Flint. There never was country like this, not in all the world. A man comes here, his heart almost bursts. He sees those thick, green grasslands and the clear water and the springs. He sees the good ponderosa black and thick up the slopes. He smells the sage, and feels the sweet air on his face, always mild. A man can hardly work up a sweat. Winters are plumb fun. A little snow now and then, mostly warm sun. Summers hardly even hot. Spring, like today, almost busting its britches. Fall, it's sweet-corn, apple-picking time. Deer and elk, wild turkey for the hunter.

"A man comes here and his heart brims over, like the cup of God, and it don't matter much if he has to wait a while to make a living. We get by because we're seeing the horizons, the sunrises. This place is sweet enough to make a bad man good. We're a little shy of cash, you bet. This place is Eden, Flint. Almost like it was made without Original Sin. You come here, settle in, and watch everything multiply in the Land of Milk and Honey. It ain't just money that brings a body here, Flint. It's the song in the sky. You won't write news here; you'll write poetry. It puts a man on his knees, thanking God."

Flint stared, amazed.

3

Sam Flint stepped into a late-afternoon cool and drew a deep breath. What was it about this air and this place? Everything here evoked a sense of well-being. The cottonwoods, in new leaf, had been here long before Payday, and were blessing the whole town with shade. The soft, dry air calmed the soul. The laughing creeks and waving grasses spoke of abundance. The scent of sage in the air intoxicated his spirit. He didn't even feel weary after his long drive.

No wonder people had come to this remote corner and stayed in spite of the isolation. Something here stirred a man to believe in the goodness of nature, and in the blessedness of life. He was not immune to any of it. The peace he felt here was unlike anything he had ever experienced. He knew that these odd tugs of the heart were interfering with his evaluation of Payday. Abel Greene had answered a lot of his questions, sometimes reluctantly, sometimes irritably, as if Flint were too dumb to see the obvious.

Payday was a town waiting for connections with the outside world. The ranches here could not sell the beef they raised. The town survived on a mountain of debt. The ranchers owed the merchants; the town people owed each other; the merchants owed their suppliers. Barter had become the favored transaction. Bales of wool bought beans and sugar; title to a dozen calves bought ranch supplies. The county paid its clerk and lawman and judge with warrants based on unpaid back taxes. Nothing would change until a railroad came, or until Payday became large enough to attract some shipping companies that would freight in wagonloads from Tucson or Albuquerque.

There could hardly be a worse place to start a newspaper, Flint mused, still standing in the wide street. On the other hand, all he really needed was enough to buy newsprint and ink, and to pay some postage. Greene had laid it all out: Payday needed a paper to boom the town, to bring in enough settlers to make it all work; a paper could plug for a railroad, make noise whenever the Territorial legislature met, and write glowing things about life in the Eden of the West. Payday merchants needed to advertise, even if they couldn't pay cash for it. Ads would stir commerce, draw in business, create demand. Payday needed a paper badly. Without one, it would probably die, and the county seat would skedaddle somewhere else.

All of which was bad news to Flint. Payday would give him no independence and permit him no criticism. Let him express a doubt, and the merchants would balk. Let him poke fun, and subscribers would cancel. It was all too desperate. He should harness up his big mules and drive out *now*, before this place seduced him any more. He'd simply ruin himself by staying here. End up broke and in debt and unable to start somewhere else because a sheriff's seizure had tied up all his equipment. It might be five years before the Santa Fe would run rails through northern Arizona, and two or three before the town would be large enough to command frequent stages and big freight outfits—and support a weekly paper properly. They wanted him a lot worse than he needed them.

He decided to leave in the morning.

It was time to eat. He headed for the café, wishing she would be there. The woman he had talked to briefly on the road. The married woman with the boy. The woman whose open face and graceful eyes, almost hidden under the straw hat, had tripped something within him he couldn't name. He would put her out of mind. He was an honorable man. It was all just a lonely man's fancy. A wave of melancholy washed through him. He couldn't satisfy both halves of his soul: the restless, traveling, frontier editor half, and the other half that yearned for a wife to love, a home and family, roots, sons and daughters, and the sharing and intertwining of lives and wills.

He would always be at war with himself. He was nothing but a lonely adventurer, an overeducated itinerant editor and printer fleeing domestic life, while dreaming of magical women who would transform him into a rooted old oak tree, giving comfort and shade to his loved ones.

There was no woman like that, no woman who would even consider a match with a man of his predilections. Hadn't he fled a lovely, gracious woman almost at the altar, back in Ohio after the war? He remembered the whole episode sadly. The pain of it had never left him. In a panic, a day before the wedding, he had fled down the Ohio River, leaving behind him a fiancée who loved him madly, was eager to care for him, and who would have been the perfect helpmeet for a schoolmaster and scholar.

Every time he thought of that shameful affair—of his desperate flight, his lame apology mailed later, his stunned family, the bride's angry parents—he was filled anew with mortification. He wasn't the sound man he wished to be. It would be a just punishment upon him if he were never to enjoy the love of a woman again, having thrown away the sweetest maiden any man could ever hope to find.

The robust, rosy woman who ran the café didn't take his order. Instead, she appeared at his rough wooden table bearing a plate loaded with a gigantic steak, potatoes, some wintered garden vegetables, and a mug of coffee.

"You looked hungry, so I cooked a big one," she said.

"But I—"

"In this place, you take what we dish out. Cobbler for dessert," she said. "It's the four-bits dinner . . . You just passing through?"

"Yes."

"I had a notion you might be the newspaper man we're waiting for. That tweed jacket did it."

"I, ah . . . was thinking about it."

"So you're him. Mr. Sam Flint himself. You eat, and you'll change your mind. I'm Vera."

"Well, thank you, Vera."

"You go ahead and make a hole in that meat. It's on the house."

"Oh, I'll pay."

"No, I'm gonna hit you up for an ad. You eat free. I get this beef free anyway. No one's got any cash around here, but that don't even slow us down."

"Why, thank you," he mumbled.

She studied him for a moment. "I want to see if you're a real eater or just a puny eater. I don't trust puny eaters."

"Oh, I'm a real eater."

He dug in, and she returned to her stove and her other customers, all of them men. They seemed an amiable lot, mostly sunscorched drovers from the ranches, and a few clerks and businessmen.

The T-bone steak had been invented in heaven. He downed it and the potatoes and the carrots out of someone's root cellar, and then the cobbler she laid before him. He pulled a few shinplasters from his pocket, but she turned indignant.

"I'm working up some space in your paper," she said. "Did I make a steak or didn't I?"

"You cooked a memorable steak, madam."

"Well, that's Payday for you," she said.

A dozen males gazed blandly at him when he left. Payday seemed to be a town without the desperado element he had run into here and there in the West.

He stepped into a darkness as soft as cotton. A half-moon had poked over the forests to the northeast, shedding creamy light upon the amiable village. He sucked in the air, wanting more of it than he could draw into his lungs. Pungent juniper and sage and pine scents drifted off the towering rims to the north and east, scenting the night as sweetly as a cedar chest. He was ready for a good sleep, after a long day of traveling and a huge meal. Something about the air eddying down from above was intoxicating him. It was early, really. Down the street, the saloons were just cranking up for the ni⁻ht's festivities. These would be pretty tame in Payday. He'd seen no sign of a sporting district, or of dives, or of the hardcases that patrolled them.

He remembered that Payday had no hotel. It would be the livery barn, then—the time-honored shelter of men as well as horses. He would spread his bedroll out on the hay and be comfortable enough. He meandered toward the livery barn beyond the courthouse square, passing the abandoned bakery as he walked. Moonlight glinted off the gilded letters of a new sign that hung above the door and window. Now there was an odd thing: a coal-oil lamp burned within. He stepped toward the window and found himself peering into a rectangular room in which his entire printing shop stood. There was his Cleveland flatbed press. And yonder, on a long worktable, rested his caseboxes. There was his paper, the ink table, the ink, the stone, the forms, and all.

He stepped back, irked at this cavalier treatment of his private property. The new sign announced "THE PAYDAY PIONEER." Moonlight glinted from the gilded letters. He found the door unlocked and entered, peering about angrily. He would have to load all his stuff in the morning.

The note on the counter, under the buttery light of the lamp, caught his eye. "Mr. Flint," it read. "Welcome to Payday. This will be your shop. There's an apartment in the rear with a good bunk in it and a cookstove. It'll be a place to roost tonight. If you don't want to stay, we'll pack you up in the morning and see you off with regret. We made up the sign a week ago, but if it don't please, we'll do another for you. Tomorrow morning, Basil Cutlip will stop by with a deed, and you can file it at the courthouse. There's a one-dollar filing fee. Mr. Cutlip's a land broker and his office is yonder in the biggest building. He's also the county judge, but there's no crime here and no one sues anyone, so he don't have much on his docket.

"Now if this don't please you, just take it all kindly and we'll keep on looking for a newspaper. There's twelve of us in the Pay-day Merchants' Committee, but it was me and Cutlip and Ike Cobb that unloaded you. The wagon's out back. The mules are in the pen out back with a good bait of hay, courtesy of the livery barn. Now you just make yourself to home, and wait for tomorrow. Sincerely, Abel Greene."

Sam Flint overcame his irritation. He found his trunk unopened in the apartment, beside the bunk. His wagon was parked in back; and Sherman and Grant, in a good stout pen, were yawning at the moon. These businessmen were a bit presumptuous, but this was a sterling thing to do, and he appreciated it even if he felt like he was walking into a baited bear trap.

He didn't know whether he would stay. But he was mighty tired of wandering; six months in one burg, eight in another, always among strangers. Maybe he should put down roots. Make friends. Meet old cronies each night for a mug of suds. Maybe . . . find a wife, start a family, build a home, acquire some property and security and comfort. It'd be tough for a few years, but it might be possible at that. He was ready for a home.

Judge Cutlip had scarcely arrived at his office after his morning constitutional before young Flint appeared at the oaken door. The newspaperman surprised him a little. Flint turned out to be a big chap, lean, with regular features and a solemnity about him that spoke well of his character. He eyed Cutlip through gold-rimmed spectacles that gave him a bookish look, along with that amazing, shapeless tweed coat that made him seem more of a dusty scholar than an enterprising editor. Cutlip had expected someone more cynical and boozy.

"You're Mr. Cutlip," the fellow said.

"Yes indeed. Basil Cutlip. Judge Cutlip. District court here, but there's not enough business in the courthouse to occupy me fifteen minutes a week."

Flint peered about the office owlishly, obviously impressed. Cutlip had designed his chambers with the intent of impressing people. For a raw frontier town, his office was something of a wonder, wainscoted with walnut imported from Tennessee; wallpapered to its high, white ceiling, where the burgundy-colored paper met a fluted cornice. A fine library of law books and other texts lined one side. Maps hung on the other walls, and a globe stood in a corner. A fieldstone fireplace added a certain bonhommie in chillier seasons, and the waxed desk offered enough acreage for unrolling plat maps and keeping subordinates at a proper distance.

Flint absorbed all that, coming to the obvious conclusion that Judge Basil Cutlip was a man of substance, which was what the judge intended, even if it wasn't exactly the case.

"Have a seat, fellow; if you indulge in fat black cigars, have one." He gestured toward a small glass cigar safe on his desk.

Flint shook his head impatiently, the motion of an ascetic. "I'm trying to puzzle this out. I certainly appreciate the quarters your people provided, sir, but I really haven't made up my mind—"

"Of course not. A businessman can't come to conclusions about a place in an hour. You'll want to know the risks and rewards, project profits, get a feel for things. You're telling me you have a good head on you, and that's the sort we want in Payday."

"Well, yes, but there's more to it than that. A newspaper that's worth anything has certain qualities—"

Basil Cutlip cut him off. "Of course, of course. You're not beholden to me or anyone else, least of all to the Merchant's Committee. Now I've got up the deed, and I'll sign it over to you. Bought the building from a baker for a modest sum—he complained about the delightful climate and yearned for something with authentic winters—and thought it'd be a perfect plant for a weekly. There's no obligation at all."

"Sorry," said Flint, "but I can't do that. If I stay here—and I'm undecided about that—I'd buy it. No gifts. An editor can't be beholden. What did you pay for it?"

"A trifle. A hundred dollars, lock, stock, and barrel. The fellow was in a hurry to leave."

"Then—if I stay—I'll buy it for that."

"Why, there's no need, Flint. As it happens, I'll be advertising. I'll just use up the credit that way."

"Advertising?" Flint seemed faintly startled.

"Look about you, young man. Is this a judge's office? Of course not. I'm a broker and an entrepreneur. I'm a land office. I also buy and sell beef. I float businesses and organize stock companies. I'm a lobbyist for certain interests. I'm the closest thing to a bank in Payday, marketing letters of credit and debt instruments for a small commission. I'm a landlord. I own this building and a dozen others. I've got three more going up that I intend to rent to newcomers."

"Where are you from, sir?" Flint asked.

"Galena, Illinois. Prettiest burg in the whole region, Mr. Flint. We—my Violet and I—were neighbors of the Grants, Ulysses, of course. Fine old brick manse there, servants, doing just fine until the crash of seventy-three when we, ah, met some serious reverses. River shipping. Lumber speculation. Lead mines. Railroad bridges and right-of-way. Things like that. Well, frankly—" he let Flint enjoy some intimacy—"my assets were all but wiped out. I brought my lady—we left behind two grown sons—out here to repair our fortunes. That's what the West's for, you know. Second chances. All a chap has to do is come here and start plucking the tree."

"You seem to be doing well."

"This? It's nothing. Wait until the railroad comes. Wait until Payday grows a little."

"I'm told the railroad is still several years away, sir."

"Oh, I don't believe it. The Santa Fe's over Raton Pass now. Southern Pacific's through Yuma and pushing east toward El Paso. I'm dickering with the Santa Fe. They plan to follow the old Atlantic and Pacific route along the thirty-fifth parallel, north of here, but there's not a soul on it; nothing but a few Navajo sheepherders. Now all they have to do is drop a little south, come through here and Prescott and follow the Bill Williams River out to California— why, here's where the people are. Or will be, anyway. There's nothing but deserts north of here. But look at this! Water, timber, coal, cattle, towns filling up.

"I tell you what, Flint. I'm buying railroad right-of-way as fast as I can get it. There's an obvious route here, all engineered. But if I can't get the Santa Fe through here—right through Payday— why, I'm mapping a spur up from Tucson. And meanwhile, I'm pushing for some settlement. Lure the settlers here and we'll have plenty of freight and stagecoach connections. I talked the government into surveying the whole basin, and they did. Just finished a month ago. The baselines are in. We can write up a legal description of any land here. Now it's all open to homesteading. Anyone can file. No more squatting. A lot of people filed on their land these past few weeks." He grinned. "Some of the ranchers don't like it a bit. Especially Buell. But that's progress.

"Now here's where you come in. Luring the settlers. I'm building a railroad to Prescott—at least when I'm better capitalized. I can't get a railroad land grant out of Congress, so I'm doing it the hard way. I've got proxies filing homesteads along the right-of-way. They get it for a dollar and a quarter an acre after six months; sell it to me for a dollar and a half. I'm getting timber-culture lands, and now we've got the Desert Land Act coming in. Irrigate a little desert and you get a section for two bits an acre.

"It'll be an Arizona empire, Flint. You'll be in on the ground floor. There's free land everywhere. File on it. You're a veteran, I take it. Get a hundred sixty. It's yours. Buy some of these town lots. Promote the railroad. Get your paper out to the whole world. Boom Payday—it's the closest thing to Eden since Adam and Eve. Bring 'em in by the wagonload and get rich, Flint. Run up the price of land. With every load of settlers we get in here, the faster we can lure the Santa Fe south, or get ourselves a spur. Give us a railroad and we can ship all these longhorns out and supplies in. That takes a newspaper more than anything."

Flint absorbed the oration. "You want a newspaper to help your fortunes along," he said softly.

Basil Cutlip caught a tone in the fellow's voice that required caution. The judge was a man of the world. He could look into souls, discover motives, appeal to dreams. That's how he had succeeded. Flint's gaze was not friendly.

"A newspaper," Cutlip said carefully, "makes a marketplace. I hope you'll share my vision, of course. I'd like to see a paper tell the world of this Eden, this demi-paradise, this opportunity, this Payday—but even if you should pursue a, ah, different policy, why, the advertising, the circulation, the notice that comes to any town that boasts a paper . . . why, those would suffice nicely. Now, Flint, please understand: a paper would be most helpful to Payday, but not the sole source of influence. I'm in correspondence with countless powerful people. Does that address your concerns?"

"Partially."

"Ah, I thought it might. You wish to preserve your editorial independence. I would too, in your shoes. I'm not insensitive to the needs of an upright editor. I'd like to be able to criticize public officials." He smiled. "A paper sometimes objects to a verdict or a ruling. Or opposes one or another faction in commerce. You would rather not be beholden. Well, you won't be. Shall I sign over the deed?"

"I'd like to talk to some people first. Who would you recommend?"

"You're a cautious fellow, but I admire that. You've a good business head on you. I'd rather see a fellow like you running *The Payday Pioneer* than some reckless fellow who's a blowhard and fool. Sure, there's some substantial men to talk to here. Some are friends, some are rivals, none are enemies. I haven't any. Now, you might start with Ike Cobb. He's a veteran, like you, and he's got the hardware and ranch-supply outfit down the street. I hear tell he's won a Congressional Medal of Honor, but he never talks of it. And you ought to run out to Clayton Buell's ranch east of town. He's the biggest stock grower in the area, more beeves than he can

get rid of. He's all for getting us a railroad but doesn't want settlers. He's a Georgia man, had a hard time in the late apocalypse,
and he's starting over. He opposes me a lot—I'll tell you that. No
love lost between us. He wants the basin to stay like it is. But talk
to him anyway. You'll get perspective.

"And you just try Nicholas Rakoczy, off to the east, between
here and the Fort Apache reserve. Now there's a peculiar case.
Hungarian from Budapest, married to an American lady, Merry-
Grace. He never saw the tail end of a longhorn before he came
here, but he bought a thousand beeves and set 'em loose; and he's
fooling with more stuff—why, it'd take a crazy Hungarian to think
'em up. Flax. He's trying to raise flax, and those peppers they use
for paprika, and some feed grains, like barley, and he's got a vine-
yard going—some green Hungarian grapes he started from cuttings—and he's planning to cut timber and mill it into planks and
two-by-fours. Plenty of pine around here.

"He should be back now. He's been driving a herd to Yuma
and the railroad. It's a break-even proposition by the time the
Southern Pacific docks him for the long haul to the coast. He has
to pay off his trail crew and take his trail losses, but it gets him
cash. It's got to be done in the early spring, when there's enough
new grass along the Gila and it's not roasting hot. Trouble is,
there're renegade Apaches along that road. Gila Road's no picnic
if Victorio's cherubs are spoiling for some loot. We can't ship beef
east—Texas licks us—but California can't get enough beef. Try
him. Try anyone in town. I'll introduce you to twenty—"

Flint held up a hand. "I'll talk to some more. But I'm getting
a pretty good idea of the place now. You're all waiting for the payday. After I look around, I'll let you know whether I'm staying."

The solemn young man with the owl eyes annoyed Cutlip, so
he simply smiled and nodded. A few moments later, the judge ushered him out, aware that he knew almost nothing about the young
editor. Hardly more than what Abel Greene had told him. But he'd

find out more, soon, and adjust his plans accordingly. Flint would stay, of course. That was the beauty of Payday. The whole gorgeous basin was tinder for the bonfires of hope, and Flint's own would catch fire soon, especially with a nudge or two.

5

Flint stepped into a bright morning. A lazy breeze rustled the new-minted cottonwood leaves, and the whole world rejoiced in its life. He peered benevolently at this Eden in the wilderness, glowing in lambent light. Dappled shade danced on the earthen street. The air had been tinctured with sagebrush, adding a faint pungency to it.

He liked Judge Cutlip. Oh, the man was ambitious, but that was usually an asset for a town. Just such restless men made towns prosper and grow, and enabled dreams of countless settlers to come true. With an amiable candor, Cutlip had described his interests, his operations, his hopes, his skills, and even his follies. He would no doubt repair his fortunes here; what was the West for, if not to put a man on his feet? From Cutlip's fertile mind had sprung all sorts of schemes for luring the Santa Fe Railroad and building up enough population to entice freight outfits and stage-coaches. If there were no markets in Payday, Basil Cutlip would create them. If markets were too far away, he would find cheap ways to haul goods.

Flint decided that this bright morning would be a good moment to further explore Payday. He knew which way his thoughts were leaning, but he just wanted a little better feel of the place. So he began a cheerful stroll through town, pausing at stores and offices, poking behind buildings, examining houses, sheds, corrals and barns, and studying the means by which six hundred people supported themselves.

Flint paced easily along alleys, past laundry flapping gently in the velvet air, past root cellars, vegetable gardens, summer kitchens, two-hole outhouses, hay piles, parked buggies, spring wagons, penned saddle horses, and flocks of chickens. Payday had been settled by families, unlike so many of the frontier camps he had wandered through. Here were women on the streets, many in white blouses and slim skirts, a few with parasols. Here were barefoot imps wheeling like flocks of crows. He saw boys chopping kindling or stacking firewood, youths grooming their paint ponies, girls shopping at the greengrocer and buying ribbons from Abel Greene. He saw no wealth, but he saw no bitter poverty either. No grand manse stood on a hill above the rest.

The fanciest place was a whitewashed square of board-and-batten with a veranda on each side but the north. He suspected it was Basil Cutlip's home, but it was no doubt nothing compared to the house the judge had left in Galena. He hunted for some grim corner—some place of shanties, sewage, depraved or corrupt people—and found none, not even in the vicinity of the saloons crowded together at the east end of Payday. He saw no Apaches, though the Fort Apache Reservation was not distant, nor did he see any Mexicans, whose country this had recently been, and wondered if any lived here.

He inspected a few stores and found the goods skimpy and high-priced, a sure sign that the supply lines to Payday were long and treacherous. People here were self-sufficient and made do. But that wouldn't help his advertising revenue. He might barter for a lot of things, but he still needed cash to order newsprint— no doubt from California—and ink, and pay the postmaster, and get new fonts as his old ones wore out. But what was a newspaper for, anyway, if not to ease the lot of the town in which it published? A lively paper inviting settlers to Payday, extolling the town's beauty and serenity, its opportunities, its almost medicinal ambience, would be just the ticket to tie the town to Tucson and Yuma, the West Coast and Albuquerque.

His meander made up his mind. He would create *The Payday Pioneer*, the name that had been chosen for him by the Committee. It would be touch and go for a while, but then things would ease; he'd have subscribers, advertising, and plenty of local news. And all to himself, too. No competitor in his right mind would try to establish a second paper in a small, isolated burg like this.

God help him if he made a mistake. He had done that often enough, moving out dead broke, unable to buy even the newsprint to start up a new paper in some other little hamlet. Once he had even lost a pair of draft mules to a creditor. On those occasions, he had bummed his way through the trouble, doing job printing— every little town welcomed a job printer as if he were a manufacturer of greenbacks. In bad times, he had left a trail of broadsides, posters, menus, programs, and notices behind him.

He should talk to more people, and yet he didn't need to. Something was stirring in him, driving him to the decision even without consulting the barkeeps—always great sources of information about a town—or the tonsorial artist, another great source, or the sheriff or county clerk.

A sheriff could be a good source. Most sheriffs could tell him exactly what troubles a town was experiencing. But Payday appeared to be a place without serious crime, and the sheriff probably did little more than collar rowdy boys and jug cowboys who'd had a snort too much.

He knew he would stay, and the knowledge had nothing to do with business. For the first time in Sam Flint's life, he had stumbled into a Garden of Eden. It promised the end of loneliness, a check on his wanderlust, and a balm for his restless itches. He would sink roots here, as deep as those of the live oaks. He would find the lovely woman he was always reaching for. Reason had nothing to do with it. Payday beckoned and seduced and whispered to his heart. He sighed, half alarmed at his lapse of caution, half delighted to be led along a primrose path at last.

Decisions always came hard. He was past thirty and aware that life was fleeting, and one could hardly retract the past. In those cruel years of war, he had seen friends and strangers die at eighteen, twenty, twenty-five, the wily veteran and the green recruit alike. Where did they go? Sometimes their souls cried to him, whispered of cheated hopes, love unrequited, dreams bled into the reddened soil of Virginia or Maryland or Pennsylvania. He had survived the war, he didn't know why, but the experience had left him restless, impatient, and unable to quiet his vagabond urgings.

Until now. Surely this demi-paradise, far from the travails of the world, was what he had always wanted, what would heal the haunting of his soul. His mind made up, he retraced his steps to Judge Cutlip's commodious office.

"I'll stay," he said.

Cutlip peered at him over a black cigar, registering that, and smiled. "This is the day when Payday begins its march to success," he said. "I'll prepare some real estate advertising. I want the honor of being your first account. It won't be long now until we all are prospering. Did you talk to a few of our good folks?"

"Not a one, sir. I walked the town. I looked at laundry on lines, children, women carrying parasols, boys combing paint ponies, outhouses, gardens, and haystacks. I hiked clear around the saloons, looking for the hidden hells, and didn't find them. I'll meet your citizens soon enough. My habit is to produce a pamphlet advising advertisers about rates and deadlines, and then distribute it, selling ads and collecting a few stories."

"I see you've a little experience at this."

Flint sighed. "Too much. I'll get started now, but later I want to consult you on freighting supplies in here—paper, ink, what have you. And where's the post office? I didn't find it."

"Inside Cobb's Mercantile. Cobb doubles as postmaster. They give the job out to veterans, you know."

"Well, I'll need to mail the paper. I use the mail and newsboys for circulation."

"He'll take care of you. And I'll be here whenever you want to sit down and learn how to move freight. There's no wire, and everything is slower than snails. Military telegraph at Fort Whipple, though. Would you like that deed now?"

Flint hesitated. "Yes, sir—as long as we both understand that my paper will not be beholden to anyone or any faction."

"It's best that way, Flint. I'd have it no other."

"Well, then, you've done me a turn. And you have a hundred dollars of credit in your advertising account."

"I'll use it in a hurry," Cutlip said, dipping his nib in the inkpot and signing a deed with a flourish. He handed the paper to Flint. "You can register it yonder in that ugly log pile any morning. There's not enough work to employ a clerk afternoons."

Flint trotted over to the courthouse, kicking up dust as he walked across its parched lawn, and found no one in the entire building. He retreated to his new quarters, feeling oddly melancholy. He usually felt that way after making a large decision, not because he feared he had chosen wrong, but because he had cut off other options.

That afternoon he organized his sanctum, as an editor's lair was called, and set his flyer, sliding letters into his type stick as he plucked them from the California caseboxes. He could set type almost as fast as he could compose. He rarely wrote up a story these days; he simply set it as he composed, and it came out just as well as if he had scribbled it all out on foolscap.

The Payday Pioneer would be published on Thursdays, cost ten cents or five dollars a year, and be politically independent.

He scaled his rates down for a very small circulation. A merchant could buy a lot of space for ten dollars, he thought. A page would cost thirty dollars; half a page, twenty; cards, or two-column boxed ads, would cost a dollar apiece. He set up some discounts for multiple purchases in three, five, ten, and twenty issues.

When he had completed setting his flyer, he found he still had some space at the bottom, so he selected a Latin motto, just to show off his classical education. He was not beyond a little vanity, especially when it came to editing.

Non sans droit, he wrote. "Not without right." That seemed about right for *The Payday Pioneer.*

6

Her enchanting Hungarian was weeks late. Merry-Grace fumed and worried. He should have had the courtesy to let her know. He was often late, but she couldn't escape the nagging feeling that something was wrong. She kept wondering whether to say something to somebody.

She loved Nicholas Rakoczy madly, and he loved her madly, and the longer he stayed away, the more she was eaten up by fantasies. He was probably dallying with some raven-haired, gorgeous Mexican girl along the trail and writing wild love sonnets in Spanish. Or maybe, in his shrewd way, he was casting an assessing eye upon lands that might grow his green Hungarian grapevines, or exploring an adobe ruin, or charming some *hacendado* with his worldly stories, or buying and selling whole herds of sheep, or telling madcap tales of life upon the Danube to cavalry officers in Tucson. Whatever he was doing, he was ignoring his own loving wife, and that made Merry-Grace cross. It also made her sad. Was she growing old and unattractive?

The trouble with being married to Nicholas Rakoczy was that

she had to share him with so many amazing people. He was invariably late because he had been having a glass of sherry with some exiled duke or mad poet or reckless cavalier or fiendish Apache chief or famous actress, and the time she had with him was always too little. She had learned to snatch those hours and enjoy them, because she would have to wait endless days for the next intimate hour with her cheerful doctor of philosophy.

Nicholas never focused on a single enterprise. He needed a dozen, all of them percolating at once, and he kept adding to the list every year. It made Merry-Grace dizzy to think of all of them. Her Hungarian lover wasn't content to raise longhorns in the Tonto Basin; he was also trying out flax and Hungarian peppers for paprika, and experimenting with exotic sheep herds, and trying out irrigation, and manufacturing oaken tables and chairs because there was so little furniture in Payday, and above all, growing grapes, using cuttings imported from Hungary. In a few years, if the blight didn't destroy the vines, he would try to produce the green Hungarian wine he loved.

In early February, Nicholas had left for Yuma and the Southern Pacific Railroad, trailing three hundred longhorn bulls, cows, and heifers—all breeding stock—for meat-starved California. He and his four Mexican *vaqueros* would drive the herd along the Gila River to the railhead, enjoying tender new grass and mild temperatures all the way. He should have been back in early April at the latest. Now it was May. He had abandoned her while he was off having a grand time. That's how he was, she thought testily. He always bewildered her.

Mostly, he left her to her own devices, letting her perform her domestic duties and raise their sons; but other times, he became her mad lover, showering her with ruby-red roses and chocolates and adoring attention, reciting love sonnets and kissing her ears and neck, his beard like scratchy wool, as if to recompense for months of neglect. But this time, he had ignored her too long, and she was going to have a stern talk with him about it. She didn't deserve such treatment, especially after resisting her parents and eloping with him.

Not that she was alone. Old Ignacio watched over the ranch as he always did. And his wife Luz helped her with food and laundry and gardening and mending. And she engaged White River Apache boys when she needed them to weed the gardens. She wished that Nicholas would let her employ half a dozen servants. She wasn't really used to domestic work and considered it beneath her station.

But Nicholas always smiled brightly, promising a dozen maids, cooks, liverymen, laundresses, and gardeners as soon as he had sold something or other, such as his herd of alpacas, imported from Peru. He always kissed her ear and told her she deserved more, said she was a princess of the blood—and never did a thing. It was a fault. She secretly thought Eastern European males were charming liars, a bit dangerous but so exciting that they could make any woman swoon—as she had swooned in Paris.

She had met him in Paris in 1863, when her parents were taking her on the Grand Tour as part of her education. It was a way for the Woolcotts to avoid the nastiness of the Civil War, with all its dreary idealism and blood. Archibald Woolcott had put himself, Merry-Grace, and his wife Louisa, on board *The Great Eastern* and sailed for Liverpool. And when they reached Paris, there was Nicholas Rakoczy lolling at the next table in a quaint left-bank restaurant, sipping beaujolais the color of overripe cherries, running a bony hand through long, wild brown hair, and seducing her with mournful looks and soulful smiles and a bouquet of snapdragons purchased from a street urchin.

She smiled wryly. That was a long story.

There ought to be news. The Gila was the great artery of Arizona, used by freighters, stagecoaches, and other travelers. They would have news. She wasn't afraid, really; hardly anything could go wrong on a well-traveled trace like that. It was just that Nicholas liked to dally. But even as she thought it, she found herself doubting. Something had gone wrong.

She resolved to head for Payday and inquire. Someone would have heard. Maybe Judge Cutlip. He seemed to have his finger on everything. The eleven-mile trip to town would consume the day, but she had nothing better to do. She left Stephen and Andrew in Luz's care, had her spring wagon harnessed, pinned her straw hat on her auburn locks to protect her fair skin, and took the wagon west through a dizzy May morning when all the birds were drunk. She scarcely needed anything in town, having been there just last week, but she might pick up a few ribbons.

She pulled up at Ike Cobb's first, to see about the mail. Probably there would be a letter from Nicholas. But Ike shrugged and said he had nothing for her.

"Ike, have you heard anything? He's weeks late," she said.

"Nope. But you know how slow the news is. You might try that new newspaper man. I hear he's paying the freight outfits to bring him news from Tucson and Prescott—other papers, even just gossip. Needs to fill his new rag."

"Newspaper?" It amazed her.

"Yeah, a fellow named Sam Flint's started up *The Payday Pioneer* in the old bakery. Bought the place from Cutlip. He's got an issue out—see here."

Ike handed her a small four-page paper, neatly printed. She scanned the columns, looking for news of travelers, but didn't see anything. "Is this for sale?" she asked.

"Ten cents. I can put it on your account, Miz Rakoczy."

She nodded, then retreated to her wagon seat to study this unexpected addition to life in the Tonto Basin. She perused a lengthy piece about the glories of Payday and its environs, and a fine statement of principles, a little local news—this editor hadn't yet really absorbed the town, she thought—and a grand editorial about the need for roads and rails between Payday and the Pacific Coast. She decided the editor was erudite. He used Latin in his stories as if just anyone could understand it, and his filler material had a decidedly classic bent, as if he had scoured the wisdom of the ancients for something profound.

Something else interested her: a boxed announcement that this paper would be mailed to a hundred other papers from coast to coast, and all those other papers would exchange news with *The Payday Pioneer.* That excited her. Nicholas was forever inventing ways to tell the world about this little paradise, mostly by brag and fulsome boasting.

She had to meet this man. If he didn't know where Nicholas was, he certainly could find out. She stepped out of her wagon, while the mangy dray yawned and peered back at her, bored with hitchrail life. She swept toward the old bakery, paused to admire the discreet new sign, and plunged into a pungent gloom, fraught with the fragrances of melted metal, ink, and things she couldn't identify. He was there, hunched over a counter dismantling type, tossing the letters back into the niches in the caseboxes, his gold-rimmed spectacles parked low on his nose. Tall! Powerful! And with a penetrating, amiable gaze that settled at last upon her straw hat—which she suddenly removed, letting her hair cascade—and finally and furtively to her left hand. She didn't miss that, and judged that he was single.

"May I help you, madam?" he asked amiably, his blue-eyed gaze so intense that it disconcerted her.

"Well, uh, yes," she replied, unnerved. Something about him galvanized her, filled her with wild curiosity, and a little fear. "I'm looking for information. I hoped you might have some news . . . "

In a rush, she spilled out her story of Nicholas Rakoczy's cattle drive to the railhead at Yuma, and his tardiness.

"Of course, Nicholas is always late, so maybe it doesn't mean a thing. But . . . have you heard anything?"

"I'm afraid I haven't, Mrs. Rakoczy."

"Well, do you think you might?"

He pondered for so long that she felt nonplussed. "I scarcely have my sources set up," he said. "I engage correspondents. In a month or two, I'll have regular letters coming to me from ranchers, stagecoach operators, and so on. But not now . . . I tell you what: I'm going to make an effort to locate him for you. There's a freighter who drives between here and Prescott. I'll have him ask at Fort Whipple. The cavalry is a cyclops. It knows just about everything. And I'll talk to every jehu and teamster coming in. And I'll talk to Basil Cutlip, if you'd like. He's a fountain of news."

"Oh, I could do that . . . " she said, then reconsidered. "But I wish you would." Judge Cutlip always eyed her a second too long, and she always got the feeling that he wanted to possess her as chattel, a part of his empire, like Alpine County, or the Territorial legislature.

Sam Flint stopped his labors and wiped his hands on a grimy rag. "I'd like to do a story about you," he said tightly.

"About me?"

"Yes, you. You've lived in the East. I can tell. You've had a lot of schooling. I know that. You're married to a Hungarian. What brings you to this remote *rincon*? And, forgive me for asking, but I'm new here—what's your name?"

When she told the editor her name, Merry-Grace had the oddest tingle of pleasure. It would be a lovely friendship.

7

Sam Flint couldn't work. After Merry-Grace Rakoczy left, he simply abandoned his labors and stared into space, a river of yearning flowing through him. He was a gentleman, and the yearning was as much as he would allow himself. The lady in the straw panama he had encountered when he first drove into Payday was joyously married, had two sons, and was utterly unavailable.

He had interviewed her at length, his newsman's curiosity doing double duty. He wanted to know all there was to know about that lovely woman. He told himself, and her, that this was so he could do stories about the prominent ranching families of Payday; but he knew that wasn't the whole truth, and he suspected she knew it too.

Nicholas Rakoczy would return soon with his *vaqueros*. The Territory might be wilderness, but a herd of three hundred, driven by five men along the greatest artery of the area, would not escape attention. Still, it was the peg upon which to hang his story. He intended to get a little more information about the Rakoczys from town people. Certainly ripples of controversy might radiate from the Hungarian, who was experimenting with so many forms of agriculture and animal husbandry, unlike his narrower cattle-raising neighbors. A vague intuition told Flint that Rakoczy was probably unappreciated in some quarters.

His yearnings returned him to Merry-Grace. What was it that made some woman attractive to him? The flesh? No, it was much more than that. Her mind? No, not that either. That she was a little spoiled and demanding, well educated, a child of affluence and culture, he swiftly discerned. But it was still more. Merry-Grace loved life. It radiated from her. When she bestowed her gaze upon him, it was as if sunlight smote him, something from the core of the universe. She was privileged and demanding; she could probably be a trial at times, and yet in the course of an hour, she had found out more about him than he had about her, and seemed to write it all in the book of her heart.

He sighed. The day was too sweet to linger inside. He was breaking up the first issue of the *Pioneer*, which had contained too much filler, including three aphorisms from Epictetus, one of Flint's favorite ancients, a gifted Stoic. He needed to absorb more of this little paradise and its Adams and Eves and write knowingly of them, instead of stuffing his sheet with the ancients.

The first issue had gone out to a hundred other papers, as he had promised Basil Cutlip it would—everything from small weeklies in the Southwest to the metropolitan dailies of the East. Many of them would begin an exchange, and his sources of news from the outside world would swiftly multiply. He had described Payday as an Eden, and he didn't doubt that a few pieces like that would draw settlers when the exchange papers picked up his work and ran it. That was how weeklies got the news in the absence of a telegraph. If they hadn't heard of Payday, they would now.

The place was so serene that he knew he would scramble for news. When there weren't events and controversies to write about, there were always people. Each person he had ever interviewed had an absorbing history, or at least one remarkable anecdote to recite, and most of them loved to see themselves in print. That sort of thing built circulation, too.

He abandoned his type and fonts, untied his printer's smock, and ferociously scrubbed his inky hands, as if they had been deep in sin. Then he headed outside. Payday was seducing him, but it didn't matter. He didn't lack time. The ambrosial air lifted his spirits as he meandered through town. He thought he might do a story about Ike Cobb. The young merchant and postmaster was a veteran like himself, and had won the nation's highest honor. That meant he had been in the thick of the worst of it, and Flint scented a powerful story. Cobb scarcely looked thirty; he must have been a mere boy on the killing fields.

He found Cobb dusting a row of stoves along one wall of his store. The merchant eyed him and smiled easily.

"Well, it's our new editor. What may I do for you, Mr. Flint? You want another ad, I suppose."

"Well, I'm always ready to sell an ad, but this time, I've come for a story."

"About me?"

"Everyone has a story. I hear you were decorated during the war. Things like that can make Payday a proud place."

The smile vanished from Cobb's face, and a certain wariness replaced it. "Oh, I never talk about that, sir. The war—it's something to forget just as fast as I can."

"But surely you don't want the world to forget the Congressional Medal of Honor. Why, I'm a veteran myself. The eastern campaigns, mostly under Meade and Grant. Seventy-fifth Ohio Volunteers, Barlow's First Division, Howard's Eleventh Army Corps. I saw more of it than I ever hope to see again. Now where were you?"

"Oh . . . " Cobb looked diffident. "Army of the Cumberland. General Rosecrans, General Thomas. Indiana Volunteers. Look, Flint, it's nothing I want to talk about."

"Well, the people of Payday certainly are proud to have a decorated hero in their midst. I haven't been here long, but that's one
thing they feel strongly about. They've told me about you, want
me to write about you. You're the only celebrity in town."

"Aw, Flint, you're a dandy editor and I appreciate your interest." Cobb smiled uncertainly. "You know how it is."

"What was your outfit, Cobb? You must've been in the thick
of it. I tell you, I was scared and dirty and cold for three years,
and half sick, too. My feet just about rotted off. You must remember some of that."

"Oh, it was terrible."

"Who was your CO?"

"My what?"

"Commanding officer."

"I've lost track. The war's a blank."

That seemed odd, but not unusual. Flint had met several men
who had blotted out the whole war because it was too horrible; they
had seen too much death, too much blood, too much horror to endure in the brain like some cancer, eating their souls.

"Well, we'll talk of it some other time. I just thought it'd be a
great story. Tell me about the Cobbs. Did any of your brothers
serve?"

"Yes, Jerusalem. He's two years younger. He was in another
outfit. I forget which."

"You're Indiana folks?"

Cobb nodded, less bewildered. "Evansville, on the river—
Ohio River. Pa's a banker. I come from a family of bankers. Maybe
I'll start a bank here when Payday's ready."

"You're single."

"Not by intention. It's just that—" He stopped, stared into
space. "I'm not a fellow to interview, Flint. You just let me mind
my store. Go find more interesting fellows to write about."

"Nothing more interesting than a hero in town. How'd it happen? What kind of action did you get into that won you an award like that?"

"Well . . . "

"I'd like to see the citation. Basil Cutlip says he's seen it. You saved some lives under fire."

Cobb reddened. "I just want you to forget it, Flint. It'd be an embarrassment to me. You tell me about yourself. No one in Payday knows a lick about you."

Cobb was certainly ducking. It seemed strange for a fellow who reputedly had bragged about his decoration, especially to a few daughters and their fathers.

"Well, I'll tell you how I got started as a newspaper man," Flint began. "I was nothing but a slogging infantryman wiping rain off a Springfield musket and trying to keep my boots dry and my blisters from crippling me and my fear down in my stomach and out of my throat. But I'm also a scholar, and I couldn't find a book anywhere in the Volunteers, except maybe a few Testaments. So one day I just pulled out my nib and wrote a long account of what it was like to soldier under fire, and sent it off to James Gordon Bennett. He's the editor of *The New York Herald*. Well, Bennett liked it and ran it and asked for more, so that's what I did. It became a feature: 'View from the Trenches.' Written by someone named Hector—I was inclined to flatter myself, I'm afraid. It was all foot-soldier stuff. What'd you do for recreation?"

"Oh, I mostly just talked with fellows. I was a lieutenant."

"An officer. That's what Basil was saying."

"Flint. That's the past. I want to see Payday bloom. We need more transportation. We need a railroad—"

"A lieutenant. Didn't they up you when you mustered out?"

"Did they what? Oh, up me." He began shuffling jars of candy. "Someday I'll tell you the whole kit and caboodle, Flint, but I'm busy now."

Flint peered about. The store was orderly. The shelves were well-disciplined. A row of dressmakers' dummies looked like an infantry column. An assortment of panamas and sombreros, all with wide brims and gauded with silk flowers, looked like the Confederate cavalry.

He realized he had been nosy. A newsman should respect people's privacy. Curiosity was a vice in him, and he always regretted it.

"You must have some sisters," Flint said. "You had to get your stylish tastes from somewhere."

"Five sisters. Abigail, Sarah, Mary, Elizabeth, and Damaris."

"Your family names run to the biblical."

"That's how my father was. He read us a chapter before supper each night. I don't hold with it. Puts too much burden on a man."

"You mean Christianity?"

"No, names like that. Like my name, Isaiah. Who can be a prophet? I sure would like to know that."

"I don't think your pa expected you to be a prophet, Ike."

"You didn't know him," Cobb said darkly. "He's dead now." Cobb turned his back, signaling the end of the interview.

Flint sighed. Not much of a story, but a little anyway, and something to develop. Some people were simply reserved and had to be drawn out. He'd have his story soon. If there was anything Sam Flint had learned over his years as an editor, it was how to pull a story out of the dark.

8

It was during one of his infrequent trips to Payday that Clayton
Buell discovered that the town had a new weekly. He picked up
a copy at Silas Frogg's Oriental Laundry and read it on horseback.
He did most of the serious things of life from the back of a horse.
He pulled out a pair of steel-rimmed spectacles, jammed them into
his iron-gray hair, and studied the new paper. The masthead said
this was the second issue.

Plainly, this was Basil Cutlip's work. Maybe it was the judge's
own paper, although the masthead announced that the owner and
editor was one Samuel Flint. It didn't matter. The message had
Cutlip stamped on it, whether or not Cutlip owned the sheet. That
lengthy front-page screed transmuting the Tonto Basin into Eden
and inviting settlement echoed Cutlip and fostered his designs.
The argument for a railroad and improved freight connections
read like it had been dictated by Cutlip. The piece proclaiming
that the basin could support any sort of enterprise, from crop
farming to cattle growing, was struck in Cutlip's mint, too. Or
maybe in the merchants'. Buell squinted through the tender sun-

light at a street full of storekeepers aching for more customers and rising real estate prices.

Yankees, mostly. If there was one truism that life had taught him, it was that Yankees were a different species of mortal, almost unfathomable and universally greedy. Buell had been trying to understand Yankees since well before the war, and hadn't made much progress at it. He didn't hate them anymore, though he had grounds to; but he tried to live his life as far from their acquaintance as possible. Almost all the merchants in town were Yankees, so he had to do business with them. But he drew the line at Ike Cobb, the Medal of Honor winner. He had never set foot in Cobb's Grocery and Drygoods Emporium, and never would.

He absorbed the whole paper silently, while his buckskin stirred restlessly under him in the rising heat. The editor was a learned fool, stuffing his sheet full of classical allusions. On a single page Buell found aphorisms or pieties drawn from Plato, Aristotle, Hadrian, Caesar Augustus, Livy, and Seneca. The ancient wisdom intrigued Buell. Once, long ago, almost upon another planet, he had mastered the literature of antiquity. But whether this learned fool had an independent mind remained to be seen. Clayton Buell would not judge the man—yet. He had always been slow to judge other mortals, and considered it an innate decency to avoid judgment until his perceptions were refined and buttressed by fact.

He disagreed with the *Pioneer*. He certainly didn't want settlers overrunning the range he had carved out of public land, and held by main force. It was bad enough having to deal with an eccentric like Nicholas Rakoczy, though they had been great friends over the years. He wasn't even sure he agreed with Flint about the need for a railroad—that was nothing but Cutlip's fantasy at work. The Santa Fe, when and if it came, would push west along the thirty-fifth parallel, as Congress had intended, and would not dip a hundred miles south to fulfill the fanciful dreams of the hustling judge.

Colonel Buell was not a Texan and not originally a rancher, but he had found his salvation in the Texas brush, where tens of thousands of longhorns ran wild. After the war, the Texans were gathering the steer and driving them north to Kansas railheads, but Buell had other ideas, arising out of his desperate melancholia.

In 1872, he'd gathered a herd of a thousand of the fractious, boneheaded beasts, enticed some drovers to help him drive them—for a share of future profits because he lacked so much as a Jeff Davis dollar—and worked his way across the dry ranges of West Texas, the acrid reaches of New Mexico Territory, and finally into the Tonto Basin, which he judged to be a cattleman's paradise. During the long drive, he had learned the cattle business from his drovers, every one of whom was a CSA veteran. The only other people with him had been his two black retainers, formerly slaves, who wouldn't dream of service to anyone else.

There in the Tonto, his herds had multiplied. He had paid his drovers with the increase, branded with their own marks and running the same ranges. Now he and his drovers commanded a herd of ten thousand beeves, which mowed the grama grasses in the placid, well-watered canyons under the Mogollon Rim, across the whole northern horizon of the basin.

He didn't want rivals. Or homesteaders. Or an influx of settlers. He wouldn't mind a railroad if it didn't come close to the basin. He needed to get beef to markets. He had found, in this sacred and blessed valley, so isolated from the rest of the world, the only thing he hungered for—an escape from the Yankees, along with the freedom that came from being left utterly alone.

He had recently patented the forty acres that underlay his headquarters buildings, and a dozen more forty-acre plots around springs, creek access points, and key river frontage, to protect himself from settlers. That was all he could pay taxes on in an almost cashless world, all he cared to own, but not all he cared to control. Of the several hundred square miles of public land he called his range, he wanted absolute control. His huge domain would not only serve to support his herds, but also to build a vast wall between himself and the Yankees, a wall that Cutlip was trying to tear down.

Maybe it was time to take the measure of the editor. Colonel Buell steered his buckskin along the unpaved Basin Street and down Prescott, studying buildings. He found the new paper easily, in the old bakery building that Cutlip had bought. The connection told him something. In a moment, the editor's response to Buell's soft Georgia resonances would tell more.

Within, he discovered a big, craggy fellow with a scholar's look about him, hunched over the type cases. Younger than Buell had supposed. The man peered at Buell, even while his hands continued their busywork, sliding letters from the caseboxes into his type stick.

"Ah'm Clayton Buell, and Ah just stopped by to pay my respects, suh. You're the editor, Ah take it?"

Flint abandoned his typesetting and wiped his hands. "Oh, Colonel Buell. The foremost rancher in the basin, I'm told, and a county supervisor. I'm Sam Flint. Mighty glad to meet you." He offered a paw to his guest and Buell shook it.

"The only way you can help me is to favor other policies, suh."

Flint paused, absorbing that. "I'm new here. I'm independent. I was invited here by the town merchants, in particular Abel Greene and Judge Cutlip. If there are things I don't know, or history I don't appreciate, or views I haven't heard, you'll find me open to persuasion."

The reply faintly astonished Buell. The man spoke with a Northerner's voice.

"Where are you from, suh?"

"Cincinnati. I'm a headmaster's son—and almost a classics scholar, until my restlessness overcame me."

"You already know where Ah'm from."

"Not exactly."

"Did we peer through gunsights at each other?"

"I was a private in the Army of the Potomac under Meade, and then Grant."

"We did, suh. Ah was a colonel with Lee in the Army of Northern Virginia. Ah suppose we'll be peering at each other through gunsights here, too."

"I operate an independent paper, Colonel Buell."

"Out of Judge Cutlip's hip pocket."

Flint reddened slightly. Buell watched him closely. All his life, he had employed razor-edged language to good effect. It cut through the niceties and got at truth. That was true at the turpentine plantation and distillery; in command of a battalion; in his domestic life; and now, in his operations as a cattleman.

"You've come to some doubtful conclusions," Flint said, shrugging slightly. "Maybe you'll learn I'm not what you think, and not staring at you through a gunsight. Now, how may I help you?"

"You can help me by abandoning this town-booming. Ah know all you editors do it. You think you'll get rich. The merchants'll get rich. More subscribers. More advertising. Ah happen to like this basin as it is, and can't find a single rational reason for inviting the whole world here. Ah abominate the boom mentality. You just may get what you want, and find you're sorry."

Flint didn't argue. Instead, he grinned at Buell. "Over there's a pad of foolscap and a nib and a bottle of India. Set to work. I'll print it. Don't know whether I agree or not. I haven't been here long enough. But this paper's going to air all views, including yours if you'll voice it." He paused. "If you want to stare down a barrel at me, you can do it in the *Pioneer*."

That was unexpected. And amiable. Buell had supposed that

most Northerners were fanatics. How else to explain the moral hysteria of the abolitionists?

"Of course," Flint added, "if your views aren't reasonable to others, you'll hurt your cause by airing them."

It was a challenge. Colonel Buell considered it carefully. "Ah'll prepare a piece for you, but not now. Ah'm a deliberative man."

"Suit yourself."

"Ah'm outnumbered here. And Ah'm against the holy grail of Progress. Ah fathom you're for it. Get the country settled, bring on the toilers, raise capital, start banks to euchre us all, harvest the forests, get rich."

"Colonel Buell, you seem to know my mind better than I do. All I know after a couple of weeks here is that the town suffers from the want of transportation—you've seen the prices in the stores. The other thing I know is that this basin is a paradise, without serious crime, without conflict, a safe place, its resources intact."

That, too, surprised Buell. Maybe Flint was simply a weakling, a trimmer. "Ah don't want a railroad through here. No capitalist in his right mind'll come this way anyway. If Ah have to drive my herds a hundred miles north, what difference does it make? Ah don't want a pack of penniless settlers—white trash and foreigners—coming here to scratch out a living. You write that claptrap and you'll wish you hadn't. Try reading Genesis. God chased Adam out of the Garden of Eden and put him to work as a sweatin' plowman. Ah don't take kindly to your notions."

"I imagine you don't. They'd homestead your range."

"They're not going to homestead. They're not going to settle anywhere except town."

Flint grinned suddenly. "You're free to say all that. I'll print it."

Colonel Clayton Buell grasped suddenly that his views, printed in the *Pioneer*, could be his own noose. He had better respect the Yankee editor. Any man who had been in war knew enough to respect his enemy. "Observe your enemies, for they first find out your faults," he said.

"Antisthenes, I believe," Flint replied.

Buell laughed. Flint laughed. Buell couldn't imagine why.

9

The barefoot ragamuffin who twitched before Flint announced himself as Elmer. The scarecrow boy looked to be in the vicinity of ten, lacked nodding acquaintance with soap or barber, and wore a linsey-woolsey shirt tucked into butternut britches cut down from an old Reb uniform. His freckles were so furious that Flint at first thought the boy had the pox.

"I want to sell papers," he announced in a reedy voice.

The proposal gladdened Flint. He had unloaded his first and second issues through the merchants, leaving a pile in each store and letting them keep two cents on the dime. He needed street sales as well, and eventually some paid subscriptions.

"All right. You're a boy with enterprise, Elmer. I'll be printing tomorrow evening. The paper needs to dry overnight. The next morning, you can pick up a batch and sell 'em. Charge a dime. You get two cents and you'll give me eight."

Elmer looked doubtful. "Not much has got cash money," he said.

"Well, maybe not dimes and nickels, but most folks have shinplasters. One bit, two bits, and four bits. Just take the paper and make change."

Elmer squirmed. "How about if I let people pay what they want?"

It was an odd request. "No, you charge a dime. You can get some pennies on credit from Ike Cobb and pay him back."

"Well, how about if you show me?"

"Sure I'll show you, Elmer. You'll get the hang of it in a minute. All you have to do is yell the headlines. You just take an item out of the paper that sounds mighty interesting and yell it at people. 'Read all about it! Mrs. Jones bit a rattlesnake!' Maybe even the advertising if you think it'll sell the paper. But it's best to yell the big story."

"Well, what's the big story, mister?"

"I don't know yet. I'll decide tomorrow. You'll find out when you read it. It'll usually be at the top of the right-hand column."

Elmer stared into the floor, and shrugged. "I guess I don't want the job," he said, pivoting on his toes to leave.

"Why not, Elmer? I'm looking for a fellow."

"I don't want it," Elmer announced. "It's too hard."

"Elmer!" Flint yelled, pinioning the boy in his tracks. "Can you read and cipher?"

"There's no one taught me yet," the boy confessed. "But I can add up to a hunnert."

"You've been dodging school?"

He shrugged. "What school?"

It shocked Flint. "Are you telling me, son, that Payday has no school?"

Elmer shrugged again.

Flint drew a breath. "Well, this paper's going to do something about that. I need a fellow who can read and cipher. You can't get into business unless you know how. If no one's teaching you, then this town's robbing you of a living—and a lot more. If you can read, you can get to see the whole world. I'm going to talk to some folks. How do I get a hold of you?"

He got no answer. Elmer backpedaled and fled into the luminous white day. Flint undid his printer's smock, washed his inkstained digits, and steamed toward the courthouse square. Basil Cutlip was usually over there this early in the morning, drinking worn-out java with his bailiff, Phil Splint.

He found the bulky judge studying plat maps in his chambers as if they were gold bullion. Cutlip waved him in. "Be with you in a moment. It's a vexation trying to put legal descriptions to real property that's been settled by squatters before the survey. These are the work of astrologers and necromancers. My right-of-way property is on the cusp of Libra and Scorpio, and the House of Cutlip is located squarely on Achilles' heel, and God lives on the thirty-fourth parallel."

Flint didn't give Cutlip the moment. "Is it true that Payday wants a school?"

Cutlip pulled his dainty spectacles off, bending earhooks, and considered the question with judicial dignity. "No, not true. There's a few home-scholar factories going just fine. Mrs. Phillips—she's teaching her three, plus seven or eight other children, every morning. And Celia Sevres, too. She's got a boy and girl in a high-school correspondence course out of some Saint Louis academic shop."

"No public school? Not even an elementary school?" Flint demanded.

Cutlip sighed. "County has no cash for it. This is a barter economy, Flint. You suppose some pale, fragile schoolmaster with patches at the elbow would take his pay in heifers?"

"How many children are there in town?"

"I don't know that anyone ever counted them. We're fertile in the Tonto Basin. The place inspires connubial bliss. More than usual for a settler place, I'd say. I suppose you'll start reporting the increase and dipping into county records each week. By the way, we have no mortician because no one dies in Payday. No one ever died in Eden. More families here than usual. Most outposts like this are all-male and restless as a gaggle of squealing boars."

"I'm going to campaign for a school."

The judge eyed him dourly. "Don't be hasty, Flint. It'll raise taxes, and we'll all suffer. I think it'd drive a lot of cash-starved outfits into the ground. Sink the *Pioneer* in a pile of McGuffey Readers and bonded indebtedness."

Flint reminded himself that the judge had the most to lose from a school tax because he held most of the patented land by far, speculating as he did on railroad right-of-way and roadways and future commercial sites. He decided not to offend his patron, at least not for the moment. "Maybe we can get a schoolmaster and people can pay in kind. That's how I'm being paid. My ads fetch me a credit at the grocery, the hardware, and all the rest. I'm saying there're ways to do this, ways to raise a schoolhouse and get a master."

Basil Cutlip steepled his hands and frowned toward a verdict. "Of course we'll need a school eventually, but it'd be wise to wait until the settlers arrive. You've put out the word for two or three issues. This is Eden. Eventually, in a year or two, we'll see some fresh faces, new business, cash money rolling in, along with an assortment of squirrelly brats. I think that'll be the time to move on it—when it's feasible."

Flint wouldn't budge. "This morning a little fellow popped in and wanted to hawk papers. Name of Elmer. I thought I had a newsboy until I found out he couldn't make change, couldn't read a headline or a story, or even an advertisement. That little fella's being cheated out of life, Judge. He'll end up a hostler in a livery barn, or a janitor, or a part-timer who'll put up the hay and never have a spare dime. No, he's a bright lad, and I won't let it happen to him."

Cutlip looked testy. "Idealism is one thing. Being practical is another. We all have ideals. I'd like to create the University of Tonto Basin and educate the redskins and ex-Rebels. But being practical about expenses and taxes is what counts, or there won't even be a Payday. If I have one grudge against newspapers, it's that they get notions and pound on them until sober people who manage budgets can't get a word in edgewise. It's easy to find lacks and wants, and stir up hungers."

Flint saw that he wasn't going to make a convert of Basil Cutlip. "I'm going to raise the issue," he said.

Cutlip sighed, glared, restored his gold half-spectacles to the massive mountain of his nose, and subsided into sullenness. "We'll make a fight of it, then. I don't make common cause with Buell, but on this, we'll be shoulder to shoulder against you."

"He's already against me. He doesn't want settlers. They'll homestead on his range. Doesn't even want a railroad through here."

"I never heard of a retired colonel who had an ounce of economic sense. They live in a hierarchy all their lives and spend government money," Cutlip said. "When it comes to making money, they're all toads."

"I offered him space for his opinions. I'll offer you space for yours."

Cutlip frowned. "A paper should speak with a single voice. Let an opposition paper speak with another voice. You don't want to addle your readers."

"I'm glad you have a theory," Flint said, departing into a dazzling day. It seemed that every time he stepped outside in Payday, he was stepping into bliss.

He tracked down Mrs. Phillips in her log house while she was instructing a gaggle of youngsters in long division, using a dusty chalkboard. He counted eight scholars, of whom three apparently were her own. She was such a wren of a woman that he wondered how she had ever borne three children, but she radiated a vast charismatic sense of rosy mission, as if her whole world centered on transmitting her skills to her charges.

"Why, you just watch, Mr. Flint," she said. "Children, this is the editor of our new paper, Mr. Flint, and we're going to show him that you can read that paper."

Most of them managed to read pieces from their primers, some with a moving index finger and hesitant lips. They had a long way to go and needed regular schooling mornings and afternoons. Then a few read shyly from a copy of the *Pioneer* —which she had supplied her classroom, much to Flint's astonishment.

He found out, after she had dismissed them, that she taught the outside children in exchange for whatever their parents could give her—milk, cream, butter, chiles, pinto beans, chickens, eggs, corn, firewood, stove kindling, squashes; and these offerings had filled the family larder when her teamster husband Orlando was away, as he often was.

"Do you know a boy named Elmer?"

"Well, I've heard of him. Elmer Kelly."

"Well, if you can lure him into your class, I'll pay you something. Mostly with credit I have at the stores."

"I'll do that if he'll come. Some children won't, you know."

"I'd like you to try. How many children are there in Payday?" he asked.

"Oh, about sixty. Not very many for a town of five hundred, you know. There're more out on the ranches. We ought to have schools for a hundred in this county, but it won't ever happen, not with Judge Cutlip. I suppose I shouldn't say that. Everyone knows he got you started."

"He doesn't want to pay property taxes," Flint said.

"And his own children are grown and gone," she added. "But I think Violet—that's his missus—wouldn't mind a school if it were named after her."

"There are always ways around obstacles."

She smiled wryly. "You haven't been here very long, Mr. Flint."

"Some towns simply raise a schoolhouse without taxes. The men of this town could build a log schoolhouse in a day. The families with children could pay you in kind, just as they are doing now . . . "

"Well, you go write that up," she said.

He did, at length, choosing to express the case as opinion. He would make enemies with this issue, but that was old, familiar turf for him. There were about sixty reasons Payday needed a school, and a hundred reasons the county should commit itself to at least an elementary school.

10

The incoming mails over the next weeks brought Sam Flint some exchange papers. He heard from remote corners of the Southwest, such as Tubac and Socorro, as well as Tucson. A little paper, three columns wide and magazine-sized, arrived from Yuma, and he perused it at once, hoping for news of Nicholas Rakoczy. He was rewarded by a standing column of shipping news that recorded freight on the Southern Pacific and steamboat traffic on the Colorado.

A two-sentence entry dated February 28 caught his eye: "293 cows, heifers, and bulls received in SP pen this A.M., bound for San Diego consignee. Shipper was N. Rakoczy of Payday." That was all. Now he had some good and some bad news for Merry-Grace. Good because the rancher had reached Yuma with his herd almost intact; bad because he should have returned two months ago. Flint wondered whether to ride out and tell her. The trip would require most of a day. He surveyed his work and decided he would attempt it later, after he had done a good stint of typesetting. That way, he would consume the evening, not the day.

The rest of the papers yielded proof that his efforts to draw attention to Payday were paying off. Many editors had reprinted intact his paeans to the Tonto Basin. Other editors poked fun, as he knew they would, but it didn't matter. A Socorro, New Mexico, editor wrote, "We have received word from Eden that Adam and Eve are prospering and inviting guests. According to the proprietor of a new rag there called *The Payday Pioneer*, the Tonto Basin, over in Arizona Territory, is a place where you can plant a seed and grow a dollar bill in twenty-four hours, and a place where a fellow can be comfortable in shirtsleeves in January and July. We're thinking of pulling up stakes and heading for this wonderland ourselves, seeing as how it had escaped the attention of the gimlet-eyed world. No serpent has been reported therein, and we have no information on whether the place contains apple trees."

Flint grinned. That sort of joshing was the lifeblood of the Western press, and once he examined his exchange papers in detail, he would fire his own sallies in various directions. The result was a sort of jocular warfare, issue after issue, which entertained readers but also brought them news from surrounding burgs and regions. Judging from the papers piling up on his workbench, he would be retailing news from all over the Southwest, California, the Great Plains, and even a few Eastern sheets. And best of all, they would be reprinting his own encomiums to Payday and the Mogollon Rim country. That was how it all meshed, and what would draw wagonloads of settlers someday soon.

The Prescott Enterprise, flying snaky flags on its mast, was having the most fun with him. Its editor, F. Jasper Bean, wrote:

It appears that an upstart burg a little east of us is laying claim to the Pearly Gates and all ensconced therein. To hear tell of it, this Payday, which has heretofore lain obscurely in the remote precincts of the Republic, is a fantastic place, with gold-paved streets and crystal palaces and pearly gates, populated by a collection of Greeks and Romans with names like Seneca and Caesar and Virgil. At least they got an awful lot of space in this divinely inspired little sensationalist sheet. The Throne of God, it seems, is situated in the sanctum of the paper, a late bloomer in the Territory and called *The Payday Pioneer*, a mast that will sound a bit peculiar after the pioneers all depart those wards. But maybe not. The pioneers of Payday are already in Paradise, and obviously going nowhere.

Flint thought that was choice enough to reprint, along with a retort admiring bustling Prescott in a left-handed sort of way. He had reason to be pleased: Payday was on the map now. In three weeks, he had made the town a recognizable place. Clayton Buell wouldn't like it, but the town merchants would. The incoming settlers would infuse the place with life, and soon freight prices would drop and there'd be something like a boom. There'd be enough new tax revenue to finance a school, too, as public land was converted into private holdings subject to property taxes.

He worked all that morning on a few choice retorts, another piece about the corner of heaven known as the Tonto Basin, some sidebars about opportunity in Payday, especially for doctors, morticians, bankers, and harness makers, and some news gleaned from the exchange papers, especially the nearby *Wickenburg Miner.*

It was a good lick of typesetting, and he took time out of his lunch break to set the galleys on the proofing table, rub ink on the type with a chamois ball, run off a proof copy, and make some corrections with his soft lead pencil. He prided himself in producing a paper almost devoid of typographical blunders and misspellings. Not for nothing had he been a scholar and schoolmaster's son.

He rented a sorrel saddler at the Cook Brothers' Livery Barn and set off toward the Rakoczy ranch east of town, the Yuma paper tucked into his baggy tweed coat. He could have chosen easier ways to get the news to her. Ranchers from that area came to town almost every day and he could have sent the paper out to her with one of them. But he wanted to see her.

On the two or three occasions he had encountered her in town since their meeting in the press office, she had further filled him with a heady pleasure. He confessed to a schoolboy crush on Merry-Grace, and reminded himself sternly that he must not cross a certain line between innocent yearning and coveting another man's wife. She wasn't his. Her children weren't his. Her love wasn't his. He decided, as he rode steadily east along a largely shaded, sun-dappled lane that broke through verdant grasslands and shimmering cottonwood copses, that if he ever came close to crossing that line, he would refuse to see her again. A brave idealism, he thought, wondering whether he could condemn himself to such a fate.

The steady jogging, relieved by occasional walks and a few canters, got him to the ranch in three hours. Nicholas Rakoczy's holdings stretched from the top of the Mogollons through verdant, grassy canyons to the well-watered bottoms of the basin, and southward into arid peaks with a totally different climate and vegetation, more like the rough desert to the south. En route to Payday, he had driven right through the ranch without knowing it, and his first glimpse of Merry-Grace, in her wide-brimmed panama, had been just west of her land in a corner of Buell's vast empire. A number of poorer and humbler ranches crowded the cedar-studded Sierra Anchas to the south; Buell and Rakoczy held the prime, lush, grassy country east of town all to themselves, while a dozen other ranchers Flint knew only by name occupied the lushest pasture west of town.

He turned into a soft, sandy lane that followed a burbling creek between massive slopes, often riding through the dappled light of noble cottonwoods that had sprung to life long before white men had settled on the North American continent. He passed herds of varicolored longhorns, majestic old fellows with great corkscrewed horns, lazily mowing the velvety meadows of grama grass.

The valley opened into a flat where cultivated lands spread wide, filled with crops he didn't recognize. Some plots had been laboriously fenced with poles hewn out of the forest on the rim-rock above; some stood unprotected, apparently because stock wouldn't touch them. And one crop that looked curiously like rows of pepper plants had been fenced with Glidden barbed wire— something Flint had heard of but never seen before. He dis-mounted to study the novelty.

In 1873, an Illinois tinkerer named Frederick Glidden had found a way to pinion metal barbs between two strands of twist-ed, zinc-coated steel wire, thus creating a cheap way to contain cattle. Flint admired the setup. Rakoczy was an innovator and experimenter. A swift flood of envy rivered through Flint. Merry-Grace had found an exceptional husband.

Just ahead, he raised the ranch complex and paused to admire it. Heat radiated from his sorrel gelding, and Flint guiltily knew he had pushed too long and too fast. Black sweat had collected at the base of the livery horse's neck and chest and around its stifles.

The main house was a spacious log structure completely cir-cumscribed by a veranda that added pleasant shade to a com-fortable, massive home. A barn, pens, and several other outbuildings that probably were barracks completed the estab-lishment. He saw no one about, and rode slowly toward the main building. But someone had seen him. An elderly Mexican in white cottons greeted him coolly from the shade of the veranda.

"Mrs. Rakoczy, please," he said.

"Who is it that calls on the *señora*?"

"I'm Sam Flint, editor of the paper. I've some news about Mr. Rakoczy."

"*¿Verdad? El Patron?* I will find the *patroña*."

"Never mind, Ignacio. I'm here," she said from a dark doorway. "Is it you, Mr. Flint? And what's this I heard?"

The sight of her dizzied him. He couldn't help it. She had rolled up the sleeves of her white linen dress and had unbuttoned it at the neck. She looked flushed from some sort of hot work.

"Mrs. Rakoczy . . . " He faltered, swept away by her grace. "I received the Yuma paper this morning. It . . . there's some word of Mr. Rakoczy."

"Oh, Nicholas!" she said joyously.

Old Ignacio plainly followed the conversation. Flint dismounted and handed her the little paper. "It's in the shipping news on page three," he said. "The last entry for February."

She found the place and pored over the column. At last she turned toward Ignacio. "Mr. Rakoczy arrived in Yuma and shipped two hundred ninety-three cattle on February twenty-eight. It was recorded in this paper."

Ignacio frowned. "A long time ago, *Señora.*"

She turned to Flint. "Surely there's more news. Other papers. He must have gone down to Tucson a while."

Flint shook his head, wishing desperately he could bring this woman gladder tidings.

"He is terribly late," she said.

"He has four *vaqueros, Patrona.* They are strong and well armed, *muy macho,* " Ignacio replied valiantly, but Flint read questions in his eyes.

"It's hard when you don't hear anything week after week, Mr. Flint." Her face clouded.

Flint hardly knew how to reply to that. Maybe Rakoczy was something of a rascal, squandering his days and his money in the sinkholes of the old city, or somewhere else. "I think, madam, that no news is good news. I'm receiving many of the Territorial papers now. They are swift to report calamities, and I've read them all since they began flowing in. There has been no great trouble except for a flash flood in a wide arroyo that stranded some travelers east of Tucson for a day. There are no reports of Apache trouble. The army would have reported it to the press."

It comforted her. "Yes, I suppose you're right," she said. "But it's been so long. Two months. Time for him to make the whole trip to Yuma and back a second time." The desperation in her face spoke of love and intimacy. "He's not very prompt—he just loves to see everything along the way, like some schoolchild . . . " She caught herself and flushed, embarrassed. "I'm sorry. I haven't even thanked you for coming all this way to bring this news."

"I know you've been worried," he said.

The moment jelled into distances. "I'm glad you came," she said. "I've been ironing—the house just isn't fit for company. But we'd be glad to give you a drink, and water your horse."

"I understand."

"But next time I'm in Payday, Mr. Flint . . . ." Her voice trailed away oddly as she looked into his face. She was seeing something there he couldn't conceal.

"I hope you have a good trip back," she said. "It was such a bother. At least it'll be cooler. It's a safe road, but they talk about painters at night—"

She was jabbering. He nodded, turned his gelding around so he could mount, and settled himself in the saddle. "If I get any word, I'll let you know directly," he said.

She nodded. She was clutching the veranda post as if it had to support her.

11

Clayton Buell sat his chestnut gelding on the banks of Pass Creek, studying the new outfit. These settlers were sheep people. Somewhere between a hundred and two hundred merinos grazed in the lush grama grasses of the best grassland on Buell's spread. Mostly they grazed silently, but now and then a ewe bleated maternal instructions to its lamb. The scene reminded Buell of the Twenty-third Psalm.

The family had almost raised a cabin cut from the surrounding ponderosa pine. It lacked only a roof. He felt a great desolation. He would have to remove them, just the way Sherman's Army had removed him—and altered his life evermore. It was the way of armies. His consisted of three of his hands: Mr. Throckmorton, Mr. Billups, and Mr. Chafee. He never addressed them by their first names, Billy, Josiah, and Clint. Neither did he ever call them "cowboys." They were men who had suffered in the armies of the Confederacy. Anyway, the idea of calling adult drovers "boys" was repugnant to him.

The family patriarch, who was returning his stare, was a gray-templed, bearded fellow as broad as an ox; his wife stood nervously beside him. Two husky boys perched on roof beams. A sheepdog lolled at the cabin door. A decrepit covered wagon sagged nearby. Four ribby draft horses grazed heedlessly on picket lines.

These were the first fruits of that miserable newspaper's campaign to bring in settlers. Here, in the flesh, were people seduced by Flint's elegaic descriptions of the Tonto Basin and Cutlip's large schemes to populate it. There would be more, a veritable migration to come. It was going to be a painful time. These people were victims of propaganda.

Buell touched the flanks of the chestnut and steered it toward the family. His men followed.

"Ah'm Clayton Buell, suh. Ah'm afraid you're on my land."

The patriarch surveyed Buell up and down from eyes that showed no warmth. "We're homesteading," he said. "My wife, my sons, and I are each claiming a hundred-sixty of this public land. It's not yours."

"Ah'm sorry, suh. You'll be leaving now."

The man bristled slightly. "I said it's not yours."

"Ah've held it for years." Buell grieved. He heard Virginia or Carolina in that man's voice and knew the story of these dispossessed people without being told.

"It's been filed on at the courthouse. I'll show you the papers."

Buell shook his head and waved away the words impatiently. "Ah didn't catch your name," he said.

"Horatio Thimble, from the Carolina highlands. Caldwell County." He waved an arm. "Mrs. Thimble. My good sons, Artemus and David." He surveyed Buell shrewdly. "I fought under Ewell, Hoke's Brigade."

Buell thought it hadn't taken long to ferret out that bond. It only made him sadder. "It doesn't matter whether you filed," he said gently. "You pack up now; get those sheep off by tonight."

"You have something against sheep, is it?"

"No. Ah don't hold with those who say they ruin pasture. Ah

have eyes and Ah've never seen it. Now Ah'll not ask again. Ah'm telling you. Get out."

Mrs. Thimble trembled and laid a weary hand on her husband's hard arm. "There's lots of land, Mr. Thimble," she said.

"I happen to like this land. Best I've ever seen. It's public. And we've made a legal claim on it."

Buell liked the man. He hadn't appealed to their common history. He eyed Mr. Throckmorton and Mr. Billups and Mr. Chafee, who were sitting their mounts uneasily, not happy with this.

"It's a pity," Buell said. "People like you need a start."

"That's the truth. The war took two sons. The carpetbaggers and Yankee crooks beggared me."

Buell stared off into the Mogollon forests catapulting upward beyond the valley, remembering. Sherman's roving jackals had burned his turpentine distillery and his home, impoverishing his family. His now mad wife languished in an asylum. Buell had been defending Richmond at the time. Sylvanus, his firstborn, had taken a spill from a cavalry mount and died at Chancellorsville. Tess, his fair daughter, had vanished in the wake of Sherman's march to the sea. Oddly, he didn't blame Sherman, whose orders had been to respect persons. Buell had watched men under him rampage in the same way the roving bands of Yankees had.

He gazed mildly into Thimble's face, meeting the patriarch's glare with his own diffidence. "Ah'm afraid time's up, suh." Slowly he slid his 1873 Colt Army revolver from its sheath on his saddlehorn, cocked it, aimed it at a ewe, and pulled the trigger. The crack shattered the peace. The ewe blatted, collapsed, quivered, leaked crimson into its wool, and lay still. Its lamb whined and bounded unhappily, nudging the ewe.

Mrs. Thimble sobbed.

"One sheep a minute dies until you start packing," Buell said, regretfully.

"You would do that?" Thimble asked.

"It's necessary."

"I'm here legally. This is my property. I'll find my remedy in court."

"Do that, Mr. Thimble." Regretfully again, he shot the lamb. The force of the bullet catapulted the little thing backward and blew a great hole in its chest. Buell wondered whether he had rounds enough. Between them, they did. His men had standing orders to carry ample ammunition. The Apache threat had not vanished.

"You will kill the flock," Thimble said, "but we won't budge. This is the end of the road for the Thimble family. There are two things you should know about us. We're pacifists. The war did that. It sickened me. I'll never do violence to another mortal. We all believe in it, my wife and boys. And another thing, sir. We've been hounded and cheated since the war. We'll not be hounded further. We'll stand here on land we've legally claimed."

"Ah regret it," said Buell. He waited. Thimble had folded his burly arms across his chest. Mrs. Thimble quivered beside him. The sons sat paralyzed on the roof beams. "Move on, while you have a flock. You can begin elsewhere."

"Colonel," said Throckmorton, "I think we ought to make room. These folks are . . . brethren."

"Life is a series of hard choices, Mistah Throckmorton. If the hard choice Ah'm about to impose on you is too large or offends your conscience, you are free to resign from my employment."

His man stared into the grasses, paralyzed. Thimble wasn't budging. "All right then, you've made your choice, Mistah Thimble. You'll let your flock die."

"No, sir. I don't choose that. You do. I don't choose to kill my flock. It is entirely an act rising from your own hard will, done in this sunlight before the witness of God. You and I are free and sovereign men. If this flock should die, it will be entirely your doing. No bullet of mine will murder these innocent creatures."

Buell liked this man, which made it harder. He didn't answer. He had no answer. Life's imperatives overrode reason. He had come west to escape. He had carved out a haven in paradise and kept the world at bay. Some days he could even forget for an hour or two Eloise's sobbed-out story, her weeping madness, the stinking, charred ruins of his distillery, which had produced essential war material for the Confederate Navy and thus was a target for Sherman's raiders. Sometimes he could even push aside the vision of his ruined home, its rock walls crumbled into dust, his pianoforte a charred mass, the Reynolds portraits of three generations of Buells gone, his black servants wailing. Lee had given him a fortnight leave with which to bury a life.

Buell shot a ram. It circled crazily and dropped. He shot a ewe and hit a leg. It shattered. The ewe bawled and wept and thrashed in the reddening grass. He began reloading.

"Shoot them, Mistah Throckmorton. Aim to kill, Mistah Billups. Destroy them, Mistah Chafee."

His drovers eyed him, swallowed, and began systematic slaughter, steering their horses through the maddened flock, casually reloading. Their sporadic volleys sounded like a string of Chinese firecrackers. Horses squealed. The Thimble sheepdog trotted among the twitching carcasses, wagging its tail. Gunsmoke hovered over the bottoms. Occasionally one of his men rode down a fleeing ewe. Lambs whined and sucked dead teat until they, too, exploded into red wool.

And all the while, Thimble stood like Gibraltar, resisting Buell with a lancing gaze that cut and lashed and scorned and spat black light. The slaughter took the better part of an hour. Buell thought it had cost Thimble fifteen hundred dollars. It had cost Buell over twelve dollars in cartridges for his Colt, along with powder, ball, and caps for the Navies used by his men. The breezes swept away the stink of powder but couldn't scrub the brassy smell of blood or the sudden odor of urine from dying lambs. Behold the Lamb of God. A man's small lease on the future, a man's dreams, lay still in the bloody grass, even as raptors flew over, laying claim to future feasts. But Buell's own imperatives remained intact.

"I suppose you're satisfied, Colonel Buell," said Thimble in a voice as quiet as a knife thrust.

"No. Ah would have been satisfied if you'd left with your flock intact."

"I think you were satisfied by the murder," Thimble said. "You are made whole by death. Now what are you going to do?"

"Remove you."

"I don't remove."

Buell felt sorry. "Then you'll suffer worse." He watched one of the boys, the bigger one, slide off the roof beam and drop into the cabin. He lifted his voice toward the boy. "Don't be foolish," he said.

The boy emerged with an ancient squirrel gun, a muzzle-loader, and a powder horn, preparing to commit his life.

"Put it down, son," Thimble said gently. "We'll live by our beliefs."

Reluctantly, the anguished boy obeyed, settling the ancient hunting weapon upon the grass.

"Please, sir," said Mrs. Thimble, weeping.

"Go," said Buell.

"You've done your worst. Be gone now. We intend to put down roots right here," said Thimble, so softly that his voice belied all that boiled within him.

"You're a fine Confederate patriot. You learned that wars are won with superior force," Buell said, not budging from his saddle. "Now leave, or your kit will be next. First the wagon. Then the dog. Then the draft horses."

Mrs. Thimble wept. "Please, Horatio, we can start over. Please don't let them burn my cedar chest."

The woman's anguish registered upon Thimble. He looked at

her. She trembled. Then, at last, his stubbornness dissolved. The resolute glare softened . . . and Horatio Thimble wept.

"It was a hard lesson, Mistah Thimble," Buell said.

But it was the woman who replied. "May God strike you dead. May God condemn your soul to damnation!" she cried.

"God already did," said Buell.

12

Horatio Thimble had done what he had to do. Some things there were that did not yield to rational argument, and this had been one of them. He could so easily have succumbed to reason: all he had to do was to find other land in this vast wilderness and lead away their hard-won flock. They had scraped dimes together from nothing in the Reconstruction South, drifting westward, slaving at any task available, a family bonded by hardship and grief. This herd they had bought in New Mexico and driven here upon hearing of the Eden under the Mogollon Rim.

Horatio might have listened to his practical Gertrude, who now eyed him as if he were a man she had never known. But nothing would alter what had happened. His reasons lay beyond reason, and he could not explain them to himself. He grieved the flock as much as she and his sons did, but they wouldn't believe it. Had she not weakened him, he would have stood his ground and forced Buell to burn his wagon and kill his dog and horses to boot. There were Rubicons in a man's life. He would have stood still on his land until they had demolished everything, just because it was what he had to do. And he would have won, too. A man who would sacrifice everything for something larger would always win.

He sighed, condemning himself for surrendering. But what was done was done. They left the incarnadined meadow under the dead stare of Buell, and scarcely afterward, a flock of turkey vultures settled on the carcasses, ripping out sheep eyes as if they were pastries. The silence of the boys and Gertrude was alive with recrimination.

"We will begin over, once again," he said softly. "There's a place on this earth for those who will do no violence, and who will flee no more, and it is here."

He knew they were disputing him in their silent hearts. Especially Gertrude, whose dreams he had crushed.

He steered the four-horse team toward Payday, conscious of the growl of the wagon wheels and the soft chatter of hooves. Zephyrs hollowed and billowed the wagon sheet, making it flap lazily like a becalmed sail.

It was in Horatio Thimble to rejoice in beauty, even at a moment like this. This land anointed his soul. He steered the wagon along a road that threaded verdant slopes of grama grass. Often the course penetrated copses of noble cottonwoods, and then the sun danced gaily like balls of light amidst the shadow. The heady air, with a breath of sagebrush and distant pine upon it, brushed dry and pleasant over his flesh and into his lungs. His eyes feasted upon the vaulting, pine-blackened slopes of the rim and the saucy creeks that tumbled out of the highland to irrigate these savannas below. Surely the Almighty had fashioned this sacred place to remind poor mortals of the sweetness of a good life. A man could not be melancholic here, bathed in birdsong; it was impossible when every vista healed the heart and refreshed the spirit.

Horatio Thimble had been drawn to this place by some force larger than his poor mind could grasp, and now that he was here, he would not let go. There were things worth dying for, and the four quarters of a section he and his wife and sons had staked for themselves were among them. Let them die at Buell's hands and he would ask only that his bones lie within his claim, so his spirit might rejoice through eternity.

He wondered whether Gertrude and Artemus and David keened what he keened, or knew what he knew. Maybe their spirits were different. His leapt to this place and danced to it. If theirs didn't, they would never understand and would always wonder about him. He couldn't help that. He had come here and no place else. Yes, there would be abundant land farther south on the rim of the desert, good enough graze if one possessed enough of it. Let his sons settle there if they would; they had both reached their majority. He would live and die under these rims.

They arrived in Payday, a village gilded with serenity and light, about midday, and drove slowly through it, as they had once before. They passed around the courthouse square and out the far side of town, and then cut across open pastures to the banks of the creek. The land probably belonged to someone, but the Thimbles would camp there in the wagon until they were chased out.

"We'll picket the horses, and each of us will find work," he said. "We'll begin again."

"It doesn't make any sense," muttered Artemus, and Horatio Thimble was glad the boy had a mind of his own. That one would do better than David. The older boy had yet to rebel. The only thing to do was to clamp down harder until David did, and then step aside.

"No, it doesn't, but we will," Horatio replied.

Gertrude knelt at the riverbank and washed the stain of tears from her cheeks. He would hear from her later, at night, when she lay beside him under the blankets, about two whispers from the boys. He was unworthy of the love she gave him.

"Check your hunger and find honest work. All toil is good for the soul, no matter how humble, and the work of the hands is more to be honored than the labors of the mind."

They had heard all this from him many times, and nodded. When the camp had been secured, the draft horses cared for, and their mongrel dog Stonewall tied, they drifted back to town, each carrying his own obligations and thoughts. They all knew how to find work. Gertrude would try the cafés. She could cook or wait tables. His sons would clerk at any store, or become hostlers. Frontier towns starved for labor.

He walked directly toward the building that housed *The Payday Pioneer*. The best way to get his land back was to learn all there was to know about the county, and the best way to do that was to work for a paper. He would wrestle a job from the editor one way or another. It was the neatly printed *Pioneer*, a copy of which he came across in New Mexico, that had started his final odyssey. He would not go farther, not even to the legendary California.

He found the offices near the courthouse square and penetrated into a cool, log-walled building. He knew nothing about printing, but a lot about writing and composing and spelling, and he thought he might make himself useful. And find out the things he needed to know.

The Pied Piper who had lured him to this Eden was proofing a sheet of paper filled with two columns of type. He was a big, clean-shaven young fellow, who read through spectacles. A grimy printer's smock shielded his shirtwaist and trousers from the hazards of his profession.

"I'll be with you in a moment," the man said. "One more paragraph." It was the voice of a Northerner.

Thimble waited. The man completed his task, stood, and surveyed Thimble.

"I'm Sam Flint. What may I do for you?"

"I'm Horatio Thimble. Yoah paper lured me to this land. I happened upon a copy of it in Socorro, New Mexico. It all but said you had to pass through the pearly gates to get here. I'm looking for gainful employment."

"The paper brought you here? Does the area live up to my description?"

"It does, sir, in every particular."

"And you want work. Are you a journeyman or apprentice? Have you been around a press?"

"I've never set foot in a newspaper office. I'm a man with some education, and my fingers would soon enough follow my thoughts."

Flint sighed. "I could use a printer's devil, but I can't pay cash. If you want a cash job, you'll have a tough time here."

"How do you survive, then?"

"Barter. A little cash, but mostly accounts with my advertisers." He smiled. "I don't suppose you have any use for credit with a milliner?"

"As a matter of fact, I do. Mrs. Thimble is always in need of a poke bonnet."

That intrigued the man. "You are schooled?"

"Four years at The Citadel. Military engineering."

Flint eyed him soberly. "You'd work for a man who wore the blue?"

"Well, I can ask the same. You'd hire a man who wore the gray?"

Flint stared into space. "That ended eleven years ago. I have no difficulty with it."

"No, sir. The shooting ended eleven years ago. The war still goes on. In eighteen and seventy-three, the carpetbaggers took all I had for back taxes. So they said. The war won't be done until they have stolen the South."

"I'm sorry, sir. I fought to preserve the Union. Free the slaves. I didn't fight for that. Not stealing from fellow citizens. Mr. Lincoln wanted a generous peace."

Thimble snorted. "Well, shall I try elsewhere? I need to feed my family."

"What's your goal? A temporary position? You're planning to homestead?"

Thimble dodged that. He smiled through his flowing beard. "You have drawn me to this valley and now I'll require a job. Even Paradise requires that I toil for my supper."

Flint seemed to make up his mind. "I can do it if you'll accept credits from the advertisers as a wage. A devil gets fifty cents a day. What little cash I receive goes into paper and ink."

"It you'll put me on, Mr. Flint, you won't regret it. Try me. I'm a man to learn swiftly, work long hours, and do a job I can be proud of."

Flint grinned and thrust a big hand toward Thimble. The Carolinian thought for a moment—he had not shaken a Yankee hand in seventeen years—and shook it.

They talked a while more. Horatio Thimble agreed to start in the morning. He would learn to break down type, proof pages, set type in the type stick, build ads, prepare the pages for the flatbed press, and run the press. He would learn as well to write stories— Flint said it was an art, and he'd teach what he knew. There would be other tasks, too: composing filler material in slack moments, pouring molten type metal into molds that made ruler lines and spacers, copying material from other papers—he called them exchanges—and selling ads if Thimble had a knack for it.

"I'm camped on the river west of town; we'll live in our wagon a while," Thimble said.

"You're not going to buy a lot and raise a house?"

"No."

"That's Judge Cutlip's land. I suppose he won't mind. He's bought or claimed land along every conceivable two-rut road, or trace, or railroad route he can imagine."

"I'll deal with him if I must, sir."

"Well, I'm looking forward to morning, Mr. Thimble. You'll master the trade in no time."

Horatio Thimble thought the man was decent enough for a Yankee. Thimble had a job. And he had more: soon enough, from this sensitive place, he would know all there was to know about

Payday. Who the prominent citizens were. Who was allied with Clayton Buell. Who might help him get his land back . . . and a new flock.

The Citadel had not taught him about this sort of war, but he would wage it. It was better than shedding blood. He could fight now with words, not bullets.

That evening he learned that Gertrude would cook evenings at the Cochise Café for seventy-five cents a shift; Artemus would become a night hostler at a dollar; and David would clerk for a merchant named Cobb for his pick of drygoods, groceries, or hardware. Between them, they'd be able to put something by. Thimble looked over his flock, pleased. He had come to believe something in his heart of hearts, a mingling of his pacifism and scripture: the meek would inherit the earth.

13

Sam Flint caught the sheriff, Arnold Betjeman, snoozing in his jail. The county lawman slowly opened one piercing black eye, then the other, and then he hoisted himself to a sitting position. He grunted. Betjeman was a man of few words but very expressive oral communication. He could say more with a growl or a snort or a sniff than most men could with a sentence. Flint interpreted this grunt not as displeasure, but as a plea for time to clear his head of cobwebs.

The compact sheriff tugged his handlebar mustache, which indicated that in due course he would actually speak, and stood. He reached barely over five feet in his stockings, but considered it an advantage: he presented less of a target, he always opined.

"I'm here for news," Flint said, pencil poised. "Have you any word about Rakoczy?"

Betjeman shook his head. Flint figured that was a hopeful sign. Usually, the sheriff just stared stolidly at angels or something floating about him that only he could see.

"Have you heard from every county?"

Betjeman nodded. A fortnight earlier, at Merry-Grace's request, he had contacted every sheriff in the Territory as well as the military at Fort Whipple, informing them that Rakoczy and his four *vaqueros* had started back from Yuma about February 28 and hadn't been seen since.

"All but Fort Grant," he said. "Nothing."

"What do you think happened to Rakoczy?"

The sheriff shrugged. Squeezing a story out of this man had turned out to be the most trying challenge in Flint's journalistic career.

"Have you followed Rakoczy's trail? He and his drovers had a regular route down to the Gila. I thought maybe you'd been out on it, at least to the county line."

The sheriff shook his head.

"Are you going to?"

"When I get some evidence." The sheriff cut off some Union plug tobacco and tucked it under his lip.

"Evidence? Of what?"

Betjeman glared at Flint as if Flint were an idiot, and sniffed. Flint read the sniff to mean that the mere disappearance of people didn't compel the sheriff to begin a manhunt. That's how he would quote him, anyway. Betjeman never protested when Flint translated gestures and snorts and grunts into words.

"Did you try Tucson? Did they show up there? Spend some of the profits in the *cantinas*?"

The sheriff scratched an ear, which was a danger sign. The man was getting impatient.

"Have you talked to Mrs. Rakoczy about it recently?"

"Uh-uh," said the sheriff.

"I will, then. It's pretty plain something bad has happened. No news. No letters to his wife. No word from the *vaqueros*. No money drafts or letters of credit in the mail. Are you going to do any more?"

"You never know about Hungarians," said Betjeman.

The remark was beyond Flint's powers of interpretation, but

he suspected it meant that the sheriff didn't much care, and probably regarded Rakoczy as a crackpot.

Flint decided to make the long trip out to the ranch himself. At her request, he had written up the story of her missing husband and pleaded in print for news. She had posted a hundred-dollar award for information. Now he would have to tell her that no news had drifted in with the mails. Merry-Grace Rakoczy had slid from worry to dread, and from dread to despair these last weeks. Now she would sink even farther. He wished he could comfort her.

"Sheriff, there's trouble here. Five men have flown from the face of the earth. Mrs. Rakoczy is probably a widow and in trouble. Are you going to do anything at all?"

Betjeman looked soulfully up at the ceiling, consulting with angels or phantoms. "It'll all come clear," he said. "Outside of my jurisdiction."

"Have you considered wiring the reservation agents?"

He nodded and smiled gently.

"Let me rephrase that. Have you contacted the Apache agents? They might know something. At the least, who's off the reservation."

The sheriff shook his head.

"Why not?"

"No crime," said Betjeman. He fired a fine brown bullet of tobacco spit into a chased-brass spittoon.

Flint sighed. He'd wrestled the sheriff all he could. It was this way every time. "All right. Anything else today?"

Betjeman was studying angels again. One had apparently landed on the butt of his revolver. "Uh-huh," he said.

"Well, what?"

"Dead sheep."

Flint waited him out. Sometimes the best way to get more than two words out of the sheriff was to cat-and-mouse it. Flint peered through the iron bars onto an idyllic afternoon.

"Stink," said the sheriff. "I rode out there. Can't get within a mile without a kerchief to the nose."

Flint itched to ask questions, but this veritable outpouring of words checked him. He studied the wooden floor halfway between Betjeman and himself, where the sheriff was observing spirits.

"Cowboy reported it. Charlie Suggs. Over to Pass Creek. One hundred seventy-seven, more or less. Can't tell. Shot. Forty-four cartridge and thirty-six ball. Wagon tracks, horse apples, no bodies."

Flint checked himself and waited.

"Sure a mystery. Maybe crime, maybe not. You might write it up and say the sheriff wants to know what's what."

Betjeman subsided into silence again. Flint intuited that he would volunteer no more.

"When?" Flint asked.

"Rode out yestiddy. Looked to happen three, four days previous. Smelt up a square mile."

"Where can I talk to Charlie Suggs?"

"Yonder," the sheriff said. He pointed westerly.

"What's your theory? Why would anyone shoot sheep?"

"Dunno."

"Whose grazing land was it—on Pass Creek?"

"Mummm."

"Was it public land?"

The sheriff didn't reply to that. "Cabin got burnt," he said.

"Sheep shot and a cabin burned? Whose sheep were they? Were they settlers? Chased off by someone?"

But Betjeman was studying angels where they had congregated two feet in front of his black eyes.

"Sheriff, this is a big story. It sounds like a major crime. There might be bodies."

"No bodies."

"What are you going to do about it?"

"Wait for a complaint. Can't act until I get a complaint from someone."

That was a real answer for a change. "There were wagon tracks. Horses. Have you looked for wagons around here?"

The sheriff sighed and nodded. "Lots of wagons," he said.

"What kind of sheep?"

"Beyond telling."

"Have you a theory? What about settlers? Whose range did you say that was?"

"Public land."

Flint gathered that the sheriff knew and was ducking an answer. He tried a shot in the dark: "That's Clayton Buell's range, isn't it? Is he driving settlers off? He can't legally do that if the land was homesteaded."

"Hummm."

"I'll get it from the judge if you won't tell me. Did you question Buell?"

The sheriff shook his head.

"Why not? He's the only one likely to know the story."

"Ask in your paper whose woolies they was; the sheriff wants to know." Betjeman turned to his desk, presenting Flint with his bony back. It was the usual signal that today's newsgathering at the sheriff's office had come to an end.

"I might. And I'm going to be asking my own questions. If you don't want to deal with the case, I'll look into it myself. That's what newspapers are for. It looks like some poor settlers got driven out and their livestock murdered because they stood on their rights. Is there anything else I should know?" Flint said at the sheriff's back.

The sheriff was trimming a lamp wick.

"If you're excusing something Buell did, or covering for him, the paper is going to say so."

The back and arms and hands froze for a moment, but Betjeman never turned.

Flint retreated into the bright day. He'd had more than his fill of a sheriff who wouldn't discuss legitimate business or make his actions public. It didn't stop there, either. He was getting less and less out of Basil Cutlip, too. They had lured him to Payday to publicize the place, but they weren't cooperating on the more sensitive stories. He felt that the new log courthouse contained secrets, or at least understandings, that he was not privy to and that were kept from public scrutiny.

He found Horatio Thimble working steadily at breaking down a page. The man wasn't gaining much speed, but it didn't seem to matter. He took after his tasks with such steady determination that his lack of dexterity wasn't important. In three days, Thimble had come to grasp the whole operation and had freed Flint to get out more.

"I wrote up a business announcement and sold an ad," he said to Flint.

"Good. You're a valuable help to me. Mr. Thimble, I'm going to be gone the rest of the day. I'm going out on a story. A flock of sheep was killed over on Pass Creek, and the sheriff isn't talking much about it. He says a cowboy reported it after the smell alerted him. I'm going to go look, maybe talk to Buell—that's his corner of the basin—and go on to Rakoczy's ranch. No word's come in, and it looks bad. I have to let her know."

Thimble was staring at Flint intently. "What about the sheep?" he asked.

"A hundred seventy-seven, more or less. All shot. Some wagon tracks, horse sign, burnt cabin. No human remains."

"Did the sheriff say anything about who did it?"

"No. I could hardly get him to admit it was public land and Buell's range. But that's how it is. Getting something out of him is like drilling molars."

"Are some gentlemen around here above the law?"

Thimble was perceptive, Flint could see that. "If they are, this paper is going to bring it to public attention. I haven't been here long enough to know. But a good paper has fangs and the courage to bite."

"Will you tell me what happens?"

"Sure, Mr. Thimble—"

"Someone was hurt," the new printer's devil said. "Some settler's dreams are feeding the vultures. The only thing most people have is dreams. Take away dreams and a lot of people die just because they can't go on. Not a step more. Lots of ways to kill people, sir."

"I hadn't thought of it just that way," Flint said. "Mr. Thimble, you'll make a great editor some day."

Flint thought the new man would like the compliment, but instead, the big apprentice whirled around, turning to his work.

14

Flint's sullen livery horse balked, and he knew he would have to go the last distance on foot. The sickening smell had panicked the horse, and it had fought the bit and refused to heed the tap of heels on its ribs. Flint could barely endure the foulness himself. He tied the horse to a limb, knotted a bandana over his nose—a pathetic gesture—and hiked up Pass Creek.

The meadow exploded with movement when at last he pushed through a stand of cottonwoods to view it. Raptors fled, wheeling upward. A bold coyote watched, and reluctantly abandoned its turf to the man.

A rancid stench churned Flint's stomach, and if he had not seen worse in war, he would have lost his breakfast. There was no point in examining carcasses; he headed instead toward the charred cabin. It was an elongated rectangle, suggesting several inhabitants. The green logs hadn't burned much, and in fact, the cabin could be salvaged. He circled widely, hunting for disturbed ground where human bodies might be buried, and found nothing. Some horses had been picketed here, and grass had been trampled around a wagon there. Faint iron tire marks indicated that the wagon had come or gone from the road to the south. What monstrous thing had happened here?

Hastily, he retreated from the abbatoir, untied his horse and rode east. The mount needed no urging. Two hours later, he turned into Clayton Buell's ranch yard. Unlike the settled, comfortable appearance of the Rakoczy ranch, this one had a raw look about it. Several log buildings dotted a flat, and Flint could scarcely make out which one was occupied by Buell. It turned out he didn't have to. Buell himself emerged from one, a lean, erect man with a determined gait.

"Mistah Flint, suh?" Buell said, staring upward at the mounted man.

"If you could spare a moment, Colonel Buell, I'm pursuing a story," Flint replied.

"Ah haven't a moment, but Ah'll spare you the question. Ah shot those sheep, and Ah chased some settlers off of my range. No one was killed. Ah was compelled to that course of action, which Ah regret. There's your story."

"Who were they, Colonel Buell?"

"If they wish to reveal themselves to you, suh, they will do so at their own discretion."

"Were they homesteading public land?"

"Ah discouraged it. Ah'll discourage all efforts to settle on my range, especially along the creeks."

"That's illegal."

"Ah'm weary, suh, of Yankee legality."

"How did they resist?"

"That is up to them to tell you."

"Did they go into Payday?"

"Ah haven't the faintest idea. There's your story complete, suh. You may print it as you wish, and say about me what you will."

"Was it an act of justice, Colonel Buell?"

"There is no justice anywhere in the universe, Mistah Flint. It was an act of force majeure."

"Do you fear indictment for this?"

"Not in the slightest."

"You are saying that no official will act?"

"No, Ah said Ah don't fear it in the slightest. Report accurately, if you will."

"Did you shoot the sheep personally?"

"Some."

"Then others might be subject to criminal or civil proceedings."

"No, suh. Good day now. You have the story entire."

"Not entire, Colonel Buell. I'll print what I have and keep on digging."

"You do that." Buell wheeled away, and there was no point in trying to squeeze any more from him.

The ex-Confederate disturbed Flint. Some deep fanaticism, or seething hatred, percolated through that man. Flint studied the ranch carefully, because a place often supplied insight into its owner. The most striking feature was its impermanence. Everything looked ready to be abandoned at a moment's notice, as if its creator supposed that it would all blow away. He saw no gardens, no flowers, no shrubs. The pole corrals were workaday affairs, with bindings of rawhide, as was the custom in the area. He sensed no roots punched into this Eden. The owner was blind to its beauty. The main cabin was not situated in any way to take advantage of the grand view, either up toward the top of the Mogollon Rim, or out upon the green savannas of the basin. A single small window served only to admit daylight, not to nurture the spirit of its occupant.

It seemed an odd thing that Buell would build himself no home, see no beauty, impose no order upon this raw camp, and yet defend his claimed range, all of it on public land, with the ferocity of a lion. This ranch exuded pain.

Buell vanished into a horse barn, where a black man was

holding a good-looking bay horse by the bridle. When it came to horseflesh, at least, Buell had an eye. Flint wished he could just talk for a few hours with the man and absorb the contradictions and antagonisms and sadness. He turned his livery-stable mount and lifted it into a jog.

The Rakoczy ranch was another two hours away, south of the road. He supposed he was going to have to report what he had found out to the sheriff, and he had a hunch that Betjeman would affect vast indifference. He wondered how Basil Cutlip would react to this open resistance to Cutlip's settlement schemes.

The road toward Merry-Grace's home danced with light. Bees meandered among the lush shrubs, along with butterflies as gaudy as a tropical garden. He passed multicolored longhorns standing belly-deep in grass; those bore the Buell brand: a large "B" on the left shoulder.

He let the plug horse drink at a ford, while crystal creekwater eddied over the nag's fetlocks. The summer sun burned down from zenith now, and this portion of the day in the Tonto Basin was becoming uncomfortable. But he didn't mind; half of his passage took him through shady bosks.

They had seen him from afar, and when he rode up, Merry-Grace was waiting for him on the veranda, her hands clenched into her white skirts. She had changed. Anguish etched her young face now. She watched him somberly as he reined his horse and stepped down.

"Bad news," she said. Her eyes were pools of blackness, drawing in the light and radiating none.

"No news," Flint replied, not quite knowing how to help her, or even how to talk to her about this looming darkness in her life. "I was coming this way, and asked the sheriff. He's contacted everyone, and no one has news."

Merry-Grace sighed the sigh of surrender. "Nicholas is gone. Something terrible has happened."

Flint could not bring himself to dispute it. "The waiting must be hard," he said.

"It was. It isn't now."

"You mustn't give up, Mrs. Rakoczy."

She eyed him impatiently. "Ignacio rode down the trail clear to the Gila and back, looking for something. He didn't see a thing. He said there weren't tracks anymore; no Apache sign, nothing. He came back filled with sorrows. '*Señora,*' he said, 'the *patron* and four *muchachos* have flown into heaven.' He asked me to be brave, as if bravery could possibly answer the gnawing questions. I . . . I only wish I could know, now. He's dead. I know that . . . but not for sure. They're all dead."

Flint had no answer to that. The woman he secretly loved had slipped into a despair that was slowly crushing her spirit and her life. "Would you show me the fields? I . . . heard he was experimenting with crops that might prosper in the basin."

She looked for a moment as if she would turn him down, and he was sorry he had added to her pain. But then she brightened and managed a smile. "I'll show you," she said. "I would like my son to join us."

The proprieties. She knew, somewhere within her, that Flint's interest went beyond journalism. Flint couldn't hide it. He accepted her discretion and approved. She returned from the interior with a son beside her, the ten- or eleven-year-old youth he had seen when he was first entering the country.

"This is Andrew," she said. "He's a bookworm and I've dragged him away from *The Three Musketeers.* This is our new editor, Mr. Flint."

Andrew acknowledged Flint sulkily and from searching eyes.

They strolled out to the fields, and Merry-Grace showed Flint a plantation of paprika peppers, and another of young, green flax, planted sparely.

"He tried to grow flax for linen first, but this climate's too warm and dry," she said. "You plant densely for that. This is a seed crop, and the plants are set farther apart so they'll spread out. Maybe we'll pioneer a source of linseed oil in Arizona, and flaxseed for the livestock."

"Your husband was adventuresome. A visionary." Too late, he wished he had changed the tense.

"Yes, he was," she said, soberly, not changing it. Gravity clung about her. She had obviously wrestled with all that for many weeks, and was not surrendering to self-pity.

She took him to a terraced slope and showed him young grapevines strung on pole trellises. "Nicholas thinks we'll have a splendid white wine they make from these grapes in Hungary," she said. "Maybe in three or four years. These cuttings came from his family's estate near Lake Balaton. But it depends on the blight. Old World grapes don't do well on this side of the Atlantic."

"I admire his imagination."

"Of course we have cattle, too. Many longhorns. He didn't know a thing about them when we came here. But now he is a fine cattleman." She smiled. "He's more careful about things than the Texans. He culls better. Our animals weigh more. And he's sold off the ones that seem very—antagonistic. These are too dangerous. He always says, 'We shall tame the wild longhorn.' "

"How did you meet him, if I may ask?"

"Why, in Paris. My parents gave me the Grand Tour and there he was, in a left-bank café, studying us the way Pasteur studies microbes, and smiling at us like a demented fool. My mother thought he was a pest and hissed at him."

"What did he do?"

Merry-Grace's face flooded with light. "He sent a street urchin to us with a bouquet. There was nothing to do but thank him—in French, of course. He didn't speak a word of English."

"And that's how it began?"

"It almost didn't begin. My father certainly discouraged it. He had not designed to have some mad wastrel of a Hungarian youth, probably penniless, marry his daughter. But Nicholas wasn't quite penniless; just temporarily. Oh, I shouldn't be telling you all this. It really isn't anything that would entertain you."

"Ah, but I want to know. I've wondered—"

"Oh, Mr. Flint, I can't answer another question." The momentary joy of her memories had deteriorated. "Andrew will show you the rest, if you wish. The stables."

The moment of heady joy had passed and she had returned to the bleak present. He accompanied her and her son back to the veranda.

"I must excuse myself," she said. "Thank you for bringing me . . . your news."

Flint felt bereft and torn. He nodded and retreated, as bewildered and tormented as she. But unlike her, he felt guilty also, loving her as he did.

15

Jerusalem Cobb, for that was his name, regretted the day that
Sam Flint drove into town with his press and fonts. Cobb should
have foreseen what would happen, but he hadn't.

Like the other merchants, he was eager to draw settlers into
the area and secure better transportation. His general mercantile
made a small, steady profit, but nothing compared to what it
should earn. He was forced to tack on freight costs larger than the
wholesale price of his goods. He often lacked grocery and hardware items because he simply couldn't get them, and his stock of
boots and ready-mades was sketchy. He needed more customers
and better transportation, and a newspaper had seemed the best
way to encourage both.

What he hadn't counted on was Flint's fascination with the
Congressional Medal of Honor given to Jerusalem's older brother
Isaiah. Jerusalem had commandeered it after Ike died from war
injuries. He should have known; newsmen were nosy. And skep-
tical. And good students of human nature. From their first meeting, Flint had visited the store several times a week. He sold
advertising space, which Jerusalem was eager to buy; he often

shopped there, and he picked up the twice-weekly mail that arrived via Prescott and Tucson. And scarcely a visit went by without Flint bringing up the subject of the war, and of the glowing story he intended to do about Ike.

Resolutely, Jerusalem had deflected the questions. "I never talk about the war or the medal," he said, over and over. He thought Flint would give up eventually, but Flint didn't. Jerusalem knew that he was getting into deeper and deeper trouble, and that his life and reputation in Payday, Arizona Territory, was in jeopardy.

In 1863, young Jerusalem had fled the war. He had done it openly, telling his banker father, Archibald Cobb, that he didn't intend to submit himself to the death, disease, and filth of the soldier's life; that he didn't much believe in Mr. Lincoln's war anyway; why shouldn't the South be cut loose? His father disapproved. No son of Archibald Cobb's would surrender to cowardice, which is all that his fancy rationalizations amounted to. "Ike is serving his country with honor; you will too," he told the younger son. "You're eighteen and an adult. You can honor the Cobbs or dishonor us. I'll not buy a substitute so you can avoid the draft. We have means, but I'll not use them to underwrite dishonor. It's your decision to make."

Jerusalem's decision was to flee. He withdrew his entire savings, mostly parental donations since birth, and headed west.

Then Isaiah won the medal for extraordinary bravery and devotion to his trapped comrades, and was gravely wounded in the process of saving a dozen lives under terrible rifle fire. By then, Jerusalem had slid west through war-torn Missouri and Kansas, out upon the plains, spending little of his hoard, until at last the death-gripped land lay well to the east and Jerusalem was a free youth with a horse, a rifle, and a good kit to take him where he would go. He had never served a day under arms. It wasn't hard to find work as a teamster with freight outfits on the Santa Fe Trail, then largely under Union control. Patrols might search wagons now and then for Confederate contraband, but never did they pull draft-dodging young men from the crews.

All went well until suddenly Isaiah was a national hero, recognized by Congress and written up in many of the papers of the North. The news reached Jerusalem in Sante Fe. The tone of his father's letters darkened. Isaiah was a hero and a patriot; Jerusalem should come home and redeem himself.

But Jerusalem didn't go home. In 1865, with the war all but over, Isaiah died of his war wounds. This time Jerusalem drifted back, ready to resume life in Indiana, only to find that he was the family disgrace. His brother had been elevated to some sort of local sainthood; Jerusalem had been demonized. People knew he had dodged. He was called the dirty coward, the wastrel brother. One veteran spat at him in the streets of Evansville. His life lay in ruins. He could never marry, and his former sweetheart, Josie, wouldn't even look at him. No one would employ him. Then one wild day, Jerusalem stole the medal—an impressive medallion on its watershot blue silk ribbon—from its shrine in the Cobb parlor, along with the parchment citation, and left Evansville behind him forever.

It didn't at first occur to him to become Isaiah. His only thought was to escape, to bury himself in the vast frontier, far from censorious eyes and public records. Maybe out there he could get a fresh start. But one day in the brawling cattle town of Ellsworth, he saw a girl who set his heart to soaring. Without premeditation, he introduced himself as Isaiah Cobb. Thus it began, almost innocently, all for the heart of a lovely, spirited girl, Lizbeth, heading west with her parents. It came to nothing; the family had detrained at the railhead, purchased an outfit, and headed for Colorado. But Jerusalem's life had changed once again. Now he was Ike, a hero of the war. He found that his reputation was bankable. When he opened up a shop, people came and bought from the war hero.

A few years and a few mercantiles later, he was a prosperous, single young merchant in Payday, with bright prospects and the admiration of the whole town, even including a few Rebs who honored courage wherever they saw it.

But he got no pleasure from it. The fraud weighed like a millstone on him. He lived in daily terror of discovery. At first, he had listened alertly to veterans reminiscing about the war, studying their lingo, their expressions, their anecdotes. But it came to him that no amount of study could substitute for the real thing, especially since Isaiah had been a lieutenant. Jerusalem then took the only course open to him: he absolutely refused to be drawn into any discussion of the war; not by other men, not by the young women he occasionally sparked.

Still, Flint's *Pioneer* made frequent mention of the Medal of Honor winner living in Payday, and thus word of Cobb filtered out with the exchange papers. Cobb lived in daily terror that some editor back East would expose the sham, announce to Editor Flint that Isaiah Cobb was dead and buried in a hero's grave in the Evansville Calvary Cemetery under a granite obelisk.

One June day, Cobb decided to act. He might spare himself some anxiety just by reducing his daily contact with Flint. When the editor came in that morning, Cobb braced him.

"Look, Sam, I'm going to stop advertising. I can't afford it. There aren't enough new people in town to make it worthwhile."

"But Ike, advertising's what draws them in."

"No, I've got the postal window. That's all I need. Sam, I owe some cash on the ads, and I'll pay it off. I don't have much, but I'll do that. Then we'll be square."

Sam Flint scratched his head, worried. "You're one of my biggest advertisers, Ike. I tell you what. I'll carry you for a while. Or I can cut down the size and just use smaller type to get your message across. You've been buying a third of a page; how about a quarter?"

"No, Sam. I've got the mail franchise, and that's all I need. It's touch and go until Payday grows some." Ike hurried to his cashbox. "I've toted up what I owe. It's a hundred and four dollars and change. I've got it right here, Sam. Cash money. You're always saying you need cash for newsprint and ink and postage."

"Sure, Ike, I do, and I'm pleased to get it, but I think this is hasty."

Jerusalem sighed. "No, I've been thinking about it for a month. Maybe someday in the future I'll start advertising again." Slowly he counted out some tens and ones and a few shinplasters and pressed them into the editor's hands. "I've got this young fellow, Artemus Thimble, clerking for me, Sam. I'll make sure he trots your mail over to you as fast as it comes in."

"That's not necessary. I'm always buying groceries and stuff anyway. Ike, this doesn't make much sense to me. Is there something about all this I'm not understanding?"

Jerusalem recoiled, and then smiled. "No. I suppose you're thinking that I've got a bone to pick with you. I haven't, Sam. Don't think it, because it's not so."

Flint seemed to see right through Cobb, as if nothing could ever be secret inside of Cobb's soul. "That may be true, Ike," the editor said at last. "Now that you've got a clerk, maybe we can get together a little. I've been meaning to have a mug with you some afternoon. We've got a lot to talk about, and you have more stories buried in you than anyone else in Payday."

"I don't drink."

"Well, have a sarsaparilla while I drain a mug of pilsner."

"I'm a loner, Sam. I just like to close up and have a bite at the Cochise Café and go home and read."

Flint smiled. "I'm going to run a card for your mercantile, just to keep tongues from wagging. You'll have a box in every issue. You won't owe me a thing. I'll just list your stock—groceries, ready-made boots and shoes, home hardware, carriage hardware, drygoods, hats. Did I miss anything?"

Cobb felt less comfortable than he had in months, and was starting to sweat. "That's fine," he said shortly. "Much obliged."

"We'll get some settlers in soon, Ike. That little paper's float-ing all over now. I've sent a few of each issue to new places—Mis-souri, Ohio, Texas, you name it. We haven't seen much yet, but Payday's on the map now. These Thimbles were the beginning. That's a family of four hardworking folks right there. Horatio said he saw my stuff in New Mexico. I'd say that within a fortnight, we'll see more like them. It takes folks some time to make up their mind, pull up stakes, and hit the road."

"Yes, well, that's progress, Sam." Cobb was perspiring as if the day were furnace-hot.

"Stop by for some of my week-old java, Ike. I still want to set you down and get the story."

"No," snapped Cobb.

Flint replied amiably, "You have a lot to be proud of, Brother Cobb. Someday you'll feel like remembering. When you do, I'll be there to write the story as modestly and carefully as you would ever wish. I'll show it to you before it runs, too. I know how it feels to be in your shoes, I think."

Jerusalem Cobb watched the editor stride out of the emporium. It was plain to him that God in His wrath was going to grind Jerusalem Cobb, young brother of a martyr hero, through the mill-stones of hell.

16

In his courthouse chambers, Judge Basil Cutlip read the new edition of *The Payday Pioneer* with a certain dyspepsia of body and soul. The judge didn't like the story about Clayton Buell, especially emblazoned on the front page, and wished Flint had had the decency to bury it on the third page, if he had to run it at all.

It wasn't the sort of story to attract settlers. Buell had not shrunk from acknowledging the deed, which seemed very like the man. Probably the isolated old Reb colonel wanted the story told as a caution to future settlers. About the only thing that Cutlip and Buell agreed upon was the need for a better transportation, but Cutlip doubted that Buell wanted so much as one more settler in the Tonto Basin.

Cutlip grunted. Whoever the besieged settlers were, they would probably demand their day in court, and Cutlip would probably have to deal with it. He confessed to himself that he might tilt the scales of justice a bit—not toward the aggrieved settlers, but toward Buell. He didn't quite know why. Surely Clayton Buell was lord of the basin, holding legally or illegally much of the lushest country under the rim, employing a large collection of well-armed drovers, and possessing sheer cantankerous willpower, along with contempt for the world. Cutlip acknowledged that he was a little scared of the man, though there was no need to be. He also acknowledged, cynically, that if Buell drove settlers off of his range, they would likely settle on public land adjacent to his own holdings, or even buy land from him. He sighed, not unhappily.

The rest of the issue annoyed Cutlip, too. There, on page one, sour as buttermilk, was yet another story about the missing Rakoczy, this time quoting rumors that ascribed his disappearance to the Apaches. Cutlip fumed. The less said about the Apaches, the better. You couldn't get in a lot of settlers if they expected to be a pincushion for redskin arrows the day they arrived.

The lengthy piece about the lack of a public school irked him too, along with the editorial on page two advocating a small levy to fund a schoolhouse and schoolmaster. Cutlip owned more patented land than anyone in the county. The burden of a school would fall largely on his own weary shoulders. It was hard enough to put his life back together after the reverses in Galena; taxes would only make it worse. The school levies would delay the day when he and Violet could abandon this miserable tract of wilderness and return to fine cuisine, good Kentucky whiskey, riverboat trips, balls at the several other mansions in Galena, and brisk profits from commodities trading, bridge tolls, and banking. Violet had soldiered well here, but she ached for just one party at which she might wear her seed-pearl ballgown and silk Parisian slippers.

The rest of the *Pioneer* seemed all right. A birth, three business announcements, and the usual quirky collection of aphorisms drawn from Aristotle, Plutarch, Hadrian, and other relics of another age. They certainly set the tone of the weekly:

Socrates thought that if all our misfortunes were laid in one common heap, when everyone must take an equal portion, most persons would be content to take their own and depart.

—Plutarch

That one decorated page one. On page three, Flint quoted Plutarch again, this time in a somber direction:

As Caesar was at supper, the discourse was of death— which sort was the best. "That," said he, "which is unexpected."

—Plutarch

Cutlip discovered a lengthy piece inviting the world to supply Payday with a much-needed cobbler, freight outfit, sawmill, brewery, dairy, tailor, dentist, doctor, jeweler, undertaker, and harness maker. All of these the town lacked, and Flint had gotten the bright notion of telling the world about it. He might have added the need for a few more restaurants, Cutlip thought. It wasn't that the Cochise Café's meals were bad; it was that the town lacked variety, half-civilized as it was. All in all, the piece was a shrewd invitation to outsiders, the judge concluded.

He discovered still more Plutarch on the back page:

Statesmen are not only liable to give an account of what they do or say in public, but there is a busy inquiry made into their very meals, beds, marriages, and every other sportive or serious action.

—Plutarch

It amused the judge. The paper would at least edify Payday, if it achieved nothing else. He decided to meander over and commend Flint. It wasn't that he approved of this issue, but he wouldn't be Basil Cutlip if he failed to understand that one influenced a man of backbone with compliments, not carping.

He found the young editor doing his books and writing up invoices, while the new assistant broke down the latest edition. Flint dipped his nib into the inkpot, added some figures to Abel Greene's bill, and then leaned back. "You've a bone to pick, I presume," he said warily.

"Ah, Flint. No bones at all. I just stopped by to tell you the issue was magnificent, especially your ongoing efforts to lure good and useful citizens to Payday."

Flint grinned. "And to let me know you aren't happy with the school story or the editorial, and wish I hadn't raised the Apache issue, and had declined to publish Buell's confession."

"Oh, now, Flint, you're too touchy. I'm a larger man than that, I trust. No, I'm here to let you know that your little *Pioneer* has done yeoman work in the vineyards. We should see an influx of settlers any day now. It takes a while, you know. People have to make the decision to pull up stakes."

"And come here and buy your town lots. Have you met my new man? This is Horatio Thimble. He and his family are our first-fruits. They've all settled into positions here; Mrs. Thimble at the café, the two sons in service. Mr. Thimble, this is Judge Cutlip, one of the committee that lured me to this wild place to publish a paper."

"I am honored, sir," Thimble said, surveying the judge with intense interest.

"You were enticed by Flint's depiction of this country, were you, Mr. Thimble?"

"Yes. I saw the story in Socorro as we were passing through. I thought it might be excellent country in which to raise stock . . . someday."

"Ah, it is. You should homestead. Lots of free land everywhere and much of it perfect for stock. I could show you whole sections, close to a future railroad right-of-way, well suited and decently watered. You and Mrs. Thimble could claim a half-section. Now if it's a town lot you want, I just happen to have a whole portfolio of them. You can buy them in fee simple. Come to me whenever you're ready and I'll make sure that you have the choicest selections. You're the first, after all."

Flint stared at Thimble, as if awakening to something, but he kept his peace.

Thimble stood stiffly. "Maybe someday I'll take advantage of it." Then he returned to his labor, dropping each Caslon letter into its niche in the caseboxes, his face averted. Cutlip sensed something deeper and darker than what had passed upon the surface of the moment.

"Sam," he said, "I've been meaning to have a chat with you about the railroad. We need a systematic campaign to bring it here, you know. I've been in contact with the Santa Fe directors and their engineering people, but it's an uphill struggle. My point has always been that if they follow the thirty-fifth parallel, they'll have no freight or passenger traffic. The line'll run through Navajo country.

"Now, of course Payday and Prescott aren't exactly metropolitan giants at this stage, but that's where vision counts. Those calculating gents in their boardrooms certainly must know that they won't get much dunnage out of the reservation. They certainly need to know that even now, well in advance of settlement, thirty thousand cattle reside here, ready to fill their stock cars just as soon as the rails are down and the spikes in the ties. Now that's something to put in issue after issue."

But Flint wasn't an easy mark. "They don't get government land coming this way, Basil; they get a lot of it if they purchase the chartered Atlantic and Pacific route."

"Well, that's a point you'll need to deal with. In fact, if you'll save me some space, I'll draft the argument and you can run it under my name. I think the basin's ready for it."

"I'll run any signed opinion, within reason. But you may find that others are opposed. I'll run them, too."

That seemed fair enough. "I'll have a draft before the day is out. You can run it in the next issue. A capital job, that's what you're doing here. Now do you mind if I correct a few impressions that people might get?"

A wry smile filled Flint's face, but Cutlip didn't mind. Flint was no fool. "Say what you will, Judge."

"All right. It'll be just a word or two about the Apaches. They're perfectly tame, you know. The White Mountain tribe is settled upon a fine reserve, and won't bother a soul. Now of course, the Chiricahuas around San Carlos are another matter, but that's just the point I want to make: Payday lies in a blessed and protected vale, far removed from tribulation."

"You go right ahead and say it, Judge," said Sam Flint. "And we'll hope that the news never contradicts you. But you know, Eden didn't lack a serpent."

17

Flint had never experienced a woman quite like the one who had entered his editorial sanctum. It was her air more than the way she presented herself to the world, although her clothing was rare enough.

She wore stiff black silk, chin to toe, her dress embroidered black upon black with roses and petals, a few black sequins adding to the effect. Black fabric buttons paraded by the score down her bosom. The blackness was unrelieved by any white lace at the cuff or neck, although she did wear a curious ornate cross of gold, with inlaid turquoise at its extremities.

Although her face was pale, flaccid, and shopworn, the black reached into it around the eyes, which reminded him of dead coals set in charcoal hollows. Her black hair had been severely subdued into a bun. But that didn't explain her either. When she entered the office, she somehow sucked all the light out of it, steeping the room in darkness and dimming the very sun, as if she were a total eclipse.

"You are the editor here?" she asked.

"Yes, ma'am, Sam Flint. What may I do for you?"

"Answer some questions."

"I'll be glad to. I didn't catch your name."

"That's because I didn't offer it. Now then. I am interested in building a boardinghouse. I wish to know a few things. Is there another?"

"Not a real one. In fact, we desperately need one. The Drover's Rest has a pair of rooms in the rear—mostly used by drummers. But we lack a proper place, especially for women. A boarding-house would—"

"How many saloons?"

"Ah, the four on the east edge of town."

"Who visits them?"

"Mostly drovers. This is ranching country. Of course our businessmen go there now and then. They're quiet places, suitable for husbands and fathers to share a mug or two with friends."

"How many drovers?"

Flint hadn't the faintest idea, but he conjured up a figure. "I'd say a hundred. The saloons on the south side are patronized by former Confederates."

"How many large ranches?"

"Oh, a dozen. But we're going to have more soon."

"Is Payday going to grow, or is it all bunk?"

The question caught him like a blow to the solar plexus. "Why, look about you. Who can resist this Eden?"

"The great majority," she said. "Who lives here?"

"This is a family place, unlike most frontier villages."

She reflected for a moment. "Families don't support boarding-houses."

"We need one. We have the courthouse, which draws people. They need somewhere to stay while doing business here. We're developing some freight routes. Judge Cutlip thinks we can lure in a railroad."

She eyed him skeptically. "A railroad? Through here? No. But you will get some teamsters."

"I take it you have some experience of this sort of place."

She smiled for the first time, and was transformed slightly by it. "How many live here? Do not exaggerate."

"Six hundred in town, three hundred on the ranches."

She sighed. "No bank."

"None. There's a lack of cash in Payday. People barter. Judge Cutlip negotiates financial instruments. We need a bank, but we're too small to support one."

"I supply my own cash," she said. "It's a gamble here. You are an optimist."

"We all must be."

"How does one purchase lots and build swiftly?"

"Why, that's easy. I'll take you over to Basil Cutlip's land office. He platted the town and owns most of the unsold lots. He's charging twenty-five for a residential lot, a hundred for a business lot."

"And putting up a building?"

"The fastest is with green logs, but you'll regret it. Dimitri Bukovich has a small sawmill west of town—cuts just about enough for a house or two. You'll want to buy what he has. Maybe import some sawn wood from Prescott."

"Carpenters?"

"Two dozen men here support themselves in various ways, including carpentering, milling, bricklaying, well-digging, stonemasonry, roofing. One fellow makes shakes. They'll do a better-than-average job."

"How about furnishings?"

"Ike Cobb at the merchantile can supply some, order the rest. Some is locally made. Rather rustic, but serviceable."

"How are the saloons supplied?"

"It all comes up from Tucson by ox train."

"Is there a saloon tax?"

"No, but there should be. The county's tax-starved."

"All right, take me to Cutlip."

Flint untied his printing smock and led her into the street. A curious ebony vehicle stood there, hooked to two black nags, rather in the manner of an English hansom cab. The two-person passenger compartment was hidden by black-velvet tasseled curtains. A cadaverous driver, as unfamiliar with sunlight as the woman, sat at the front, idly undulating a whip. He wore a black-silk stovepipe hat, boiled white shirt, black cravat, and black suit, along with shining black boots.

Moments later, Flint ushered the woman into Cutlip's handsome real estate office and found the judge whittling a Havana cigar.

"Ah, Basil, this is—" It struck Flint that he didn't know her name.

"Odie Racine," she said.

"Ah, yes, enchanted, madam. Welcome to our fair and prosperous and blooming metropolis."

"It's Miss. Miss Racine."

"Ah, yes, of course. These things are always a tad awkward."

"Miss Racine wishes to build a boardinghouse," Flint said.

"Ah, indeed! A boardinghouse. Why, we have a need. We lack a hostelry of any sort. We could use a true hotel. You'll do a splendid trade, especially when the growth we anticipate—"

"I never wait for trade."

"Oh, yes, financial wisdom if ever there was some. Now, I would recommend a lot on the square, privy to the courthouse."

"Are there lots next to the saloons?"

The judge was taken aback. He raised a bushy eyebrow. "I don't think you'd have the trade there—"

"Drovers, Judge Cutlip."

"Ah! You're ahead of me, Miss Racine. Yes, drovers do board, at least overnight."

"I wish to know whether the four saloons are considered a public nuisance in Payday."

"Not at all. We're a quiet town, and they're quiet men, many of them veterans, who come for a mug or a shot and some whist or euchre. No, our good sheriff, Arnold Betjeman, is never troubled by any of them."

"What sort of gentleman is he?"

Cutlip studied Miss Racine carefully, inflating his knowledge and his suspicions. "I daresay that Sheriff Betjeman is a live-and-let-live sort. Now, if things get out of hand, he'd be the first to wade in. But Payday isn't that sort of burg, if you know what I mean. This is Eden, you know. People gaze out upon the wooded slopes, listen to the crystal creeks and the singing birds, step into the friendly sun, and their spirits are subdued and calm. You might say that the Tonto Basin is, ah, a sort of church in its own right. We haven't much organized religion here, although I suppose some circuit rider will eventually conduct a revival or two. I'm sure you'd welcome the public edification."

The angle of Cutlip's discourse amazed Flint.

Odie Racine smiled graciously, more expression on her face than Flint had seen so far. "Show me the plat map," she said.

"Why, of course, of course." Cutlip could move his bulky carcass in an awesome hurry when he wished. "Now, while I unroll it, I'll ask you what brought you here."

"Mr. Flint's exaggerations."

Cutlip laughed. "He didn't exaggerate a thing. I think you should ride around. You look in need of some sun. You're probably a night owl, like me, and miss the glories of nature. We shall have to take you on a picnic beside one of our sparkling creeks."

She eyed Cutlip mockingly. Flint watched the faintest curl of amusement lift the corners of her lips. Then she bent over the plat. All the lots had been numbered. Most were unsold. She pulled out a lorgnette from her small handbag and studied the town as if it were a cadaver.

"My gracious, Miss Racine, you're getting in on the ground floor. See how Payday'll grow! I'd suggest that you acquire lot number seventeen, there, or twenty-one, here. I think they'd be close enough to your drovers and still draw other traffic, families in from the ranches, drummers, people with courthouse business. As I say, they're a modest hundred dollars and we can work out terms. There's not much cash here, but we have our ways. And you may wish to purchase a residential lot also. A woman of sensitivity may wish to reside apart from her place of business. I could sell the pair, the commercial lot and a residential one, for a little less— say, a hundred fifteen, and on generous terms, low interest."

Odie Racine straightened, stared into space for a moment, and came to her decision.

"Judge Cutlip, I will purchase thirty, thirty-one, thirty-four, thirty-five, forty-seven, forty-eight, fifty-one, and fifty-two. That's eight commercial lots. I'll want a discount, of course." She pulled open her little bag again, and extracted a roll of greenbacks. From this she peeled seven one-hundred-dollar bills and pressed them gently on the plat. Flint glimpsed a nickel-plated derringer within the bag.

Flint craned to see what lots she had purchased, and discovered that she had chosen the two lots on either side of the saloons on each side of the street. The woman obviously intended to operate more than a boardinghouse.

Judge Cutlip stared at the amazing little stack of greenbacks, as limp as wilted lettuce, and then at her selections. "Done," he croaked. "I'll draw up the deeds in a trifle, and you can register them at the courthouse for a dollar apiece."

"That will be fine," said Odie Racine. "Now, Mr. Flint, kindly summon this sawmill man. And then the carpenters. And I shall need to see Mr. Cobb about furniture. I wish to open my boardinghouse in two weeks."

"Two weeks!"

"Money talks."

Flint sighed. "I hope you'll advertise."

"There never is a need," she said.

18

The hills above Merry-Grace crawled with Colonel Buell's cattle. She watched helplessly as a giant herd, thousands of longhorns, drifted like a grasshopper plague down the long slopes, mowing the tender grama grasses. They were being pushed by unseen hands; though she never saw a drover, she knew they were just over the ridges. Cattle didn't move like that save when they were herded. In this lush country, the kine rarely abandoned their own well-watered bottoms unless there was a drought—which there wasn't.

Colonel Buell was taking advantage of her, enjoying her helplessness now that Nicholas and his drovers were gone. It made her bitter. Her dear Nicholas was probably dead. As the days drifted by, that conclusion had forced herself on her. And now her neighbor was driving his ten thousand beeves over her ground.

Andrew, Stephen, and old Ignacio were out in the fields, trying to keep the beeves from destroying the flax plants. But what could two boys, eight and ten, and one old man do? Already, Buell's invading army had tested the barbed wires and no doubt would break them, trampling the pepper plants. At least the grapes, young and vulnerable on the terraced slope above the house, didn't interest the cattle, but they had knocked down some of the trellises.

A great brindle longhorn bearing Buell's mark meandered straight toward her like a lord, its giant horns swinging back and forth. Even her ranch yard wasn't sacrosanct, and if she didn't watch out, they'd break into her fenced vegetable and herb gardens.

She ran straight toward it, waving a broom. "Go!" she cried.

The bull turned and trotted away, leaving green piles in its wake.

In the midst of all this, she espied a visitor approaching in a black buggy drawn by a smart-stepping trotter. She waited impatiently. If it was Buell, she intended to appeal to his conscience—if he had any. She had supposed he was a civilized and honorable man. But it wasn't Buell. She could see that. As the buggy approached, she realized it was Basil Cutlip, massive in his dark suit, his face shadowed by his broad-brimmed straw hat. He steered the conveyance right toward her on the veranda and drew to a halt. The lacquered black buggy, with gold filigree, had been talcumed with red road dust.

"Ah, Miz Rakoczy, I've come for a little visit. May I join you on the veranda for a tad?"

She nodded. She needed a visitor. He emerged from the buggy, tilting it sharply as he avalanched to the ground, and then studied the fair hills, burnished green with early summer grass.

"Why, I have never seen so many kine. You must be prospering."

"I'm glad you came, Judge," she said. "Those aren't mine. They're Clayton Buell's. He's driving them over our land. You're witnessing something so awful I don't have words for it. He's taking advantage of my helplessness."

The judge frowned. "I never imagined Buell would do something like this. You have no way to stop it."

"My boys and old Ignacio are out trying to protect the fields."

"It's an outrage," the judge said, but the tone seemed perfunctory. "May I have a word with you?"

She eyed him, troubled. He wasn't really very interested in the crisis that was eating away her ranch from under her. It was almost as if he were shamming sympathy, like some lightning-rod drummer or sewing-machine peddler, just to get a sale.

"Yes, of course," she said quietly, remembering to be a hostess. "Would you like a glass of springwater? We have very good water here, sweet and cold."

"Why, later, I imagine. I've been worried about you—Mr. Rakoczy gone, and all. I thought to come out and make sure that things weren't amiss. I see that they are." He dropped a black carriage weight to the red earth and hooked it to the trotter's bridle.

After he'd settled into a squeaking wicker chair, she joined him in another. The veranda was a blessed place during the high-summer heat, always cool, and with vistas that quieted the soul. The judge had something on his mind, and she wondered if it would only mean more grief for her. Without Nicholas, she felt so helpless, so *naked*.

He lifted his broad straw hat, releasing his long locks. He looked like a supreme court justice, or a great senator, she thought.

"It must be very hard on you, the waiting," he said tentatively.

"Nicholas's often late, Judge Cutlip."

"You've considered the alternatives, I trust."

She nodded.

"But have you really? There comes a time to come to decisions. A time to prepare for changes."

"I'm not ready for that, Judge Cutlip. He may come home. He . . . maybe he's not dead. Indians capture people, you know."

He smiled somberly. "'And what do you think the chances are of that?"

"I don't think in terms of chances. I just keep the faith and wait. My Nicholas will come home." It was bravado, but some intuition made her say things she no longer could support within her heart.

"My dear Merry-Grace, how long do you suppose a man—five men—can lie wounded? Or how long can they be kept captive without being discovered by the cavalry? Or how long do you suppose Nicholas could tarry in Tucson, or Northern Mexico or wherever, without writing or letting you know?"

She didn't reply to that. He was rehearsing all the thoughts she had entertained for months. "I have no proof of his death," she said.

"That's so, and it kindles hope. But it also leads to, ah, a lack of planning, which leaves you vulnerable. If I may say so, what we see before us—" he waved at the drifting battalions of cattle— "is the destruction of the Rakoczy ranch before our eyes. I'm afraid our friend and neighbor Colonel Buell has abandoned all honor. You're a young and desperate widow."

"You're calling me that; I don't call myself that."

"Ah, my dear, there's the crux of the matter. When will you acknowledge it? Today? In a week? Next year?"

She eyed him quietly. "What did you come here for?"

"I believe you're in trouble, and I came to offer help."

Somehow, the answer didn't satisfy her. "I'm going to stay here, talk to Colonel Buell until we come to an agreement, and wait for Nicholas."

"Let me say, plainly, Nicholas is dead. Nothing is accomplished by pretending he isn't, and much is lost."

"Neither of us know that—unless you came to tell me something you've learned about him."

"Believe me, no matter how hard the news, I would share it instantly. No. Nothing new. But the situation requires mature judgment. You have your sons to think of. And your own life. Were you cut out to live in isolation, in hard labor on a remote frontier? I think not. The Woolcotts, I gather, enjoyed quite another life. Rather like our own—Violet and mine—in Galena. You may find yourself yearning to return to that life, if only you peek beneath your most admirable and gracious sense of duty and loyalty. Most admirable. One can discover a wealth of good examples in the conduct of Merry-Grace Rakoczy."

She felt very still, as if the earth had paused, as if that army of invading cattle weren't demolishing the Rakoczy range. "I like it here," she said.

"Of course. Idyllic. This home, so exquisitely planned and built, is a work of genius. I've always admired the Hungarians, who build with their souls."

She liked that, even if he troubled her. She began to feel herself in the jaws of a vise, with Buell twisting one jaw and Cutlip the other. It became hard to breathe. She waited for him to continue, offering him no encouragement.

"I took the time to examine the county plats and homestead claims and other items. Nicholas homesteaded what he could, once the county was surveyed. You have your homestead quarter and Nicholas his. We sit upon private land. Your crops are on private land, I believe. And by other devices and proxies, you've acquired, or are homesteading, three sections, and claim ten of public land as your range. Squatter's rights. You've gone much farther than most. Buell's patented only a few forty-acre pieces, and avoids almost all taxes. He squats on a hundred square miles of public land."

"My husband comes from a place where land is scarce, and he thought differently. We've preferred the taxes—and the titles."

"Ah, yes. That makes this ranch especially valuable. I'd say it might yield you three thousand."

"There is no price that can be put on a place you've built with your own hands, out of your own dreams, Judge."

"Ah! I understand the sentiment exactly! But practicality comes creeping in on cat's feet, does it not?"

"No," she said sharply. "I don't give up dreams so easily."

"Well, I wouldn't want you to. I would want you to begin new dreams—sending those fine boys to Harvard or Yale—having the comfort and security of a trust. Getting on with living after so large a loss."

She sighed. "I don't believe a missing person can be declared dead for seven years."

"Oh, the law has multitudinous ways, my dear. One can establish a conservancy, or assign right-of-attorney to someone you trust to take care of your interests. If you should desire to rebuild your life elsewhere, why, I'm at your service. I can pay you cash, even in this cashless place. And I can dispose of your livestock for you at a nice gain. You might go East with a very princely five thousand in hand."

"I have not even buried Nicholas. I have not even arranged for a service. And you come with this!"

He looked stricken. "Ah, forgive me. I've been insensitive. But truly, some good has been served here if I've focused your mind upon matters that cry for attention."

She wanted to tell him he was thinking of his own gain; of the profits from selling the land to the settlers drifting in; of dividing it into a dozen places for nesters; of showing crop farmers that crops could be raised in the basin—and selling the bottomland and hay fields for a large gain. He'd buy it for five and parcel it out for twenty. She clenched her fists and released them, waiting until she could control her tongue.

"I'll consider it. Thank you for coming. I'll make my decisions in my own good time. When I arrive at my answers, I won't regret my choices." She stood, clearly inviting him to leave.

He worked the brim of his straw hat around, placed the hat

on his head, grasped her hand between his big, warm, comfortable ones, and squeezed. "You are a splendid lady, and I rejoice to be of service," he said.

She watched him drive off, feeling the clutch of her aching heart.

19

The grim look on Merry-Grace Rakoczy's face suggested new grief, Sam Flint thought.

"What brings you to town, Merry-Grace?" he asked.

"I want to buy two ads," she said. She handed him two sheets of paper. One read: "Drovers wanted. Immediate employment. Inquire at ranch or leave word at newspaper. Rakoczy Ranch, east of Payday." The other read: "Experienced ranch foreman wanted. Immediate employment to qualified man. Rakoczy Ranch, east of Payday."

"These make sense," Flint said.

"Make them big type. I'll pay when I can. I am sending more cattle to the railroad."

"How many men are you going to employ?"

"Ten or twelve."

"So many?"

Something hardened her face. She stared uncertainly at the new printer's devil, Thimble, at work setting up the press, and decided to confide in the two men. "I've been overrun with Buell's cattle. I need men to drive them off before they eat my whole range.

It's deliberate. He's pushed his entire herd—thousands and thousands—onto my land."

"Colonel Buell did that? Taking advantage of a widow?" Flint wished at once he hadn't said that.

She bridled. "I don't know whether I am a widow or not, Mr. Flint. But when I'm ready to be a widow, I'll let you know."

Rebuked, Flint apologized. Mrs. Rakoczy seemed unusually distraught. Near the press, Thimble listened intently.

"I'm also sending some men with a small herd of my own to the railroad. I have to raise cash," she said.

"Have you talked to the sheriff?"

"No. It's public range. Colonel Buell isn't doing anything illegal. We were all squatters until last winter, when the federal surveys were completed. Then Nicholas and I filed on what we could. And so did Colonel Buell. The first ranchers simply divided up the public land into ranges. The colonel and my husband worked out a boundary line. It ran along a wooded ridge. Cattle hardly ever cross it. He squatted on his piece of public land, and we squatted on ours until we could file on it." She paused uncertainly. "And I don't think Sheriff Betjeman is the man for the job, anyway. He's . . . not adequate. And furthermore, the colonel's a county supervisor."

"What have you done so far?" Flint asked.

"It's all my boys and Ignacio can do to keep the cattle out of the flax field and the pepper plantation. That's the reason, you know. Colonel Buell doesn't want crop farmers to settle here. There's so many cattle, and we can't guard at night. His cattle have never experienced barbed wire, and they just push in. We can't keep it up anymore. So there goes Nicholas's dream."

"Your crops are on your patented land, aren't they?"

She nodded. "We patented our cropland every way we could. Homestead, Timber Culture, proxies. You can't enclose public land, and we needed to protect the crops. The fences are all on private land." She paused, seeking ways to explain her dilemma.

"Nicholas worships land. It's scarce in Hungary, and every hectare is treasured. We were going to add steadily, in spite of the taxes and burdens. He always said he loves to stand on his own ground and feel his own dirt under his feet."

"Have you thought of a civil suit? Colonel Buell's clearly causing damage to your private land."

She seemed to swallow back something. "It won't work," she said. "Even if I could afford a lawyer."

"But Merry-Grace, it holds promise. Make him pay!"

"No!" she cried. She stared at him uncertainly again. "I'll tell you something, even though you're a part of the town's Merchants' Committee and you'll be against me. Judge Cutlip tried to buy me out for a song yesterday. Oh, he oozed sympathy and kindness, and said it was all for my own good, but he wanted to make a killing. I told him most of the property belonged to Nicholas. We'd have to wait seven years to declare him dead—if he is—and the judge said he had all sorts of legal snake oil to get around that. I know you're on his side; you're friends. You're all trying to develop Payday and bring in people and freight outfits and a railroad, and I don't suppose a woman like me—"

"Merry-Grace!" Flint interrupted. "Listen! I run this paper as I see fit. It's independent. I told Basil Cutlip he wouldn't like some of my reporting or my opinions. He knew I meant it, and he accepted it. At least he said he did."

Something softened in her face. She seemed near tears. He could see the desperation in her, but also the iron will. This remarkable woman wouldn't give up without a fight, if she ever gave up at all.

"Anyway, I'd like the ads put in this issue, and I'll pay you when I can. And I'd like you to let me know if anyone applies here. Or send them out to me. I'll take anyone I can get."

"Merry-Grace," he said gently, "I'd like to do a story. Would you mind?"

"About what?"

"About what Colonel Buell is doing. And that you've been pressured to sell. I'm going to press tonight. I don't have time to go out and interview Buell—not that he'd say much anyway. I'd have to ascribe everything to you, but I can still do it."

"What good would a story do?"

"It's news, and I report all the news. I don't know what good it would do, except shine light on your troubles. A newspaper isn't a lawyer, isn't a sheriff, and isn't a weapon—except in one or two respects. A truthful newspaper can awaken public feeling, appeal to the decency of people. The other thing it can do is alert officials to trouble."

"They'd gang up against me. They all think Nicholas was an eccentric, a foreigner, and they just barely tolerated him. And Basil Cutlip—well, what chance have I in court against a judge who sits in the center of the county spiderweb?"

"I'll do the story."

"All right," she said. "Not that I have any say in it."

"I prefer consent," Flint said. "The story will do you no harm, and might help. It could even draw cowboys to your bunkhouse. They're mostly romantic young men, I'm told. There's another thing a paper does: it makes a record."

"Oh, Sam," she said. "You're the only friend I have in town."

"No, ma'am," said Horatio Thimble. "You have another friend."

She eyed the middle-aged man with surprise. "Why, thank you, Mr. Thimble. I don't know how I've earned that."

"I'm a man who wants justice."

Flint stared sharply at Thimble. For some while he'd suspected that it was Thimble's herd and cabin that had been demolished by Buell, but the man never said a word and Flint respected his silence. "I'm glad you do, Horatio. This paper stands for justice, wherever it may lead. But we must always be careful of our facts. We aren't partisans of any faction."

A look passed between him and Thimble, as if each knew the

other's thoughts. But Merry-Grace missed it. She appeared worn to the bone. The brightness had fled her, and she seemed a decade older than when Flint had first encountered her. "I wish I had news of Nicholas for you," he said. "Any sort of news would help."

She dissolved again into desolation, and he wished he hadn't brought up the subject. "Thank you," she said, so softly he barely heard it. She hurried out into the hot day, and Flint thought that his editorial sanctum was suddenly robbed of light. Even in her grief, Merry-Grace shed illumination upon his heart. He could not answer his own question: why did he care so much? And what did he really feel about Rakoczy's disappearance, and the emerging reality of Merry-Grace's singleness? He shoved those scorching, dangerous thoughts out of mind.

"I'm going to tear up the front page and pull my school editorial from page two," he told Horatio. "I'd like you to build these ads. Make them two columns by four inches each."

Thimble withdrew the completed forms he had shoved onto the press and loosened the wing nuts so he could remove the type.

Flint plucked up his type stick, set an empty galley tray before him, and began a new front-page story, composing it as he slid the upside-down letters into the stick, adding lead slugs between words to justify the line.

He wrote dispassionately, ascribing everything to Merry-Grace. It didn't ever pay to use inflammatory language. A spare account of a great cruelty to a bereaved woman would be tinder enough to ignite public sentiment. He didn't stop with the cattle invasion either, but continued on with the rest of her story: Cutlip's pressures on her to sell out. He mentioned her advertisement for ranch hands, and told of her plans. The story wasn't long; ten column inches. He found space high on the front page by pulling a weather story, wrote a headline, "Neighboring Cattle Besiege Rakoczy Ranch," and put the page together again.

On page two, he inserted a new editorial: "The devastation of the Rakoczy ranch comes at a painful time for the bereaved Mrs.

Rakoczy," he wrote. "That the act, taken by Colonel Clayton Buell, who ranches northeast of Payday, was deliberate can scarcely be questioned, and is strange conduct from an honorable and admired county supervisor. While the cattle migration was from one portion of public range to another and thus has an aura of legality, the reality is that it devastates Rakoczy range. The cattle have all but demolished Rakoczy's experimental crops, thus ending for the time being any hope of diversifying the economy of the Tonto Basin.

"But the act was not only a cruelty upon a woman in distress, it was also a moral wrong. Much of the damage has been inflicted upon private, patented landholdings. The purpose that Mrs. Rakoczy alleges, that the colonel opposes settlement in the basin, may or may not be the case, but that will be the effect of his actions. If the colonel is truly an officer and a gentleman, he will settle generously with Mrs. Rakoczy. If not, he deserves public scrutiny.

"Mrs. Rakoczy has been under pressure to sell out at a price far below the market value of her holdings, this from the interests represented by Basil Cutlip's land office. Surely this is equally unsuitable pressure, unbridled opportunism. She will not budge, she tells us. She is not ready to concede that her husband is dead, along with the ranch's four employees. She points out that there has been no report of trouble or the discovery of any remains. That buoys her optimism, and she intends to keep on waiting for news. It is the hardest task given to any spouse, but she remains resolute and courageous in the face of deepening doubt. That is entirely her decision to make, and this paper applauds her fortitude. Let her alone, we say, for the sake of decency. And let her tormentor know of his shame."

He sighed. That was a strong opinion piece. He had written nothing like it since arriving in Payday. Every merchant in town would hate to see it and the front-page story, knowing the account would reach the exchange papers and all but shut down the trickle of immigrants arriving in the Tonto Basin. Flint knew, grimly, that his advertising would suffer when the merchants retaliated. But he had been in corners like this before and knew that even if he lost every advertiser in Payday, he would continue to pursue justice.

And that went double for the woman he loved.

"That's a fine editorial," said Horatio Thimble after proofing the page. "I'm proud to work for you. You believe in the things that count."

20

Flint knew he would be hearing from people about that issue of the *Pioneer*. And he was right. The very afternoon the paper reached its readers, Basil Cutlip meandered in, masked in cheerfulness. He eyed Thimble back at the composing bench and drew Flint off to a corner, out of earshot.

"Ah, Sam, that's quite a paper, this issue."

Flint anticipated him. "Not every bit of news I run is going to make Payday look good, Basil."

"Well, of course. And I'm grateful my name wasn't directly mentioned, even if I was the obvious subject. You might have consulted me before running Mrs. Rakoczy's accusations."

Flint nodded.

"You know, I grieve for her, Sam. I thought maybe I could help out. Rakoczy's dead as a stump, but she's not facing up to it. Widowhood's a responsibility. She has children. I wanted to give her a way out."

Sam grinned suddenly. "At a profit."

Cutlip beamed. "Of course. Who'd deny it? That's the wonder of business. When two parties strike a deal, each benefits."

"Sometimes," Sam said.

"Well, that's not why I'm here. I told you from the start that the paper could say whatever it wanted about me. But I'm concerned about Payday. You know. Cutting off the flow of settlers. That issue is going to scare dozens of people away. It just seems to me that some judicious caution might have been in order. Now, if you'd consulted with me first—"

"It wouldn't have changed much of anything, Basil. I would still have run those stories and the editorial."

"I see," he said. "Well, you've done magnificently so far. I've sold four city lots and put half a dozen businesses on their feet here in two weeks. We'll have a cobbler shortly, and a pastry maker, and a fire-insurance agent. I'm talking to a horse trader. So you see, bit by bit we're getting there. I've started some talks with two freighting outfits, and the stage line, too. And here's the best of all, especially for you: there may be a wire going in from here to Fort Whipple if I can get the capital together. I'd like the paper to be the Payday terminus."

"Really? That's good news, Judge. A wire puts us in touch with the world. I've noticed a few strangers. You'll have to introduce me. I'll do some stories about them, and write up some business openings."

"That's not all, Flint. There's some homesteaders staking claims south of town. I've privately warned them away from Buell's land, of course—they all want some of that lush grass and good water. I'm turning them toward drier country, but it's still good ranch land. And doing it privately, Flint. Without airing Buell's intransigence for all the exchange editors in the Territory to see."

"I understand," said Flint. "But news is news."

"Well, you're bullheaded, I'll say that," Cutlip said. The mask never slipped from his massive features. "I just thought I'd pass the time of day. Let you know how splendidly the paper's coming along. You have the business community at heart."

Flint smiled and saw Cutlip to the door.

"What was that about?" asked Thimble.

"That was a complaint about the stories," Flint said.

"Did he threaten you?"

"No, he wouldn't do that. If they—the merchants—were to start pulling ads, they'd just do it and let me see my profits vanish and figure out why. There wasn't a threat."

"You'll hear from Buell, too."

"I imagine."

"But it won't be civilized."

"How do you know that, Horatio? Have you met him?"

"I just know it," Thimble said, compressing his lips into a thin line.

"Horatio, you're doing well. Gaining speed faster than I ever thought you could. If you want to make a career of it—not just wage labor to get you and your folks going—I'd welcome it."

Thimble looked for just an instant as if he were going to crumple, or even weep, but the moment passed so swiftly that Flint doubted he had seen it.

"Sam, I haven't made up my mind yet. I like it here. I want to write about things like justice."

"Justice?"

"Yes, sir. I think justice is the most important thing there is—save for personal liberty."

"Someday, Horatio, I'd like to plumb your whole philosophy. But just now, I've got to take a look at the new boardinghouse . . . if that's what it is."

"It isn't," Horatio said. "I walked over there. It isn't that, Sam. It's something that'll change this quiet town. Odie Racine's no boardinghouse-keeper. I'm waiting to see how it all falls into place before I make any decisions about staying here."

"I'm afraid you're right," Flint said. The woman was erecting a two-story frame building. Rumor had it that the lower floor would house a saloon and gambling emporium, and the upstairs would be divided into cribs where soiled doves would ply their trade. It wasn't exactly the sort of business expansion that Payday's merchants had had in mind, and it might be something he would be taking up soon in news stories and in his opinion columns. Once the enterprise opened, Payday would never be the same, and Arnold Betjeman would have a tough job—if he could handle it at all.

But before Flint could shed his printer's smock, Clayton Buell darkened his door, entered, peered around at the entire plant, studied Thimble, and finally Flint himself. The man was leaking thunder but said nothing, and Flint noted that the colonel was not young, and really no larger or brawnier than himself.

"Flint," said Buell, striding close. Flint balled his fists, expecting to defend himself. But the colonel stopped just short of arms' length. When he spoke, it was in a tone of voice so low that Flint strained to hear him. "Ah'll tell you just once, Flint. If my name ever appears in this sheet again, Ah'll flay you with a bullwhip. Ah'm good at it. Ah'll make you regret the day you were born. You won't even have to use my name. It applies to any story in which Ah'm recognizable."

Flint could see Thimble straining to hear. Flint didn't budge. In every town he had ever published, without exception, he had received physical threats. They seemed to be a part of frontier reporting. "I will publish the news," he replied softly, surrendering nothing. "And if you come, I'll be ready for you."

"You are warned, suh."

"I appreciate it. But it won't deter me. Was Mrs. Rakoczy right?"

"It is not your business."

"Why did you do it?"

"My conduct is not for public scrutiny."

"Had you given any thought to her bereavement?"

"Ah will not subject myself to an interview."

"They tell me you fought honorably for your side, a true officer and gentleman."

Buell reddened. The purple veins in his nose—the man was familiar with barleycorn—seemed darker to Flint. Some swift epiphany led Flint to see the man not as a bully, but as one carrying unbearable wounds, so terrible that his spiritual pain was making him lash out at a benign world around him. But the moment passed under the glare of Buell's smoldering brown eyes.

"Ah repeat, suh, one lapse and Ah'll flay the flesh off of you."

"And I repeat, Colonel, that if you abuse that desperate woman, it is news and I will report it. And if you abuse settlers or new neighbors, I will report that too."

They stood there at loggerheads, neither budging an inch. Then, from some underground river of the heart, Flint found himself saying the unexpected. "You've become a hero of mine, Colonel. You picked up a shattered life and started anew when other men would've died of loss and grief. I'd love to write that story someday. All this will pass, and the time'll come when we'll share a whiskey and branch together, maybe in one of the saloons south of the road. I was a private in the trenches, and I'd like to hear your side of it, as long as the war is so alive in both of us."

For the smallest moment, Buell's imperious glare softened, only to harden again. "You heard me, suh," he said. Then he turned to Horatio, who was standing as rigid as a statue behind the ink table. "And that goes double for you."

They knew each other.

Stiffly, like a wooden soldier, Buell scowled, turned, and walked out, leaving an odd vacuum and a terrible silence in his wake. Flint watched him stride purposefully along the clay street and finally vanish into the livery barn.

"You stood up to him, Sam," breathed Thimble.

"I've stood up to a lot of men. People who don't like to see their behavior in print get mad. I was almost shot once—until I talked the man out of it. Turned out he had a grievance. I had gotten a story all wrong, and damaged him. It's a tricky business, Horatio. Getting a story right requires a certain dedication. And more. I'm always humbled by how much I get wrong in nearly every story. Mostly it doesn't make any difference, but the errors, the twists, are there. Newspapering's a business that I won't master in a lifetime."

Horatio Thimble nodded and returned to the ink table to proof a galley, but Flint stayed him.

"Horatio, it's time for you to tell me about the butchered sheep . . . and what you're going to do about it."

Horatio Thimble clenched and unclenched his fists, and began to talk.

21

Flint listened as his bearded, gray-templed, flinty printer's devil quietly recounted the entire story of his confrontation with Buell. It left him puzzled.

"Why didn't you leave with your herd, Horatio, and take the matter to court? You have a valid homestead claim."

Thimble peered at him sharply. "I refused to retreat one step more."

Flint could understand that, and nodded. "But it cost you everything."

Thimble's face crumpled. "Yes," he whispered. "My pride and my hatred overruled me. I lost my senses. I should've backed off. Now I've cost my dear wife and my sons a year of labor." He looked at Flint from eyes radiating pain. "I was wrong," he whispered. "I just couldn't bear being pushed anymore."

"You faced firearms?"

"Only the threat of them. There's something you should know about the Thimbles. We're pacifists. We saw too much of war. I vowed never to do violence to another mortal for the rest of my life. My wife and my sons share my beliefs."

"Did you tell that to Buell?"

"I did. I told him we were pacifists and entirely at his mercy, and that whatever happened would be on his conscience."

"Buell wore the gray. It made no difference to him that you did also?"

"Yes, it made a difference. I could see it in his face. It turned bleak with his own darkness. I pitied him."

"You . . . pitied him?"

"He has obviously suffered all that mortal man can suffer. I don't know what."

"After the sheep slaughter, you came here, crushed and penniless. Why didn't you report the episode?"

"Mr. Flint, you're as innocent as a babe. You haven't experienced the Reconstruction South. The last thing one does is go to Yankee officials, carpetbaggers, tax collectors. We didn't get home rule until two or three years ago, after they'd raped us for all we had left."

"This isn't the South."

"Is there even one Southerner in the courthouse?"

"You could have appealed to a federal marshal in Tucson."

Thimble grunted. "What's done is done. Yes, I should have retreated for my family's sake. Have you never done something you regretted later? That doesn't mean I've given up. I intend to homestead our claims, one way or another."

"You'd face Clayton Buell again?"

"That land is my paradise. You didn't exaggerate. This basin is the place of my dreams. Someday my flocks'll graze the good sweet grasses. We'll be safe. My sons'll marry and live close. Gertrude and I—we'll be good neighbors to all souls. I started as a military engineer and ended up a pacifist and a shepherd."

"How?"

At last, Thimble's despair overtook him. "I don't know. We have a right to homestead. Our claims are filed over there in the courthouse. We'll settle here. Peaceably if Buell wants peace. If not . . . I'll find ways. Pacifists aren't toothless." He peered sharply at Flint. "You going to dismiss me now?"

Flint didn't reply to that. "Did you have more in mind than a wage when you came to the *Pioneer* for a job?"

"Yes, sir. If a man needs to know how a town works, who's the friend of whom, where to pull a lever, one comes to a newspaper. It all becomes plain to newspapermen. This is where I'll find a way to return to my land." Thimble stood straight, not yet bent by his crushing burdens. "I've already learned some things. Even if I earned the means to go to court against Buell, and got a judgment out of Cutlip, it wouldn't matter. The law's too weak to enforce a court decision against Buell. A newspaper's the place to learn about how things work."

That was candid enough, Flint thought. People used newspapers in various ways. Cutlip, Greene, Cobb, and the rest all had their agendas, things they would like to see *The Payday Pioneer* support or oppose. Flint had his own agenda, such as his campaign for a tax-supported school.

"There's no harm in that—within certain bounds, Horatio," Flint said. "There are lots of partisan papers around, especially out here, where editors trade words like bullets. Some editors are fierce Democrats, others strong Republicans. Some color their news with their views. This paper doesn't. I keep my opinions confined to a regular space on page two, and I sometimes publish opposing views, on the proposition that I'm no Solomon. Can you work peaceably within those boundaries?"

"I admire them, and you, sir. Yes, I can."

"You're an able writer and reporter, and soon you'll be a journeyman compositor. Would you like to continue here?"

"I would. I've discovered a joy in it. I'd like to do it even after I win my land back. For as long as you'd want me."

"Well, let's get to the nub of it. There'll be times when I'm gone, when the paper's in your hands. Would its basic principles remain intact?"

"Sir? Mr. Flint—"

"Let's say the news is that Colonel Buell has given some patented land to found a veterans' home. Would you write it generously, and give the man his due?"

"Yes, sir. And not because he's suffered more than I have, either. It'd be because the story is what makes the paper a trustworthy source of news."

Flint, filled with a sense of brotherhood, eyed the bearded, worn man before him. "I'm promoting you. You're no longer a printer's devil. You're the assistant editor. And your pay is now a dollar a day. It'll improve when the paper prospers. We'll put an announcement in this issue." He smiled. "Meanwhile, you'll still be doing the same things."

Thimble blinked. Softly, he said, "You're a man to make the world a better place, Samuel Flint."

"There is no other reason to be a weekly newspaper editor," Flint said. It filled him with a curious emotion. A person residing in Eden must possess a soul residing in an Eden of the spirit, or all would be lost. His own soul was as light as air.

"You're a man of conviction, Sam. You also seem to be quite alone in the world. Has there been no woman?"

"There was. I was to be married in sixty-six, but I broke it off just before the wedding, much to the dismay of her family and mine. The war made me too restless. I hurt her, hurt myself, and saved my life. I left Cincinnati."

"But have you no friends?"

"Horatio, editing a paper's the loneliest business in the world. A paper draws conflict to it. Some people want their ideas trumpeted. Sometimes they want to avoid public notice. Many's the man—or woman—who's come to me asking that I not print something they find embarrassing. I usually turn them down. Why, this very eve I might share a mug or two with Abel Greene, or Ike Cobb, and they'll urge me to keep something out of print, or to put something in. I'll refuse. Then my friends Abel and Ike suddenly become my antagonists Abel and Ike. That's how it is. You don't make many friends, not the kind who stay with you through all kinds of weather. To answer your question—I have friends. They're all temporary. That's what life is for an editor. Temporary friendships."

"I hadn't thought much upon it. It'll happen to me too, I suppose, working here. At least I have a family."

"There you have something I'd be very lucky to have in this lonely calling."

"Then why? Why'd you choose a hard vocation?"

Flint had no very good answer. "Some of us drift through life without marriage, without friends, without brotherhood. I'm one of those, mostly by choice. I'm no loner, but I'm alone. That's all the answer I can manage."

Thimble laughed. Flint had never heard him laugh in all their weeks together. "I like a stubborn man," he said affably. "You remind me of me."

Flint laughed too, but uncomfortably. "Well, Horatio, we've a lot of stories to collect and write this time. Judge Cutlip tells me there are some new homesteaders, and a few new shops about to open. He's been selling land and town lots, helping people homestead south of town, well away from Buell. Lots of stories in all that. But first, we have two stories to do."

"Two stories? About what?"

"One'll say that the owner of the sheep slaughtered by Clayton Buell has been identified as Horatio Thimble, who with his wife and sons made Homestead Act claims on Pass Creek and were driven off by Clayton Buell."

Thimble was thunderstruck. "But Flint . . . I thought we were talking confidentially. How can you do this? Let me live in peace."

"Because that much of it is news. Readers should be informed about that much of it."

"It's my private business, Flint. You disappoint me. I entered into this candid conversation assuming we were talking privately, man to man."

Flint didn't budge. "Let me tell you something about this paper, Mr. Thimble. If Sheriff Betjeman should haul me off to his jug on charges of public drunkenness, the matter would appear in the next issue, exactly as written in the court record."

"Is it not possible to have private conversation or friendship with you, Flint?" Scorn oozed from the question.

"Of course, Horatio—I may still address you familiarly?"

Thimble stood there, his passions rolling across his granite face like thunderstorms. "What's the other story?" he asked at last.

"That Colonel Buell came to the *Pioneer* office to protest the article in the present issue about his running his herd over public and private range controlled by Mrs. Rakoczy. And that Buell threatened to horsewhip the editor and his assistant if his name ever again appeared in *The Payday Pioneer.* "

"You would do that?"

"It's absolutely necessary."

Horatio Thimble glowed like a sundog. "Sam Flint, I reckon I've never met your kind. You figure we can give as good as we take from the old bull?"

They laughed, they stomped, they wept . . . and became friends.

22

It was hard for Flint to believe that Odie Racine could erect a building that covered an entire town lot in only three weeks. But there it was, a raw, two-story board-and-batten rectangle, with wood so green that sap leaked from the planks. Her cash had done it. When it became known that she would pay in greenbacks, half the men in town had turned themselves into carpenters or sawyers. It was said that the little sawmill west of Payday had run night and day the whole time.

It certainly wasn't a building built to last. Soon enough those green planks would shrink and warp. But a place with a climate like Payday hardly needed tight, winter-proof buildings. Then, one night without fanfare or advertisement, the place opened up as the Golden Calf. Flint had heard several earfuls of gossip about it, but he always discounted gossip as a dangerous source of news. The one thing he was sure of was that Odie Racine had not built a rooming house or a hotel.

He corraled Judge Cutlip that evening for a little tour. Usually, when a large business opened in a town the size of Payday, there would be a celebration. A committee of merchants would perform an opening ceremony with a few speeches about the rosy future of the place, and a ribbon-cutting ritual that was supposed to mark the beginning. But not Odie's place. She had scarcely met any of the town's merchants and had imported virtually all of her furnishings from mysterious and distant places. It all looked like an important story to Flint.

It was a particularly lovely summer evening. In a balmy, purple twilight, they walked along Basin Street, past the small, oddly quiet older saloons that were now dwarfed by the big yellow box of a building. A glance through batwing doors told them that this night, at least, the world was paying homage to the new queen. Horses stood hipshot at hitchrails, but scarcely a soul wandered the dirt street, or crossed the clay from one honky-tonk to another.

They stood at last before the palace, and Flint discovered a freshly painted sign proclaiming "The Golden Calf." The name struck a note with him, and he recollected the golden calf of molten jewelry fashioned by Aaron in Exodus, and the worship of the idol while Moses was away, and the death and plague that followed. Would death and plague come to Payday?

It didn't look like it. A crowd packed the Golden Calf, but it wasn't noisy, and all Flint discerned was a cheerful hum.

"Well, Judge, it isn't what I'd call rowdy," he observed.

"That's good. We can't afford a new deputy."

"I suspect there'll be some pretty wild times, though," Flint said, peering through the open double doors.

"I'm a student of vice, Sam. A wild place runs to petty vices, such as a tad too much red-eye. The ones that cause trouble are as silent as tombs. Serious vice is as silent as a stalking cat. Murder and highway robbery and that sort of thing aren't begat where people are having a party."

"I never had that perspective," Flint said as they pushed in. The place had drawn at least two hundred drovers and townsmen, yet seemed only moderately crowded. Several things struck Flint at once: it was poorly lit, with a few lamps hanging from the rafters here and there; it was as raw as a building could get, with the studs showing; and the lengthy bar and backbar had been fashioned from planks. And people weren't noisy. The sleazy building could burn to the ground or its denizens could be driven out of town, and Odie Racine wouldn't lose a lot. But one glance told Flint that the proprietess was going to mint money every hour this joint stayed open—especially on ranch paydays.

There weren't many at the long, dark bar, but scores crowded around every imaginable gambling apparatus known to man. Flint spotted four faro layouts, two chuckalucks, four roulette layouts, and a raft of poker tables. Tinhorns presided over them all, some in black suits, some in their dress shirts with sleeve garters. Smoke from their cigarillos drifted lazily through the lamplight.

"Some boardinghouse," said Flint.

"From what I hear, it gets worse," Cutlip said. They surveyed the tables, one by one. Judging from the way the stacks of chips stood, the sharks were swiftly gulling the cowboys, especially at the green-oilcloth poker tables and faro layouts.

"I'll buy some tonsil varnish," Cutlip said, sliding toward the bar. "It'll be a test." He corraled a mixologist whose pitted face had suffered the pox. "Two of your best bourbon, neat," he said.

The barkeep nodded, poured something yellow-orange from a green bottle without a label and slid two tumblers before them. "Two dollars," he said, coughing.

"Two dollars!"

"Two dollars."

Cutlip sighed and slid four four-bit shinplasters toward the man. "I haven't paid that much since a charity ball in Galena," he said. "I suspect I'll regret it." He lifted a tumbler to his lips, sucked, and gagged. "Ah!" he cried. "Turpentine, or a facsimile. Rotgut. Red-eye. Popskull. Busthead. Forty-Yard. You know how that got named? It makes you walk forty yards and drop." He turned to the barkeep. "My compliments. An outstanding selection."

Flint tackled his, wondering if it would make him blind. At least two sips didn't. But he wondered how to snuff the fire in his tonsils.

They turned their backs to the bar so that they might watch the action. Flint discovered a stairway at the far wall, which seemed to lead into blackness; at least no light filtered through the blue haze. Several gents, drovers all, ambled down the steps, looking sheepish. Someone laughed. A kid, barely fifteen, bravely mounted the stairs, driven by the raillery of some of his drover friends.

"Don't come down until you lose it," a bull-like top hand bawled.

"I don't suppose this will improve the local economy," Flint said to Cutlip, his tone more solemn than usual.

"Oh, it might, it might."

"I think most of it'll go into Odie Racine's purse," Flint said relentlessly. He tried another sip of that varnish. It was making his throat parch. "Either that or into the tinhorns' treasury. It doesn't bode well for the merchants."

"Ah, but it's a magnet. Payday will now draw drummers and travelers, teamsters and drovers, for a hundred miles around. It's going to be good for business. We're going to sell town lots."

"There's the lady herself," Flint said. Odie Racine was descending the steps from the mysterious reaches above. She paused halfway down, studying her clientele, dressed as usual all in black, with about a town lot's worth of decolletage. Her milky upper chest showed not the slightest sign of age. The elaborate cross hung in its appointed nest. Her lips were painted. She fastened upon the editor and judge at her bar, descended the remaining eight stairs, and headed their way.

"Do you like my boardinghouse?" she asked in a sultry voice Flint had not heard issue from her before.

"Your tenants don't stay long. About ten minutes," Cutlip said.

"I like turnover," she replied. "Here, dears, make yourself at home." She dipped into a little black thing that hung from one wrist and placed a brass token the size of a silver dollar in the hand of each.

"Consider it a bribe," she said.

Flint read his token. It said, "Good for One Screw."

"Will it buy some good bourbon?" Judge Cutlip asked.

"Anything and everything is for sale, including the building and the lots and me," she said.

"Ah, you've evaded my question. Will it buy some good Kentuck?"

"You're in the wrong place," she said, a vague disdain leaking from between her words.

"I'll give it to Violet," Judge Cutlip said. "Perhaps she can find some use."

"Everything's for sale," she retorted. "My god is money."

"Very good. You'll fit right in as long as you pay your taxes."

"I knew it'd come to that. It depends. I'm expert at leaving little dumps like this behind me."

"We've been needing a school, isn't that right, Flint?"

"Uh, Basil, I don't think this is the right tax base for a school."

"We already are a school, dearie. I employ five teachers." She didn't really laugh; it was an odd cackle.

"I think, Miss Racine," said Judge Cutlip with serious demeanor, "that you can expect some taxation for more law enforcement, at the very least. That's how it's done. And I think resistance would result in, ah, disestablishing you."

She eyed him knowingly. "See this joint? It's bare studs. I'll earn enough in a week to pay for it. It'll take that long to pass an ordinance to boot me out. I'll pick up and go, any time. Don't think that you'll squeeze me, because we'll just roll out. I'm a travelin' road show anyway. I'm betting on Payday. It looks like a jackpot. But that don't mean a thing when we get right down to greasing your county officials."

She seemed almost truculent, and Flint sensed she had conducted this sort of negotiation in several outposts over many years. He wondered how old she was: thirty to fifty, but he couldn't nail it down.

"It'll all be a good story," he said cheerfully.

"Keep me out of your rag," she said, "or I'll make trouble. I have ways you never thought of."

"When you or the Golden Calf make news, I'll cover it," he said. "Up until tonight, this was a town without serious vice."

"I don't believe it," she retorted.

23

Merry-Grace lay abed dreading the day. The world was closing in upon her. Each day it seemed less likely that she could last. The house itself felt alien now, as if she didn't belong there. The great log building was hunched down, poised to spit her out.

Nicholas had designed it, and even though it was a frontier log building like all the rest in the Tonto Basin, it was a Hungarian building, too. He had given them a huge, bright bedroom, larger than the parlor downstairs, so big that it gave them a private world of their own, with desks and armoires and stuffed chairs. In it was an oversized four-poster, empty and forlorn now. Often she would lie down on it, trying to salvage some courage from it, pick up his scents, or his spirit, or whatever it was of him that lingered there. But now that room seemed as alien as the rest of the great ranch house.

She could admit to herself that Nicholas was dead, even though she had not yet admitted it to the world. In Payday, they all thought she was clinging to fantasies. He would never come home. One thread of hope—that he was a captive of some Apache renegades—faded daily. At the moment, all the Apaches on the

reservations were accounted for and peaceful. The only other possibility, that he had been abducted by Mexican Yaqui Indians,
fierce cousins of the Apaches, was really beyond serious consid-
eration. She knew that, but still she caressed the idea as a way of
postponing the inevitable.

She would have to arrange a memorial service, an acknowl-
edgment that Nicholas Rakoczy had departed from the living.
Even that posed problems. He was Catholic, she wasn't; there
wasn't a priest north of Tucson, except for an occasional mis-
sioner. She would find a minister. Such services were more a consolation for the living than for the dead.

But wrestling with her grief—her love for him had been deep,
true, and filled with delight—was only a part of her deepening
struggle. She had to preserve what was left of their property. Each
day her world seemed to crumble, and now these very walls
seemed alien to her.

The advertisements in the *Pioneer* had failed. Not one drover
had applied for work at the Rakoczy ranch. Flint had sent no one
out, either. It seemed very strange. Surely there were cowhands
in the basin who lacked work or wished to change employers. The
last time she had been in Payday, Flint had told her that about a
hundred new people had come to the Tonto Basin, mostly as a result of his paper's efforts.

She needed the drovers desperately, not only to separate her
cattle from those of Clayton Buell and to push the trespassing
stock back to its own range, but also to drive a herd to the Southern Pacific yards, so she might get some desperately needed cash.
She had bought the ads for the second week, but she knew what
the result would be. Somewhere at the bottom of this was Clayton
Buell, the man feeding upon her grief and helplessness.

This day she would go visit him. Not because she expected
any good to come of it, but because it was all that was left for her
to do. It would be one of the harder moments in her life. She threw
back the coverlet and sat up, feeling the weariness in her young

body. She poured some lukewarm water from the pitcher into her basin and washed her face, wishing the water might drive away the pain in her heart as easily as it cleansed her flesh.

She chose a black linen dress, though it was midsummer and gauzy white cotton would be normal. Let him see her in mourning. She had not worn black before; defiantly, she had worn white or lemon, some brightness while she had waited for Nicholas to come home. When Merry-Grace emerged from her room at the rear of the long house, Luz glanced at her sharply, her face a mask.

"Please tell Ignacio to harness the spring wagon," she said, avoiding their usual morning intimacy when she and Luz chattered like jays in the lingua franca they had evolved. She wasn't hungry, but managed some sharp, hot coffee. Later, the servants and boys watched silently, their faces question marks, as she climbed onto the wagon seat. She rode away without explaining herself and drove the old horse through a pleasant, breathless morning.

It wasn't far to Colonel Buell's ranch buildings—two hours if she pressed along. She saw his cattle everywhere, fat and contented, chewing their cud while they lay near bosks of cottonwoods. Any other morning she would have rejoiced at these visions of Eden.

She discovered the colonel standing on the porch of his cabin. Several hands were at work in the corrals, where cattle bawled unhappily. Big, multicolored longhorns crowded every pen.

"Morning, Merry-Grace," he said neutrally.

He didn't invite her in, which she considered a small blessing.

She nodded, gathered up her courage and addressed him without any preliminary niceties. "I'd like you to remove your cattle from our range," she said.

"Ah don't think so," he replied.

"I'd like to borrow some of your men to cut out my cattle from yours, brand calves, and drive some to the railroad. I'll pay you from the proceeds."

He smiled suddenly, his face crinkling into crow's-feet. She hadn't expected that. "You just step down, Merry-Grace, and we'll walk over to the pens."

Puzzled, she stepped down, lapped the lines around a hitchrail, and followed him. When they reached the pens, she realized that the crew was branding. Several irons lay in a fire. Gifted hands were roping calves, dragging them away from their bawling mothers. Others wrestled the bleating calves, wrapped piggin strings around their feet or pinned them down while dirty, worn-out men swiftly applied a red-hot iron to the calves' flanks. Acrid smoke billowed up, smelling of burnt hair and seared flesh. She watched them brand a heifer and release it. The indignant creature hastened back to its mother, somehow pairing up.

"Yours," he said.

She stared again. The heifer wore the Rakoczy brand. Its mother bore the Rakoczy brand. She stared at the rest. Every cow-calf pair in the pen was hers. Every branded calf or newly made steer bore Nicholas's R-Bar brand on its flank. She stared at Buell, bewildered.

"Ah thought time was getting ripe to put your mark on your cattle," he said. "No one there to do it. You've lost a few slick calves already. Plenty of drovers around looking to put their own mark on a maverick. None of mine, though. Ah won't permit it." He pointed. "Look there."

She saw a big brindle Rakoczy cow suckling a bull calf that bore a rafter-J brand.

"Theft. Ah didn't much like these newcomers stealing Rakoczy beef, so Ah took steps."

"Please explain the rest," she said quietly, not happy with this odd show of neighborliness.

"A ranch has to be looked after, Merry-Grace, and Ah decided to look after it."

"Why are your cattle all over my grass?"

"Ah'm running everything together, ten thousand of mine and

a thousand of yours. Yours'll be eating over here when your place is eaten down; some already are."

"But why?"

"Ah'm keeping settlers off your place. It'll save you grief. You're not able to put up much of a fight, not with Nicholas gone. Now that Judge Cutlip got the basin surveyed, and he and the newspaperman are begging for settlers, we've got our hands full. Ah'm grazing the Rakoczy place right to the roots. It won't look good to some settlers. Poor grass, overgrazed. They'll pass you by, mostly."

"You might have asked me," she said softly.

He stared off into space. "Grieving needs to be let alone."

"I advertised for a ranch foreman and hands. Did you discourage men from hiring on?"

He nodded. "You've never run that ranch. Nicholas did. You're wrestling with loss."

"You might have let me decide that. I'm being treated like a child."

He grinned suddenly, and it was as unexpected as the first time. "Well, Ah suppose the Woolcotts fitted you out to run a big frontier outfit, handle a dozen men, fight off nesters. Ah guess the Grand Tour did it. You picked it all up in Florence and Naples."

The answer didn't mollify her. "You've made me your prisoner. You did all this without even consulting me. I need cash and I have no way to get it. You control my beef. I wish to plan my future, but you hold all my assets."

He stared over her head, and then into her eyes. "Merry-Grace, Ah'm not keeping you from anything. If you want to sell me some beef for cash, Ah'll pay you directly out of my safe. Ah thought to give you some time. Maybe six months, maybe more, for you to see how this all works out. Hold it for you until you've made up your mind. Ah'd hate to see Judge Cutlip walk away with your place for a fraction of its value. Ah thought if Ah just took away the worry and let you decide, let you come to some belief about Nicholas, why . . . " His voice trailed away.

She put a high-button shoe on a corral rail and pondered it. His intentions had been kind. He also had been imperious, if not insulting. But just now, relief flooded through her, lifting her heart, removing weight from her chest. "I'd like to sell you ten calves. I need money for groceries. I need to pay my servants. Pay me, and you can put your own brand on ten of these."

In minutes, the transaction was completed. She stuffed greenbacks into her pocket and watched his drovers brand the Rakoczy calves with a big B on their shoulders.

She knew she should thank him. A dozen of his men were doing Rakoczy work, but he was charging her nothing. It was hard to thank him for it. He remained an unfathomable, grief-ridden man, and she probably had become his puppet.

"I'd like you to come for dinner tomorrow night," she said. "I'll bake a pie. Nicholas loved pies."

"Ah'm afraid Ah'm going to be busy with branding, Merry-Grace. But Ah'd love to sample some pie."

She drove the spring wagon back to her home, through a world that seemed less threatening.

24

The assault rose so swiftly that Flint had no time to defend himself. He was composing a funeral story—Mrs. Schmidt had died of summer complaint—when Clayton Buell burst in, an uncoiled bullwhip in hand. The first lash broke over Flint's back, a streak of fire. The tassel popped his forearm, cratering his flesh. Flint howled. His type stick sailed to the floor, scattering the first clause of a compound sentence. The second lash caught his upper arm, bloodying it, and seared around his chest. Flint tumbled backward, his world aflame with pain.

Horatio Thimble bulled toward Buell, only to be driven back by the snapping, crackling whip. The colonel was a master, creating a lethal screen of braided leather and leaded tassel around himself, keeping both his adversaries at bay.

"Ah told you, suh, if you published my name in your rag again, Ah'd be here with the whip. Ah'm a man of my word. Ah'll be back again if my name appears one more time."

With that, Buell calmly strode out the door, his back as straight as a pillar, his broad-brimmed hat still glued to his head.

Flint slowly stood up amid a sea of fiery pain. He leaked

blood from a long red welt on his arm, and knew from the wetness on his back that blood was staining his shirt. His chest hurt, but had been somewhat protected by his duck-cloth printer's smock.

"Sam! Are you badly hurt?" Thimble cried.

"Don't know," Flint muttered through searing pain. He examined himself. The worst damage was to his left forearm, which dripped blood and stung so much it made him faint. Thimble helped him out of his printer's apron, with Flint gasping at new insults to his flesh with every movement.

"This shirt's soaked to your back, sir. It's not worth much now. I'd like to cut it off."

Flint nodded. Thimble gently sliced through the fabric with a scissors and laid Flint's back bare, then led Flint into his quarters, where there was a pitcher and washbasin. He set to work with a damp cloth while Flint groaned at every touch.

"Two welts, both bleeding. The cuts don't look deep, sir. But that's a nasty hole in your arm."

"They feel like they go down to bone," Flint muttered. "All right. Let's get me bound up."

It consumed a whole pillow slip, which Thimble quietly tore into bandaging. Flint sat silently, enduring the torture because he had to. He fought back tears, but finally surrendered to them, and they slid down his cheeks.

"Is this a hazard of the profession?" Thimble asked at last.

"It's my first acquaintance with a whip. But two or three times I've looked down the bore of a revolver. I've been threatened many times. Most unhappy people just bluster."

"People take the printed word seriously."

"It inflames some people."

"Buell wasn't inflamed," said Thimble. "I'd wager he was as cool and collected as any man could be."

Flint sighed. Even drawing air into his lungs set his back to throbbing. The relentless pain never lessened. "At least he gave me warning. Most don't. They just nurse their grievance until they decide to attack. They always have reasons, you know. It never occurs to them that most editors would print their side of the story."

"It's revenge, I guess."

"It's often more. It's punishment. This wasn't revenge; it was punishment for throwing light on his conduct. Buell saw it as a violation of his person. Most of them do."

"I suppose most editors just cave in. They don't want to be shot."

"Most do; I don't. Once it's known that an editor's afraid, it's all over. That paper's going to be the cat's-paw of some interest or other." But he wondered about himself. He knew he couldn't endure much more of this. Maybe he'd be a cat's-paw, too. A man could bear only so much, and this had pushed him to the brink. The knowledge disappointed him. He was weak, like all the rest. The stinging of his flesh would soften his paper. Unbidden tears welled in his eyes again, this time from his disheartening self-assessment.

Thimble finished his work and stood back. Flint's pain had reached his head, which now hurt wickedly. He wouldn't be much good for several days.

"It's going to be up to you for a day or two," he mumbled. He wanted to lie down. "You'll do fine. You're coming along, Horatio."

"Thank you, sir. I swear, if I could have gotten my hands on him . . . I owe him, sir. I owe him a thrashing he'll never forget. My pacifism doesn't include my fists."

"You can start with a story about this. Every detail."

Thimble gaped. "This? The whipping?"

"It's news."

"But he warned you again."

"That's right." Flint glared at him. "If you won't write it, I will." He flinched, anticipating more black pain.

"I'll write it! Everything! I admire you, Sam. But I hope you understand the consequences."

"I do."

Thimble stared into the gloomy room. "I wish I knew what drives the man. I know a little. Something in the war ruined his soul. My soul, too. But all this darkness he heaps on his neighbors—his cruelty to poor Mrs. Rakoczy—has no design in it that I can fathom. For the life of me, I don't see the colonel as an empire-builder, driving away competition. This is something else."

Flint's head throbbed, but the puzzle interested him. "Maybe he's driving away friends, Horatio. A man who's been wounded in the soul might not want friends. Might not want anyone around who reminds him of love. If that's Buell, then his business is to make sure not a soul on earth will remain a friend. Especially a Confederate veteran like you. Or a beautiful widow. Or settlers hoping to plant crops."

Thimble's face lit up. "You have something there. He's a hurting man. I saw it. When he found out I'd worn the gray, it only made him darker. That's when he shot the first ewe."

"Do you really think there's something in it?"

"I *know* there's something in it," Thimble said. "But I don't reckon any of us can do anything about it. And I reckon I'm not done with him."

Flint spent a long, agonizing day in his quarters, scarcely able to move without subjecting his flesh to new hurts. Thimble left late in the afternoon, and Flint decided that he was going to hurt as much abed as up, so he slowly dressed and wandered into the shop. Thimble's story lay in a galley tray, under the heading, "*Pioneer* Editor Whipped." The military engineer had done a workmanlike job, describing the whipping, the wounds, the previous threat and its fulfillment—and the promise to whip Flint again if Buell's name appeared again. Flint intended to bury it on page three, but run it he would.

He ventured into the late-afternoon sun, walked a block in close, hot air, and found Judge Cutlip still commanding his office, doing his accounts in the light of a double coal-oil lamp, all alone.

Basil's eyes raked Flint, missing nothing. "You seem to have lost an argument with something," he said. "I suppose an irate subscriber."

Flint managed a smile, and then a careful explanation, leaving out nothing. As far as he was concerned, it had been a rout.

Cutlip frowned, opened his humidor, offered Flint a cigar, which he refused, and lit one of his own with a lucifer.

"You're a glutton for punishment, but I admire it in you. That's what separates you from any of the scribblers I've met. Now, I'm going to offer you some advice. You're probably here to find out about legal remedies." He shook his head. "I don't think you'll get far. Oh, there're a lot of theoretical things you could do. Fetch a lawyer from Prescott since Buell employs Culbertson, file charges, ask for a restraining order, bring suit. I could grant you everything you ask. Mind you, I'm not saying I would. I happen to be just as independent up there on the bench as you are in your sanctum. And it wouldn't be ethical for us to be making arrangements. But as I say, I could. And then what? Send Arnold Betjeman out with a summons?" Cutlip laughed cheerfully. "Clayton Buell's his own law, and that's a fact of life in Payday."

"I was wondering about that," Flint said.

"He's an ornery cuss, and if you don't want to get hurt, you'd best avoid trouble."

"I can't do that."

"You're not an editor; you're a masochist."

"Call me what you will. I'm going to try to find ways to help people he's hurt. Especially Merry-Grace Rakoczy."

Cutlip exhaled a fine blue plume. "Law can't help much, I'll tell you that. They both were using public range. Buell and Rakoczy carved up the best chunk. But their agreement has no status in law. Or with public officials."

"His cattle have ruined crops on homesteaded or patented land, Basil."

"Well, that's actionable if she can pay for a lawyer, and if she's willing to suffer worse. You can count on it. If she takes him to court, she'll be hit harder. I know the old wolf."

Flint sat on the edge of his chair, unable to settle back upon his wounds. "Then there's only one thing left. Public opinion."

Cutlip laughed softly. "How many bullwhips and cannon does the *Pioneer* have, eh?"

"No guns, just convictions. And sometimes the power to persuade people of the justice or injustice of something."

Cutlip turned serious. "Sam, you've got to understand your limits. You're getting into trouble."

"Thank you, Basil, but I won't back down. Thimble and I have an idea or two. We don't think there's design in any of Buell's acts. They're all random and don't lead anywhere. Not to land or power. Not to wealth or privacy. We think it's something else."

Cutlip eyed him skeptically.

"He's just a mean sonofabitch," Flint went on. "He's not trying to achieve a thing. He's just ornery. It's his nature. Whatever goodness he had, the war wrung it out of him. If that's how he is, the *Pioneer* 's going to say so."

He left the judge at his desk, blowing smoke rings and shaking his head.

25

Abel Greene was bucking the tiger. The one-armed drygoods merchant and head of the Payday Merchants' Committee had discovered that Odie Racine's Golden Calf could be the place to while away an evening. It beat boredom.

This warm night, he was cleaning up at faro. He liked the game because it was hard for the tinhorns to cheat and because the odds were almost even. His pile of chips had grown steadily all evening, putting him in a capital mood. It was almost as if some intuition had been steering him toward the right numbers.

The tinhorn operating this layout, Red Queen, looked consumptive and was. He coughed politely into his grimy white sleeve now and then. He was cadaverous, black-haired, with burning black eyes that suggested fever, and was probably not yet thirty. His casekeeper, operating the wooden beads of the abacus-like contraption keeping track of cards that had been played, looked moronic but seemed bright enough to keep abreast of the play.

One by one, the tinhorn slid cards out of the oak casebox, decorated with a gaudy tiger: loser first, winner second. Greene had been playing losers all night, coppering his bets. The game was

simple enough: to bet, you placed chips on a layout with the cards
depicted in the spade suit. If you bet a number to lose, you put a
copper token on your chips. By keeping an eye on that case-
keeping device, you knew what had been played and what remained in the deck. The house had only one advantage. If the
dealer drew two cards of the same value, say sevens, the house
won. Other than that, the odds were always even. Since the cards
were drawn from a port in the box, it was hard for a tinhorn to
cheat. Greene thought that was pretty sporting, given all the ways
those table lizards could skin their victims.

Odie Racine had wandered past a dozen times. She always
looked like a funeral wreath, and always trailed a scent behind
her that reminded him of rotting apples. She rarely smiled, she
didn't greet her clientele, and her agate eyes bored into every table
game and every customer. A ruthless lady, Greene thought. Maybe
an asset to Payday, but probably not. Every few minutes, she
glided up those stairs over on the yonder wall, to look after the
other side of her business.

Greene had seen not a few townsmen he knew slither up the
stairs and then descend, staring straight ahead, hoping the dark
wrapped them. The light over there was so low that he could
hardly make anyone out, but he knew the gaits of some of the men
around town. There wasn't a lamp anywhere near that stair, keeping all that action anonymous. He had yet to see one of the ladies
and didn't know whether they were plain or fat, black or yellow
or white, pretty or loco, opium fiends or boozers. Miss Racine
never let them wander around the lower floor. None had ever entered his drygoods store to buy a ribbon or a yard of calico. It was
as if Odie Racine locked them up in iron cages during the day.

Gossip said she had five doxies up there, and five or six tinhorns and bruisers worked the lower floor. He saw two at that raw-
plank bar and three dealers working the tables—one poker, one
roulette, and one faro. A couple of other games stood idle. It
struck Greene, as he slid his chips out on the black images, that

almost all the men he saw in this joint were strangers. He knew Payday; he'd lived here since the town was nothing but a huddle of log cabins. These people were new to him. Some looked big and rough; some looked like sewer rats. Ranch hands probably, but there was no way of knowing. Several wore side arms, which made him faintly uneasy. They didn't really look like cowboys.

The big campaign to draw in settlers was netting a sort of drifter that no one had much thought about before it all began. The Territory boasted a lot of them. It made him wonder about all the horses hitched outside, bearing more new brands than he'd ever seen, some likely the artistry of a running iron.

He studied the cases and realized that no three had been played, and there were ten cards left in the box. That suited him fine. He shoved a stack of ten one-dollar chips onto the three and coppered the bet. The two other players bet on seven and jack to win. The dealer drew a four and a nine. Nobody won, nobody lost. The bets rode. The dealer drew a three, loser, and a jack, winner.

Greene smiled. His ten had doubled. Red Queen paid off Greene, and then paid off the winning jack. Greene figured this was a good time to vamoose, so he plucked up his chips, nodded at the lunger tinhorn, who smiled through yellow, gapped teeth, and cashed in at Racine's brass-grilled wicket. A thick dude with his hair pomaded to his skull paid Greene off, with dour whispers. The evening's take came to forty-nine dollars. Greene tucked the swag into his billfold and walked out past the batwing doors.

The night wasn't late, but it was black and moonless. He passed the Drover's Rest—all the old saloons seemed empty these days—and turned down Prescott, heading for his comfortable three-room log home beyond the business blocks.

He heard a faint noise, turned, and then his head exploded. He tumbled to the clay. It was hard enough to keep his balance with half an arm missing, harder when his head burst like a sky-rocket. He had been hit with a knout, or the barrel of a revolver. He couldn't see, but he felt hard hands grapple him down. He thrashed, kicked at the dark, and flipped like a flopping fish, but it didn't help any. Someone big and rough got his purse, yanking it from his trousers, and took off. He heard boots on gravel, and then nothing.

Nausea descended upon him. His head throbbed. He lifted a hand, felt gingerly along the left side of his skull, and found wetness. Blood. He sat up dizzily, suddenly aware of his hurt. The only thing in his world was the pain bursting in his skull.

It took him a while—he didn't know how long—to reach the point where he could stand up. The few shards of light in Payday all seemed to have a halo around them. He walked gently—every step shot pain through his head—toward the courthouse. He circled around the black building to the sheriff's office, but Betjeman wasn't there and it was as black as the rest of the building. His head cleared a little. He'd been robbed. It was the first crime of any consequence that he could remember in Payday.

He walked gently along Mogollon Street. Betjeman's would be the last house—a cabin, really. It was dark. He hated to roust out Arnold, but a crime was a crime. He hammered on the door and waited. Arnold Betjeman eventually opened. He wore a nightshirt; his hand wore a revolver.

"Been robbed," Greene said, leaning dizzily into the door frame.

The sheriff grunted disapprovingly. Greene didn't know if the disapproval was directed at him for waking the sheriff up, or at the criminal, or neither. Greene told his story in the dark, in the door, while the sheriff grunted and grimaced.

"That's it," Greene said. "What're you gonna do?"

"Nothing."

"Nothing! I was robbed!"

"You identify him?"

"No."

"Can't do nothing, then."

"You can go into Racine's and study any big-time spenders."
Betjeman grunted.

"You can make everyone in that joint put everything in their
pockets on the tables. Do the same in the saloons."

The sheriff smacked his lips.

"You can light up a lantern and have a look at the place I got
hit. I'll take you. Maybe the yegg left something behind."

Betjeman yawned. "Might in the morning."

"It'll be too late," Greene growled.

"See me tomorrow," Betjeman said, yawning. He shut the
door in Greene's face, none too gently.

Greene's night turned sour. He'd lost his winnings plus another
dozen dollars. His head throbbed as much with his rage as with
his wound. What was just as bad, he knew for a fact that there
wasn't enough law in Payday to help him, or anyone else. Arnold
Betjeman was obviously afraid of all those men with guns hanging from their waists.

Back in his home, Greene lit a lamp and studied his head. An
egg-sized lump decorated the left side. The bleeding was nothing
but a few scalp lacerations. He dabbed cold water on the mess,
wishing the water were an elixir, like laudanum, that would float
away the hurt.

He lay awake that night, his head pounding, his mind awhirl.
He'd call a meeting of the merchants. He'd corral Basil Cutlip.
There ought to be a tough deputy on at night, and the salary
should come out of a saloon-and-gambling tax—and also from a
tax on those dollies Odie Racine kept upstairs. That's how all the
new towns did it. Licensed the sporting places. The trouble was,
committees argued and debated and ate up time. Cutlip had his
own agenda. Two of the county supervisors, Severance Jackson and
Seth Pollack, were as timid as toads. Rudy Farquehar, the county
clerk and assessor, was a bureaucratic obstructionist, born to
stamp forms and say no. And Clayton Buell, the other Alpine
county supervisor, had gone mad, from all accounts.

That left Flint.

About nine the next morning, Abel Greene walked into Sam Flint's sanctum. He knew he looked the worse for wear. The left side of his head had puffed up, and his left eye was buried in inflamed blue and purplish flesh.

"Holy cats, what happened, Abel?" Flint asked.

"I've got news, and I've got some things to talk about," Greene said, easing himself into Flint's uncomfortable wooden chair, which had obviously been selected to keep people from pestering the editor overlong. "And not a word of it's private. I want it plastered from one side of your sheet to the other."

Greene narrated; Flint took copious notes.

When it was over, Flint toyed with his gold-rimmed spectacles and sighed. "That's a story, all right. You know, Abel, when we set out to draw folks to Payday, I hadn't even given a thought to getting ones like this."

"I hadn't either. I had good solid settlers in mind. Families, churchgoers, people with gumption and vision."

Flint grinned wryly. "Other types can read, I guess."

"I don't know how. Light's so bad in Odie's, you can't hardly see the cards. Well, what're we going to do about it? You've got the paper. I'm out a lot of money, and others will be, too. I'm just the first. You're the one to ventilate all this—and make some suggestions."

"Just between us, Abel, what do you make of Arnold Betjeman?"

"Oh, he's a good old boy. Perfectly all right locking up a drunken cowboy, or chasing some smart aleck who's been scaring carriage horses. But Sam, this burg's changing by the day. Tough owlhoots. Plenty of them wearing artillery. They could terrorize a peaceful little village like this. Those fellows in Odie's, they're not cowboys on a lark. Betjeman's outnumbered and outclassed, and this town's in trouble until it gets some muscle in that office."

"My thoughts exactly," Flint said.

26

Sam Flint knew he was putting out an explosive issue of the *Pioneer*. He had two big stories: one was the robbery of Abel Greene; the other was the assault upon himself by Colonel Buell. The latter story he buried on page three, preferring not to be in the limelight. But he knew it would not escape most people.

The Greene robbery gave him the chance to editorialize about change in Payday, and the need for more law enforcement. He pointed out that:

> This is the first crime of consequence since the town was settled. Our peaceable days are over. No doubt those of us who promoted growth and settlement did not quite realize that we might receive into our midst the dregs of humanity that roam the frontier.
>
> We have witnessed the construction of a large enterprise devoted to vices of various sorts, run ruthlessly to exploit the weaknesses of mankind. One need only tour its precincts to see the sort of citizen that Payday could do without. There are few in that place who will help Pay-

day prosper or are here for the long term. The very building looks like it might blow away in the next windstorm.

The migration to our once-safe city is well underway and cannot be stemmed. Nor should it be. Most of our new settlers work in honorable trades, and have come to sink roots into a paradise that promises a good life.

But as the brutal assault on one of our eminent merchants reveals, we are facing change. We need to hire deputies at once, and we must request more aggressive law enforcement from Sheriff Betjeman, including regular night patrol of what may soon become a notorious district. The sheriff is an elected officer, and if he fails to measure up to the new demands on him, he should suffer defeat when he faces the electorate.

As for the employment of deputies, it is the custom in frontier communities to license the establishments that cause the trouble and to devote the licensing fees to law enforcement. Alpine County has the source of revenue at hand to deal with our public safety problem. There are various approaches, but the common one is a quarterly license to be paid in cash by the proprietor of each saloon, each gambling table, and each of the denizens of a house of ill fame, to be collected by the sheriff or his deputies.

The *Pioneer* suggests swift action by the county supervisors to impose such license fees and collect them. Any delay will subject innocent men and women, people pursuing their honest vocations here, to harassment and worse. Voters should consider inaction to be tantamount to negligence, and demand an immediate remedy.

Flint proofed the editorial, believing it was almost unarguable. Something had to be done, and fast, with two or three dozen people drifting into Payday each week. Basil Cutlip told him he had sold three more lots along the budding tenderloin, for what purpose he didn't know. But it was clear that the sporting fraternity, or sorority, considered the drovers from all the surrounding ranches fair game. If this editorial didn't move the supervisors, he would repeat it in every issue, and highlight every crime. One weapon a newspaper possessed was repetition: the power to keep something before the public as long as it wished to.

Flint completed the pages by plugging the holes with filler material, mostly from Plutarch, his favorite source of ancient wisdom. He leaded out some paragraphs to fill the available space and then turned the forms over to Thimble. The apprentice locked up the forms, hammered the type down with a block of hardwood so it would print evenly, ran page proofs, and checked them over. He discovered that they had failed to change the date and edition number in the masthead, and made the corrections. Then he slid pages one and four into the Cleveland flatbed press and began printing. Flint watched, well satisfied that the able man he'd employed and befriended would do a fine job.

Thimble didn't say much until they had completed the four-page paper and begun wiping down the press.

"I expect you'll be hearing from Odie Racine," he said.

"I usually hear from anyone I propose taxing or licensing. And maybe we'll hear from Buell, since I've written up the story about his attack. Are you ready?"

"If you mean am I armed, no, I'm not. And I hope you're not either."

"I'm not. But I think we ought to do a little planning." Flint's wounds still ached viciously, even after several days. "I'm inclined to rush him. If we go after him together, we might tackle him. Don't wait an instant if he walks in."

"You're not going to file a complaint, Sam?"

"I've thought about it. It's assault, and I could. But we run up against a plain fact: Arnold Betjeman's not going to lift a finger. For one thing, Buell's one of his bosses. For another, Betjeman's likely to get hurt. I don't think the colonel would balk at giving the sheriff a whipping. I'm hoping that publicity will corral Buell. He's a vicious man. Maybe he's gone a bit mad. Who can say? He's hurt you, hurt Merry-Grace Rakoczy, and lashed into me."

Thimble grinned sourly. "You're sure a glutton for it."

"No, I don't ask for it. I dread it. But it's a hazard. You either put out a true paper, or you put out a piece of trash."

Later that day, they toted copies to the post-office wicket in Ike Cobb's store, handed a hundred to the newsboy, the leather-lunged Elmer, and hand-delivered a score more to the merchants so they could check their advertisements.

Thimble headed for his wagon, where he and his family still lived, leaving Flint alone to begin writing his invoices, which he would do until twilight and an empty stomach overwhelmed him. He liked that time of day, and he especially liked the fulfillment of delivering another issue, something comparable to childbirth. Once a week he delivered an almost totally new product. A newspaper was the ultimate custom business, a little like tailoring. Each issue was different.

Like most other weekly papers, the *Pioneer* had a few ads on page one. He began writing an invoice for each. When he had finished with page one, he would prepare invoices for each ad within, except for the standard-sized cards, which were paid in advance. Most of his advertisers were one or two issues behind, but he carried them anyway.

He was interrupted by Odie Racine. He watched her glide through the door and knew she was going to object to his proposal to license the sporting places. The new issue was only four hours old. It was all too familiar to him; he had dealt with this sort of thing constantly, from his first paper in Kansas.

But she didn't seem very angry. She smiled, if anything like a smile could be ascribed to Odie Racine, and nodded toward an empty wooden chair. "Mind if I sit?" she asked gently.

Flint knew this approach, too. The lady had some sophistication. "Have a seat. You didn't like the editorial, I take it."

She settled into the chair with a rustle of black silk. She seemed to have half a dozen dresses for all seasons and all moods of blackness. This one had a faint iridescent sheen, and a string of pearls had replaced the gold crucifix. A faint musty scent clung to her, like year-old rose petals. "Well, dearie, I'm used to it. They call it a 'sin tax.' I just thought I'd explain a few things."

Flint nodded. This tough cookie was playing it soft and low.

"That was an awful thing that happened to Mr. Greene," she began in that gentle, whiskey-graveled voice of hers. "It was none of our people, I assure you. I don't hire people like that. It's bad for business. I can't control customers out in the alleys, though."

Flint nodded, and waited. He had learned to absorb these protests the way a sponge blots up water.

"I've been in lots of dumps, and they all want to put a license on me. Or lots of licenses. You want a saloon license, one for each of my five tables, and another for each of my girls. You're a regular licensing fiend. Sort of a license addict, ain'tcha?"

Flint nodded. "About enough licenses to pay for a couple of deputies," he said.

"I just hate to ladle out a dime," she said. "I'm a money fiend. You've got to make your entire bundle in ten or fifteen years in my business. Otherwise, you'll have nothing to retire on. You don't have money, you start sliding, and by the time you're forty, you're in fifty-cent cribs wishing you could croak."

"It's not a happy profession."

"Yes, well, I didn't invent male lust," she said.

He waited.

"I can see you aren't a big talker. Look, there's no need for all them licenses. I'll hire a full-time guard. Not one of my people. Someone you and your business cronies pick. I'll have him on every night, six to two in the morning. He'll wear a deputy badge. Keep the streets nice. The county don't pay a dime. I don't pay licenses. It's cheaper for everybody. Me especially."

Flint shook his head. "We're going to need a lot more than that.

You're just the first. Judge Cutlip told me he's sold three more lots along there. Sorry, Miz Racine, I just don't like the idea of a private business paying for a deputy. He'd be working for you, not the public."

"I'm sure not getting anywhere," she said.

"No, I'm afraid not."

"How can I persuade you?" She smiled suddenly.

"Intelligent arguments. Write me something that would change my mind. I'm flexible."

"You're a stick-in-the-mud, is what you are. You a bachelor or something?"

He nodded.

"I thought so. Men with wives, they're more reasonable. I can deal with them." She eyed him so thoroughly that Flint felt he was being sized up for a burial suit. "You come by for a drink any time. On me. I like to have friends around. Me, I don't play games, dearie. I need a newspaper editor now and then. I'm in a rough business. Sometimes just a little sympathy does it. You don't need to be on my side. Just know what I'm up against."

"I'll come by for a drink, but I'll pay for it, Miz Racine."

She eyed him again. "You got any vices?"

"Several."

"I thought so. Lissen. For you, everything's free." She untied a small black bag and extracted a handful of brass tokens. "Here, take these. It's on Odie, dearie."

He stared at the tokens. Each bought a girl. He shook his head.

"Don't you like girls? You got a problem?"

"I like women," he said.

"Well, you think it over. Everything's for sale, including me. But for you, it's free." She parted her lips slightly. Flint confessed to himself that Odie Racine laid a powerful magnetism on a man. He sat rigid, surprised at how vulnerable he was feeling. "You think about it," she said. "Rome wasn't laid in a day." She laughed, gritty and funny, and he laughed too.

She stood, straightening out her silk skirts. "Just remember Odie," she said. "I'm a businesswoman like everyone else. I can solve your problems. Darling, I'll fix it so there's never any trouble."

He sighed, almost believing her, as she walked out into a balmy evening.

27

Sam Flint stepped into a new log church put up by the recently organized Baptists, feeling sure that this would be one of the most unusual services he had ever attended. Merry-Grace Rakoczy had finally surrendered to reality, and had arranged a memorial service for her husband. She had placed a small ad in the paper announcing the event. The Rakoczys had been close to the town's earliest settlers, and now the pews were filling swiftly.

The strange quality of holding a service for those who had simply vanished—the ceremony was as much for Rakoczy's Mexican ranch hands as for the Hungarian—gave it an odd cast. There were no coffins, and no true assurance even of death. It was as much to help Merry-Grace get along with her life as to notify Payday of her widowhood.

That alone would make the event strange, but there was more. She had daringly asked Colonel Buell to deliver the eulogy, and much to Flint's astonishment, the dangerous man had agreed. He and Rakoczy had been amiable neighbors once, and he perhaps knew Rakoczy better than anyone else in town. But it simply stunned Flint that Merry-Grace had driven over to Buell's place and asked him. She didn't explain why she had, but he sensed that she thought better of Buell than he did. He wanted to talk to her about this, but the opportunity had not arisen.

The final oddity was that Rakoczy had been a Catholic, but this service would not reflect it. No priest was available. These little congregations had no organ, so the townspeople settled quietly in the pews. Flint saw Basil and Violet Cutlip near the front, Abel Greene, and all the merchants and their wives.

At last Merry-Grace, a soft whirl of black, filed in on the arm of her elder son Stephen, followed by Andrew, and then by Ignacio and Luz Santamaria. Merry-Grace wore a veil and he could not quite see her expression, but it seemed as if she were serious and resolute and wholly in command of herself.

Following them came Colonel Buell, gray and erect, weathered and worn, military and fierce even when he was not trying to be fierce, looking neither left nor right, as if no one else existed. He wore a black suit and a stiff, high white collar. Flint looked for signs of madness or vicious conduct, and saw only a face wreathed in grief and hurt.

The minister, an ascetic young man scarcely out of seminary, followed in his black robe and opened with a prayer. Flint listened patiently to the prayer for the souls of five men he never knew, and then to the verses that promised life hereafter, and to the words of comfort the young man bestowed in all earnestness upon the presumed widow. He was treating Rakoczy's long disappearance as death, and Flint knew that that was what Merry-Grace wanted.

The fierce August heat oppressed the room, and women fanned themselves metronomically, their attention divided between their comfort and the curious spectacle before them. Everyone was waiting for one thing: the words of the neighbor who had driven his entire herd over the range of the man he would eulogize. Thanks to Flint's careful reporting, not a person at the memorial service was ignorant of Buell's transgressions. They had read each story: the one about the murdered flock of sheep; the follow-up story identifying the homesteading victims; the stories about the invasion of Merry-Grace Rakoczy's ranch; and more recently, the account of his bullwhip assault upon the editor. Flint suspected that half the people in that crowded little church had come for the spectacle, not to honor the gracious and enterprising young Hungarian.

Then, at last, it was Colonel Buell's moment. He walked stiffly and positioned himself below the pulpit. A silence deepened. The fans stopped. He stared at the crowd, somehow looking like a judge about to try the whole congregation.

"Ah've been invited by Mrs. Rakoczy to say something about the late Nicholas Rakoczy," he began in a commanding voice. "And so I'll do my duty."

An oddly military way to look at it, Flint thought.

"I'm going to talk here of a great and good man who came from abroad. The Hungarian came here, took up a place, and turned it into his Promised Land. Ah always thought that if any mortal could wrest paradise out of a wilderness, Nicholas Rakoczy was it. To this basin he came with his young wife and infant sons, and bravely fashioned the best and most commodious home, the finest herd, the most adventuresome crops, and the most legendary hospitality in the Territory."

Flint smiled within himself. The colonel would not embarrass Merry-Grace, and would pay Rakoczy his due. Which made his odd aggressions all the stranger.

"Ah could not set foot to his land without being shown his latest innovations—the struggling little pepper plants, the tender grapevines, the crossbred cattle he was experimenting with, fat and big on the grama grasses. He was a man to try everything, and to learn from failures, and to give to a passerby the sense that miracles were in reach of everyone. He was a man to draw a stranger to his hearth, pour generous libations, talk learnedly of God and crossbreeding and the history of war, all in ten minutes, while lay-ing gracious compliments upon his wife and any ladies present. Ah've never met his kind, and am stricken by his passing."

Some subtle change came over him.

"Nicholas Rakoczy was one of those rare mortals who was filled with light. Whenever Ah was privileged to enjoy his com-pany, Ah felt myself peering into a mind that loved knowledge, and loved life. He wanted to know everything, not just the things in books, but the things he could see and touch and hear. He loved people. He was boldly curious. He asked me endless questions about myself, and Ah answered them. He asked questions about my beliefs—the personal kind, whether Ah believed in the virtues, whether Ah held a brief for life after death, whether Ah lived for gain or for something else—and Ah answered him. Then he would pause and give me some new insight into myself, as fresh as springtime. Ah never left his home without feeling lifted up."

Colonel Buell spoke for ten minutes, outlining Rakoczy's life, praising him in terms so endearing and generous that Flint was dumbfounded. How could this be the same mortal who had tor-mented the widow, and was even now crushing her ranch? He had no answer. Clayton Buell was a man so complicated and troubled that no one would ever fathom him. Was this the mortal whose wis-dom and judgment had won him a supervisory seat in the county's first election, and yet the man who would slaughter a settler's herd of sheep without the slightest hesitation or regret?

When at last the minister dismissed them and people were fil-ing out, Flint caught the colonel's eye and did not see bullwhips in his gaze. The colonel nodded stiffly and marched out. Flint lin-gered, wanting to give his condolences to Merry-Grace, who was receiving people in the vestibule. He confessed to himself there were other reasons. He loved her. He couldn't help himself. The press of her hand, a glimpse of her troubled face, a word from her, would be precious to him. He placed himself at the end of the line so he might have more than a word with her. He had taken a few notes during the ceremony, and now he carefully hid away his foolscap in his old suitcoat. Editors were always at work.

"Thank you for coming, Sam," she said. She had lifted her veil, and he beheld the face of a woman in rigid control.

"I'd do anything for you, Merry-Grace. What's next?"

"I don't know."

"Can you last out there?"

"Yes. I've gotten help."

"Some hands ever show up?"

"The colonel discouraged it. But he's helping me."

"Helping you?" Flint asked dumbly.

"He's an old family friend, Sam."

"Is that why you asked him to do the eulogy, Merry-Grace?"

"He knew Nicholas better than anyone. They talked by the hour at our hearth, especially during winter evenings."

"But—"

"I knew he would do it beautifully. Don't you think he did? Clayton Buell has the soul of a gentleman and a poet."

"Yes, it was beautiful, but forgive me, I don't understand why you chose him."

"I'll explain some other time," she said simply. She turned to leave the church, but he stayed her.

"Were you hoping this would change things? Make him reconsider?"

"Sam, he's taking care of me. He's branded my calves. He's bought some of my calves and paid cash."

"Are you and I talking about the same man?"

"Sam, some other time. My mind's been filled with Nicholas."

"I'm sorry," Flint said, knowing he had pressed too hard to unravel this new mystery, and at an inappropriate time as well. "You'll be wanting to think of your husband and remembering the good times."

"Yes," she said, lowering her veil again.

She left him there, puzzled, unsatisfied, aching for some way to make sense of all this. Editors needed to make sense of things. Editors had orderly minds that required reasons and rational behavior, and here he had no reasons and a fierce old CSA colonel's double vision of the world—one tender, one vicious.

He watched Merry-Grace and her two boys squeeze into the rear seat of a buggy, while Ignacio and Luz settled in front. It all seemed unfinished. There had been no graveside service. No reception. Ignacio slapped lines over the croups of the two horses, and Flint watched Merry-Grace slide into obscurity.

He walked back to his sanctum, bemused. He would write the story while it was fresh in his mind. He had admired Buell's eloquence, and would say so in a separate piece in his opinion column.

"How did it go, Sam?" asked Thimble.

Sam told him.

"I never would have thought it. I don't understand Clayton Buell," Thimble said. "And I'll never know why Mrs. Rakoczy invited him to deliver the eulogy."

Flint pondered it. "Horatio, some people think that newspaper editors are on the inside of everything, that we have all the facts and reasons. The truth is, we're always on the outside, looking in."

28

Clayton Buell stopped at a creekbank looking for wildflowers. He wished to fashion a bouquet for Merry-Grace, but he found no flowers in the August heat and finally gave up. She wouldn't appreciate them anyway, not with a home that seemed to rise out of a riot of blooms that Rakoczy had planted around it. He climbed onto his favorite mount, a sixteen-hand blood bay, and continued toward the Rakoczy ranch, his spirits buoyant.

There were moments when Buell wondered whether he were mad. He considered it a possibility, but doubted it. He suffered no delusions and understood his conduct perfectly. He sometimes subjected himself to rigorous scrutiny, placing himself in the dock as if he were the defendant. Then he conducted his courts martial, using military rules of evidence, and found himself not mad.

What the tribunal of his soul finally came up with was evidence of a susceptibility to his emotions, which sometimes ruled him and rendered him their slave. In some dark cauldron of his heart there bubbled and boiled bitterness, anger, and helplessness, and these had occasionally governed his conduct and rendered him unworthy as a mortal, and less than the gentleman he had aspired to be. These feelings had been born in January of 1865 and had never gone away. And while he controlled or masked them most of the time, there were periods when he was as prostrate before them as Georgia was before General Sherman's Army.

Knowing he wasn't mad only deepened his private sorrow. If he were mad, he would not be responsible. But he wasn't mad, and he was wholly responsible. His conduct had rational purpose. He had deployed his vast longhorn herd like foot soldiers, by division and brigade and battalion; and his drovers like subalterns, putting them in command of his army of ten thousand. It was scorched-earth tactics, not unlike William Tecumseh Sherman's, and it would keep settlers out of the whole north and east quadrants—the well-watered and thick-grassed sectors of the basin. What settler would claim poor, gnawed-to-the-roots grazing land when there was so much virgin country nearby? He was protecting Merry-Grace's spread from settlement, but he wasn't sure she grasped that.

She was almost like a daughter to him, and when he contemplated her tragedy, wave after wave of pity overwhelmed him. He had suffered much the same agony years ago, and it had forever altered him. Merry-Grace was waiting for a husband who would never return; he had searched for a daughter who had vanished, and had waited for a wife to regain her senses, though she never did.

His turpentine plantation had been squarely in the path of General Slocum's left wing of Sherman's Army on the march to the sea after the burning of Atlanta. Sherman was living off the land, sending out foragers, or bummers as they were called, to provision his vast army as well as to destroy everything of military and civil value—including the turpentine works. He had pieced together the story from his former slaves, who clung to the place when it lay in ruins. The bummers arrived on the twentieth, burned the turpentine works to the ground and pillaged the house, pocketing valuables and taking all food. But they had left his wife and daughter alone.

At one point after the war, he had thought of taking a revolver in hand and shooting General Sherman and then himself, but being the cautious officer that he was, he took time to study Sherman's orders to his command. They were to destroy everything of military value, including foodstuffs, but they were to leave private homes and their residents unharmed; they were not to loot private citizens; they were to respect women, and leave enough food for households to subsist.

Once Buell read Sherman's orders, his fantasies of vengeance vanished. Armies would do what armies would do in spite of stern orders. Had his own foragers in Maryland and Pennsylvania obeyed his restraining commands? No. They had provisioned their pockets as well as the Army of Northern Virginia.

Sherman's bummers had burned Colonel Buell's lovely old plantation mansion, against orders, and stolen his treasures, also against orders. He knew the reason. It was because Buell had been a victor at Fredericksburg, the most hated defeat of the Yankees, and no officer could restrain the Union troops from wreaking their vengeance on Buell's household. But even then, his servants told him, a lieutenant protected the two women, wife and daughter, with a pair of revolvers. They were gentlemen; the North and South had gentlemen.

What was more important and desolating, it was not the Union Army that had inflicted the ultimate grief. That, too, he had garnered from his weeping ex-slaves.

In the terrible vacuum left behind the advancing Union Army, all civil authority vanished and the Georgia countryside was at the mercy of another kind of bummer: deserters from North and South, organized in gangs, rampaging, violating, turning the world into hell. A gang of twenty Confederate deserters had walked in the next day. That was when the servants heard his wife's screams for most of the night, and when they saw his dear daughter Tess being led away into the deep pine woods, somewhere, never to be seen again. These jackals, these barbarians, had worn his Confederate colors. It was a grief beyond bearing, and he lived through 1865 and 1866 in a haze of rage and helplessness, fitfully trying to find Tess—or her grave—and realizing he had no way to care for his demented wife. The good Catholic Sisters of the Sacred Heart in Savannah finally took her into their haven.

The rest of Reconstruction was darkness. Blueclad soldiers re-occupied Georgia when it refused to ratify the 14th Amendment, and didn't return it to civil government until 1870. The voracious carpetbaggers lingered for two or three more years, looting and taxing. He lost his pine forests to fraudulent taxes, and the last he knew, some corrupt carpetbagger from New Jersey owned them.

He wasn't mad, he thought—just unbalanced. He walked a fine line, a prisoner of war. He couldn't stand anyone near him except Rakoczy, and that was because Rakoczy was a Hungarian, exempt from his fevered hatred and hurt. With Rakoczy gone—God knows where—he had to push his perimeter outward, ever outward, to free himself from his seething soul. By expanding the Buell ranch to some undefined boundary, far, far from his cabin, he won peace and tranquillity; he could be his own master at last. He meant to protect Merry-Grace while he expanded the boundaries; she was the bright brand snatched from the ashes, and he loved her in his own way.

He hoped his eulogy had pleased her. He had studied how to do it, how to praise the man and his works as graciously as possible. He had watched her and had seen her face soften, her eyes signal their gratitude there in the first pew. He had given her everything back. She had always known how much Buell and her husband had shared and enjoyed. She had come to the right man to give a eulogy for Nicholas. He hoped she would come to understand that he was also the right man to protect and nurture her and her holdings.

He found her at home. She was always at home. Her boys were in the fields. She worked hard to keep their minds off the loss of their father.

"Merry-Grace, I should like a private word," he said.

Her eyes searched him, and then she led him silently into the study, deep in cool shadow. "Your eulogy of Nicholas was a sweet gift to me, and to his memory, Clayton," she said gravely. "I'm glad you came. I have wanted to talk to you. I realize you're looking after my interests in your own way, but I'm not comfortable with it."

"Why, Merry-Grace, Ah've come for an entirely different purpose. Ah've come to worship at your feet. You're the loveliest woman in the universe, and Ah'm proposing matrimony."

She gaped at him, speechless, but he'd expected that.

"He's not coming back, madam. Ah'm fifty, lean and hard from a robust life, and I'll see eighty. You're a tad younger, still in your bloom. The boys need a man about, so they'll grow up with a stiff spine and learn honor."

"But Clayton . . ." she whispered. "I don't love you. And you don't love me."

"Ah do love you."

She rallied suddenly. "Clayton. This is impossible. I can't marry. I have to wait seven years before Nicholas is legally dead."

"Oh, Ah thought of that. Ah'm inclined just to take up together and live in bigamy. Ah'm not one to mince words."

"What?"

"Well, we're both in the same fishpond, you know. Ah've got a lovely wife back in Savannah, mad since the twenty-first of January, eighteen and sixty-five. No lovelier woman on earth, my Eloise. Loving and gentle. Attentive to my needs. Strong and capable, guiding my sons, greeting our guests, winning the servants with her own dignity; beautiful, beautiful as magnolia blossoms, and fun, too. She never neglected her wit, and many's the jest that set us all to laughing. But she's left this world for her private one." He paused. Merry-Grace looked utterly shocked. "What I'm proposing is just taking matters into our own hands and making a match. The world'll call us a scandal. But we'll just make us a match, and enjoy some flamin' bigamy. You're lonely and uncertain, and looking for a way to live. As for me, Ah don't suppose a man could be happier, having Eloise in Savannah and you in Arizona."

"And what will happen if I refuse?" she asked tautly.

"Why, nothing at all."

"Clayton Buell, you're unspeakable! You toy with my virtue and intend to ruin my good reputation. You have no honor. The answer is no, not now, not ever." She clenched her small fists and glared up at him.

"Ah thought you might feel that way. Ah was hoping you'd see you can't run this place alone and that Ah'm offering you a life of comfort."

"I'm not ready to make choices, Clayton. But I can't imagine that living in bigamy could be one of them."

"Seven years is a long time, Merry-Grace. You won't be able to marry, or sell this place, or make plans until the courts declare Nicholas dead. Ah designed a way out for us both—springtime and sunlight and years and years of birdsong."

"I'd like to be alone now," she said. Tears rose in her eyes.

"Think on it, madam," he said, bowing deeply before he found his way to the blood bay at the hitchrail.

29

Horatio Thimble wondered how Sam Flint would take the news, and whether there was any way to soften it. He was going to resign, and it would be a blow to Flint, who had counted on Thimble more and more.

But Thimble couldn't delay any longer. His family had camped in the wagon outside of Payday all summer, and now they were restless and irritable. With Gertrude cooking at the café, and Artemus and David employed, they had repaired their fortunes somewhat and had both cash and credits at the mercantiles. That rock of stubbornness within his breast was insisting that they return to Pass Creek and take up their homestead once again, Buell or no Buell. The boys insisted on it. Gertrude was eager, dreaming of a home, a spacious cabin, her own land under her feet, even though she loved company and the life in Payday.

They had talked it over endlessly in the light of the evening cook fires. The Thimble family would claim its rightful land, and now was the time. This time, they would take it step by step, testing Colonel Buell but never making themselves vulnerable.

Artemus and David had ridden out to Pass Creek several times and knew that the cabin was scorched, but repairable. The family had fashioned a plan: they would not buy livestock only to have it murdered at Buell's hands. Instead, they would build the cabin, add outbuildings and corrals, and await Buell's response. They would have a roof over their heads during the winter. They had funds enough until spring, and could earn more if they had to. Later, they would stock their range.

Each of the four Thimbles would file additional Timber Culture and Desert Land Act Claims, and these together would blanket the whole Pass Creek valley, giving them a full-sized ranch. It would deprive Buell of about five percent of the public land he claimed as his range. They couldn't squat on vast tracts, the way Buell had done prior to the government's survey, but neither did they have to limit themselves to homesteading.

Horatio approached Flint one Friday, hating what he had to do. The editor had been good to him. "Sam," he said, "I'm afraid I've got hard news for you. I'll be leaving your employ in a week."

Flint set down his type stick, stared, and nodded. "I always supposed you would," he said. "A family can't live in a wagon forever. I don't know what I'll do without you. Hire a boy, I guess. But no one can replace you, Horatio. You're ten times more than a printer's devil." He gazed at Thimble knowingly. "You're going to go out to Pass Creek and try again."

Thimble nodded. "It's our land. The closest to Eden I've ever seen. It stirs us up. Even Mrs. Thimble's eager to start over."

"Your stock'll be killed and you'll be driven off."

"We're not buying stock for a while. We'll build a homestead and a barn."

"You know the risks, Horatio. It could be your blood."

"We won't be driven anymore. We've been pushed and shoved by carpetbaggers and soldiers and tax collectors. We're going to Pass Creek and stay or die."

Flint was taken aback. "Die? Are you sure you know what those brave words might mean? The heartache? Buell's a deadly man."

"We'll see. I'll trust in pacifism. Not even Colonel Buell would shoot unarmed people in cold blood."

Flint stared into space for a moment. "You know, Buell's a complex man. He's vicious, but apparently he's been treating Merry-Grace Rakoczy quite decently." He eyed Thimble. "Frankly, I fear for you."

"I tell you, Flint, it no longer matters what kind of man he is. We're putting roots down right there, even if we water that soil with our blood. That's not just my feeling. My sons are itching to begin."

Flint gazed solemnly at Thimble. "You know, Horatio, there are two Clayton Buells. That eulogy he gave for Nicholas Rakoczy was written by the angels. But the bullwhip and the sheep-shooting—those are the acts of a hellish man. I still feel his lashes. This whole basin suffers. The town suffers. New settlers like yourself suffer. I don't know what can be done about it."

"Well, Sam, I do have one thing in mind. I'd like to buy a two-column ad. It's going to announce that the Thimble family's returning to its holdings on Pass Creek, and it's going to say that the land's posted against trespassing."

"Do you think that'll help?"

"Yes, Sam. It puts the light of day on everything. The colonel will know that whatever he does, it will be subject to public scrutiny. You taught me that's what a newspaper can do. It can shine a light. If the Thimble family should come to a violent end, God forbid, the law'll know where to go, and everyone will know what happened."

Flint sighed. "It won't come to that. Buell's not that kind. Horatio, that ad's free. The least I can do for all your help. And I'm going to write a frank editorial about it. Your private problem is also a public problem, and Buell's conduct deserves public review. Maybe it'll help keep you safe."

"Maybe it'll bring you a whipping."

Flint replied quietly, "If you and your family can risk death on Pass Creek, I guess I can risk a bullwhip."

"You're a strong man, Flint."

"I wish I were. I'm mostly a man who sees what needs to be done. It's amazing how many people in this world don't want anyone to know what they're doing. That's why newspapers are powerful and hated. I could write better if I didn't dread being hurt or ruined."

"Well, you're a friend, Sam."

"Horatio, would you be available part-time?"

"I reckon we'll be too far from Payday."

"How about just occasionally, when I need to get away for a day or two? Would you come in, stay here?"

"I'd do that."

"Good. It's settled, then. Why don't you compose your ad and put it on page four? And I'll start that editorial about Buell. I mean it to be amiable, but a warning, too. It's coming to a head. Buell's going to have to give ground or face trouble in Alpine County."

On press day, Thimble helped Flint run off an issue that openly called Clayton Buell's conduct a problem for Alpine County and its hopes of progress. A front-page story announced Thimble's resignation, and his intent to return to his homestead in spite of what had happened in the spring. Flint had done what he could, and now it was up to the Thimble family.

That Friday, Thimble broke down type, wiped the press clean, collected a final pay envelope—cash this time—from Flint, and walked out to his wagon, where his good strong sons and brave wife awaited him.

They had hitched the team and were ready to roll. Stonewall raced in circles, his tail up, looking for sheep to herd. But there would be none for a long while.

"We'll go now," Thimble said. "We'll claim our land. I'm proud of all of you. What we are doing takes a special courage, the type that comes from standing our ground and trusting in God and justice to make things right."

Gertrude said nothing, but she clasped her hands over his and peered into his eyes with such love and courage that Thimble counted himself one of the world's most blessed men.

With that, he clambered into the seat and hawed the team eastward toward their Eden, not knowing what to expect. The *Pioneer* had probably reached Buell, if anyone from the ranch had come to town.

He drove through a long summer's evening, his sons and wife silent around him. The passage of three hours took them to Pass Creek, which seemed uncannily lovely in the soft twilight of August. Horatio saw his land again, and loved it as much as he had ever loved anything on earth. The creek bottoms lay velvet with grama grass. The meadows rose in steps, folded into the timbered foothills and then into the towering ramparts of the Mogollon Rim. Above, the sky glowed with a lambent light from a setting sun.

It wasn't only the beauty that struck him; it was the peace that lay sweet and low over his hills. God had blessed this land, consecrated it to the Thimble family as a Promised Land. He reined up the team so they all could gaze upon their home and absorb the laughter of Pass Creek, which would solace them and water their sheep.

"This is a good place," he said to his family.

There was no army of Buell's Texas cowboys ready to turn them back. He steered the creaking wagon, burdened with all their small treasures, toward the fire-charred cabin a quarter of a mile up the creek, and there he did spot something. A blood bay horse stood nearby. A familiar figure stood beside it. Buell appeared to be alone. The man wore a black suit, white shirt, cravat, and a side arm.

"Let me handle this, boys," Thimble said softly to his sons. "It looks peaceable enough. Don't do anything rash."

Thimble drove up to his cabin and tugged the lines.

"Mr. Thimble, get off my range," Buell said calmly.

"It's our land, and I'll have to say the same to you, Colonel. We have a proper claim. We've also filed Timber Culture claims up the creek, and Desert Land Act claims below. You may have squatted here, but it's no longer yours."

"Not your land and never will be. This is Buell range and will be to my dying breath. Pass Creek was where Ah came first, out of Texas with my men. We camped here, made it our home for the first half year. Ah claim prior right. Ah won't argue it further. Prior right. Now leave peaceable, or die."

"And die, Colonel? You mean it?"

"Ah do. You'll turn around now and never come back or Ah'll shoot you."

"You're aware we have no means to defend ourselves? We have come here unarmed, because that is our way."

"Ah have eyes. Ah'll shoot you anyhow, right here and now, upon this soil of mine, before Ah retreat an inch."

Something flat and stubborn built in Thimble. He stared a long time at the colonel, coming to conclusions. Then he turned to his sons. "You get down and water the team. We'll start unloading now. We've nothing to fear. This man won't shoot in cold blood."

"Ah'm warning you, Mr. Thimble."

Horatio Thimble nodded to his sons, who reluctantly slid off the seat, put a foot to the hub, and landed in the grass. Gertrude leaked terror, but slowly climbed down. The boys edged toward the traces, intending to release the team.

Thimble started to clamber down. Buell's shot shattered the twilight, followed by a terrible moan, and Horatio Thimble started, wondering who had died because of his stubbornness.

30

A haze of blue gunsmoke drifted toward Pass Creek. Horatio Thimble gaped. His sons and Gertrude stood paralyzed. Clayton Buell calmly restored the revolver to its sheath.

Then Thimble saw it: Stonewall lay bloodied and quiet. One of the dog's rear legs slowly straightened. A great sadness filled Thimble.

"Oh!" gasped Gertrude, tears welling up.

"Ah told you the dog'd be next. Then the horses. Then the wagon," Buell said calmly. "Now git."

"And after that?"

Buell didn't answer.

"Go on, then," Thimble said relentlessly. "The horses. The wagon. And then what? Your bullwhip on us?" He crossed his arms and waited.

"No, Pa," David said, seething. "We can rush him."

"We won't. We'll respect this man."

"But he doesn't respect us!"

"I think he does."

David and Artemus didn't like it. But Horatio Thimble simply stood there, his gaze locked with Buell's.

"We're not moving. We've been pushed out of the South. We've been taxed and bullied and beaten down. Everything we owned was stolen. Everything we had when we arrived here, you shot. We're not budging an inch. Do what you will. Bury us here. It's our home."

Something like a shudder rocked Buell. He formed words but didn't say them. He glared, sulfurous and malignant, but Thimble held his ground. "Ah'm telling my men to shoot your stock on sight, and to burn you out," Buell said.

"All right," said Thimble. "You do that."

Buell's lips compressed. Thimble had never beheld such a flinty, malevolent glare rising from another mortal. Buell exuded brimstone and hate. Then he turned toward his bay saddler, looking ten years older.

"Colonel, wait," Thimble said.

Buell didn't. He pulled a stirrup around, slid a boot into it, clasped the reins, and settled himself into a polished Confederate cavalry saddle. He looked born to it. He wasn't wearing gray, but Thimble could almost see it on him, the wide slouch hat, the tunic with the elaborate Confederate gauds at the sleeves, the epaulets at the shoulders bearing his marks of rank, the dangling sword, the shining boots. The proud horse pranced under him. Buell was more than a man; he was a Force of Nature, radiating willpower.

Thimble swallowed hard and gathered his courage. "Colonel, we've filed on most of the land in this valley. Our patented range will run from the forests of the Mogollon down to desert country."

"So Ah've heard."

"You're subject to the law like the rest of us. Those aren't carpetbaggers in the courthouse. We'll defend our rights by law or whatever peaceful means are at hand."

Buell leaned forward calmly. "Mistah Thimble, suh. Ah ignore such trifles. Betjeman won't find me to serve process papers. And if he does, Ah'll ignore them. Ah won't hire a lawyer and Ah won't show up in Cutlip's court. And if you win a default judgment, Ah'll ignore it—but you won't win, Ah'll tell you that. Basil Cutlip won't cross me. He's afraid of me. And if that clown of a sheriff comes out to enforce the court's will, Ah'll chase him and all his ragtag posse off my range. In short, suh, you'll see me in Hades before you see me in court or collect a dime."

"Sorry, Colonel. That won't help you. I'm not running another foot. This is our land and our home. You can bury us here, but you can't drive us off."

"Ah won't have a bit of trouble getting rid of you."

"Colonel Buell, there was a day when you could have your way, just as you say. But those times have passed. This country's being settled. A young man—a Yankee I worked for and came to ad-mire—started a newspaper. He's not for us or against us. He's for a good commonwealth. Everything that happens here will become part of a public record. That's what a newspaper is for. It creates public opinion. If you defy public opinion and the law, it'll be known not just in this county, but also in Prescott."

"Ah've never paid heed and never will."

Thimble sighed. Trading threats didn't come to much, other than to let the colonel know that he faced a resolute man. It was in him to make peace with this desperate, ghost-driven man, mad-dened by long-ago events that had crushed them all. "We're neigh-bors now. We'll be good neighbors. Right now we're grieving a beloved dog, and we're going to shed some tears. We've shed so many since the War of Secession, a few more won't matter. His name was Stonewall, named for a great man you served under. Let us alone now. We want to grieve privately."

Something in Buell's face crumpled, and for one searing mo-ment, all Thimble could see was pain and desolation. But then Buell's face stiffened.

"Ah'll be on my way, suh," he said.

Gertrude said, "Colonel, I've learned to make a good pot of tea over a campfire. Sometime, when you're ready and we're ready, and we're no longer so hurt, stop by."

She still had tears on her cheeks. Thimble fathomed the courage she had drawn upon to say that. Stonewall had been her dog, mostly.

Buell reddened, looking fierce and sad, and then shook his head. He wheeled his bay and rode off.

They watched him walk his horse up a gentle grassy slope, and when he reached the crest, the horse lifted into a jog and Colonel Buell vanished.

"You didn't even get mad. He killed old Stonewall!" Artemus bawled.

"I feel as bad as you do about Stonewall, son. We won today, even though a part of our family is dead. We'll bury our old friend and say good-bye. And then we'll say hello to our new home."

Gertrude edged toward the dog, not wanting to see what lay there. She stared. Her shoulders slumped.

"I'll bury him proper in a bit, Gertrude," Thimble said softly. "He'll have an honored place here."

She found his arms awaiting her and fell into them, clinging tightly for a moment. Then she let go. "There's a lot to do," she said.

"It can wait a moment," Thimble said. "Boys, you come here."

Curious, Artemus and David drew close.

It was ceremony that Thimble sought. The moment was sacred. "Take your hats off, boys."

They did. He took his off, too.

"We've reached our Promised Land," he began. "We've wandered many years and have been led here. This is a good place. We've lost creatures we've loved. But their blood sanctifies this place. Here we'll put down our roots, and no force on earth'll ever dislodge us. This is the beginning. We've seen war and death and sickness and theft. Now we'll build. We'll each do our work quietly, in fullness and industry, and without slacking. I'm going to bless this place with a prayer of thanksgiving. Our long journey is over, our tribulations are being lifted from us. So let us bow our heads."

He waited for them to do so. Then he spoke in a sonorous voice that somehow might carry over the ridges, beyond the skies and beneath the depths. "Almighty God, the Thimble family has come to the place You prepared for us. We will build here, by being good neighbors, and by contributing all we can to You and this community, and by hard work. Bless this place, and ourselves to the task before us. Amen."

Gertrude smiled at him through her tears. Something about that moment was the benediction she needed.

"We'll begin this very evening," Thimble told his family. "We'll unload the wagon. Tomorrow, Artemus and I'll take the team and begin hewing trees for the cabin. David, I'd like you to take the drawknife and cut away the charred wood on the cabin logs. If you weary of that, split some of that dry wood yonder into shakes for the roof. We'll finish this cabin in a week. We'll build corrals. We'll scythe prairie hay and stack it for the horses. We'll build a barn. We'll construct a pole fence that'll keep stock out of a garden. We'll plow up the soil for the spring seeding. We'll build a stoneboat and drag in rock for a fireplace and chimney—winter's coming.

"It won't be all work, either. Each Sabbath we'll ride up Pass Creek and study our land, all that we're claiming. We'll locate the springs rising in the rimrock and keep an eye out for catamounts and other dangers. We'll learn this country before we put a single lamb upon it, and know what it holds for us."

It occurred to him that he was handing out a lot of orders without asking Gertrude or Artemus or David whether they approved, objected, or had better ideas. He didn't mean to. At times, during their long odyssey, he had been the only one with the courage to go on.

"Is there a better way?" he asked.

For an answer, he got smiles. David was with him; Artemus looked agreeable. Gertrude appeared eager to begin unpacking her kitchen.

"All right," he said. "Let's bury Stonewall, and remember that this land came to us through fire and blood."

31

With Thimble gone, Flint found himself working desperate hours. The paper had grown; the town had grown. It took longer to sell ads and collect the news. He built an ad seeking a printer's assistant. If that didn't work, he intended to go the other route and advertise for a person capable of selling ads, collecting news, and doing some billing. But he preferred to hire a devil for the monotonous typesetting so he himself could develop the stories.

He felt a sense of loss. Horatio Thimble had been good company and a hard worker, seeing things to do and doing them without waiting to be asked. There weren't many like him. The Thimbles would be good neighbors, honest, strong, productive, and caring. If only all the newcomers were like them, Payday would bloom into a good community.

But most of the newcomers weren't. Much to Flint's regret, his town-booming seemed to be bringing in a stream of mean, greedy, hardcase types who threatened to overthrow the good order of Payday. There were more reports of nighttime trouble: brawls, street robbery, drunkenness, and even occasional mysterious gunshots, all from the growing sporting quarter along Basin Street.

So far, nothing disastrous had come of it, but Arnold Betjeman avoided those precincts at night and strutted bravely into empty dives by day, pretending to be the lawman he wasn't. Judge Cutlip had started calling him "The Sunlight Sheriff." All the sheriff's records showed was a slight increase in drunks detained at the jail and two or three complaints of muggings. Flint suspected there was a lot more, but since it occurred when the Sunlight Sheriff was snoring, it didn't get reported.

Flint was going to have to cover that, and keep covering it, and hammering at it, until the supervisors did something about it.

He was building a new ad promoting some freshly arrived, ready-made men's kangaroo shoes at Ike Cobb's when Merry-Grace walked in. She wore white again, gauzy and light, the shadows falling through it, vaguely hinting of a slender form within. That was how she had dressed when he first laid eyes on her, coming to Payday that April day. But now, as she approached, he saw the pain collecting around her lips and under her eyes. She looked almost ravaged. His heart melted. It always did when he beheld Merry-Grace Rakoczy. And lately there was something new in his feelings. She was a widow, probably; single, probably; and his yearnings had exploded into a wild longing—too soon, improper, disrespectful.

"Merry-Grace," he said, wiping his hands with a grimy towel.

"Sam, have you a few minutes?"

"I'll make a few."

She headed for his battered desk and sat in one of its chairs almost hesitantly, as if she was about to commit ink to her whiteness. He followed around the workbenches and settled into the remaining chair, across the battered pine.

"Sam, you're the only person I can talk to. I . . . I'm in a dilemma. Could this be just between us? Not for the paper?"

He nodded reluctantly.

"Is that a promise?" she asked urgently.

"Yes." It irritated him. He treasured his integrity, and she was questioning it. But one look at her told him she was suffering something unbearable. He'd surrendered a lot of stories this way through a lifetime as an editor. He'd regretted keeping what he'd heard out of his papers, but he had not once violated his promise to keep a secret. It had cost him several grand stories and sometimes made him seem slower than the competition.

"Clayton Buell came over," she said, then stopped. Whatever she wanted to say, it was troubling her.

"Yes?"

"He came over and wanted to talk."

Sam Flint watched this lovely, grieving woman wrestle with words that came and went upon her lips.

"He proposed to me," she blurted out. "Only, it wasn't a proposal. You know." She stared at the plank floor.

"I'm afraid I don't know, Merry-Grace." He felt anguish flood through him. He wasn't the only man in the Tonto Basin yearning deep in his bones for this woman in white.

"He wanted to move in with me. He wanted me to be his consort. His—you know."

"But Merry-Grace, why?"

"Because he's married. And because I can't marry until the courts say that Nicholas is dead. Seven years from now. And for my own good, he said!" Now she turned feverish. "He didn't seem to worry much about my reputation or my honor."

"And you said what?"

"I said no. It's too early to think of another man. And just imagine him coming to me like that! Oh, Sam, he's been good to us. His crew has done all our ranch labor. They branded our calves. He buys beef from me when I need cash. He's trying to keep nesters off. He's been a father to my boys, too. He's given them ponies and saddles. I . . . I owe him a lot, Sam. But this! This thing that has no name. Don't you see? I don't love him, and I—" She quit suddenly, almost spent by her outburst.

"I don't know what to do," she whispered. "I'm sorry I bothered you. You must be busy. Where's Mr. Thimble?"

"He's left me, Merry-Grace. He's going to try homesteading again."

"Oh," she said somberly. "I don't know what I came here for. I guess I needed to talk to someone who wouldn't gossip. I have lots of friends, but they'd gossip and ruin my reputation."

"Please stay. I want to hear the rest."

She leaned toward him. "Clayton's married, you know. His wife's mad, and some nuns in Savannah care for her. He said he wished to be a bigamist and we'd live in defiance of man and God. That's what he said."

"My God, he said that? What'll happen now, Merry-Grace?"

"He said he'll wait. If I'd consent to—you know—he would be a good steward and protect me, protect my sons and me, from everyone. Sam, I don't know how long I can last. I'm all alone there. And selling a few animals to Clayton doesn't help me much. Ike Cobb, Abel, and the rest have been very gallant, letting me charge things. But it can't go on, you know."

Flint felt his longing flood through him. He wanted her more than he could say, and here was a powerful rival. He realized he didn't earn much. He knew nothing of ranching. And he had scruples about his arrangements with women. But he sensed that love might triumph over all—if she had any feelings for him.

"Merry-Grace," he said carefully, "these arrangements aside, what do you think of Clayton Buell?"

"He's a kind, good neighbor. He and Nicholas spent hours . . . But now he wants to disgrace me."

It mystified Flint, unless the colonel was simply catering to his lust. "Has he made . . . advances?"

"He's never touched me, if that's what you mean."

"I don't fathom him."

"What should I do?" she asked, tears welling up.

"Follow your conscience. His proposition, and his conduct toward his wife, aren't exactly virtuous."

She cast her gaze elsewhere. "I just needed to talk," she said, rising.

"Please don't go," he said. She settled back into the wooden seat reluctantly. "Sometimes people are driven to do things they wouldn't otherwise do. Sometimes people mean well. Maybe he's trying to protect you."

"He is. He said it would keep me from harm. That I needed a man. I do. If Nicholas doesn't come back, I might have to leave the ranch and do something else."

"Is that what you want?"

"I don't know. But I don't want to make the decision under pressure. Well, now I've made a fool of myself."

"No, Merry-Grace."

"I wish Nicholas were here. Everything was so lovely then. He was my sun and my evening star. Strong and romantic—I mean, brimming with feeling. Sometimes he just poured it all over me, and I felt safe and loved. What other man would wake me up with a bouquet he'd picked while I was sleeping? Or tell me the boys would be handsome because they had my blood in them? I could never love anyone the way I loved him. We had moments . . . He melted me into wax. There was only one Nicholas, and no other Nicholas could ever replace him."

Some small, dark pain burrowed through Flint's heart. "You have good memories," he said.

"More than memories! Maybe you think I'm mad, but I know he's present!"

"How do you know that?"

"I just do. It's written across the sky." She eyed him shyly. "Sometimes at night I feel his spirit beside me. When the moon's bright, I see him on the wind." She smiled wryly. She rarely smiled lately. "I'm being crazy right before your eyes."

She stood. "I remember the first time I saw you, Sam. Back in April, on the road."

"You do?" It amazed him.

"I knew you'd be a friend. I don't know what it was. I didn't know who you were or where you were going. But we talked a moment and something about you caught me, and I thought about you all the rest of the way home. I thought it would be nice if you came to Payday, and I thought when Nicholas came back, I would invite you to our house for dinner."

"You remember the moment as well as I do, then. It's been in my mind."

She looked knowingly at him, as if they had come to an unspoken compact. He felt a flood of love and yearning he knew he couldn't express, something he had dammed up for as long as she believed Nicholas Rakoczy might live and hold her love and loyalty.

"You're the only person I can talk to. I read every issue of the *Pioneer*. You shine through on every page, in every article. In all your opinions. I had to come and talk to you because you're the one who stands up to be counted."

He nodded, feeling heady. "If there's a way for a newspaper to help you, Merry-Grace, this paper'll help. Mostly, a paper records events. But sometimes a paper can change the world. If I can change your world for the better, I will."

She smiled and offered her hand. He took it. Her handshake was firm and warm, and the pressure of it left his fingers tingling with joy. Then she smiled wordlessly and walked into the dazzling sun. But he felt a seven-year sadness slide over him.

32

The farther Jacob Miller penetrated the Tonto Basin, the more he liked his surroundings. His twenty beautiful, fawn-colored Jersey cows nipped the lush grasses as they traveled. Frequently they forded sparkling creeks. Surely this was the very Eden he had been looking for, and if Payday needed a creamery, he would start one.

He and his four girls and his wife Evangeline had left Evansville early that spring, intending to build a new life on the frontier. He had a veteran's land allotment coming to him, and they could also homestead one-sixties. They could claim more than enough pasture. He was using four bulls as draft animals, and now the big, slobbering, trail-broken beasts were pulling the heavy wagon forward. They would soon fill out on grass like this.

They had stopped in Socorro in the heat of August to inquire where a good creamery might prosper. Miller's practice was to talk to the local newspaper editor. In this case, an English-speaking Mexican named Trujillo helped him.

"We have a creamery here," he said with a shrug, "but there's a town in Arizona Territory that's growing fast. The editor calls it

Paradise. Ah, Paradise! What a thing to say of someplace in this world, yes? Mother of God. I read his paper every week. He's a good editor." Trujillo extracted a couple of copies of the *Pioneer* from a heap lying in a corner. "Now, Señor Miller, let's look for an advertisement for a creamery. Or for a store that sells milk and butter, yes?"

Miller studied the Payday paper, blotting up all he could of the place. He thought it was intelligently written. The ads were plentiful, but he didn't spot one for a dairy. The name of a mercantile caught his eyes, though. Cobb's General Store. That was a name he was familiar with in Evansville. Old Cobb was his banker. That family had experienced both glory and shame during the war. Miller would gladly have encouraged a match between either of his older daughters and the Cobb boy who had died a hero.

Miller had done his time in the Indiana Volunteers in spite of being a little older than most. He was never wounded, but almost died of typhus. He recovered and fought again, finally being discharged a month after Appomattox. The government had taken three years out of his life, and now the government would pay him back with some land. Not that the government could ever pay him back. But freeing the slaves had been a just cause, and he didn't regret aiding it. He abominated slavery in a free nation. Slavery had made him seethe inside, so he had signed up, fought, and won a veteran's bonus. So that he would have good milking hands, he had waited for his girls to grow before starting west.

After a parched, hard trip across New Mexico, he walked into Payday one afternoon, liking what he saw except for the strip of gaudy sin parlors along Basin Street. This was no desert; it was God's own secret hideaway. The town certainly looked prosperous. He had the girls and Evangeline herd his gentle, brown-eyed cows on the edge of town, in the shade of majestic cottonwoods, while he walked in. He wanted to talk to people. That editor, for one. A land office for another.

But he passed the Cobb Grocery and Drygoods Emporium on Prescott Street first. The sign read "Isaiah Cobb, Proprietor." That startled Miller, and out of curiosity, he went in. Maybe this fellow would be distantly related to the Evansville Cobbs. He spotted the man in a white apron brooming the floor at the rear. On closer inspection, he realized that he knew this Cobb, and that it wasn't Isaiah; it was Jerusalem the coward, the boy who'd stolen Isaiah's medal and run off. And apparently stolen Isaiah's name and honor to boot. It all came to Miller in a rush.

Jacob Miller was a big, burly man. Cobb saw him coming and froze. "It's Jerusalem Cobb," Miller said relentlessly. "I always wondered where you were hiding."

"Mr. Miller," Jerusalem croaked.

"Well, you have quite a store here. Look at it. You left without a dime. I don't suppose being a Medal of Honor winner has anything to do with it."

"You don't know how it was," Cobb whispered.

"I think I do. I'll bet my last dollar that this town thinks you won that medal, that you're a local hero. I'll bet my last cent that you encourage that impression. And I'll bet that not a soul knows your real name or what kind of coward you are."

Jerusalem Cobb peered wildly about. But the single customer in the front of the store was studying ready-made blouses out of earshot.

A vast, black contempt filled Miller. "Your father and mother didn't grieve you much. She died last summer, proud of one son, ashamed of the other. They never talked about it, but when you and the medal disappeared, they didn't need lessons to figure out what happened. They didn't entertain for a year. The Cobb home was closed to company. I think it killed your father. He was dead in two years. I heard he wrote you out of his will, but I can't prove it."

Jerusalem had paled so much that Miller thought he might faint. Cobb was actually a fine-looking, slender young fellow, and Miller suspected that he was as ingratiating as ever. The boy had always made his way in the world with a ready smile, a compliment, and a strong dose of charm. "Ah, are you staying in Payday?" Cobb asked solicitously.

"I don't know if I want to, with a rotten apple like you in it," Miller said. He was relentless and wanted to be. "I suppose you've shown the medal around. Impressive-looking, on its blue ribbon. You're a hero here."

Mockery oozed from that last. Cobb listened, twitching and distraught.

"Well, I know what you're thinking, Jerusalem. You're wondering if I'm going to spread the word. It happens I don't know a soul here, but I always like to talk to newspaper editors about a place. They're a shrewd bunch. I was heading that way anyway. Maybe I'll talk about you."

Cobb nodded stiffly. Something sad drifted into his face, and Miller thought Cobb was seeing his exposure and disgrace and planning his flight to some other obscure frontier town.

Miller laughed and wheeled out, while Cobb gripped his broom, knuckles white. The air smelled cleaner outside. Miller breathed it in and got the stink of cowardice out of his nostrils. He'd fought beside witless men who had never fired a shot in battle. He could understand that; at least those men were there, and hadn't deserted. But Cobb was something else: a robber of reputation, glory, and courage.

Miller found the log offices of *The Payday Pioneer* near the courthouse square and marched in. The man who greeted him wore a blackened printer's smock and a curious, observant gaze.

"I'm Miller. In from Evansville, Indiana, on the Ohio River. I might settle, and I've a few questions. You're Sam Flint. I saw the name on a copy of the *Pioneer*."

"That's me. I'm from Cincinnati. It almost seems like we were neighbors," Flint said. "We've a fellow from Evansville here, a brave young man named Cobb."

"Yes, Jerusalem. I stopped there."

"Ah, no. It's Isaiah."

"It's Jerusalem. Well, I've driven my little dairy herd here—nice, gentle Jersey cows and some bulls. I'm fixing to homestead, use my veteran's allotment, and start up a creamery. Tell me the ins and outs of it."

"Why, we could use a creamery, but you'll have some competition. The Polks, south of town, have a few cows and we're not lacking for milk and cream, but times are changing. You have to go out there to get it. They don't market it in town, don't have any bottles. We don't see much cheese here, and the town's growing fast, and maybe you could build a nice business.

"Judge Cutlip—Basil Cutlip from Galena—has the best land office. There's places to settle, and places I'd advise against. All the best grass, with the creeks running through it, is up against the Mogollon Rim, and that's claimed by one big ranch. But there's lots of land if you don't mind drier country."

That wasn't entirely good news to Miller, and he decided that the situation would take some investigating. "This Cutlip's a judge?" he asked.

"That takes an hour a day. Peaceful place. He's just around the corner and down the street. Have a good talk with him. He'll not only sell patented land, he'll help you homestead public land, file for your veteran's claim, and get you settled besides."

"We'll see," said Miller. "I want the complete lowdown on everything. Who owns that good grass on the north side?"

"Clayton Buell. He has a big outfit. He got here first."

"That's a familiar name. I don't suppose he's a Reb colonel? Fredericksburg, Chancellorsville?"

Flint nodded.

"And he's hogging all the good grass, while a loyal veteran corporal like me, who risked his life to free the slaves, gets the dry country. Have I any remedies?"

"You might if you have courage. Buell's holding public land you can claim, but he chases people off."

Miller didn't like that. "I've got four girls and a wife and no sons," he said. "Fat chance."

"Well, your best bet is to talk with Basil Cutlip. He won't mislead you. I think you could settle here profitably. We'd sure welcome you."

"I'll look into it, Flint. There're some things I don't like about the town, and one of them is that strip of dives along Basin Street. I'm not sure this is the place for decent young women. Now, I've read your paper, two issues, and I didn't see anything about that."

"I've covered it." Flint pointed at a table. "You can study any issue over there."

Miller didn't quite trust the man. This editor seemed too tricky for his own good. "I'll see about it. It looks to me like this is one of those towns so inbred that outsiders can't get a foothold. This Buell and this Cutlip, and maybe this Cobb. I know the fellow. His real name's Jerusalem, and as long as I'm here, I'm going to tell you a story about Cobb and you can print it up. It's something a newspaper editor just better know and write about. I don't know what he's been telling folks around here, but that fellow never won the Medal of Honor and never fought in the war . . ."

That sure got Flint's attention.

33

There were times when Sam Flint didn't much like his position in town. If he were to draw a Thomas Nast cartoon of himself, it would be a grotesque one in which each of his ears had grown into a giant ear trumpet, sucking in all the whispers and darknesses of the human race. It had happened in every town where he'd start up a paper. Sooner or later, someone's dark past would reach Flint's funneling ears. A lot of people had done things that they were ashamed of and tried to bury.

Flint set himself to composing again, plucking letters from the California caseboxes, laying them upside down into his type stick, adding a space between each word, leading out each line until it was justified, sliding the completed line into the galley tray. But his mind was on Cobb. Flint didn't doubt that Jacob Miller was right. Cobb's becoming modesty about his bravery under fire wasn't becoming and it wasn't modest; the young man knew that if he talked much, he'd arouse the suspicion of any veteran—and especially of a wary editor.

The matter puzzled Flint. If Cobb had merely run away from

the war, he would have done nothing more than thousands of other men who figured they would sit it out in safety on the frontier or deep in the wilderness. But Cobb had stolen his dead brother's glory, flaunting a medal and reputation he had no right to possess. That's what separated Jerusalem from the others. Maybe Cobb couldn't cope with the comparison; a heroic older brother esteemed by his parents and all of Evansville; a younger brother privately terrified of war, squirming at danger, and ashamed that he didn't measure up, branded a coward. Jerusalem Cobb was a fraud and a reprobate.

Within the hour, Basil Cutlip walked in. Flint didn't stop composing. With Thimble gone, he couldn't stop for anything. Cutlip knew that and drifted back to the workbench.

"You talked with Miller, I take it," Cutlip said.

"I sent him to you. I laid it out for him: we could use a good dairy here even though there's some competition. I told him that the lush grass he coveted would be tough to claim, and I told him he could still do well south of town."

"Well, I told him the same thing. Tried to get him to stay, but he didn't like the looks of Basin Street, and I can't say that I blame him, four daughters and a wife. He decided to head for Prescott."

"Odie Racine's costing us growth. And it's going to get worse, Basil. Did Miller tell you anything else?"

"No. Should he have?"

"I guess not."

"It's not just Racine's joint anymore. Three more are going up, and it seems I'm selling a lot a week along there. That's getting to be Hell's Half Acre."

"It's three acres now, Basil."

"Several gunshots last night. An injured man, tough fellow, shot through the right lung. He'll probably die. We don't even have a doctor in town. Here we are, prettiest valley in the West, nicest town anyone could ask, and we haven't a sawbones."

"I'll make a note of it. Maybe the exchange papers'll pick it up. Your Merchants' Committee could solicit someone. Maybe get one up here from Tucson."

"We haven't got a proper undertaker, either. Tony Stapleton never took to it. He'll build a box, but he hates handling bodies. And there's not a place in town to pay one's respects except the church."

"Well," Flint said, "you don't need doctors and undertakers in Eden. When they read all my talk of Paradise, they figured they weren't welcome."

Cutlip laughed, but quickly turned solemn. "Violet's ailing. She's just shrunk down and lost weight and turned quiet. She's got black circles under her eyes. It worries me. And there's not a doc closer than Prescott."

"You'd better take a few days off and take her over there. At least you'll have some kind of diagnosis."

Cutlip sighed. "I dread it. Maybe she'll get better."

Flint doubted that many people simply got better from something that wasn't fever. "Now tell me what was done with this injured man, and who he was," he said.

"The Transfer Company made room for him on top of the Prescott coach," Cutlip said. "They pulled out an hour ago. I doubt that the fellow'll make it. His lungs are filling up. He'll die before he gets there."

"Who shot him?"

"No one's saying. Arnold Betjeman's been questioning all those people, but no one's talking. He says the tinhorns just grin and shrug, mocking him. They know he's old and tired, and it's all a joke to them. He hates that. Say what you will about Arnold, he wants to be a good man at the job. But his enemy's rheumatism and lumbago and gout more than anything."

"I'll get the story from him, but you can help me now. When was this, where, and who witnessed it?"

"In Odie's gambling hall. Around midnight. Not one person

in there claims to have seen it happen, Arnold tells me. Now, if
we had a real sheriff, he'd rattle their teeth and shut down the joint
until he got the story."

"Who was the injured man?"

"Someone called Black Reilly. No background on him. About
thirty. Wasn't carrying much cash. Probably a drifting bum. Left
a sorrel horse at the hitchrail with a Box Three brand that looked
blotched—who knows where that came from."

"Was he armed?"

"No, but he had a revolver in his kit. He was one of those tough
characters we've been seeing around here. We need two or three
deputies. And we need a new sheriff. I know, I know, you said that
in your paper a few weeks ago."

"And no one did anything."

"Sam, we didn't think it through very carefully. The Committee wanted settlers, and we got you in, but we never gave a thought
to who'd show up. We don't even know how to pay some new
deputies."

"I suggested a way—licenses. Every border town I've been
in has them."

"Yes, well, Odie's opposed, and she's joined the Merchants'
Committee, and—"

Flint laughed. "And she's handing out tokens."

Judge Cutlip nodded, suddenly discreet.

"I'm going to do a story about all this, Basil. If Odie Racine's
got the town's businessmen in her palm, and if the county supervisors won't act, that's news. I'll be embarrassing you businessmen and all the rest, but I'm going to do it."

"I thought you might. It's going to anger your advertisers, but
you'll weather that." The judge turned solemn. "Sam, I think Odie
Racine's gone a lot farther than handing out tokens. She knows
exactly who's climbed those stairs to her second floor—and she's
using it. Blackmail. You should see some of those fellows stick up
for her. Lafe Short's one, and even Clay Wiley's mewing over her.

They know better than that. She's got 'em where she wants 'em. She's also waving money around, not quite bribes, but you get the idea."

"Has she tried to influence you? You're the one who'd be conducting any trials. If she has, she could be indicted on it."

"Yes, I suspect so. She's offered to buy up any business lots on Prescott Street at two hundred a lot. Now, there's still eighteen left, Sam, and that's twice what I've been selling them for. You can call it whatever you want. And our fine county attorney, Badger Culbertson, is looking prosperous suddenly."

Flint had the sensation that dry rot was eating away at Payday, and maybe it was already too late. "What've the supervisors done to curb her?"

"They talked about a midnight curfew—slow her income down some. But Jackson and Pollack didn't want it. They said her cash's prospering the whole town. Trade's up at the greengrocer, the cobbler, the lumberyard, the feed store, the smithy, and everywhere else. She's a regular cash cow, they said."

Flint smiled. "Cash cow. That's a name for her. In other words, they're already in her palm and now we've a town filling up with thugs. No one's safe, especially our women. And we've one harebrained sheriff to enforce the law, which he barely does even when the sun shines. Where are you on all this?"

"Oh, in the middle. I'm making money fast, Flint, and I'm not opposed to it, and I don't care where it comes from. But I think we've got to protect Payday, and that means deputies, and it means licenses on those dives, so we can pay for some law."

"Have the supervisors bought her idea of hiring her own deputy?"

"Well, yes, they just about have. Most of the merchants like it—no new taxes. Even Greene and Cobb."

"Where's Buell on all this?"

"He hasn't attended the last several county board meetings. But he hates all forms of government. Especially law enforcement.

He's got his own loyal men out there, and right now, to be candid, they're the most powerful armed force in Alpine."

"You have any inkling of the end of all this?" Flint asked intently.

"I'm afraid I do."

"Can you talk the town merchants into a little less greed and more safety?"

"I'll try, but . . ." The rest faded from Cutlip's lips.

Flint sensed he was going to be largely alone the next few weeks. And in mortal danger. "I'm going to fight," he said.

"A delicate hand would be best," Cutlip said. "A lot of wealth's involved. And you don't want to scare off settlers and new subscribers."

"Payday isn't safe, and you know it. There isn't a strongbox in town beyond Odie Racine's reach. You'll be opening yours at gunpoint. Others will open theirs to avoid being exposed by blackmail. And others'll have theirs blown open."

Cutlip settled his broad-brimmed straw hat over his graying locks. "You're too much the pessimist," he said. "You forget I'm a judge. I can lay down some tough sentences. See you, Flint."

Flint watched the judge step into sunshine so bright it looked as if the man were ablaze. Tough sentences. Assuming anyone was brought to trial, or anyone cooped up in that log cell room wasn't sprung out. A bad joke.

He knew what he had to do. He eyed his forms, seeing that this edition was well along toward printing. Just a few holes to fill up, mostly on the front page. He could hold back some stories and make room. He'd get the shooting story—it probably was murder by now—from Betjeman, and maybe a little more from Odie. Then he was going to roast about half the town—at least the half that owned the stores and ran the county government. He was going after Odie Racine, too: her brass tokens, her pressures, her probable blackmail, and all the rest, including her attempts at not-very-subtle bribery of a judge. He was also going to hide his cash, not that he had much. And he was going to put the heat on, issue after issue, until civil authority was established in Payday.

People didn't like papers that said such things. It was an odd thing. He'd lose a lot more than the advertising. He'd lose his friends.

34

Before putting the paper to bed, Flint made a hurried trip to
the courthouse. It took Rudy Farquehar, the county clerk, no time
at all to answer what Flint wanted to know: whether Odie Racine
had sold off the lots she'd bought. She hadn't. All that frantic
building going on along Basin Street was on her property.

Then Flint hoofed over there for a closer look. Even though
he'd known about the frenzied construction there, he hadn't been
paying much attention. Half a dozen new places were either open
or about to open, including a big gambling hall called "The Bo-
nanza," chock-full of roulette, faro, chuckaluck, and poker tables.
A new, dark-lit saloon called "The Bucket of Blood" had opened
up next door, and beyond that, a dubious-looking boardinghouse
with an all-night diner on the first floor. "Two Bits a Flop," the
sign read.

Across the street, still on Racine lots, squatted a mysterious,
small log building, whose purpose he was unable to fathom until
he smelled the sweetish scent of incense drifting from a window:
a den for hop fiends. And next to that was a new hurdy-gurdy, a
dime-a-dance joint called "The Shebang." He peered into the sour

gloom and saw a few haggard, varicosed strumpets in calf-high full skirts, lounging at a table. At night, they would transform themselves with paint, stomp with cowboys to the music pounded out of an old upright piano, hustle drinks—rotgut for the gents, tea that looked like whiskey for themselves—and maybe pilfer coin from their guests' pockets while inflaming their carnal instincts. Here, too, Flint could see a dark stairway rising surreptitiously to a second floor.

He gazed amazed at the numerous strangers, all of them scruffy males, loitering on the boardwalks, drifting from one joint to another, even in mid-afternoon. When the area exploded into life at night, their number would multiply several times over. The evolution of Basin Street was breathtaking: these wild venues now occupied two blocks and formed an entire district on the east edge of Payday. People coming into town, like Merry-Grace, would have to drive right through the worst of it.

He added some material to his story at the last minute, citing each joint by name, asserting that the lots were still owned by Odie Racine, and that the district was crawling with unsavory sorts who posed a menace to the good people of Payday. With the new paragraphs in place, he locked the form again and began printing. The next morning, he took a load of papers to the post office, gave his cheery newsboy Elmer a stack to hawk on Prescott Street, delivered a few dozen more to merchants, and returned to his sanctum, where he began to break down type with a revolver not far from hand.

He expected Odie, but instead, found himself facing a pair of torpedoes in derbies and shiny worsted suits, each built like a gorilla. One was black-haired and swarthy; the other, freckled and carrot-haired.

"Yeah, Odie Racine sent us," said the dark one, rotating a mauled yellow cigar around his lips. "She mostly likes what you're saying. She likes law and order."

That surprised Flint. "She'd go for a license fee?"

"Nah, that's not it. She's hiring two deppities on her own, and wants the merchants to pay the salaries. That'll keep order around the place."

"Two private lawmen?"

"Yeah, us."

"You? Who would you report to?"

"Her."

"Not the sheriff or the county?"

"Oh, we'd cooperate. Betjeman'd pin a star on us. We'd divvy it into three shifts. The sheriff, he patrols from eight in the morning to four in the afternoon. Then I take it from four to midnight. They call me 'The Punch,' which I'm real good at. And Fauntleroy here takes it from midnight to eight, because he's junior and gets the graveyard shift."

"What's your salary?"

"Hunnert a month, each of us. Starting now, we're collecting fifty clams a month from each merchant, you included. We've already squeezed most of them. We got twenty-eight on the list. You want protection?"

Flint sighed. "Do I want protection from you?"

"Yeah. If you don't pay, we won't help out if you get broken into."

Flint eyed them. "Your salaries cost two hundred a month. Arnold Betjeman earns fifty from the county. You're lining up twenty-eight businessmen to pay fifty each—which is nineteen hundred a month. Who gets the profit?"

"Odie does. She's thunk it up, and that's her profit."

"Is Judge Cutlip paying?"

"Oh, yeah. He's got that town-lot business that needs protection."

Flint felt icewater run through his veins. "I guess I'll decline, gents. I can't afford six hundred a year, and I'll just protect myself."

"You're better off not protecting yourself. No telling what can happen if we're not patrolling here."

"Sorry."

"Odie won't like it, Flint. She wants everyone to be safe and happy."

"I can imagine."

"She don't like newspapers very much."

"She'll like mine even less when I report the news."

"She'd like a nice story, Flint. She's making a civic contribution to Payday. Us."

Flint laughed. The torpedoes laughed, too. "You tell Miss Racine that I'll publish whatever is true."

"Well, Flint, maybe you won't publish at all if we can't protect you. Streets are fulla real bad criminals these days, real hardcases that need bopping over the bean now and then."

"Yes, you're right. But I'll take my chances."

"Yeah, that's a pity, Flint," said the bigger torpedo.

"What's your real name?"

"Danny Drinker. The Punch. And he's Gerald Fauntleroy. The Knuckle."

Flint watched them lumber out. That pair came out of Hell's Kitchen probably. He realized he was alone. Greene, Cobb, even Cutlip, had caved in to extortion. He knew he didn't have much time: maybe two or three issues, and he'd either be the victor or he'd be dead. And in between, he'd probably see his plant and equipment ruined. It was a temptation to surrender. He could pay the extortion, keep his editorial gaze askance, write about christenings and store openings and the price of cordwood, and not stir up the hooligans. Easy to do—but he'd hate himself and feel he was letting down Payday.

He pulled apart his columns for a while, pondering matters, and then decided to confirm what was happening to Payday before coming to any decisions. He hung up his smock, scrubbed his stained hands, and walked down the street to the land offices of Basil Cutlip.

"I know why you're here, Sam," Cutlip said from behind his desk.

"You paid?"

Cutlip shrugged. "Violet's very ill, and I haven't time to deal with these matters for the moment. I intend to, later on."

"I guess you're saying you paid the extortion money. Have you talked to the county attorney about indictments? Extortion is a crime."

Cutlip laughed shortly. "Badger Culbertson's paying fifty, too, to protect his lawbooks. He, ah, values his health."

"Just like that? We've let Odie Racine and some thugs out of the East take over Payday and begin to squeeze the town dry? Just because some merchants got greedy! What's the sheriff done?"

"He's quieter than ever."

"Has he gone in there and arrested these torpedoes?"

Cutlip glared. "You know better than that."

"If Betjeman pinches one, and he's brought before you in court, what'll you do?"

"Flint, don't ask questions that a man can't answer."

"I'm alone, then. I didn't pay, and I won't quit."

"Then no one can help you, Sam. Look, let the tidal wave roll over, and after that, we'll get rid of these crooks. I intend to summon help from Prescott. Maybe even ask for the militia."

Flint stared at Cutlip, disgust building in him. "A few days ago, you were telling me we could all profit from having a tenderloin. Now you know you'll be beaten out of everything you own."

"I've hidden my assets," Cutlip said calmly.

"And when those torpedoes start working you over, you'll howl out the name of every hiding place."

Cutlip peered into space. "We should've heeded your editorials weeks ago. A stiff license fee for all sporting places, two sworn county deputies, and maybe a new sheriff, with some muscle and courage."

"Well, you didn't, and now you'll lose every cent unless we all act fast . . . and together."

Cutlip didn't argue. "We came out here to repair our fortunes, Violet and I," he said. "That's what the West is for."

"It's not too late."

Cutlip stood dismissively. "It might be. I hear that Miss Racine is collecting more tinhorns and bartenders, most of them handy with revolvers, scatterguns, derringers, knives, baseball bats, and brass knuckles. It's the devil's army. But we can get through this. Lay low. Go along for a while. We'll quietly organize a way out, maybe hire some noted shootist to come in and clean up. Don't be reckless, Sam. I'm intending to get word to the governor, hush-hush of course."

"Well, it's all going into the next edition," Flint said.

"Please don't say a word—for your sake. I prefer you alive."

Disturbed by Cutlip's gloom and passivity, Flint wandered into the evening. He spotted Ike Cobb locking up his store.

"Ike, could I have a word?"

Ike turned, and Flint was amazed to see terror in the man's face. "I want nothing to do with you," Ike cried. "You're stalking me like a painter."

"Ike, I want to talk about Odie Racine's thugs."

"No you don't. You're going to ruin me." He fled down Prescott Street, his stride spastic.

Flint sighed. Ike would be no help.

He went back to the office and worked into the evening under the coal-oil lamp, putting display type away, rebuilding ads, and thinking about the story he would run about the doom of Payday. He went to bed in the rear apartment around midnight, but he wasn't there five minutes when he heard the crash of glass and, moments later, saw wavery yellow light radiating through the door from the shop.

He bolted up from bed, rushed into the shop and found a yard-wide pool of coal oil and shattered glass feeding a fury of flame near his composing bench, even as the pool grew wider and wider.

Water wouldn't work on coal oil—he knew that. He plunged back into his quarters, yanked up a threadbare carpet in the parlor, and returned to his shop, which boiled with dazzling yellow light and thick smoke. He threw the rug over the pool of oil and flame, stomped hard wherever flame broke through, cutting his feet on glass, until at last his shop lay in blackness and acrid smoke.

Sobbing, he studied the smoking rug, looking for the one ember that would start the flames up again. Finally, he retreated on bloody, smarting feet to his bedroom, washed and got dressed. Then he slowly cleaned up the mess, dragging the rug into the street and sweeping up shards of glass. *The Payday Pioneer* was intact—for the moment. He dragged a rocking chair and a blanket into the shop, shed his clothes and clambered into his bathrobe, and rocked through the quiet, smoke-choked night, his old Navy revolver in hand and his gaze darting from window to door to window.

He was no quitter, and he believed that the best defense was a good offense. He would take the war to the very doorstep of Odie Racine.

35

Sam Flint knew of weekly newspaper editors who would ruin their businesses and bankrupt themselves rather than moderate their white-hot opinions. He never counted himself as one of those suicidal types. He could be stubborn, but sometimes he had to bend a little just to survive.

Now he chose to bend a little. If he dogged Odie Racine and her growing hooligan army issue after issue, he'd only end up with a ruined plant, wrecked equipment, and little prospect of ever recovering enough to operate his own paper again. To buy himself some time, he intended to back off for an issue or two. But that didn't mean he would abandon the fight.

Life in Payday continued serenely, and outwardly nothing seemed different. Odie's two "deputies"—wearing county stars making them actual lawmen—kept peace in the sporting district, or so it seemed. Everything ran wide open. One could buy a drink or a pipeful of opium or a shuffle with a weary woman any time. One could lose at faro, play poker, lay money on the red or black roulette numbers at eight in the morning or eleven at night. There was actually some good in it: plenty of actual cash, greenbacks mostly, appeared in cash-starved Payday. In practical terms, Odie Racine had become the town banker.

But Flint knew it wasn't the same. Every business in town, save his own, was laying out fifty a month in "taxes"—actually, extortion money. Flint knew that the price would rise. And not a soul outside of the district was safe. Nor would there be justice done when frightened county officials, in peril of their lives, went along with Odie Racine. Sadly, that included Judge Cutlip.

Nothing more happened to his plant. He supposed he had been warned. They were watching. He sensed that they would let him operate as long as he left them alone. A paper had it uses, even for people like Odie Racine.

Flint felt strangely isolated now. Businessmen, treasured friends and acquaintances, hurried by him. His meals at the Cochise Café turned solitary, even when he sat next to old friends. But there was still news to gather, and he made his rounds, collecting stories about the daily lives of people. There were always newcomers to write up; visits from relatives; the topics of last week's sermons; the prices given for cattle. And news and quips from the exchange papers to copy. This he did, making a show of it.

Then, on an August Wednesday, Violet Cutlip died. Since the town had no doctor, all anyone could say was that she died of natural causes. It reminded him that he should write another editorial pleading for a sawbones to come to town. He learned the news about Mrs. Cutlip from the judge himself, who simply walked in, dressed in solemn black, sat down, stared at Flint for a dozen ticks of the clock, and announced the death of his wife shortly after midnight that morning.

"I haven't the faintest idea what took her, Sam. She wasn't fevered; she just failed, shrank down to nothing, turned gray, professed to have a hard time breathing at the last, and gave up the spirit very bravely. I was holding her hand. Her final thoughts were about our next life. She believed she'd see me again."

"I'm sorry, Basil. So sorry. You and she tried to rebuild your lives and now you're alone here."

Cutlip sighed. "It changes things. I don't know what I'll do. I'll confess to you that someday we intended to go back to Galena and pick up our life there—you know, recoup here, go back there. But we hadn't known that the Tonto Basin would be an Eden, and this last year we didn't talk much about going back. We had a certain, ah, status there. Wealth, comfort. It's an odd thing, but I've no plans to return to Illinois now. If Violet had wanted to, I would have. But not now. Payday's my home."

"Are you all right, Basil? Would you like company? What may I do for you?"

"I'm all right, Sam. I came to give you some facts about Violet. Could you write up a good obituary?"

"Why, Sam, I'll give it everything I can bring to it. You tell me about her—start at the beginning. I didn't know her well, so you just assume you're asking a stranger to do this. And I'll put it right on page one."

"If you have a page one by the next issue."

"I think I will, Sam. I'm concentrating on business for a few issues. Making money, keeping afloat."

Cutlip smiled slightly. "I thought maybe you'd get up on the stump and wreck your paper. You're the type. You're full of ideals, like the Abolitionists. How can you compromise?"

Flint shrugged. "I haven't. I'm just choosing the time to act."

Cutlip talked for an hour about Violet—how they met at a cotillion, how he courted the belle of Galena at a time when the frontier lay just across the wide Mississippi, how they had raised sons. He described her tastes in literature; she couldn't abide fiction, which softened the brain, but was a glutton for books that expanded her horizons. He talked on and on, his voice turning gentle with memory, or excited with pleasure at Violet's gift of dancing and her blithe indictments of fools, or heavy with loss when describing her swift, wasting illness.

At last, Basil Cutlip, the squire of Payday, arose. "I'll let you know about the service after I make some arrangements. It'll be in the church," he said.

Flint rose. "Basil, Basil," he said softly.

Judge Cutlip's eyes glistened. "I'm not as brave as I thought," he mumbled.

Cutlip left, looking suddenly diminished. Men without wives always looked incomplete and less adequate, Flint thought. He expanded his notes, then set his pencil aside. It was midday and he had some business down the street.

He hiked through blinding sunshine to Cobb's Grocery and Drygoods Emporium where he spotted Jerusalem hunched over his books in his railed-off office at the rear. He was alone.

Cobb watched him coming with a trapped-rat look on his pale face. At one point, he looked ready to bolt. But Flint stayed him.

"Ike," he yelled across what seemed an acre of bedclothes and underwear. "Wait."

"I know what you want, Flint. I'm already being blackmailed by Odie Racine's thugs, and now you want another piece of me. You and your lousy articles inviting immigrants to Payday."

"Hey, slow down, Ike."

"I'll shut this down and leave. I know how to hide. Is that what you want? When will it come out? Next issue? Or are you going to toy with me, the way a cat toys with a half-dead bird? Let me sweat for a month. Eh?"

"Ike—"

"Well, I'm not going to buy another ad. Why should I? I'll sell this place. That's what you want, isn't it? You'll expose me, make a fool of me. Shut down a good mercantile with a twelve-thousand inventory, just for fun. That's how you operate. You print everything and call it news! Well, Sam Flint, I won't tell you what I think of that, or of newspaper parasites like you, feasting on people's private lives like vultures."

"Ike, whoa."

"You'll call it an act of virtue. Expose the man, clean the town up. Why aren't you after Odie Racine instead? She got you in her claw? No, you're going after me. A man from Evansville comes to town, and my life's ruined."

"Ike! Stop it!"

This time, Jerusalem Cobb did stop. Waiting for the news of his ruin, he glared sullenly at Flint.

"I'm not going to expose your secret," Flint said quietly.

"Oh, you're just going to blackmail me!"

"No, I'm not going to publish a word of what Miller said."

"You'll hold it over me like a sword."

"It's not anything of public interest," Flint said. "Actually, most editors don't print private dirt. All it does is hurt someone. You were young. Driven by things I don't know about. I don't excuse it. I suspect you've suffered every day since. You must loathe yourself, Jerusalem."

"There you go, moralizing."

"Actually, offering sympathy. I wouldn't like to be in your shoes. One reason I won't touch that story—or spread it around in any way—is that you've grown into an asset to Payday. There're a lot of solid citizens who wouldn't like the world to know how they got started."

At last, the hot pain in Jerusalem's eyes faded. "Maybe I'll tell you my side of it . . . sometime," he said, not acknowledging Sam Flint's charity.

"I don't know that I want to hear it. The past is dead. But what about the future?"

"Well, what about it?"

"You could hide the medal—or send it back to Evansville."

Cobb grunted.

"We've larger problems, public problems now, Ike—I'll just keep on calling you Ike. Odie Racine. Two sworn-in deputies who are thugs and could hurt any of us. They could throw you into the jail if they felt like it. Or me. I'm looking for a few allies, strong and silent, who'd do some housecleaning at great risk to themselves. Let's call it a committee."

"You're asking me to join?"

Flint nodded. "Can I count on you?"

"What do you want me for? You think I'm a coward."

"Ike, people grow. You've been surviving on the frontier for what, ten or eleven years now?"

Cobb nodded.

"All right, then. I hope we can clean up this town. I'd like your support if worse comes to worse. That fifty-a-month extortion is enough to break most of the town's businessmen. It's their profit, what they live on. If Odie Racine ups the ante, it'll ruin them."

Cobb nodded curtly.

Flint grinned. "Good. I'll get back to you. Now, how about next week's ad? Same, or something new? Sell the shoes again? Did the last ad clean you out?"

"You'd trust me?" asked Jerusalem.

"Yes," said Flint.

Jerusalem Cobb looked as if he had been taken down from the cross still alive.

36

It suddenly became tough to sell space. Flint wandered from merchant to merchant, expecting them to run their usual ads, only to find them cutting back or canceling. A few who ran standing advertisements were locked into long-term insertion agreements, and that was all that kept the *Pioneer* profitable.

Sam learned that Abel Greene was one of those cutting back.

"Sam, those gorillas are taking fifty a month right off the top. That's my living. This place yields me about eight hundred a year," he said over the battered counter in his drygoods store.

"You didn't resist?"

Greene looked annoyed. "If I had both arms I might have."

"I'm sorry, Abel. I wasn't thinking."

"Well, in fact I did resist. I told them to get out. But then one of those thugs slipped a pair of brass knuckles on. Sam, do you know what brass knuckles do to mortal flesh?"

"I can imagine, Abel."

"By God, if I had two arms, I would've anyway. They just marched in here and extorted the money, knowing I was helpless. Arnold Betjeman's as useful as a cowpie. We've got a county attorney who's afraid to prosecute and a judge who won't convict."

"Are you sure?"

"I'm sure. They're both too old to cope with brass knuckles, and poor Cutlip's grieving Violet. I suppose they got fifty outa you, and maybe a few editorial suggestions."

"No, they tried, and I refused. They did try to burn me out that night, but I caught it."

"You refused? No brass knuckles?"

Flint shook his head. "Newspapers are somewhat protected—sometimes. I can't explain it, but there's a fear of newspapers. I'm not saying editors are immune to violence, but hurting an editor or wrecking a paper can be the start of big trouble."

"That makes sense. Anyway, Sam, I'll buy a little ad, a few column inches, almost like a card except I want to push some crinoline." He squinted at Flint. "Are you going on the warpath?"

"Not this issue, Abel. They've let me know they'll burn me down if I do."

That somehow delighted Greene. "Ah! So you're made of flesh and blood too! I was starting to call you 'Saint Samuel the Lesser.' Now I don't feel so bad about caving in."

Flint grinned, took the order and left. That's how it went all morning. There'd be less advertising and more filler in the next issue. Plutarch was going to come to his rescue again.

That afternoon he attended Violet Cutlip's funeral, quietly making a few notes, especially on the Reverend Burnside's eulogy and observations about the final passage of the soul. Flint returned to his sanctum in a melancholic mood late in the afternoon and immediately added several paragraphs to his front-page story about Mrs. Cutlip's death. He hoped it would please Basil. The judge had looked drawn and old as he sat in the front pew silently absorbing the rites. No hearse existed in Payday, but the coffin had been taken in a bunting-draped wagon out to the little cemetery west of town. A church sexton had dug the grave. There weren't many graves there; Payday hadn't existed very long. They buried her near an unsolved crime, an unmarked grave housing one of the drifters who had been shot in the new tenderloin.

He had one more item to write: an editorial about the need for a volunteer fire department in Payday, and the standard measures frontier towns took to keep from burning to the ground. He had been meaning to tackle that topic for weeks, but not until he barely squelched the fire in his workplace did he finally attack the issue. And when it did form in his mind, he saw a subtle way to fire a shot across Odie Racine's bow:

> It is time for Payday to organize a volunteer fire department. The risk of fire increases with each new building arising along Prescott or Basin Streets. Many of these, especially the new structures on the east edge of town, are scarcely a yard apart, and a fire in one will swiftly spread to all.
>
> Alpine County lacks funds for such a department, and Payday is unincorporated and levies no taxes. So the task befalls the merchants, whose stores are vulnerable and unprotected. The safety of property here requires, at the least, the usual water barrels on every street corner of the business district, along with a trained company of volunteers and some equipment, including buckets, ladders, and fire axes. This paper believes that if these precautions are not soon undertaken, Payday may burn to the ground at any moment, and its merchants will incur terrible losses.

Then Flint turned the editorial in a slightly different direction, which he hoped might have its impact on Odie Racine.

> Especially vulnerable is the new sporting district, if "sporting" is a proper word for it, on East Basin Street. Unlike most businesses, these establishments run nonstop all

night, requiring numerous lamps and the burning of large quantities of coal oil. The slightest accident or carelessness could result in the leveling of that whole district. And while some citizens would consider that a desirable result, the conflagration would harm the innocent along with others more culpable. These establishments are also vulnerable to disgruntled clients. All in all, this district more than any other needs substantial fire protection, lest its investments and profits all go up in smoke.

Flint supposed that Odie Racine would get the message. There were ways that the disgruntled might get even. Flint didn't doubt that some wounded citizen, perhaps a businessman she pressed too hard, might do whatever damage he could. Surely those who ran sporting palaces designed to squeeze the last drop of juice out of a customer were aware of their special risks.

Flint concluded by arguing that if the town's merchants would make a one-time investment in some water barrels and equipment, the volunteer department would require very little funding after that, and might prevent huge losses.

He went to press that evening with an edition that avoided all mention of Odie Racine and her private police, an edition innocuous and bland. It did include an account of the firebombing of his workroom, but he played it down. The lead story was the funeral. He reprinted an entire Sunday sermon given by Ebenezer Parkhurst, a Methodist circuit rider. There was a speculative piece on the new population of Payday, and his educated guess that the town now topped a thousand. And the happy news that the Payday Forwarding Company would soon begin daily Celerity Wagon trips to Prescott, and three-a-week coaches to Tucson. And a further piece detailing Judge Cutlip's continuing negotiation with the Atchison, Topeka, and Santa Fe Railroad to divert the line south of its projected path.

And, since he had too much space, the issue contained a rare assortment of Epictetus, Plato, and Plutarch, including one of his favorites:

A Roman divorced by his wife, being highly blamed by his friends, who demanded, "Was she not chaste? Was she not fair? Was she not fruitful?" holding out his shoe, asked them whether it was not new and well made. "Yet," added he, "none of you can tell where it pinches me."

—Plutarch

The next afternoon, about the time the paper had been read and absorbed throughout Payday, Odie Racine darkened Flint's sanctum. She wore spangled black as usual, spreading blackness around her the way a joyous bride spreads light. She came alone, entering the newspaper as bleakness enters the soul. It occurred to Flint that she lived a life without sunlight of the heart.

"You threatened to burn me out," she said without preamble, her gaze upon him like dead rocks.

"No, just the opposite. I pointed out that you're vulnerable."

"It was a threat. I don't lack intelligence." She watched Flint digest that. "I'm starting a volunteer fire department. The merchant fee will be twenty-five a month for fire protection. I see you've already had a fire. You need protection."

"I'd contribute to a real department. Not to yours."

She smiled. "Then I guess you'll risk fire. The other merchants will contribute."

"I doubt it. They can't afford it on top of your fifty-a-month extortion."

"Too bad for them."

"Miss Racine, when a parasite kills its host, the parasite dies too."

"Aren't you brainy? Wrong, dearie. I pack up and leave."

"That would be good."

She eyed him. "I own Alpine County now. Everything but you. When am I gonna own you?"

Flint ignored that. "Does it make you happy?"

"I have never considered the question."

"The happiest people are those who give. Who love and nurture others. It's a paradox of life. Taking is less a joy than giving."

"That's what I like about you," she said. "I come to do business and find I'm in church."

"You're not happy," he repeated, sensing he had struck a sensitive area.

"There's no room for it in my profession. If I were happy, I'd know I'm in trouble. Happiness is blinding, and I keep my eyes open at all times. I discourage it among my employees. But I always have my moment of pleasure. When I've won."

"I'm afraid I can't pleasure you."

She eyed him with cold mirth. "You wouldn't know how," she said. "But I could teach you."

He ignored that. "Madam, I've no doubt that your thugs can hurt me. Burn this place to the ground. Ruin me. But you won't let it happen. You don't want to risk a lynch mob with some hemp. They'll come for you one of these days if you don't pull back. The fastest way to get yourself into a jackpot is to burn down a newspaper. People don't like that."

"You don't have nine lives," she said.

"An editor in these frontier towns lives with that reality every day. It becomes a part of publishing an honest paper. In an odd way, it makes me satisfied with my calling. I'm sorry you're not happy, Miss Racine. I believe everyone should enjoy happiness."

"Don't threaten," she said.

"Happiness is a threat, eh?" That somehow filled Flint with cheer. "You go back and skin suckers, and leave Payday alone, Odie."

"You called me by my first name," she said. "That puts us on intimate terms." A twisted smile filled her face, and she left without another word.

Flint wasn't sure, but he suspected she had backed off. He guessed that no one talked like that to Odie Racine. He also suspected she would give up her latest extortion: pay to keep from being burned out.

That woman, he thought, had been incubated in Hell.

37

Fear laced Merry-Grace Rakoczy. The merchants wouldn't extend her credit, and several had asked her to pay up. Apologetically, Adolph Zeppel, the greengrocer, Lafe Short, the baker, Nels Gulick, the hardware man, and even Abel Greene, her old friend, had hemmed and hawed and finally refused her trade, not meeting her eyes. Her spring wagon remained empty.

"But Abel," she said, "I need to sew some shirts for the boys."

Greene stared at the plank floor. "I've some bolts of lavender stuff that isn't selling. I'll give you some," he said. "How many yards?"

"I don't want charity. I want to put it on account. I'll get things straightened away and repay you."

"Times have changed, Merry-Grace," Greene said, sadly.

"But how?"

"Just take my word for it. There's not a merchant in town making money."

"But the town's grown! I passed seven new buildings on Basin Street!"

Greene's mouth compressed and he slid into silence that mystified her. He just stood in the middle of his drygoods, shaking his head back and forth like a pendulum.

"I don't know what I'm going to do," she said. She hurried into the bright day, baffled by a subtle bleakness she couldn't put her finger on.

She had been living on the cash Clayton Buell had paid her for a few beeves now and then. But there were substantial debts outstanding, accounts with many of Payday's merchants, that Nicholas would have settled with the money he brought back from Yuma. But he had never returned. She owed Ike Cobb, Abel Greene, and especially Clay Wiley at the feed store, where the ranch bought its oats and salt.

The only way she could satisfy these debts would be to send another few hundred Rakoczy cattle to market. And for that, she would have to depend on Clayton Buell. He shipped periodically, driving huge herds to Yuma in the winter, and to the Colorado mining camps in the summer. The Colorado trips had been risky, and he'd taken a beating once or twice.

She would have to ask him to include her cattle in his next trip, and to pay himself some of the profits for doing it. She dreaded the thought. Ever since he had come to her with his odd proposition, she had desperately looked for other options. There weren't any that seemed tolerable. She didn't want to be dependent on him, even though he had been kind to her.

She admitted, numbly, that he had seen what she couldn't face: she needed him to run Nicholas's huge spread. She couldn't even pay off her accounts without Buell's help. She didn't love him, and certainly didn't approve of his proposition. But the only other option was to sell to Judge Cutlip for pennies on the dollar. Events were trapping her, and now something sinister was spreading through the basin.

Seeking answers, she walked over to the newspaper. Sam Flint had always told her everything that was going on in Payday and had tried to help her. She sensed that his feelings went deeper than friendship, but he had respected her widowhood and had never voiced them. She suddenly wished he would, if only to bolster her sagging courage.

She found no one within. "Sam?" she cried. "Sam?"

She was about to leave when he emerged slowly from the apartment in the rear.

"Merry-Grace!" he said, rubbing sleep away. "You're a vision. The woman in white. Always white. How beautiful you are."

"Oh, Sam. You were sleeping? I'm sorry."

"A nap. I have to work to midnight these days. Need a new devil. I haven't found one I want to hire. I didn't mean to sleep—just to take a ten-minute break—but I'm worn out trying to keep up."

She settled into the chair he offered her, wondering if she would get ink on her white skirt.

"Are you all right, Merry-Grace?" he asked.

She felt a flood of emotion just because Sam Flint cared. No one else in town seemed to. "No, Sam. I'm in trouble."

"Nothing could be that bad."

"I've lost my credit at all the stores. I have to pay cash now. Something's happened here, and the merchants have all shut off my credit."

Flint blinked, still chasing away some cobwebs. "It's not you. They'd all carry you if they could. It's a bad story, Merry-Grace," he began. "After you hear it, you may not want to stay here."

"I don't have enough money to go anyplace else."

She listened to a strange story about a disreputable woman named Odie Racine and some evil men she controlled, and about her extortion of the town's merchants.

"She's cleaning them out," Flint said.

"And you?"

"No, I haven't surrendered."

"But won't they hurt you?"

He smiled and pointed to a circle of charred plank floor near his workbench.

"They're cowards," she said at last.

"No, a man facing brass knuckles is no coward for caving in. Is one-armed Abel Greene a coward, Merry-Grace?"

"You faced a bullwhip not long ago."

"I wouldn't want to face one again. Or brass knuckles."

She knew he was right about the merchants, and nodded. "I don't know what to do," she said in a small voice. "I dread selling more calves to Clayton Buell. There must be another way."

"I've some credit—some of the merchants pay for their advertising that way. Let's go make a few arrangements."

"Oh, Sam—I can't let you do that."

"I want to."

She sat silently for a while. "I'll take you up on it. But I have no way to repay you until later. When Nicholas didn't return—"

"You've already repaid me."

She peered at him earnestly, understanding the grave and tender look in his eyes. "If I were free, Sam Flint, I'd return your love. But seven years . . ."

He gazed at her, his eyes, shooting light, blinked back something tender, and turned away. "You knew," he said.

"For a long time."

"I must have been obvious."

"Yes. But you never looked closely enough at me to see what was in my face. I cherish you, Sam. If I were free . . . You've been my courage and my help. I loved Nicholas. I've clung to his image, to the memories. But now . . ." Her voice was shaky. "I'm very confused. I can't do anything. I'm in a prison made by law."

"Seven years is a long time."

"I can't bear the thought of being alone for so long. I can't seem to think straight anymore."

He leaned toward her. "Let's walk over to Cobb's. I'll arrange for you to use my credit," he said. "After I load you up, I'll rent a saddler and go out to the ranch with you."

"But you're busy."

"I want to be with you."

She didn't argue. She welcomed his company. She had lived day by day, hour by hour, with more burdens than she could bear alone. His company would lift them for a while.

An hour later, they drove eastward through the beautiful basin, the grasses brown and tan now, she with her burdened wagon, he with his private thoughts. They didn't speak for two hours. Then they forded Pass Creek, and Flint stared up it.

"I wonder how the Thimbles are doing," he said.

The road took them through Buell's vast savannas, and at last they came across his multitudes of cattle, grazing quietly on the golden grama grasses.

"Some of those are probably Nicholas's," she said.

Around a bend, a hundred or so longhorns blocked the road. They rose slowly, rear end first, and stared at the intruders. She saw calves among them, and cows with the Rakoczy brand.

"See, Sam? Clayton's been good to me."

"What?"

"The calves. Those are my cows, and those calves have my brand. Clayton Buell branded them for me."

She stopped the wagon. They stared. She counted a dozen newly branded calves, some of them paired up with their mothers.

"You're right, Merry Grace. He's been a good neighbor—at least to you. I wish I could say the same about his treatment of the Thimbles. And me."

"I don't understand Clayton Buell," she said.

Sam Flint closed his eyes, and Merry-Grace supposed he was peering at some interior landscape. When at last he looked at her again, she found warmth and tenderness in his expression.

"I think you should take Clayton Buell up on his offer," he said. "It's unorthodox, and tongues would wag. But in his own way, he's been protecting you from the world. There's nothing you can do for seven years—call it six and a half now. But he's giving you his love in the best way he knows."

Flint flabbergasted her. "What? You want me to be his paramour? Without marriage? Openly bigamous? When Nicholas might still live? The man who bullwhipped you? Shot the Thimbles' flock? Do you know what you are saying?"

They resumed the trip, scattering cattle that snorted off, tails high, as they rode through.

"Yes, I do," he said.

"Have you considered my feelings?"

"Yes, Merry-Grace. Have you considered mine?"

She stared at him as he rode beside her, and saw love and surrender and resignation and sadness written upon him. He was letting go of something he could never have.

38

Colonel Clayton Buell was enjoying one of the few pleasures left him, a pipe bowl full of Virginia tobacco on the stoop of his cabin, when Sam Flint rode up in the setting light on a livery-barn horse.

Buell resented the loss of his peace. He both loathed and admired the approaching editor.

"State what you want to say and be off, Flint," Buell said harshly. "I won't ask you to light."

"It'll take a few minutes," Flint said, lighting anyway, which irked Buell. Flint stood and stretched, holding the reins.

Buell furiously knocked ash from his pipe.

"You haven't been coming to the country board meetings," Flint said. "Things have happened in Payday that you should know about."

Buell nodded. He knew what this would be. His men kept him apprised.

"A while ago, a madam named Odie Racine purchased eight town lots next to the saloons. She's thrown up buildings on all of them, transforming the area into a regular tenderloin."

With that as a start, Flint quietly spelled out a story of ruthless expansion, a crime explosion, the capitulation of county officials, the employment of thugs as deputies, and the extortion of merchants. And then a new twist: extorting more money for a volunteer fire department—or being burned out. And Flint's newspaper war against all of it.

"What it comes down to is, she's got Alpine County by the throat, the town by the throat, and absolute power over the entire town."

"No concern of mine," Buell said.

"You know it is."

"I don't know anything of the sort," Buell growled.

"Judge Cutlip's grieving. You may not have heard that Violet died. He's lost in grief. They're getting fifty a month out of him, and he'll run into brass knuckles if he makes any sort of ruling in court that Odie Racine doesn't like."

"I always knew Cutlip'd cave in at the first sign of trouble."

"I'd like to think you never said that, Buell."

"I said it."

Flint paused, somberly. "I want you to make Odie Racine your business. The county's corrupted. The merchants who supply this ranch are pressed to the wall. There'll be more graves soon, maybe mine. I survive on sufferance because a paper's useful, but if I say the wrong thing, it's all over. They've already tried to burn me out. You're an honorable man. Odie Racine's dead wrong. She doesn't own Alpine County as long as she doesn't own you. And me."

"If you're done, get up and leave," Buell said. "My twilight pipe's my only consolation, and you've robbed me of it."

"There's more."

Buell hawked up a great round of juice and spat it in Flint's general direction.

"The merchants have cut off Merry-Grace's credit. She's on the ropes. I supplied her with groceries today."

"Then you only delayed the inevitable. She needs to come to some decisions. She can get cash from me any time she wants it."

"But there are strings attached."

"It's none of your business."

Flint ignored that. "I want to thank you for protecting her."

"What? Are you crazy? I'm pushing as hard as I can to get her out. I'm starving her out."

Flint shook his head. "You'd like me to think that, but I won't. Some of what you do's a puzzle, but not all of it. She told me she has no options. She's legally married until a court declares Nicholas dead. She can't even dispose of his property until then because she hasn't inherited it. Her older brother back East might take her boys, if it comes to that. Her father's dead; her mother, on a small annuity, can't shelter her. You've given her an option if she's desperate enough—and strong enough to defy social convention.

"It comes to me that you loved Nicholas Rakoczy as a friend, the only one you've had for years, and you've admired Merry-Grace from afar. I think you love her. Your ten thousand cattle ate that range down to the dirt; she told me her place carries about a thousand beeves, and your cattle ravaged it. That discouraged settlers, didn't it? Not a one of the hundred who've come here have filed a claim on that naked, overgrazed Rakoczy range. It looks awful. As for her crops, they're tramped under now, and not one honyocker's filed a homestead claim. You've discouraged plowmen, too.

"You haven't starved her out; you've helped her. You've protected her. You've offered her a haven. There's no strong man over there to fight off settlers and thieves. At best, she'd slowly sink, selling off her cattle while rustlers and settlers and opportunists chipped away at the rest of her holdings. She's a strong woman, but she's alone. And you're offering her a shocking salvation— which I've urged her to accept."

Buell rose from the stoop in a rage. "Out!" he roared. "Right now, or I'll fetch my bullwhip."

Flint smiled. "You didn't deny any of it," he said. He mounted nimbly. "Sometimes you're a good man, Clayton Buell, even if you're hard on most of us."

Buell snorted. "What I am, Flint, is a madman. Go print it."

He watched Flint vanish into the murk of evening. His pulse raced. Off at the bunkhouse, a dozen of his men were idly observing. They hadn't heard much.

Buell settled on the stoop again, raging against phantasms, smacking his pipe against the step, over and over. He hated Flint. Buell considered himself mad, or nearly so. He had a foul well in his soul, bottomless, in which all the evil of the universe crawled.

Only he didn't really believe that. Flint was nearer the mark, God damn his good eye. Way back in May, one of Buell's men had picked up a rumor out of the San Carlos Reservation. Some young renegade Chiricahua Apaches had jumped Rakoczy and his four *vaqueros*, killed them, hidden their bodies in the vast fastnesses of arid rock to the east, blotched the brands of their horses, driven them to Sonora, and traded the horses and stolen cash for other horses and rifles and ammunition. Now they waited quietly on the reservation, brooding and dreaming of the day when they would drive the white devils away.

Buell didn't doubt it, though it had been only a rumor. He never told Merry-Grace. If it could be proven, he would have told her. But it was nothing but an old Apache's whispered tale to a friendly cowboy, told to Buell's man over a campfire. Buell had written to John Clum, the San Carlos agent. Clum had written back: no young warriors had been missing from San Carlos as far as he could ascertain. But Buell didn't believe it. He had chosen not to destroy her hope. Maybe it had been a mistake, but as the months passed, he couldn't redeem the decision. and now he was sure the rumor was true. Merry-Grace was a widow.

He wasn't sure when the idea came to him to protect her ranch for her. It was some of the choicest land in the basin; settlers would file homestead claims on it like vultures waiting for a cow to die. She wouldn't have the will or the means to resist, and she'd sell her herd piecemeal until it was all gone, then watch the great spread die, partitioned by invaders.

Neither could he say just when his idea of an illicit liaison came to him. That's why he was a madman, of course. His courtship consisted of being a guardian, scaring off settlers, helping Merry-Grace brand calves, selling stock, keeping going. He didn't know any other way to woo her. And he couldn't honorably get around his own marriage or her seven-year ordeal.

He thought he was plainly imbalanced. He mocked himself suddenly. His was not the way to a woman's heart. It was nothing but an old man's voluptuary dream. He was fifty; she was thirty. His attentions would horrify her. He had never imagined he would be drawn to another woman, with poor Eloise demented in a convent and the love of her alive in him.

But in his own way, he was a widower, and even when he and the mad Hungarian were the best of friends, Buell had paused now and then to admire Merry-Grace, fighting back a soft, gentle yearning he could not deny. Nor could he escape admiring the graciousness of the home the Rakoczys had erected out of their dreams; how sharply it contrasted with his own mean cabin, the product of a dreamless, ruined life.

Now Flint would feed her for a while. The younger man had moon-eyes for her, too. Flint's help had to be a temporary arrangement. The young editor couldn't long afford to buy food for five people and still feed himself. The problem would be self-liquidating anyway, because Odie Racine's gorillas would destroy Flint or his printing plant sooner or later. Flint was nothing but a fly in the ointment.

Buell hated to admit it, but Sam Flint was a remarkable man, and one to be reckoned with. Merry-Grace might go for him. A lot of women would—a strong, honorable, hardworking fellow like that. Flint had a brain, too. He alone grasped what Buell was up to, or understood that he and Buell were rivals for the love of a woman. She could live in sin with a crazy old colonel, or she could wait seven years—slowly losing her range and her cattle all the while—for Flint, the editor of a shaky little weekly.

Or, Buell confessed to himself, she could find her own way out. She was strong enough to leave them both in the dust.

39

Sam Flint worked quietly all the following week. He had to rebuild most of the advertisements, using smaller display type. Odie Racine's exactions from the merchants were costing him almost a page of advertising each issue.

Even though he yearned to launch a crusade against the corruption of Alpine County, he checked his impulses. He had to bide his time until the right moment, and then expose the whole mess in a way that would ensure results. If he so much as mentioned the extortion, or the suborning of county officials, or the demise of proper law enforcement, he would swiftly feel the effects of two pairs of brass knuckles, artfully employed by masters, and witness the demolition of his press and equipment, putting him out of business and leaving him penniless—if he still lived.

So he censored himself. He was as much a businessman as an editor, and the will to survive and to publish on another day remained paramount. He found plenty of other things to write about. He had taken to interviewing the new settlers when they came into town to shop, and had prepared amiable stories about seven families that had recently settled in the area. With good cheer, he introduced them all, parents and children, to the community.

Payday had acquired a tailor, a smith, and a teamster. The latter, a burly, bearded chap, Stanley Gordon, intended to compete in a small way against the two big freight outfits hauling supplies up from Tucson. The fellow had two good Pittsburgh wagons and several span of oxen. That was especially good news, because freight rates would probably drop and shelves would be better stocked.

But while he wrote of these things, he kept a careful eye on the new tenderloin and the black widow at the center of its web. In spite of the money coerced from the merchants to create a measure of fire protection, Flint noted no water barrels, no company of volunteers, and no equipment. The cash simply vanished into Racine's coffers. When the moment came, he would speak out. But not just now.

He continued to editorialize for a schoolhouse, knowing that neither the county nor the merchants could spare a cent. There would be no school or schoolmaster until Payday had sent Odie Racine packing. But at least he could keep the issue before the public.

The editor in him rebelled at the businessman in him. The editor wanted to mount a white horse, grab some Excalibur, and attack. The businessman eyed his gloomy ledgers and told the editor to wait. So the next issue was filled with a vast blandness. To the unwitting, Payday appeared to be the capital of Eden as it always had been.

His shrunken advertising taxed his ability to fill the gaping space on his pages, so he copied material from exchange papers. This issue contained news from Tucson and Prescott, and a story on the discovery of promising silver lodes in the southeastern corner of the Territory. Nor did he forget his beloved filler material, drawn from antiquity:

Though the boys throw stones at frogs in sport, yet the
frogs do not die in sport but in earnest.

—Plutarch

Flint thought that was good enough for the front page. It was
a sobering idea, and he favored sobriety.

Thus, willy-nilly, he created his paper, proofed it, and clamped
down the forms to prepare them for his usual evening printing. But
just as he ran off the first copy by the light of a coal-oil lamp, he
found he had visitors. Madame Racine herself this time, in stern
black gabardine that made her white face almost ghostly, and her
two torpedoes, each sporting a deputy sheriff's circlet on his black
suitcoat.

Flint knew at once what this would be about. The timing was
so perfect that he didn't doubt he had been spied upon all along,
and probably for days, so that she knew everything about him,
down to his trips to the outhouse. It gave him a strange feeling,
that his labor was so well understood and his schedule so well fathomed.

He stared at the three of them. Odie Racine's eyes glowed like
ice in her white face, and it occurred to Flint that the woman was
a hop fiend herself, or at least imbibed some opium on occasion.
The two thugs peered at him cheerfully, like wolves waiting to be
unleashed. Flint's stomach turned in anticipation of the wild red
pain he might soon experience.

"Let me read it, Flint," she said, pointing at the first paper.
"You're the only weed left in my garden."

Wordlessly, Flint handed it to her. She plucked a lorgnette
from her bosom and studied it, page by page, while time ticked
by. Now and then her soft lips pursed. Once in a while, Flint could
trace his text on her lips. "Oh, oh, oh," she said at one point. She
grew weary of standing and settled her black-clad body into one
of his wooden chairs. The torpedoes shifted weight from one shiny
shoe to the other.

She spent a long time studying Flint's opinion pieces on page two. She skipped news from exchange papers altogether, but examined the advertisements and cards. At last, she put the paper aside. "You're learning, Flint," she said. "You have the right idea."

Flint nodded curtly. He hadn't learned anything except to bide his time and collect the real news.

She fumbled in her beaded black bag, which glowed iridescent in the lamplight, and extracted a piece of paper.

"Put this in on the front page," she said.

It was an order. Flint went blank and cold inside. He examined the item: half a page of writing in a spidery, black-widow hand, no doubt her own.

"Sheriff Arnold Betjaman has decided to resign, effective Friday. He says he is not in good health and is ready for retirement. The County Board of Supervisors has appointed Deputy Sheriff Gerald Fauntleroy to the post, and will shortly appoint a new deputy.

"The supervisors agreed to give Fauntleroy a salary increase of $100 a month, to be financed by a new property-tax levy on agricultural land and homesteads."

Flint read and reread it. "I have to check this out," he said. "I'm a stickler for accuracy."

"Run it."

"I can't run something that hasn't been verified. If it's correct, I will run it next week."

"Run it."

Flint saw no give in her. The two torpedoes, one of them Fauntleroy, grinned. "Did Betjeman resign, or did you boot him out?"

"Run it."

"Is he in ill health?"

"Run it."

"What supervisors voted to put Fauntleroy in, and when? There hasn't been a regular meeting. And what was your role in this? Why does this come from you?"

"I ordered it, that's why."

"Then this piece is untrue. Am I right?"

"It doesn't matter. Run it or face the music."

Flint felt icy. "A newspaper that lies is not trusted. I don't publish lies, at least not knowingly."

Fauntleroy spoke up. "The lady says run it." He pulled brass knuckles from his lumpy suit and slipped them on, exuding cheer.

"Yes, you could do that to me," Flint said. "But a press is tricky to run, and takes a lot of skill and muscle. It is not anything you could do. And setting type is a delicate process. If you hurt me, I wouldn't be able to set the story. I think I choose not to run it."

"Flint," said Odie Racine, "be a good boy. You don't want to spend the next week in the jug, do you? Our new sheriff doesn't like bad boys."

"Your story's a fabrication. Arnold's not a very good sheriff, but he's an honest man, and you've thrown him out, scared him off. He's not in poor health, unless you've pounded on him. The supervisors don't even know it. I don't publish things like that. Most attempts to use a paper are more subtle."

Flint eyed a long iron pry bar he used on the press from time to time. If they came after him, they'd have to wade through that. He edged backward a bit. "No, Odie, I'm not going to do it. If these torpedoes pound on me, the paper doesn't get published. If you throw me into the pokey, a lot of people will take notice—including public officials in Prescott. A silent paper shouts. So does a paper that stops publishing suddenly.

"If I'm manhandled, I'll pull out. Pack up my wagon and roll out. There'll be no paper here. Towns without papers go downhill fast. You'll have a ghost town before you know it, and then where will you be? You won't get a skilled printer to come in here and print lies. Not even the drunks. You'll have a county seat without a voice. Without advertising, most of the businesses will fold. Then where will you be? You may think you control the county, but you don't."

He was back now, within a quick lunge of the pry bar.

They looked at each other. Odie seemed unsure of what to do next.

Flint grabbed the heavy bar. The goons saw him and inflated with joy. A brawl. The Punch looked ecstatic. Flint knew he couldn't hold off both, but he knew he'd hurt them before he got hurt. He held the bar like a lance. It felt massive in his hands.

"Get out," he said.

Odie Racine stood, her lifeless black eyes sucking him into some cave within. "It doesn't matter," she said. "Betjeman's out. I'm the law. What does it matter?"

She nodded, and the three drifted out. The goons looked sad.

Flint watched them vanish into the dark. He was shaking. He eyed the press, not ready to start the printing again. He tried to console himself: it would soon come to an end. The woman was overreaching. People like Odie Racine and her thugs always did, supposing themselves supreme. With Betjeman out, they'd lock up and work over anyone they felt like damaging. Payday had drifted from a sleepy village to a wilderness hell. He drifted to the door and stood there, peering into the black street, still holding the iron pry bar as if it were a rifle. The street looked peaceful.

He began printing what he supposed would be the *Pioneer*'s last issue. He hated to give up, but he could think of no reason to stay on in Payday—not alone, without allies and help, printing lies and censoring the real news.

40

In the morning, Flint handed a stack of papers to Elmer Kelly, his newsboy. The little red-haired hellion knew how to hawk papers. He had leather lungs and a instinct for drawing people to him. And thanks to Mrs. Phillips' tutoring, he could read now.

"Not much news, Elmer. Could be tough." Flint paused. "Watch out for trouble. Might be some of those thugs wanting to chase you off."

"I'll yell like a banshee," Elmer said.

Flint thought the boy would be all right. Flint had won last night. He sensed it. Maybe it was nothing but the pry bar held murderously in his hands, but maybe it was more. Something about a newspaper separated it from selling shoes or baking bread or slicing meat. A paper was a business, like all the rest, needing sales and profits to survive. And yet it was different, and Flint had often puzzled over the difference, not quite knowing why a newspaper was the exception, why it commanded respect and was treated as something beyond ordinary business. Publishing was one of the world's sacred callings.

Maybe it was because a paper bore news, crucial to any community. Maybe it was because a paper could mobilize the opinion of the community. Most papers were loved and hated, especially those that stuck as close to the truth as possible. The *Pioneer* was loved and hated. Whatever it was, Odie and her thug deputies had backed off, and Flint sensed he had won an important victory. He anticipated no more trouble—as long as he dodged everything that was happening in the sporting district, law enforcement, and county government.

He broke type for a while and then, curious, grabbed notebook and pencil and headed for the courthouse. He discovered Betjeman there, staring into space. The sheriff nodded. A nod saved a word.

"Did the supervisors fire you?" Flint asked.

Betjeman looked astonished. "Huh?"

"Did you resign?"

"Nope."

"You feeling well?"

The sheriff nodded and belched.

"Odie's after you. Tried to have me run a story like that."

"What good would that do?"

"It'd make it official. If the paper says it, it's official. Then they'd chase you out. The supervisors would cave in." Flint eyed him. "They obviously want you out. They don't quite control this corner of the county."

"Been trying for weeks. I got my ways."

Flint waited. The best way to get Arnie Betjeman to blab was to pretend you didn't want him to say anything.

"I hid the jail keys. Except for one right here." The sheriff pointed at a key hanging from his belt. "They can't lock anyone up without my say-so. Cutlip has one, too."

Flint smiled. Old addled Betjeman had his ways, like he said.

"They belong in there themselves," Betjeman said. "Throw away the key."

"They tried to lock someone up?"

Betjeman nodded. "I don't let 'em," he said. "They think they can push me around. Got a surprise coming someday." He leaned forward irritably. "You think I've caved in. Well, I got a few things up my sleeve. I got the rest of the deputy badges hidden. I've been deputizing some people. Adolph Zeppel, he's a sworn deputy. So's Ike Cobb. So's Nels Gulick. And Driggs, who runs the Drover's Rest, he's one. All young and tough."

It surprised Flint. "Who else knows?"

"No one. And don't print it."

"What are you going to do?"

Betjeman grunted. He had retreated into grunts and flapping gestures again.

Flint probed further, but the sheriff only snorted and muttered. Flint didn't think the new deputies made much of a force. Not against skilled thugs backed by a mob of tinhorns and bullies. A businessman could get killed that way. But one thing was certain: Odie Racine didn't have a lock on law enforcement. Not yet. No wonder she'd tried to prize Flint open.

Flint left Betjeman, feeling depressed. Deputizing businessmen and hiding the keys to the jail wouldn't slow Odie Racine. He trudged along an orange-varnished corridor to Cutlip's chambers and found the man there, soaking up the morning. The judge had aged ten years, and Flint suspected that the collapse of law in Payday had as much to do with the decline as Violet's death did.

"I don't know what I'm here for," Cutlip mumbled. "I haven't tried a case in two weeks. Culbertson hasn't brought one. Not even a misdemeanor charge."

Culbertson, the part-time county attorney, owned a surveying business, running two crews to keep up with the flood of incoming settlers. Odie Racine had gotten to him with fifty-dollar extortions and brass knuckles, the same as she had all the rest.

"Basil, you're looking fine," Flint said, stretching truth a lot. "Can we talk?"

The judge waved him in. Flint shut the door behind him.

"Alpine County's reached a state of anarchy," Flint said. "Who's in charge?"

"No one, Sam."

"Have Jackson and Pollack caved in?" Flint asked. "What're the supervisors doing about it?"

"Both Severance Jackson and Seth Pollack are in the same boat I'm in, Sam."

"And what boat is that?"

"If they defy that woman, they'll be ruined. As it is, they pay her extortions. Seth's feed-grain business is vulnerable to fire. Severance's saloon sits next to Racine's Golden Calf, and he can hardly breathe without her say-so. It isn't just their livelihood and mine; it's the threat of injury. Those are experts. They can batter an old man's bladder, jamb his limbs around until they ache for the rest of his life. They know how to cripple. I pay her extortion. If I don't, my office goes up in flames—all the records, maps, plats, correspondence. So do the duplicates in the courthouse. Leaving me with nothing." He eyed Flint wearily. "There is no law and no justice here. I'm very weary. I keep wondering how you escape."

"I haven't. I've been unable to report the real news." He didn't say that he was younger and tougher, or that he'd faced the hooligans with a big pry bar. "Basil, has anyone contacted the Territorial governor?"

Cutlip laughed derisively. "What's the governor going to do?"

Flint had to think about that for a moment. The Territory had no militia or armed force. "Ask for help from Washington," he said lamely. "Get some U.S. marshals in."

"That's right. Fat chance," Cutlip said.

"Please do it. You're defeating yourself with pessimism."

Cutlip stared into space, and finally nodded. "You're right. Violet's death has blinded me. I'm not my old self. I'll write."

"You're a magistrate; they'll listen to you."

"I'll write. Maybe the letter'll get through."

"What do you mean, 'get through'?"

"Some masked bandits stopped the Prescott coach and pulled off the mailbag last night. They held the coach while they pawed through mail, looking for something. Then they robbed the passengers. Got seven hundred dollars cash from Lafe Short. He was trying to slide his life earnings out of Payday. Thought you knew."

"I hadn't heard. How did you find out?"

"Betjeman."

"I'll go get the story."

"You won't get it. He won't tell it."

"Then I'll try the Payday Cartage Company. Or Short."

Cutlip smiled sourly. "Good luck. Racine gets fifty a month out of the cartage company, too. And another twenty-five for fire protection. Even those teamsters and jehus have knuckled under. And Short's not opening his doors. You can't buy a loaf of his bread today."

"You think she's behind it?"

Cutlip shrugged. "Her type doesn't allow rivals. She's going to suck the town dry and leave when there's only a husk left."

"Basil, what does she get out of it?"

"Who knows? You might ask her."

"I think I will," Flint said. "I'll interview her for a story. Might as well go directly to the black-widow spider."

He left the courthouse even more discouraged. It was odd how the light had vanished from Payday. Maybe it was only the changing seasons. The nights were chill now, and Thanksgiving wasn't far off. But he knew it wasn't the season. It was the collapse of an orderly world that darkened the place, as if everyone in Payday saw life through smoked glass.

Odie Racine rarely stirred before late afternoon, that being the nature of her profession, so Flint broke type all afternoon, sold a few small ads, and waited for the right moment. He had a glimmering of an idea: interview her, let her hang herself in print. He sighed. Words formed into stories didn't stack up against extortion and brass knuckles and knouts, arson and robbery, thug deputies and an army of crooked tinhorns.

And yet, he thought, truth was the most powerful weapon of all.

41

Sam Flint walked over to Odie Racine's big sporting palace thinking about the paradoxical position of any chronicler of the world's affairs; sometimes admired, more often feared and despised, often by the same people. Editors had lots of acquaintances and few friends. People didn't know how to deal with editors, and usually held them at arm's length. He was always hearing prefatory things such as "Don't print this, Flint . . ." or "Keep this under your hat, Flint . . ." or "I'll tell you something if you promise not to publish it."

He was almost alone now. Odie Racine had effectively clamped her puffy white hands around the throat of Payday. The only bright spot was Arnold Betjeman's sudden courage. The man might be ineffectual, but he was honest and in his own way, trying to marshal some resistance. Odie Racine was quick to sense it, and had tried to maneuver him out of office.

He entered the Golden Calf mid-afternoon and found it webbed in gloom. A single coal-oil lamp glowed over a faro table. A fat tinhorn and a pint-sized bartender manned the place. Later, it would all come alive. A place like that thrived in darkness. Daylight rebuked it. Poker tables and roulette and faro layouts stood forlornly, like factory equipment out of use. The sour smell of stale beer and cheap cigars hung in the air. The stairway leading to the second floor looked dreary and abandoned off in its corner. A few grizzled men leaned into the raw wooden bar, sipping red-eye and saying nothing, but they were watching Flint through eyes that revealed their own emptiness.

It certainly wasn't a fancy sin parlor, Flint thought. As utilitarian as the girls upstairs, strictly for use, not beauty. Odie Racine didn't waste a nickel.

He approached the tinhorn, who smoked a cigarillo and lazily shuffled a stack of chips one-handed. "I'm Flint, from the *Pioneer*, and I'd like to interview Miss Racine," he said.

The tinhorn studied him through cobalt eyes, exhaled a plume of smoke, and rose silently. He waddled through a door at the back, where she had an apartment, and eventually reappeared.

"She doesn't wish to be interviewed, but she'll see you," he said.

Flint padded to the rear, knocked, and heard a muffled voice urging him in. He found himself in a parlor, a sort of twilight place decorated lushly in ashes of roses, tones that exuded sadness, like a dried flower.

She appeared in an archway, puffy and white and wearing a black-velvet wrapper. Her soft jet hair hadn't been combed.

"I don't want an interview," she said.

"Then why did you ask me in?"

"Everything here's for sale. Five dollars for me. I thought it'd be amusing. Especially you."

He ignored that. Her remark was really intended to put him off balance. "You're the town's leading entrepreneur. I thought readers might enjoy a glimpse of you in print."

She eyed him shrewdly, then settled herself on a silk settee of weary pink. "I know you. You won't even mention that I run a bordello. All you'll talk about is the gambling and the saloon. Actually, I'm a whore."

"It'll take some discretion, yes. Do you want to talk?"

"I never talk about myself. Nothing I say will appear in the *Pioneer*, understand?"

"Unless I have your permission," Flint said, an unspoken question in it.

She shrugged.

"Do you prefer to be called Odie or Miss Racine?"

"Neither's my real name, though I was married to a tinhorn named Racine. He broke me in. But my real name you'll never know. Nobody knows." She eyed him. "If you can't write about me, why are you here? Looking for some way to resist me?"

"Yes," he said.

"One thing I like about you, you're halfway honest."

"You're getting rich fast. Is that your goal, getting rich?"

"Yes."

"What happens when you've milked the town dry?"

"I'll destroy it. Bleed it white. Ruin it and you."

"Why?"

"It pleasures me."

"Are you happy?"

"There's no such thing, Flint. But there's pleasure. People who believe in happiness only impede their progress. I enjoy pleasure and sell pleasure."

"I'm happy," Flint said.

"People delude themselves. I could tell myself I'm happy, but I know better than to lie."

"I don't really understand your hostility to Payday. What have we done to merit it?"

She shrugged. "It's not just here. I've often thought about it. I live for revenge, Flint. I live to destroy, to bleed, suck, drain life away."

It puzzled him. "Revenge for what?"

"For being born a woman."

"That's a nice excuse."

"Flint, the trouble with you is that you think most people are nice. That we all have consciences, like you. That when we do something wrong, a little voice tells us not to, or makes us feel bad. You're wrong. You're the oddity. No one's nice. The Golden Rule hardly occurs to anyone. And it doesn't make any sense anyway. Can you give me one good reason why I should treat others as I wish to be treated? One reason?"

"It keeps tyrants off our backs. When we govern ourselves, we don't need harsh laws and police to do it."

She shrugged. "If you're gonna get governed, what difference does it make who does it? Especially here." She waved vaguely toward the small window.

"Nurturing others is the root of love," he said.

She laughed. "Love," she said. "Another delusion. Flint, you're too good for the human race. That's your trouble."

Actually, she was interviewing him, not vice versa, he thought. "What are you going to do with your money?" he asked.

"I suppose you want some."

"You're ducking me."

"I'm going to get a fat pile of it. Money's the yardstick. If I have it and you don't, then I have the power. I'm somebody and you're not. One thing you never learned, Flint. With money, you buy anything you want and do anything you feel like doing. But that's not all. If I have a million, they bow and scrape and pretend they like me. I like that."

Flint thought for a moment. "All right. That covers your private life. I won't write about it. Now we'll talk about your public life, and I'll write about that."

"You're not going to write anything, Flint. Unless you want your press broken to bits and your face turned into hamburger."

"There you go, trying to intimidate me again. From now on,

whatever you say is for publication. What are you doing with the money extracted from merchants for your little police force?"

"Paying the deputies."

"They're certainly well paid. And what happens if a merchant doesn't wish to employ the services of your big galoots?"

"Well, I'm afraid the dude would likely get robbed. My fellows only serve our customers."

"And what about your fire protection? How have you spent all that money?"

"On my fire department, Flint."

"And who's that?"

"Come upstairs and I'll show you. They love fires."

She was playing with him, but it didn't matter. "What happens if a merchant doesn't pay for your protection?"

"Oh, Flint, he'd be a fool not to, with so much that's valuable. We won't put out fires for people who don't pay." She attempted an imitation of a laugh.

She was fencing with him. Banter. He wanted information. The kind of material that would help him free Payday from her scourge. He eyed her apartment. Here, at least, she had spent some money, unlike her bare-studs emporium. "You must be doing well, Odie," he said. "This is lavish."

"Not as well as some places. This is nothing. You should see me when I'm really raking it in."

"Where was that? You've been around, I take it."

"Oh, Ellsworth. Fort Griffin. El Paso del Norte. Denver."

"Those were your best places?"

"Fort Griffin and Denver. Ah, Flint, a lady can make a pile in places like that."

"Fort Griffin? You had a place?"

"A big place. All those buffalo hunters and cowboys and soldiers and tinhorns. Ah, that was the best. I threw up a joint. It could've been canvas and poles and it would've done just as good. But it was a big place, board-and-batten and adobe, and I had a dozen girls, and I charged like a bandit, and I had a whole floor of tinhorns working for me, table games, poker tables, the works."

"What happened?"

She turned quiet. "I got pushed out. I wasn't very bright. You've got to keep people either paid off or scared off."

"What about Denver?" he asked.

"Oh, Holiday Street. I had a regular house and charged the young bucks plenty. Oh, yes, I had the best house in town. Mostly white girls there; I'd get 'em off the immigrant trains. All those gold kings, and then the silver kings, and then the merchants. It was like living in red heaven."

"What happened? You didn't stay?"

"I've got a weakness for rotten men," she said.

"You have a man here? A gambler?"

"Flint, I gave up men long ago. I can't afford 'em."

"You're not doing as well here."

"Not like Denver. Not like Fort Griffin. That's where they'll never forget Odie."

"Why did you pick a little place out in the middle of nowhere like this? Not much money here."

"Because of your flowery prose, Flint." She smiled again. "Or maybe I had to hide for a while."

Flint knew, suddenly, that he had something of value. He hadn't wasted his time after all. She had a past. He probed a little more, and then bade her good-bye.

"Don't print a damned word, Flint," she said.

"We'll see," he said.

42

Flint met Merry-Grace at the Cochise Café for lunch. She looked especially elegant, wearing stiff white linen this day, and he was very glad to bask in her company. She had brought the boys but they were tearing around Payday, so she was alone with him, which also pleased him.

"Your wagon's full. Are things better?" he asked.

She shook her head ruefully. "I traded an old Hungarian clock, a beautiful thing with a glazed-tile façade. It's a treasure. I hated to part with it, but . . ."

"But you don't want to trade any more cattle for Buell's cash. Merry-Grace, I'm good for lots more groceries."

She nodded, embarrassed. Flint knew she didn't want to depend on him. "I'm all right for now," she said gently. "Luz knows how to live on nothing. She makes marvelous meals out of pinto beans, corn flour, and chilies. The boys hunt wild turkeys so we have meat now and then."

"But it won't last long."

She agreed with a nod. Vera served them beef and new potatoes, and placed cups of coffee before them At the Cochise you took what she offered.

"Is there any news?" he asked, sipping the hot java.

"Yes. A German family named Grosskopf tried to settle on Rokoczy range. A nice bottomland along Almond Creek. They filed the claim, but Clayton rode over there and chased them off. They couldn't understand much English and he simply terrified them. I felt . . . I don't know, my feelings are all mixed up. Nicholas would have gotten rid of them, too, but he would have charmed them into doing something else. Maybe even helped them settle somewhere."

"Buell's still protecting your range?"

"Yes, ever since Nicholas disappeared."

"It all fits. In his own way, he's a caring man. At least he cares for you," Flint added, remembering the whip.

"I know. And he's given me an out. It's just that what he's suggesting appalls me so much that I can hardly stand to think about it."

"Merry-Grace, instead of looking at public appearances, maybe you should examine your private feelings. Does he love you? Do you care for him? Could you be friends and lovers?"

She smiled. "You're right. I must think about those things."

He wished she would give him a clue, but she kept all that veiled from him, perhaps not wanting to hurt him. "Don't think about the world's disapproval. Think about your happiness and his, and your children. That's what matters."

"I think it's easier for men to say that than women. If we lose our reputation, we're ruined. It's a double standard, but every woman lives with it."

"That's so, Merry-Grace. I forget that. I don't know much about you. If you hadn't met Nicholas, what would you be now?"

"Married, probably, and living on the East Coast."

"Is that what your parents had in mind for you?"

"Oh, yes, Sam. They wanted me to be cultivated. That's what

the Grand Tour was all about. Symphonies, opera, plays, readings, Venice, Rome, Florence, Salzburg, Paris, London." She smiled wryly. "But then I met Nicholas."

"And you both dreamed of coming here?"

"No, I never dreamed of coming west. It was just some barbarous place. But Nicholas was full of romantic ideas—wilderness and wild Indians. It just fired his imagination. And wherever he went, that's where I wanted to be. So . . . here I am."

"Does Clayton Buell know all this?"

She nodded. "He must wonder why I stay here. Well, I like it. I miss the civilized things, but I like it. Oh, if I could just hear an orchestra playing Beethoven again. But mostly, I want the boys to grow up here. They'd wither and die if we went back East."

"Merry-Grace, I can't fathom what's in his head. But I'm pretty sure he doesn't think you can manage alone."

She pouted. "That seems to be men's opinion of women."

"Did Nicholas run the ranch, or did he leave it to you?"

"I was the mistress of the household and the boys and the vegetable garden."

"You're mostly squatting on public land, running cattle on land anyone could claim. If settlers started claiming that public land, would you drive them off? What Clayton does is illegal, you know."

She stared, silently.

"It's some of the best in the basin," he said.

"I'd try to buy them out."

"If neighbors' stock drifted onto your range, what would you do?"

"I'd have my men push it back. Or fence my range. Nicholas thought that this barbed wire was going to change ranching."

"Will the government let you enclose public range?"

She shook her head.

"Could you afford a manager, half a dozen drovers, and fence too? With a thousand-head ranch?" He didn't wait for an answer.

"Is running this ranch for at least seven years, until you can inherit it and dispose of it, something you'd *like* to do? Are you qualified? Could you keep it intact, even with a hired manager and crew? All I'm doing is looking at it from Clayton's viewpoint, Merry-Grace."

She gazed into space. "The birdsong I hear in this valley is like a Mozart symphony," she said. "Yes, I'd like to stay here. I've come to love it." She laughed. "Imagine Merry-Grace Woolcott loving a place like this!"

Her face had become animated, and she looked all the more ravishing to him. The desolation had left it. The haunted look had vanished in spite of cruel uncertainties. It was as if she were emerging from her cocoon of sorrow and becoming a radiant young woman again.

He was stricken clear through by a barrage of Cupid's arrows. He had a yearning almost palpable to reach out and touch her, hug her, fever her with his buried passion. What's more, he sensed she was awakening from widowhood. It was in her glowing eyes, her cheerful, intimate voice, in the way she held her hands together, as if to keep herself from reaching out and holding his in her own.

She looked at him intently. He realized that her food had gone almost untouched. She focused on him as if he were the only thing on her mind. "I don't know much about you, Sam," she said softly. "Mostly I know you through your writing. A person shines through the things he writes."

He felt suddenly uncomfortable. "Writing can be a mask, too, you know. The purveyor of the loftiest ideals can be privately vicious. I could name an editor or two . . ."

"Tell me about your family. About who you are." He had never seen her so intent.

"Schoolmaster's son," he said, curiously reluctant to talk. "We ran a private academy for boys. In Cincinnati. Not a lot of money, but we were always comfortable, and the pleasures of that life made it good."

"You were a classics and antiquities scholar."

"That's where I started. I intended to carry on, maybe at Princeton. But I didn't. The war came along."

"What were your parents like?"

"My father was very severe but very fair to the boys in the classes, and more so with me. He wanted each young man to be self-governing. If a man governs himself, he always said, he can live in perfect liberty, the slave of no vice such as drinking or sloth, and the master of the world around him because he can focus himself upon goals and achieve them."

"That must have been hard for a boy to live up to."

Flint sighed. "I never succeeded. But I have bits and pieces of my father's ideals floating in me."

"And your mother?"

"Every boy in the academy was her son. I sometimes had fifty brothers. They came to her for sympathy, especially when my father was impossible. He wasn't really impossible, but the things he asked of the boys seemed too much at times. My mother loved them all, smiled, listened, and sent them back to their dormitory knowing they weren't alone in a strange place. I guess the same goes for me."

She liked that. He could tell. "Well, how did you become a frontier editor?"

"That's a long story," he said, and told her of his restlessness after the war, when the whole wild world wouldn't fit into a quiet academy. He told her of his engagement and of breaking it and his ensuing flight. He didn't spare himself. She deserved to know. She became very quiet as he spoke of the canceled wedding and the aftermath. Then he described his wandering life as a newspaper man in Kansas, New Mexico, Texas, and now, Arizona Territory.

She sighed. "You mean you've started eight papers in eleven years?" Worry filled her face.

"Yes. I'm still restless."

"Will you stay here?" she asked in a small, tense voice.

He dodged. "It's a very beautiful place," he said.

"But will you stay here and settle down?"

"I don't know, Merry-Grace. I can't predict the future."

"Why did you leave those other towns?"

"I got chased out of some. Or boycotted into folding up. But mostly I got bored when the town was settled and the churches came and the place was just as quiet as a village in Ohio. I guess I liked the *founding* more than the humdrum life after a place got settled."

He discovered a subtle new distance from her side of the table to his. She wasn't focusing on him anymore. He'd known, in a leaden way, that it would end up like this. If he could have promised her he'd stay, wait out the seven years and offer marriage, she would have glowed, he thought, and waited, come what may.

"I guess I'd better round up the boys," she said.

43

Basil Cutlip reread the letter from Porter Allen, chief engineer, Atcheson, Topeka and Santa Fe Railroad Company. The letter advised that the railroad would not build along the alternative route proposed by Judge Cutlip even though there were impressive increases in population along that route. Right-of-way construction in the area would have to include a bridge over the Verde River and many smaller bridges, along with difficult grades and a sinuous, indirect line around numerous ranges. The company would stick to the old Atlantic and Pacific route along the thirty-fifth parallel. But it would certainly consider a spur line in the future if circumstances warranted it.

Basil Cutlip knew that all the land he had bought along the proposed right-of-way would be worthless, a tax drain. He would probably have to unload it for less than he had invested in it. The loss wouldn't break him. He had his fingers in so many pots that ill fortune in one area merely slowed him down. He still owned land along the best routes to Prescott and Tucson, and every little while made a sale to some settler or another. A new freight company had just bought forty acres for a yard, as well as a half-section of grassland for pasture.

But the news from the railroad put him in a reflective mood. Violet was dead. This was now his home. His sons were in Galena, and he could always return there. But he wouldn't enjoy returning alone, and he didn't feel like remarrying. Payday would always be his home, and Alpine his county, and Arizona his Territory. Which put him in mind of the deep disorder around him and his role in creating it.

He, after all, had formed the Merchants' Committee, with Abel Greene at its head, to bring settlers to Payday, and especially to invite a newspaper to the town. It had all succeeded beyond his expectations because they happened to reel in Flint, a truly gifted and persuasive man. Within weeks, the *Pioneer* was sailing all over the Southwest, extolling the new Eden. Within a month, the first settlers had appeared.

And then Odie Racine arrived, swiftly reminding them all that expansion could cause problems. In his quiet office, Cutlip admitted to himself that he had been the major culprit, his eye upon quick killings, his intent to pull out as soon as he and Violet had repaired their fortunes.

Now all that was a shambles. Not only did the madam openly extort money from him, but threatened him with bodily harm if any of his court decisions displeased her. He remembered the showdown well; those two thugs, grinning and sliding their thick fingers into the brass knuckles. Cutlip wasn't young. He doubted he could survive such a pulverizing. They didn't hit him. They didn't have to. Between that and the same treatment of County Attorney Culbertson, and their domination of Arnold Betjeman, Odie Racine owned the county. She was above the law.

It appalled Cutlip. He had been greedy, but he was also an honorable man. He had succumbed to weakness. There were excuses, of course. He was grieving Violet and hardly cared about the outside world. But every moment that he surrendered to those thugs, he loathed himself. He wished he had Flint's grit. Flint not only risked his body, but showed courage of mind as well, and somehow couldn't be bought or intimidated.

Cutlip felt shame, but he didn't dwell on it. The true use for shame was to impel change and reform, not self-flagellation. He knew he didn't have much to work with. Softness, middle age, neglect of the virtues, all of these things had eroded the man he once was. Violet's death had really started all this. There she was, deep in the ground, and here he was, a widower wondering why he was alive, and to what purpose was his life. Luxury? Suddenly alone, he didn't give a fig about it. Wealth? He needed only to be comfortable. Ah, but the other questions. Was he proud of himself? He wasn't; he desperately wanted to be. Had he served his fellow mortals? No; he had been too obsessed with gain. But now he would.

He felt better just for thinking through his troubles. He eyed his comfortable office with all its solid furnishings and look of substance, knowing that it was a sham. Nothing protected him. An ineffectual sheriff didn't. An intimidated county attorney didn't.

He sighed, plucked up the railroad's letter, and hiked the block over to the newspaper. He found Flint at his ledger and settled himself beside the young man while Flint completed his sums. When Flint at last looked up and smiled, Cutlip handed him the letter.

"Here's news," he said. "There was a time not long ago when I would've hidden this from you. Bad for business. But you've shown me a thing or two."

Flint read the communication. "It's a story," he said. "I doubted we'd ever get the railroad. But there's good news, too. We're well connected by coach and freight outfits, and maybe we can start pushing for a wire. A telegraph is really just as important as a railroad." He smiled. "At least to a newspaper."

The judge leaned back in his chair, gathering words from the edges of his mind. "I suppose you're disappointed in me," he said.

Flint eyed him sharply. "You're grieving . . ."

"I'm disappointed in myself. I've kowtowed to those brutes. Those knuckles are enough to make a man's stomach flop."

"You're not young, Basil . . ."

Cutlip sat up straight. "I'm young enough to be a man." He pounded a heavy fist on Flint's battered desk. "I won't bow to them. I'm here to talk about ending the reign of terror."

"Well, you're not alone. Together, we can do it. I've interviewed Racine. Newsmen get to do things like that. I found out some things. She's plied her trade in Denver and El Paso and Fort Griffin. She's moved quite a bit—so much so that it looks like she's been required to leave. I've asked Arnold Betjeman to make inquiries now that we know something about her."

"Arnold's not worth the time of day."

"No, Basil, that's not so. Arnold's getting his courage up, just as we all are. He's put some letters in the mail asking about her. He wrote them within an hour after I told him what I'd learned. She might even be a wanted person. But that's not all. Arnold's been secretly deputizing some of our leading men. He's even made Ike Cobb a deputy."

"Why do you say even? Tough fellow, Medal of Honor winner."

Flint smiled. "I misspoke. Ike's going to be a help when the showdown comes. Now, here's some more news. Betjeman's keeping the key to the jail on his person. The two thugs can't stuff anyone in there unless Arnold approves. He's still sheriff, and they know it. What I'm saying is, Betjeman's really kicking. And he's gathering his forces."

Much of that pleased Cutlip. "Yes, he gave me a jail key and told me to hide it," he said. "Well, if you and he can take risks, I can too. I'm going to talk to Culbertson and just see about some indictments. Maybe if he knows he's not alone, he'll show some sand."

"Good. But we've got to expect that word will get back to the black widow. Someone's going to talk."

Cutlip grunted. "It's a funny thing how fear of pain turns men into jelly," he said. "Including Judge Cutlip."

"Including Sam Flint. You don't see me publishing a word about the woman."

"But that's a tactical retreat, Sam, so you can keep on going."

"That's what I tell myself," Flint answered wryly. "It's not what I believe down inside. I think I'm a coward."

They talked a while more, and Judge Cutlip found himself drawing strength from the young man. It wasn't that Flint did anything spectacular; he was simply a rock, a man who refused to budge or compromise. The editor knew evil, resisted, and thus made himself an inspiration to others.

Cutlip stood at last, knowing he was eating into Flint's precious time, and stepped out into brilliant fall sunlight. The basin glowed with beauty. The autumnal air was sharp and crisp and sweet. He had an odd thought: Odie Racine could not take pleasure from sweet, crisp air, or from nature, or from the thing the judge was feeling now—a cleansed and hopeful spirit. Flint had almost been a church for him.

Now, after months of floundering, Basil Cutlip found himself with a mission. This day, at long last, he called Payday his home. This day, he would begin to sweep it clean, braving whatever hell the black-widow spider and her thugs might mete out to him. Surely it was worth the risk. He knew where his newfound happiness came from. It rose out of a cleansed heart and renewed will.

He walked briskly to the courthouse, looking for the sheriff. But Betjeman wasn't there. Instead, one of those grinning hooligans—Danny Drinker, he thought—in his lumpy, black-woolen suit and bowler, sprawled at the sheriff's desk.

"Where's the sheriff?" Cutlip asked.

The thug grinned. "He's at home nursing a few bruises."

"What happened to him?"

"Fauntleroy and me, we was jailing an awful criminal, and Arnie got in the way."

"Got in the way?"

"We needed a key to lock this toad up, and he wouldn't give us one, so he got in the way of these." The bruiser pulled out his brass knuckles. "After that, he done give us the key."

"Who'd you jail?"

"Cobb. He didn't feel like paying his taxes, and that's a criminal offense. Wanna see him?"

"Ike Cobb?"

"Yeah, himself. He stays there until he pays his taxes."

"His store's shut?"

"Who knows? We just dragged him out of it."

"Has he been charged?"

"Charged, haw."

The judge loomed over Racine's paid deputy, wishing he could pound him into submission. "Release Cobb. That's a court order."

The hooligan stood, towering over Judge Cutlip. "You want to go in there, too?"

"I'm the Alpine County judge. Release him or stand in contempt of court."

"I think you better step in there yourself, Judge, sweetheart. We're starving the louse into submission. Pay, we sez, or you'll starve to death, if you don't die of thirst first. I suppose that applies to fat old judges, too, eh?"

Cutlip felt a cold dread seep through him. The courage he had acquired from Flint seeped out of him. What was moral courage of Flint's sort against a man who could and would pulverize him? His pulse lifted. Somehow he fought back his terror and stood unyielding. "I'm a magistrate," he said in a low tone that surprised himself. "If you touch me, you'll end up breaking rock in the Yuma Territorial Prison for twenty years. You and your henchman. Do you think you're not watched? Do you think that you can take over an entire county and run it? Do you know what the governor would do to you for jailing a Territorial judge without cause? You're in trouble. Release Cobb. That is an official court order from the bench."

"Sure, boss."

"What's your name? Just so I spell it right on my complaint."

"Danny Drinker."

The hulking idiot squinted, rubbed a meaty thumb across his nostrils, and nodded. Cutlip felt sheer exultation when the bruiser lumbered toward the cell door, unlocked it, and released a frightened Ike Cobb.

"Come along, Ike," the judge said. "We'll talk." He turned to the bruiser. "You're not the law. Remember that. You're an inch from a life spent breaking rocks."

Drinker chuckled, but he radiated doubt.

The judge steered Ike Cobb into sweet air, and no hand stopped them.

44

Merry-Grace found Colonel Buell out at the corrals, where his men were weaning calves. The blatting of lovelorn calves and the bawling of bereft cows deafened her. She knew it would keep on for a week or more, but slowly die away. Eventually the cows would drift off to feed themselves instead of guarding their imprisoned offspring. She watched closely for a while and was rewarded with information. Her own calves, carrying the Rakoczy brand, were being weaned too, as the drovers ruthlessly herded the calves into the pens. That was, she supposed, good.

Colonel Buell watched her wordlessly. One could scarcely talk amid such a racket. She peered through the high pole fence, across the bawling multitudes, and eventually their gazes met. He abandoned his post on the far side and walked around to her.

"Merry-Grace?" he said. There was great gravity in his face.

This was the moment she dreaded and yet sought, the fulcrum of the future. "Would you walk with me?" she asked. "I can't hear myself think."

He nodded, and they strolled to the creek. She felt his presence beside her acutely. The racket slowly subsided as they put the cattle behind them. She began to hear the purling of the crystalline creek that rose from springs high up in the Mogollon Rim.

"Sam Flint thinks I should take you up on your offer," she said.

"Flint? Flint does? Ah ought to horsewhip him for it. He must think you're a loose woman."

She glanced at him, trying to find humor in it, but he showed no sign of levity.

"You've asked me to defy the laws of God and man," she said. "I was shocked at first. But not now. This is a new land. Maybe a woman should make her own decisions, no matter what law or tradition says."

"You'd be a scandal," he said. "Tongues would wag. You'd be ostracized. You walked into a church and arranged for Nicholas's funeral and received nothing but love from the congregation. When Ah die, you couldn't do that."

"I've thought about that."

"Ah think you should know the future when you make a choice of this sort."

"I knew it would take courage, but I hadn't thought enough about the loneliness."

"It'll all fall on you, not me. Men escape unscathed. You'd be treated very like Odie Racine. It's how life is."

She reddened. They scared up a flock of gambel's quail, and the birds whirred away into the bright blue heavens.

"You haven't give me much confidence that you'd consider my happiness, or my liberty."

"On the contrary, Ah've shown my very soul to you, but you didn't have the vision to see."

"No, I didn't."

"It was necessary for you to see the future before you could even consider an . . . alliance with me."

"I haven't come to any decision. A few bouquets, a single loving discussion sitting in my parlor, in which you trusted my adult judgment, might have helped."

"Ah'm not much of one to deal with something like this. Ah'd be a traitor to Eloise, my poor mad wife. Ah love her just as dearly this instant as Ah always have."

She eyed him thoughtfully. She liked his abiding love for his wife.

"Ah suspect you love Nicholas as much, and he's sacred to your memory. It'd hardly be wise for me to intrude."

"Then, why—"

"Because an alliance would be the way out for each of us. Ah give you my word of honor, you'd be treated with all the love and respect Ah accord my wife."

"But not freedom."

"You'd be at total liberty."

"And if I chose to leave, what would become of my property?"

"Ah'm only a steward, looking after Nicholas's assets for you. Their disposition is up to you. You have my word of honor on that, too."

She didn't argue. She knew there were plausible reasons why Buell had savaged the Rakoczy grass and kept the Rakoczy herd in his care. To protect her from loss. There was something dashing and cavalier and Southern about it that oddly appealed to her.

"You . . . would expect me to take up with you as man and woman?"

"The other option is seven years for you, eternity for me."

She blushed again, but it had to be dealt with. "What if I conceive a bastard?" she asked softly.

"The child will carry my name. If necessary, by adoption. And will be my heir. Ah . . . have none. Ah lost my sons and my daughter. Ah'd consider an heir a miracle of such grace and loveliness that it would seem like the beginning of a new life, a return to my youth here in this place. Ah'd plumb spoil that child. Ah'd look at you, Merry-Grace, with our child in your arms, and Ah'd worship you and that babe, and Ah'd go outside and fall upon the earth and draw my hands through it, and Ah'd thank God for gifts for an undeserving old fool."

Something breathless hung in the air. She turned to him and found a hint of tears in the furrows of flesh around his eyes. She felt her own spirits lift in her body. She seemed to float along the path, in blithe peace.

"What of my sons?" she asked. "They're reaching an age now when they'll understand what our arrangement is. They'll hear things in town. Maybe they'll be teased, or hurt."

"Your dear Stephen and Andrew'll be like sons to me. Ah'll do my best, and stint nothing. Ah can't guarantee that result. They may resent it. Nicholas will always be their father and your husband. It's a decision for you to make."

She stopped beside a pool formed by a rock ledge and peered into the mysterious water. It reflected puffball clouds back to her, scurrying across its surface like floating cotton.

"I'd like a ceremony," she said. "Vows are important to me. No one can marry us, but we can make sacred vows to each other. Would you make the vows to me? For richer or poorer, for better or worse, in sickness and in health, until death do us part? If . . . I agree to this?"

He stared into the forests high above. "Ah broke a vow once," he said.

Her heart went cold.

"When Ah entered the United States Army as a lieutenant, after West Point, Ah vowed on my sacred honor to defend the United States against all her enemies. That was a sacred oath, Merry-Grace. Ah broke a sacred oath. So did many others when the time came in eighteen sixty-one."

"What are you saying, Clayton?"

"Life's cruel beyond anything Ah ever thought when Ah was young."

"Are you suggesting you might not keep the vows we make?"

"No. Only that sometimes we must make choices so sad and bleak that we shatter our honor. If Ah should somehow pass to Paradise, which Ah won't, and Eloise is there waiting for me, a sane and sweet angel, then what?"

"Don't think of such things."

"Ah do."

She gazed softly into the water. "I face cruel choices, too. But you've given me a lovely choice, if I can find the courage to go ahead."

The creekside bower seemed unbelievably soft and gentle, and the place cupped her and held her. She saw not a living thing, not even a moth or a bird. Only Buell, wiry, lean, lumpy, with eyes like black marbles and unkempt graying hair. Those black-marble eyes radiated a gentleness, and his worn and ravaged face seemed to exude peace. She had never seen him quite this way. All the years when she and Nicholas had entertained him, there had been pain in him, radiating hotly out upon them both; pain enough to melt rocks and strike fires.

She made up her mind then, scarcely realizing that the decision had come and gone. "Clayton, would you hold me?" she asked softly.

He seemed hesitant. She opened her arms to him. He entered them and tenderly drew her to him as if she were as fragile as an eggshell. But she knew it was because he wanted her to be at ease. She slid her arms about him and clasped them at his back, feeling his hard, wiry frame. It had no give or softness in it. Hugging him was almost like hugging a block of wood, and yet it was infinitely more. She needed a hard, hard man, and found comfort in it. Then, after an eternity, he drew her tighter and she felt their bodies crush each other. She lifted her head and found his hard lips with hers, and drew her hand over his hard, furrowed face.

Some long while later, he released her.

"I'll welcome you in a few days," she said. "I must prepare

my family. Ignacio and Luz—" She stopped, realizing she had never brought up the subject of her beloved servants. "They might not approve," she said weakly.

"Ah will talk to them," he said.

"What will you say?"

"That Ah love you, Merry-Grace. They'll understand that."

"Oh!" she cried. "Clayton Buell, we love each other. I'll tell them that. And I'll tell Stephen and Andrew that, too."

"Merry-Grace, Ah hope that everything Ah do honors Nicholas. That was my intention."

"What if he returns, Clayton?"

He laughed easily, and she felt him shaking with it. "I don't rightly know, Merry-Grace."

45

An autumnal rain drizzled over the Tonto Basin and leaked through Sam Flint's roof. The steady dripping endangered his supply of newsprint, which he pushed to a dry area while keeping an eye on the wet floor. But the water didn't pool; it simply slid away between the floor planks. A mist blurred the street, and the sunny skies he had become so used to now lay gray and sodden, obscuring the Mogollon Rim. Water dripped onto the Cleveland press, but there was little he could do about it.

For days, he had sensed more than the change in the weather. The town's earliest settlers, who had supposed themselves to be living in Eden, were coming to a decision: they would fight. They would overthrow this reign of terror. Flint had seen it in Judge Cutlip, who was openly defying Odie Racine's bullies. Arnold Betjeman, still wearing the black and yellow flags of his beating, seemed resolute and determined to throw the phony deputies out of his office. He had quietly deputized several more businessmen, including the big farrier, Billy Bravo—a brute of man and one to be reckoned with when it came to brawls. Ike Cobb had become a firebrand. Now he kept shotguns under several counters and threatened to shoot any of the thugs who stepped into his mercantile. Ike Cobb! The young man who had disgraced himself was showing signs of courage.

But Odie Racine was no fool, and she was taking her own measures. A pale, rat-faced killer had appeared, flamboyantly flaunting a brace of Navy revolvers hung low from his belt. She had upped the ante from beatings to murder, and the town's businessmen and county officials knew it. No one had been shot—so far. But the threat hung there, paralyzing further resistance.

For a while, it looked like County Attorney Culbertson would stiffen, too. He actually brought some complaints. For a day or two, the county court system actually functioned. Betjeman dragged some bullies out of Odie's emporium on various charges; they were charged, tried, found guilty, fined, and jailed for a week. But then Culbertson caved in again. Racine's hired killer probably had threatened the man.

Flint knew that all the quiet progress would be lost unless he could rally the town's timorous merchants. It was up to *The Payday Pioneer*. He alone had the weapon: public exposure of wrongs. Daylight! That was the magical thing about newspapers, especially those that went out on an exchange basis to the surrounding world.

He sighed. Odie Racine knew that just as well as he did. And he didn't doubt that that funereal woman would just as soon lay another black wreath upon the town. His own. For three weeks, he had published pussycat papers, tame as a tabby, knowing that her cyclops eye studied each issue looking for offense. But as far as the world knew from those issues, Payday went serenely along. No terror stalked its streets; no extortion racket bled its citizens; no anarchy ruled Alpine County.

It was now or never.

He had no intention of dying if he could help it. He had seen enough of that in the war. He knew what death was. He had had friends who had planned to marry their sweethearts as soon as their enlistment was over—but who had never seen their beloved again. One day, they were there beside him, dreaming dreams and complaining about generals. The next day, they lay still and cold, gone the dreams and the hopes. Flint knew what that pasty-faced man who lounged at the rear of Odie's saloon was about. He was Odie's death's-head, skeletal and murderous, as blank-eyed as she.

With some cunning, Flint could get an issue out. Twice they had pounced on him just at press time, studied the pages and walked out. He could get around that by printing and publishing at a different hour or a different day. It would take some deception: displaying galley trays full of bland stories that would not be used; hiding trays full of the real stories. He would need to get bundles of papers to the post office and put on the stagecoaches before the world knew of their contents. He had done that before in other towns. It took extra work, but he could do it.

The real problem, though, would be to stay alive after he had published the issue. He could defend himself with arms, or he could hide. If he hid, they would burn or demolish his plant. In the hours following publication of an issue like that, the merchants would either band together in a posse and drive out the thugs, or quail in their homes. The county's officers and courts would either enforce the law boldly, or cave in. If they caved in, and if the town's merchants wouldn't fight, then the paper would cease publishing. With luck, Flint might escape Odie Racine's web of informers radiating out from East Basin Street, but he would own only the clothes on his back.

It would be a do-or-die issue of the *Pioneer*.

He could not risk telling a soul about it in advance. Some of those businessmen would spill the news to Odie Racine. Or Odie's thugs would twist the information out of them. Still, he had to let one merchant know, one who would take the lead and form a posse and put an end to the menace. Who?

The answer came to Flint almost as a bad joke. He would tell Ike Cobb and ask him to form a posse the moment the paper hit the streets. And he would tell Arnold Betjeman, a man who was quietly growing into his office and beginning to show some authority. Why Ike? Why had that name risen from the mists of his mind? He knew why. Ever since he had taken pity on the young man and kept his secret, something sweet and strong had bloomed in Cobb, rising from a hunger to redeem himself. Ike Cobb was filled with the resolute courage the job would require. Maybe. Flint sighed. Could lead be transmuted into gold?

Quietly, he began to plan his big issue. The headline, "Anarchy in Alpine County," would say it all. He would do a number of related stories. The first would be on the usurpation of the sheriff's office by phony, privately paid deputies. It would cover the beating of Betjeman, the incarceration of citizens who were not suspected of any crime, the use of jail threats and beatings to extort money, the theft of Betjeman's jail key—taken from his person by force—and the growing number of crimes against persons in Payday, from robbery to murder, for which no arrests were made or investigations begun.

Flint decided on another story about Odie Racine. He expected information about her history at any moment. He would connect her to the illegal deputies, describe her life history, especially her hasty exit from Denver, and any outstanding charges against her. The story would include her effort to suborn the district court and intimidate the county attorney, thus nullifying the whole process of law enforcement. He hadn't gotten much out of Odie Racine during the interview, but he would use what he had.

A third story would be devoted to the extortion racket: the selling of alleged protection from crime and fire, at a price no merchant could afford and enforced by brass knuckles; threats of jailing; and, most significantly, robbery and arson. It would trace the extortion to Racine, and its enforcement to her two thugs. It would mention the new shootist, too. Flint would do a sidebar to that one, recording threats to the newspaper, to freedom of speech, and the prior censorship of several issues without the slightest pretext of legality.

A fourth story would deal with the mushrooming sporting district. He intended to describe each building and detail exactly what sort of vice it catered to. He would indicate the legal owner of each lot and building, including Racine's eight. He would also describe the sort of dregs of humanity the district was drawing to Payday: a growing army of lawless men that threatened the peace and safety of good citizens.

He set to work quietly, mostly by lamplight, trying to organize the enormous amount of information he wished to convey not only to the paper's regular readers, but to the whole Territory and its officials.

Two days after he began, Sheriff Betjeman brought in three responses to his queries about Odie Racine's history—from El Paso, Denver, and Fort Griffin.

While Flint studied the reports, Arnold Betjeman eyed the front door nervously.

"Let's go back to my apartment, Arnold. I'll copy these in longhand. They're not long. If anyone walks in, you won't have to worry."

The sheriff sighed. "Sorry. Scares me." As usual, he was saying as little as possible. "But I'm getting my dukes up," he added.

"You're stronger than you think," Flint said.

The letters delighted Flint, but also worried him. Odie Racine had a Colorado warrant outstanding on charges of attempted murder, extortion, and operating a house of ill repute. She was also wanted for questioning concerning the disappearance of three women and two males. She was known as Marvella Ogle in Denver, one of several aliases. But the letter from Fort Griffin, Texas, called her Odie Racine, and said she catered to buffalo hunters and soldiers, running a tough bordello, along with a saloon-and-gambling joint. She made a lot of money fast. A number of her customers had been fed drinks laced with chloral hydrate, and had found themselves awakening in the alley behind her joint, robbed of everything, including their clothing.

The El Paso sheriff had record of her as Francine Odie, and said she had had a male partner, a gambler, who suddenly vanished, probably into Old Mexico. The local constabulary had finally shut her down as a public nuisance, but the day afterward, the town marshal had been murdered by parties unknown. Nothing could be pinned on her. She was believed to be rich, but no one could say where her money went. She carried a double-barreled, nickel-plated derringer-type weapon on her right calf.

Carefully, Flint copied the most important material, then returned the letters. "Thanks, Arnold. I'll be using it shortly. I'll let you know when. I'm going to blow the lid off."

"Hate to bury you, Flint," Betjeman muttered.

46

The man slipped into the sanctum of the *The Payday Pioneer* just after sunrise, surprising Sam Flint at his typesetting. No one came this early, and the caller had opened and closed the front door so silently that Flint hadn't even been aware of it.

A single glance told Flint who this man was, though they had never met. A swift panic rose in the editor. He had been working on his Odie Racine story, and it lay half-finished in the galley tray, incriminating him. He thought to slip the tray beneath the counter, where he was keeping his big stories, but willed himself not to. He set down his type stick and waited.

The man glided across the floor as noiselessly as he had entered. The jet eyes in his skeletal white face never wavered from Flint. He wore black corduroy britches, a tan frock coat of the same fabric, and a pair of sheathed holsters, from which projected the slim grips of Navy revolvers. There were largely hidden by the frock coat, but they flashed out like lightning bolts hidden by clouds. Flint saw his own death approaching, and gripped the worktable to steady himself. A false move would kill him. "Yes?" said Flint.

"Odie sends a friendly warning. If you print any of it, you won't like what happens." The voice was as velvet as Odie's dresses.

Did they know about the edition he was planning? Had they snooped in here? "Print what?" Flint asked shakily.

The man smiled, revealing even, white teeth. They were his best feature. "You'll learn soon," he said.

"Learn what?"

The man smiled. "Wait and see. And remember what I said."

"Look, Mr.— I don't know what kind of game you're playing. I don't know what you're talking about."

"Adolph Zeppel declined to pay his taxes."

That mystified Flint all the more. "Is that news?"

"It will be. Remember what I said."

"You said I won't like what happens. What on earth do you mean by that?"

Instantly, Flint found himself staring into the muzzle of a cocked revolver, and thought he was dead. His pulse shot high. The bore lifted toward his forehead, lowered to his chest and then to his belly. But the gunman merely smiled and silkily returned the weapon to its nest.

"Now you know," he said, and wheeled away. "Remember. Not a word. And that includes funerals."

"What's your name?" Flint asked.

"They call me The Hired Man."

"I mean the name you were born with."

"I forget," he said. He nodded, an act of odd civility, and walked out.

Flint watched him go and then collapsed into a chair, unable to stop the trembling that racked his body.

The mystery resolved itself a few minutes later when Arnold Betjeman walked in, dour and prickly and bristling with silence.

"Murdered Zeppel," he said. "Beat him to death last night. In his quarters behind his store."

"Adolph Zeppel?" The mild, middle-aged greengrocer with

the shock of unruly white hair tortuously parted in the middle, beaten to death?

"With brass knuckles."

"Drinker or Fauntleroy?"

"I don't know. Likely both."

"Literally pounded to death?"

Betjeman nodded. "Not a pretty sight. Couldn't pay, I suppose."

That was no doubt true. Zeppel rarely advertised, saying he couldn't afford it. His fruit-and-vegetable business constantly suffered from uncertain supplies shipped by wagon from Tucson and Yuma, often arriving just before they spoiled. And he had competition from Ike Cobb.

"That hired killer just warned me not to print anything. Not even a funeral notice. Waved a revolver in my face. Scared me witless."

"He made the rounds," the sheriff said. "Told me that if I arrested anyone, I'd wish I hadn't. Stopped by Basil Cutlip and told him that if he started anything, it'd be his last act. Stopped at Culbertson's house and told him if he wanted to see the next sunset, to keep smiling."

"Where's Adolph?"

"Still there."

"How'd you find out?"

"Odie's killer told me."

Flint felt a deep sadness. Zeppel had come to these shores a decade earlier, trying to make a new life. He had lost his wife to typhus. He had struggled along, speaking with a heavy accent, a grave man who smiled rarely.

"Anarchy," Flint said.

"Not quite. I've bench warrants that Cutlip wrote out. I'm going to lock up those two. Drinker and Fauntleroy." He sighed. "Take some doing, though. That killer means business. Don't know how yet."

"Who's going to take care of the body? Who'll do the coroner's report?"

"I will. Wanted you to know before I'm shot."

"Has he relatives?"

"In Strasbourg. I'll write."

Flint stared out the window into dawn light. "The entire story will go into my big issue. If that killer had bothered to look at what I was setting when he walked in, I'd be leaking blood into the floor now."

"It's not anarchy. Not yet, Flint."

"You'll take on that killer and those two thugs? And the mob behind them?"

"Not alone."

"You know of anyone who'd face that killer?"

"Yup."

"Who?"

"Have to take a trip," Betjeman said. "Be gone today."

"Where are you going? Arnold, we've got to keep each other informed."

"To Clayton Buell," he said, and padded out.

Clayton Buell? Confederate colonel, with twenty or so drovers, all of them veterans. The idea delighted and awed Sam Flint.

"You'll have this paper's endorsement," Flint yelled, but he doubted that the sheriff heard. He returned to his work, making a note to write up the story in full, including each threat to a public official. Once again, the safety of each official depended on the one thing a paper could do: shine a lot of light into dark corners.

But he had his doubts. The Hired Man would shoot Buell without a second thought. And he doubted that Buell would take on the task. The man lived in deepening isolation, and wasn't even attending his county board of supervisors' meetings. Buell would listen, shrug, and invite the sheriff to leave.

If there was any hope at all, it lay in Betjeman's new deputies, the merchants. Not that they'd be any match for The Hired Man either, but eventually they'd catch the killer and his two thug lieutenants, or maybe Odie herself, off guard.

Flint glanced at his Seth Thomas seven-day clock on the wall, discovering it was after eight and normal business hours were upon him. He slid the galley tray with its half-done story down to a dark shelf beneath his composing bench.

For the rest of the day, he would stick with routine business. Remaining on the composing table were stories about the new mail service promised by the Prescott postmaster, an editorial on the town's continuing need for an undertaker and a doctor, a new county population estimate, based on some figures by County Clerk Farquehar, and some statistics on cattle shipments, sheep shipments, and November prices in Tucson for them both.

He stepped outside. He didn't like to be gone long from his plant, knowing how easily it could be searched, or destroyed. But he had to gather news. Betjeman usually helped, keeping a shrewd eye on the place. From the stoop of his building, Flint studied the town. Autumn rains had washed everything clean. The sky was transparent. The distant Mogollon Rim crowded the heavens, a staircase of black pines vaulting upward. The city was stirring. He watched Lafe Short sweep the doorway of his bakery, and Nels Gulick unlock his hardware store. His life and safety were inextricably tied to them: would they take heart and form a posse when asked? He didn't know. A lot of men never risked their skins for anything.

He wondered whether the town would react to the exposé issue in the way he hoped. Though he had been here a while, he couldn't yet fathom whether ordinary citizens would rise up and slay the dragon in their midst. He could publish the facts, but his life would still depend on how the town responded.

Payday might let him down. People might just shut their doors and hide. He was tempted to destroy the galleys, pack up, and leave. He was too young to die, and other towns beckoned. He could so easily throw harness over Grant and Sherman, load his wagon, and drive out of Payday, head off to safer places.

But he wouldn't.

He still felt weak and tired. Looking down the muzzle of a cocked revolver held by a killer did that to one. He wished he could simply retreat to his narrow cot and forget the day. But he couldn't do that, either. He was tempted to get his pad and pencil and wander over to the sporting district and roust Odie Racine out of her silken ashes-of-roses apartment and get her story about the hammering and torture of Adolph Zeppel. But that was boyish fantasy. Flint was a newspaper editor, not some U.S. marshal armed with warrants and a posse.

Still, a newspaper could be a shield. Once this issue was out, in the mail, on the street, circulated to the whole Territory, it would throw a screen of protection around Betjeman and his allies. Yes, it could do that—save their lives, and maybe his own. Murderers preferred darkness and secrecy. But Flint wasn't sure that exposure would stop Odie Racine.

47

Horatio Thimble had come to the crossroads. It was time to put stock on his land or abandon this place. He and Gertrude, and Artemus and David, had toiled unceasingly all summer and fall, building the cabins, a generous barn, and livestock pens. They had dug a well, fenced and plowed a garden tract, dug and roofed a root cellar and a springhouse, and cut deadfall into firewood against the coming cold. Now, at last, he was done with the building. The homestead had a solid look about it. The cabins had shutters thick enough to stop a bullet, but his real defense would be his pacifism.

He had been to town several times to buy a wagonload of supplies, but he had not seen Flint. Now he needed to see Flint, who would probably know more about Colonel Buell's mood than he would. From time to time, Thimble had seen one of the colonel's men gazing down from some distant height, and in those moments, Thimble had quietly alerted his sons. But Clayton Buell's riders never descended the long slopes to threaten, or even to talk, and simply vanished over the crest of the ridges, no doubt to tell their boss how the Thimbles were progressing.

But the Thimble family could scarcely survive without stock on the land to bring them an income. The grass on his homestead had not been touched except by their horse, and neither had the grass that lay clear up Pass Creek Canyon, deep into the rimrock. None of the Buell cattle had drifted that way. It was almost as if Buell's men were keeping his huge herds out of there. Was it a courtesy to Thimble, or was it merely to preserve that vast tract of land as winter pasture? That's what Horatio Thimble itched to find out.

He set off for Payday one crisp fall morning, enjoying the rain-washed crystalline air and the premonitory bite of cold. Again, as always, the basin seemed an Eden to him. The cotton-woods blazed golden now, and soon would lose their leaves. The grasses stood tan and lush, good winter pasture. The thickets teemed with mule deer and wild turkeys. A love of this place came upon him, so strong and stunning that he wanted to step down from the wagon and hug the fertile, generous land, or kneel in the sun-gilded fields and thank his God for delivering the Thimbles to this sweet haven after their years of torment and war.

As he approached Payday, the size of the sporting district astounded him. In the bright sun, it seemed innocuous enough, but Thimble didn't for a minute believe that it was. The district, slumbering through a golden morning, was like the biblical whited sepulcher, stately outside, foul within. He'd had little contact with anyone all summer, but even so, news had drifted in on moth wings, hints of darkness and brewing trouble. Two solid blocks of Basin Street contained saloons, hurdy-gurdy dance halls, gambling parlors, boardinghouses, and buildings whose nature and purpose he couldn't fathom. A few horses stood at hitchrails, but no mortals were about.

He found Flint bent over his type stick. What a slow and painful labor it was to place each letter of each word, along with the spaces between words, into a metal device that would fabricate a line of type. It took patience and full absorption, especially if you were also composing the story as you went along.

"Horatio!" Flint bawled, setting down his work.

They clasped hands, and soon Sam Flint was asking all sorts of questions about Thimble's prospects. Thimble answered those questions and more, detailing how the summer had gone for the Thimble family.

"I've come to buy stock, Sam," he said. "I've some cash in Ike Cobb's safe. The time's come to risk ourselves again. What can you tell me about Clayton Buell?"

"I wish I could tell you something certain. That he's changed. That he's happier. That he's letting homesteaders settle. I can't say that to you. I don't understand him any better now than before. I can't assure you that if you run stock—more sheep, I suppose—he'll not slaughter them."

That didn't sound good to Thimble.

"He's a county supervisor, but never comes to board meetings and seems more isolated than ever," Flint continued. "But, Horatio, there's been a little change. He's been kind to Merry-Grace Rokoczy. He's helped her. Branded and weaned her calves, bought stock from her when she was pressed for money." Flint looked solemn. "There's more to it than that. Buell's got his heart set on her. I don't know how that'll all come out, but Mrs. Rakoczy's listening to him."

Thimble nodded. "That's fine, but it doesn't help me. I can't expect anything, and I'll just have to take my risks. I'm putting sheep back on if I can buy some here. There's a pretty regular market over at Wiley's Feed Store."

"There's less prejudice against cattle, Horatio."

"Cattle don't supply two crops, wool and mutton. We figure two-crop animals are safer. Wool's always in demand. Meat isn't. This is natural sheep country, couldn't be better. The boys know how to shear. We can bale up the wool ourselves."

Flint sighed. "I wish I had better news for you."

Thimble nodded. "It's not bad news. Buell isn't on some sort of rampage, driving people out, burning houses, the way he was when we tried to get settled. I'm going to go ahead."

Flint grinned wryly. "Well, you can have your job back if it doesn't work."

The offer somehow offended Thimble. "Sam, I am going to make it work. We refused to budge. We still won't budge. We'll defend our sheep the same way."

Flint eyed him soberly, and the matter was settled. "All right, Horatio. Now, I've some things to talk to you about. Alpine County is no longer Eden; it's a branch of hell. You'd better know what has happened, and what's likely to happen, before you lay out cash for a single four-footed animal. You may choose to flee while the fleeing's good after I fill you in on some things."

Thimble listened to an account of a county's capture by criminals, some of which he knew about. But he hadn't realized that matters had deteriorated to such a degree. Then he listened intently to Flint's plan for a big exposé issue, and Flint's hope that it would trigger reform.

He knew that Flint was asking for help, and he resisted. He would not take up arms or do violence to any mortal. He had fled here to escape just such things. He and his family had found a haven at last, and if he kept to himself, it would still be a haven. Only, on reflection, he didn't believe it. If Odie Racine triumphed and drove Flint out of town or killed him, her swindlers and enforcers would find Thimble soon enough and take what was his. The knowledge rested heavily on Thimble because he knew what he had to do: live by his ideals, no matter what.

"Sam," he said wearily, "I'll help, but not with arms. Call on me when the time comes. I can print in your absence."

Flint didn't say anything. Instead, he took Horatio Thimble's big, rough hand in his own hand and held it tight. "I hope I don't have to call on you, but I know you'll be a stalwart if things go badly. You're a friend and more, Horatio. You're a good man."

Thimble clasped the younger man's hand, knowing that Payday was lucky to have a fighting editor, willing to risk his life and property to root out the corruption of one of the loveliest places on God's green earth. Nothing more was said. Thimble knew, too, that if word came, he would set type and write a story at the risk of his own life if necessary.

He stepped into the stiff fall sunlight, feeling anew that his life was at a crossroads. It wasn't just the decision to stock his land and face Clayton Buell. It was the decision to clean out Alpine County. He retrieved his sack of coins from Ike Cobb's safe and headed for the feed store at the north end of Prescott Street, where buyers and sellers of livestock often made a market, usually by leaving word with Clay Wiley, the proprietor.

It didn't take long. From Wiley he learned that several outfits south of town had sheep for sale and would offer a good price to local buyers. Thimble steered his big draft horse south down a two-rut lane into drier country dotted with juniper brush, and turned east at a crude sign announcing the Praxiteles Ranch. He passed herds of fat merinos, big and healthy, guarded against coyotes by several cantankerous mules, and eventually found himself dealing with Apollo Praxiteles, whose herds they were. The venerable Greek, it turned out, was cash-starved. In half an hour, in spite of a language barrier, Thimble acquired about seventy merino sheep, mostly ewe-lamb pairs, with a few good merino rams thrown in.

"You have a bargain, yes?" the wiry old man asked, his blue eyes bright with pleasure.

"It's the usual two dollars a hundredweight," Thimble said.

"Ah, but these are fat and make good oily wool!"

The purchase amounted to less than half the herd he'd started with, Thimble thought gloomily. But he would not surrender to pessimism. These were fine animals, and he expected they could all be moved the few miles without loss. And he had a bonus: Apollo's two sons would drive the herd to the Thimble ranch, arriving tomorrow.

He watched Praxiteles's dozen alert sheepdogs circle the little herd, and knew that shepherding was an ancient tradition among these people. "Mr. Praxiteles," he said, "are any of those good dogs for sale?"

"Ah! You are a wise man, Thimble. I send along two puppies, a lady and a gentleman five months old, with my great respect for the Mister. They are a strain I bring with me, Macedonia they come from." His eyes shone with delight.

"The herd will be well guarded, and I thank you."

Thimble drove north thoughtfully, thinking that seventy sheep, thirty of them lambs vulnerable to wolves and coyotes, would not be a living. He needed at least three hundred, and that would take a few years. But he had to start somewhere. Clayton Buell might destroy these, as he had the others. But Thimble sensed that he had already won, and Buell would not trouble him.

He didn't get back to the homestead until well after dark, and hours later than he said he would. Gertrude held back tears, and he saw in her face the unspoken relief that Clayton Buell hadn't hurt him.

After he unloaded the wagon of his purchases in town, he gathered his small family around him in the light of the single coal-oil lamp. He was proud of his sunburned, weathered sons and his smiling, resourceful wife.

"Seventy good merinos will arrive tomorrow, along with two young sheepdogs of ancient lineage to replace Stonewall. I bought them from the Praxiteles family, south of Payday, good sturdy Greeks. We've crossed our Rubicon. Every cent we possess has been invested in them. What comes next will require daily courage and constant care. We'll stick together, keep up our spirits and prayers, deal firmly with Clayton Buell, and soon we may prosper. Our strength is pacifism. We must never threaten another human being."

They were all listening. He had raised his sons to be serious and mature, and it was not in them to ever be dandies. Neither did they waste their hours. He knew he could count on them when trouble came.

"We've waited for this moment. We'll know soon whether we will prosper here and have a good neighbor, or whether we will see more blood. I have strong, wise sons and a strong, loving, and wise wife, and we will endure. But I'll say now, if we fail again, we will keep on. We'll find jobs. We'll keep on and on and on. The Thimbles will not surrender."

48

It had gone badly. Merry-Grace had summoned her courage and addressed Ignacio and Luz in the kitchen. She had told them that she and Colonel Buell would live together as man and wife. They had stared silently at her. They knew the colonel's story. It had never been any secret that he had a mad wife. Finally, Ignacio had nodded, wordlessly, and it seemed to be over.

But now Ignacio stood gravely before her, and his very first word revealed worlds to her: "*Patrona,*" he said hesitantly. Neither he nor Luz had used that formal term since the first year they had joined Nicholas and her. Nicholas had hired them only weeks after arriving in the Tonto Basin. Ignacio had been among those who had helped build the great home and outbuildings.

"*Patrona,* we have decided to leave your employment," he said, his umber eyes mournful.

"But Ignacio! I'll be able to pay you soon. As soon as the colonel comes. I'll make sure."

He shook his head sadly. "That is kind of you, *Patrona,* but we have decided to live in *Nuevo Mexico,* in the *placita* where we grew up."

"But I can't just let you go! You're so dear. You're part of my family."

He stared away from her, and when he spoke, it was so softly that she could barely hear. "It would not be proper."

She knew then. Her decision to live outside of marriage with Colonel Buell had disturbed them so deeply that they could not ratify it with their presence here. She felt that sinking, vertiginous feeling that comes with helplessness. She could not keep them without abandoning her plans. She would lose them.

It had been a little easier with her sons. They were too young to know that her choice lay beyond the laws of God and man, and in fact, it pleased them that their old uncle, Colonel Buell, would come and be a father to them. They had always gotten along famously with him, and he, in his courtly way, had paid close attention to all their hopes, once giving Andrew a paint pony, and Stephen a saddle and a lariat. To be sure, the colonel's longhorns had demolished the crops, but that did not turn her children against him. He was still the old family friend and frequent guest.

"We will stay until the day comes, *Patrona*. Let us know."

"But won't you . . . reconsider? Is there anything I can do?"

"No, it would not be the same."

She surrendered. "It will be December first, Ignacio."

He nodded.

She could almost read his mind. This was sin, and they had to retreat from it. This sin would doom the ranch. Evil things would happen. The wrath of God would descend upon them all.

As if to confirm her thoughts, Ignacio suddenly made the sign of the cross upon his ancient homespun shirt, and bowed. He had never bowed. She desperately wanted him not to bow. It utterly changed their relationship.

The next days ticked out in a strange, tense manner. The colonel obliged her request to pay the couple by bringing twelve pregnant heifers, a bull, and a horse and cart to Ignacio, who received them stiffly, his eyes opaque and his thoughts mysterious. On the last day of November, Ignacio and Luz loaded their few belongings into the cart and hitched the horse to it. The colonel wasn't present, but Merry-Grace, Stephen, and Andrew watched silently. Both boys were so stricken that they could barely fight back tears. Ignacio and Luz had been almost a father and mother to them, and it tore the youngsters in two to lose them.

At last Ignacio and Luz were ready. The cattle had been released from the pen. Ignacio would herd them; Luz would lead the horse and cart. The solemnity only deepened. The couple was not old, or careworn, or aged or frail, but robust and golden-fleshed and in good health. But Merry-Grace noted grayness in Luz's hair, and wondered why the streak of silver in Ignacio's hair had escaped her. Luz wore black, and upon her bosom rested an ornate silver crucifix, as if to ward off the evil of this place.

Merry-Grace studied their impassive faces, wondering what lay beneath. Did they grieve? Did their sense of sin, and the wrongness of Merry-Grace's choice, drive away all the memory of love and joy, the hearty meals, the shared Christmases, the careful instruction of the boys?

"Vaya con Dios," she said to them when they stood before her, ready to go.

Those particular words seemed to strike them oddly. How could a Godless woman, plunging herself into sin, wish God's blessing upon them?

"Gracias, Patrona," Ignacio answered at last.

No one hugged. No one shook hands.

"Adiós, Ignacio. *Adiós,* Luz," whispered Stephen.

That evoked a small, controlled smile from Luz and then from Ignacio. The child didn't share his mother's guilt.

Merry-Grace clasped the hands of her sons, Nicholas's sons, and held them tightly while Luz tugged on the reins of the horse. The cart creaked away, and Ignacio clapped the little herd into its slow walk east. A deep, ineffable sadness filled Merry-Grace. It was as if the last of Nicholas's world had crumbled, and now she faced an entirely new one.

The next afternoon, the colonel arrived, along with some of his crew. These he directed toward the bunkhouse, while Merry-Grace and her sons watched quietly from the veranda. Some deep grief filled Merry-Grace as she watched the silent transition that made this the Buell ranch. He kept part of his crew at the old place, but this would be the headquarters and home. This wounded, loving man, this old friend, this uncle to the boys, was to be her mate now, and yet there would be no ceremony, no vows recited, no pledges given before all the world, no reception, no dance, no recording of this event upon a church ledger or courthouse record. She felt hollow, cheated, and yet determined. She watched the colonel direct the move, wondering what life with him would really be like; whether he would be kind, whether he would be as generous and romantic as Nicholas, whether he would treat her sons well. These things had nagged at her, along with the great question: did he love her?

She knew that in his own way, he did. A man so stricken by grief at the loss of his beloved Eloise was a man brimming over with love. Oddly, it comforted her that he loved and respected his wife and grieved her every hour, just as she grieved Nicholas. It spoke of goodness in him.

At last, he turned to her. "Well, Ah'm here, for richer, for poorer, for better and for worse, in sickness and in health, till death do us part," he said, something kind and affectionate in his black-marble eyes. She loved the declaration. It was a small attempt to make this moment sacred. She wanted the sacredness more than anything just then. But would this hard man treat her well? A thin edge of fear remained within her.

He turned to the boys. "Your mother and Ah'll be making a home together. Ah'll be here for you, helping you grow, helping you find the way to manhood. Ah'm not a hard man and not an easy one, and Ah'm not much different from your dear father, who set you an example. Ah'm not much at husbanding or fathering, but Ah'm here to do my best."

"Yes, sir," said Andrew.

"I'm glad you're here, sir," said Stephen.

That was hopeful. Merry-Grace hoped her sons meant it.

"Please come in, sir," she said. She hadn't meant to say "sir."

He looked sharply at her. "Ah'm quite capable of staying in Ignacio's house," he said.

She smiled as warmly as she could. "I wouldn't think of it, Clayton." She used his given name deliberately.

He smiled. "Ah believe Ah will," he said.

In a few minutes, he had carried some heavy portmanteaus upstairs to . . . their room. She watched silently.

"Would you like me in the spare bedroom?" he asked.

A small coil of emotion spread through Merry-Grace's belly. "No, Clayton," she whispered.

"My men'll go back to the old place for supper. They'll stay there tonight," he said. "Tomorrow they'll return, along with the cook."

He was making it easier for her, she knew. She would not face that embarrassment this night. He was a man of surprising sensitivity.

"Ah thought perhaps Andrew and Stephen might enjoy a night with my drovers, talking the business of cattle. They'll be in good hands. My foreman, Mr. Throckmorton, would look after them as if they were his sons."

"Why, Clayton!" The idea delighted her, and she suspected the boys would be enchanted.

It was swiftly arranged. Then she watched her two boys, filled with all the excitement their imaginations could conjure, ride away on handsome paint horses, accompanied by Buell's men.

Then she and her man, Clayton Buell, stood alone in the big, silent, sunlit, empty house. Her pulse lifted, whether with fear or anticipation, she could not say.

A clock struck two, and he noticed it. "Ah guess this is a time of day when a lot of people walk down the aisle," he said. "Ah thought maybe we could do this our own way. Ah have a sense that something is needed just now."

She nodded, utterly agreeing, and felt his hard hand clasp hers. It reminded her of how hard his body was; no softness, no fat anywhere. He drew her to the big, sunny bedroom where she and Nicholas had lived out their joyous, private existence, in a suite separate from all the rest of the large house. The sun poured in through gauzy white drapes, whitening the whole room and turning the big four-poster bed into a pool of molten gold.

"Merry-Grace," he said, "Ah'm glad you keep on loving Nicholas. Ah'm glad that Eloise is a shrine and an altar within my soul. Ah can't offer to be a new Nicholas, nor could you be a new Eloise. Ah know you're feeling a little cheated by life. This moment needs something, and so Ah'd like to give you this."

He slid a hand into his coat pocket and pulled out a plain gold ring. The ring finger of her left hand still bore Nicholas's ornate band, but she eagerly stretched out her hand to him. Slowly he tugged and pulled, and finally slid Nicholas's ring off and gave it to her. Then he held her left hand in both of his big, strong hands.

"Ah wish we had God's blessing—maybe we do. God's mysterious. But all Ah can offer is my own blessing, since there's nothing in civilization or religion to help us. So, Merry-Grace, take this ring, and with it, my word: Ah'll love and respect you all my days. Ah'll support and help and honor you all my days. Ah'll help you face a hard world all my days. Ah pledge my undying love and devotion all my days."

With that, he slid the gold ring on her finger. It fit perfectly, and she wondered how he knew her size, or what small conspiracy he had engaged in to find it out. Or whether this was some uncanny magic, born of destiny.

"Clayton, this ring weds us," she said, "no matter what the world thinks. You are my dear husband. My vow is sacred: I'll love you always, and bless you always, and make your days as joyous as I can." She paused, seeing his warm, alert gaze. "Kiss me, Clayton," she whispered.

49

In the gray light of dawn, Sam Flint held up the first copy, thinking it sputtered like a fuse. Its headline, "Anarchy in Alpine County," was set in the largest display type he possessed. And beneath, a dozen damning stories spread from page one onto page two, where the reporting was reinforced by stinging editorials demanding action.

He felt almost giddy. This issue had been the culmination of a lot of digging. It missed nothing that he knew of. He was producing it a day early to throw off the hounds of hell. He was printing it in the predawn hours, when he was least likely to be discovered burning midnight oil.

He set to work printing the reverse side of the sheet, and after he had finished twenty copies, he hid the batch in his outhouse behind the building. Two hours later, he had an issue drying in a heap beside the press. Even as he worked, he found himself glancing at the windows, at the barred door, awaiting assassins. He scarcely knew what he would do if one showed up. But of course they didn't know. His fevered imagination was concocting menace that didn't yet exist. Soon enough, menace would exist, but not at this moment. He calmed himself with that thought as he planned his next step.

He knew that he would need to get the issue on the stagecoach and well away from Payday before he released it locally. He tried to imagine what Odie Racine would do. Obviously, her first move would be mail robbery. She could not permit this issue to reach Prescott or Tucson, where it would swiftly reach the eyes of Territorial officials. He considered the problem while wiping down his press, and decided on a course of action.

Some mail would go out on the morning stage to Prescott; other mail would go out on the afternoon stage to Tucson and points south. He would need to get copies on both stagecoaches before releasing the edition in Payday late in the afternoon. He wondered whether Ike Cobb, who handled the mail from his mercantile, would keep the secret. He decided he would have to risk it, and would explain to Ike the need for silence until the issue reached the streets. But that wasn't enough. He wrapped ten copies in butcher paper, addressed them to Silas Marnier, editor of *The Prescott Review*. Silas would know what to do. These would go via the Payday Transfer Company freight. If all else failed, they would get through.

He delivered them to the freight office as soon as it opened, and paid the dollar-and-sixty-cent tariff. Then he watched the clerk take the bundle back to the forwarding yard. Satisfied, he carried his usual load of exchange papers over to Ike. It was still early in the morning, and Payday was hardly stirring.

"You're a day early," Ike said, walking to his postal wicket.

"Ike, this is the big one. I want it dispatched and out of here before it reaches the streets. You understand why."

Ike nodded.

Flint handed him the bundle, each with an address in its corner. Ike glanced at the headline and whistled softly. "Good God, Sam."

"Ike, my life depends on you. So does this town."

Ike paled. "What if they show up?"

"They won't, because they won't know. I'm not releasing this until the Tucson stage has gone. Maybe around four this afternoon."

"Do you think this'll help?"

"Read it, Ike. But don't let a soul see it."

"What about afterward? When Odie and her killers see it?"

"I'm depending on Arnold Betjeman and you deputies to keep order—and keep me alive."

"You'd better make yourself scarce."

"And lose my plant? They'll demolish it."

"At least arm yourself, Sam."

"I will. Not that it'll protect me from that fellow—The Hired Man, he calls himself. He'd empty all six chambers before I could lift a shotgun. I know that. I'll arm myself, but it'll be up to you fellows to keep the lid on. I won't be safe until they've been driven out . . . and maybe not then."

"Does Arnold know?"

"I'm on my way over there."

"You're going to have your boy, Elmer, sell it?"

"For a while. He'll take an hour. After that, I'd like to have you merchants keep on selling it from your counters. You'll be putting all my mail copies into the boxes."

Cobb whistled. "You're asking us to commit suicide."

Flint boiled. "I'm risking my life for this town. Maybe you should share the risk."

Cobb reddened. The past hung between them. "You should maybe just take a few issues on the stagecoach to Prescott yourself. I don't know why you do it this way."

"It's the town's fight, Ike. It'll take a few dozen brave and determined men, and I'm counting on you to be among them."

Cobb reddened again and nodded curtly.

Flint left the store worrying about Cobb. Doubts crawled over Flint like an army of lice. He grabbed a copy of the big issue and headed for the courthouse, where he would let the sheriff in on his plans. Betjeman was there all right, but so was Danny Drinker. Too late, Flint tried to slide the paper under his suit jacket. But Danny loomed over him.

"Whatcha got there, Flint?"

"Nothing," Flint said. "Arnold, would you meet me later?"

"I said, whatcha got there?" Drinker stood there, massive and immovable, grinning.

Flint turned to leave, steadying his footstep, but Drinker's huge paw clamped his arm. "No, Sammy, you're staying here."

Flint glanced at Betjeman, who sat behind his battered desk making no move whatsoever. Plainly, the sheriff feared the bruiser.

Flint felt himself pulled by an irresistible force into the center of the office. Drinker's other paw dug into Flint's coat and extracted the issue. He flipped it open with one hand and studied it.

"I don't read so good," he said. "Never saw the use. I'll take this over to Odie. Get in there." He shoved Flint toward the jail cell.

Flint staggered into the bars, hitting his head hard. It had all been for nothing. A moment's carelessness had cost him his life—and imprisoned Payday in Racine's grip for years to come. Drinker pulled open the cell door.

"In," he snarled.

Flint weighed the chances. They weren't very good. But he had no chance at all once the door closed. He gathered his strength and pounced straight at the brute. It felt like butting a stone wall. Drinker rocked slightly. A massive blow hit Flint's head, dizzying him. Another shot pain through his shoulder. He sagged to the floor in a haze of pain. Then he heard a sharp crack. Drinker gasped and staggered. Through blurry eyes, Flint beheld Betjeman looming over Drinker, a nightstick in one hand, a revolver in the other. The stick landed on Drinker's skull a second time. Drinker sighed and slid into oblivion.

"You all right?" Betjeman asked.

"No," Flint said, peeling out from under Drinker's weight.

Betjeman grunted. He tried to drag Drinker into the cell, but the brute's sheer weight was too much. Flint, still reeling, attempted to help, and between them, they got Racine's thug into the cell, retrieved the issue, took away Drinker's jail-house key, knout, brass knuckles, and revolver, and locked the door.

Flint sat on the floor, holding his aching head, feeling wild pain course through his shoulder.

Betjeman studied the paper, grunting like a hog.

Flint pulled himself to his feet. All his plans had been blown. There was little time. The other bruiser, Fauntleroy, would drift in here, and so would that killer, The Hired Man. All Drinker had to do was start bawling like a bear to attract attention.

"This it, huh?" the sheriff asked.

"Yeah." Flint eyed the apparently unconscious Drinker, not trusting the situation. He motioned the sheriff into the hall and explained his entire plan: the postal copies, the freight copies, and the distribution beginning that afternoon after the issue was on its way to Prescott and Tucson.

"Now it's all shot," Flint mumbled through the pulsing pain.

Betjeman grunted. "We've got an hour. Fauntleroy usually shows up around ten or eleven."

"Could you get him into that cell, too?"

Betjeman grunted. It sounded like a "no" to Flint, but there was no knowing.

"Posse, maybe," Betjeman muttered.

"You've deputized eight businessmen."

The sheriff grunted.

Flint understood that grunt. Who among them would stand against the hired killer? "I seem to have an hour to get the issue distributed and copies out of town. And then I'm on my own?"

Betjeman nodded.

"All right," Flint said.

"Sorry," Betjeman said.

"What're you going to do?"

The sheriff grunted again. Annoyance built in Flint. The sheriff had been acting like a sheriff should—until now. But in the pinch, he was fading fast.

"Hold 'em off. Lock the door. I need time," Flint said.

Betjeman pursed his lips.

"Arnold. I'm spreading this paper from one end of Payday to the other. I don't have any choice. After that, I want all the protection you can give me."

Betjeman slid into his usual silence, and Flint gave up trying to prod the man. When they returned to the sheriff's office, Drinker was standing up, his paws threatening to pull the iron rods apart. This time, he wasn't smirking. His stare bored into Flint like a drill. Flint thought the man would gladly commit murder.

50

Sam Flint could not remember a more hectic or desperate moment. He raced to his press and scooped up an armload of papers, then plunged into each store.

"Put these under the counter. Give one to every customer," he said to each surprised merchant, and didn't stay to explain.

He shoveled papers into Abel Greene's place, the Cochise Café, Billy Bravo's smithy, Lafe Short's bakery, Nels Gulick's hardware store, the Tonto Basin Drayage Company, and Clay Wiley's feed store, and then ran out of copies. He ran back to his shop, his heart thumping, his throat burning, and ran mail subscription copies through his addressing stencil. That took a while, and he peered fearfully at his locked door as he stenciled the names and box numbers of his customers on each copy. Ike Cobb already had the exchange papers; they were probably in the mail pouch for the morning Prescott stage. But not these city and county papers.

They came to a hundred fifty-nine. He finished the stack and peered out the window into a serene, late fall day, with the friendly sun driving away the morning chill. Payday looked quiet. No one was out. The numbing sight he dreaded, The Hired Man stalking catlike, like an emaciated panther, didn't materialize. He had spent over an hour. Time had run out. He looked about, hefted his papers into a canvas sack, and walked doggedly through the morning to Cobb's store.

Jerusalem Cobb eyed him sharply.

"Here's a hundred fifty-nine, Ike. Put it on the tab. You got thirty-four exchanges earlier. I'll pay you when I can. Don't have time now."

"Against postal regulations. No credit. Got to be paid, Sam."

"Just do it!" Flint roared. "Bill my personal account at the store."

Cobb reddened. "You'll get me killed," he said. "Your Prescott papers are gone. In the mail pouch. The Prescott stage's loading; it'll be off soon." He dragged the canvas sack into his postal cubicle. "All right, I'll put these up," he muttered. "I got enough hardware in here to fight off the Confederate Army."

Flint stared. He spotted an over-and-under shotgun, two revolvers, and a rifle inside the wicket.

"I figure I'm barricaded in here," Cobb said. "They won't tamper with the U.S. Mail."

"Likely nothing'll happen," Flint said. "But I like your attitude. Like it a lot, Jerusalem."

Cobb glared at him.

He stepped out into the chill sun, feeling prickly. Three men formed a knot in front of the café, all of them studying a copy of his exposé issue. A woman was carrying a copy tucked under her arm. Word was out now. There could be no turning back. He still had a hundred or so copies, ones that his newsboy Elmer would sell, but he didn't want to expose the kid to the sort of trouble they would bring. Flint thought he would gather another armload and stuff them into various doors. Drop off one in Cutlip's chambers at the courthouse. Another to the clerk, Farquehar. He was beginning to feel a little better. The issue was out, gone to the four winds.

He started toward the courthouse, only to see a thing he dreaded. Danny Drinker and Gerald Fauntleroy emerged from the courthouse door, a copy of the issue in hand, and trotted swiftly along Basin Street. Flint ducked into shadow and they missed him. He noted that both men wore revolvers.

Flint watched sharply, and then slid into the courthouse. He found Betjeman locked in the cell. The sheriff stared at him.

"Have you a key, Arnold?" Flint asked.

"Nope."

"Need anything?"

Betjeman pointed toward the gun rack. Flint nodded, handed the sheriff a shotgun.

"More," Betjeman said.

Flint handed him four more weapons: two rifles, another shotgun, and a revolver in a sheath. Then he added a pasteboard box of bullets and some paper shotgun cartridges and caps.

"Water, and my lunch in that pail," Betjeman said.

Flint handed him those. "I'll try to find a sledgehammer. Break you out. What happened?"

The sheriff grunted. "Take the revolver in my desk, Flint."

Flint did, stuffing it into his belt. "I'll be back," he said.

"You'll croak," Betjeman countered. "Before you do, tell Billy Bravo to break me out. Cutlip should have a key. Try him."

"I will."

Flint hurried to Cutlip's chambers, realized the judge had not yet arrived, left a copy of the *Pioneer* on his desk, and raced across the courthouse lawn toward Prescott Street. The Prescott stage, a Celerity drawn by six broncos, was just pulling away from the express office, to the music of the jehu's whip. It headed straight toward Flint. It would round the courthouse square and head west on Basin Street. But then the driver tugged the lines, and the coach sagged into its leather thoroughbraces. Slowly, the jehu raised his hands, and from a shadowed gallery in front of Zeppel's, The Hired Man stepped into the street. Flint couldn't hear a word. The killer had stopped the stage without even removing a revolver from a holster. Bystanders gawked.

Flint felt a prickle. He stood a hundred yards away from the assassin, but the man seemed all too close. Flint slipped into shadow himself, between Short's Bakery and a new structure half-built. The jehu, who was driving alone, clambered over the roof of the coach to the boot at the rear and extracted the gray mail pouch. He threw it down to the ground. Odie Racine's hired killer didn't bother to pick it up. He invited the passengers to step out, and they did. Even from Flint's distance, their terror was palpable to him. The killer casually examined them all, having each male open his suitcoat. Then he waved them back into the coach. He hadn't taken a dime from them.

He motioned the jehu on, and the driver took up the lines and started the broncos forward again. Flint ducked back between the buildings that concealed him. The coach rolled by, raising dust, and then the killer opened the mail sack and extracted the newspapers.

Odie Racine's jackal left the bag in the middle of the dirt street and hiked toward Cobb's mercantile. Flint wondered why the multitudes who had just witnessed mail robbery didn't simply shoot the man. But such was the man's lethal aura that no one even imagined doing it—except for Flint, who was a block away. The Hired Man, as he fashioned himself, calmly walked into Cobb's building, only to meet gunfire. The roar of a shotgun erupted through Payday, followed by several soft snaps of a revolver.

"Good God," Flint muttered to no one in particular while peering out of an unglassed window in the new building. "Jerusalem—"

No one moved. Then everyone moved, and the street emptied.

Some moments later, The Hired Man appeared, this time with his revolver in hand. He studied the empty street, his gaze sweeping from alley to window to door, and finally he stepped into the sunlight. Blood leaked into his green shirt at the left shoulder. The wound did not prevent him from carrying a heavy load of *The Pay-day Pioneer*. These he heaped in the middle of the street, then went back into the mercantile. Flint was pretty sure that the heap of papers would include every copy Cobb had posted to the mail-boxes, and probably the copies Flint had given Cobb to distribute free.

The man emerged from the store with several tins of coal oil, which he poured liberally over the papers, kicking some of them aside until they all got a good soaking. He scratched a lucifer across his denim britches and lit the *Pioneer*'s funeral pyre. He grimaced with satisfaction, only occasionally studying the windows and alleys of the silent, deserted avenue. He paid no attention to the shoulder wound, but watched intently as the billowing orange fire consumed most of the copies Flint had printed.

Then the man walked calmly down the center of Prescott and headed toward the courthouse square, his obvious next stop the *Pioneer* offices. And Flint knew he could not stop that deadly killer from doing whatever he intended to do. His only solace was that the twenty copies hidden in the outhouse would probably be overlooked.

Cobb was on his mind. In anguish, feeling helpless against this unleashed force, Flint slid through back alleys, sticking to shadow, angling toward the mercantile. He wasn't the first to arrive. Abel Greene had beaten him, and also Lafe Short and Nels Gulick. They were staring into the wicket. Jerusalem Cobb lay there in a spreading pool of blood. He had been shot four times, once in the forehead, once over the heart, once through the neck, and once just below the sternum. His mouth formed an O, as if death had overtaken surprise. He had fired one barrel of his double-barreled shotgun. The weapon lay beside him, soaked with his blood.

A rush of sadness flooded through Flint at the bloody spectacle. A crowd gathered around, peering mutely at the carnage.

"Brave man," Greene said. "Medal of Honor winner once, and

he proved his mettle once again. Lost our finest citizen. It's murder, Flint. Murder, postal robbery, and the death of Payday."

"Jerusalem, Jerusalem," Flint said softly.

"What's that?" Greene asked.

"Ike. Ike," Flint said. "I was thinking of his brother."

"Didn't know he had a brother."

"Both brave young men," Flint said. "Good family back there in Evansville, Indiana."

Greene stared at Flint. "I read that issue. I have the notion, Flint, that your life may be short if you don't move fast."

"That killer's at my shop now. Hunting down the rest of the issues. It's the two thug deputies I'm worried about. They locked Arnold in a cell. We need to get Billy Bravo to go over there and free him. Cutlip has a key if you can find him."

"Flint, you vamoose. I'll send Billy over. Abel and I'll get some help here, take Cobb to Tom Stapleton for a box. You shouldn't be here, dammit. For you, every minute counts. Fetch a horse from the livery and get out of town, before we lay you out beside Cobb."

"No," said Flint. "I started this. I have to finish it. If I don't, Jerusalem Cobb will have died in vain."

"Don't know why you keep calling Ike Jerusalem," Greene said.

"Because he was a holy city," Flint said, tears welling up.

51

Basil Cutlip studied the extraordinary issue of the *Pioneer*, unaware of the turmoil on the streets. What an issue! Flint had systematically detailed the slide and collapse of order in Alpine County, pulling no punches. Here was a piece about the extortions; there was a piece chock-full of information about Odie Racine's past. And over here was a piece about the collapse of law enforcement and the legal system.

That incredible young man was risking his life, producing an exposé issue like this. This courageous act won Cutlip's unstinting admiration and respect. The issue was all the more powerful because Flint had used subdued and civil language. There wasn't a rabble-rousing word in the paper. Each story focused on facts and situations, and avoided the rhetoric so common in overheated frontier newspapers.

Several feelings flooded through Cutlip. One was that he must do something, fast, before Odie Racine's hired thugs pinched out the flame of this brave candle. Cutlip wanted to act. He was a magistrate; he had the power of the Territory and common law and public opinion behind him.

He sighed, knowing that he had scarcely been a shining light himself. Flint's charisma radiated so powerfully that Cutlip felt inadequate in the bright light. He had not thought much about the treasures of the human spirit: courage, idealism, honor. Instead, he and Violet had come to the Territory simply to repair their fortunes. They had arrived without the slightest intent to build a good community, but only to get rich fast and leave.

But then Violet had died, and in the quiet wake of her burial, Basil Cutlip learned that he loved this place. This had become home. Someday, not so distant, he would lie for all eternity beside her in the Payday cemetery.

He peered into a bright, quiet morning, watching the Prescott stage roll out of town twenty minutes late. The log walls of the courthouse muffled the sound of its passage. Soon there would be trouble. Maybe blood. Quite likely Flint's. Maybe he could do something to avert that if he could summon some mettle. It occurred to him that he could strike directly at the heart of the evil. He sat down at his enormous desk and began filling out bench warrants. The first was for Odie Racine herself, for extortion and half a dozen other crimes he could think of. He completed additional warrants for Danny Drinker and Gerald Fauntleroy. He wrote a John Doe warrant for that gunman whose name he didn't know. He added other John Doe warrants for some of Racine's lieutenants.

With each scratch of his nib pen, he knew he was risking his life. But if Flint could risk his, Cutlip could share the risk. The town wouldn't be freed of this octopus of crime until brave men risked their lives. A newspaper editor had shown the way; now a magistrate would act. When he had completed his bench warrants, Cutlip pulled open his desk drawer and extracted an over-and-under derringer he kept there for emergencies, checked the loads and the caps, and slid it into the hip pocket of his suitcoat. He folded the warrants, tucked them into the breast pocket, and walked across the silent courthouse to Arnold Betjeman's offices.

He found no one within, which annoyed him. But of course the sheriff would probably be out, no doubt having read Flint's paper. But as he turned to leave, a voice from the cell stayed him.

"Basil."

The judge turned and discovered the sheriff standing behind the bars. "Arnold—what happened? Are you all right?"

"Locked in. Drinker done it. Get me out."

"I can do that," Cutlip said. He had the jail key in his chambers. Moments later, Cutlip unlocked the cell door with a metallic snap of the bolt and Betjeman stepped out.

"Who armed you?"

"Flint. He couldn't get me out."

"You all right?"

"Sound as a Confederate dollar."

Cutlip eyed Betjeman, wondering how the sheriff would respond. "Arnold, I've drafted bench warrants for the whole crowd. I came here to get you. I'm planning to walk straight into Odie Racine's Golden Calf and I want you to arrest her."

Betjeman blinked, squinted, sighed, and picked up his double-barreled, sawed-off scattergun. "Might as well croak there as here," he said.

"I'll back you."

A faint glint of humor filled the sheriff's face. "Best to watch your own back," he said. "Just as well there's no doc in Payday. It'd give me the hope of living."

Nonetheless, the judge picked up a Remington shotgun and helped himself to a few paper cartridges and some caps lying on a shelf.

The pair walked into the delicious Arizona sun, feeling its welcome rays warm their black suits. Cutlip suddenly felt his years. He had grown soft and portly with age. His hair had receded and was gray now. The man beside him was just as old, skinny, bent slightly, and he limped a little. A pair of sixty-year-old warriors going after cutthroats.

Not a soul stirred around the courthouse. But when they looked down Prescott, they saw smoke rising from the middle of the street—and the street strangely empty of people. Something was amiss there. Betjeman grunted.

A big man slid out of the shadows between Frogg's Oriental Laundry and the next building. Cutlip swiftly swung his shotgun in that direction, but then pulled it away.

"Flint!"

The young man trotted over to them. "You're out," he said to the sheriff. "What are you two doing here?"

Basil Cutlip felt a rush of affection and something akin to love for this strong young man. "Long as you put the match to the fuse, Flint, we thought we'd go for Racine. I've a pocket full of bench warrants and an itchy trigger finger."

"Just you two?"

"All there is."

"I'll join you."

"You've done enough, Sam. What's happening down on Prescott Street?"

Flint filled them in. Mail robbery by that silky gunman, in front of scores of witnesses. Ike Cobb dead, defending his postal wicket.

"Ike dead!"

"A brave death, Basil. A brave, brave young man who gave his life to protect the mail. He wanted my newspaper to reach the world."

"Ike Cobb!" Cutlip could scarcely believe it.

"The gunman burned all the issues he took out of the post office and off the coach. The crowd's just left. The man's headed for my office."

"Where's the two bullyboys?"

"Don't know. Probably protecting Racine. But maybe wrecking my plant." Flint stepped in beside them. He had extracted a revolver tucked in his waist. "I'll trade this for the shotgun, Basil. I can use a long gun best. Army training."

The judge handed the shotgun and some shells to Flint. "I can't work a firearm anyway," he said. He took the revolver from Flint.

Then the three of them padded through the silent sporting district, past the amiable old saloons where drovers and townsmen had gathered for years, and on to the newer part, where jerry-built buildings, still leaking pine sap, hulked. They were three men, without help, determined to rescue a town, a country, and the lives and fortunes of many good citizens.

Cutlip wished suddenly that they had gotten the deputized merchants together, but soon realized that none of them would have willingly walked into this, not after seeking Ike Cobb's lifeless, bloodied body lying in the post-office wicket. It had come down to a judge, an editor, and an old sheriff.

He wondered if he had the courage to aim that revolver and pull the trigger. He had never pointed a firearm at a man. He wondered what it would be like to be hit, thrown backward, hurt, die. He pushed the images aside. He would do what he had to. That shining light beside him was somehow leading him into the greatest test of his manhood. Cutlip didn't mind. For the first time in his long life, a sense of high purpose and joy flooded through him. And if he died, maybe the death of a magistrate would galvanize the Territory. His death would not be in vain.

They pushed through the double doors into the Golden Calf and let their eyes adjust to the perpetual dismal light that made every act within the place seem furtive and sinister. Cutlip made out a bartender and a single pock-faced tinhorn at a faro layout, and two customers who looked disheveled and drunk. The bartender glided leftward along the bar like a cat.

"Stop," said Betjemen suddenly. The sheriff's shotgun aimed directly at the mixologist.

Slowly, the barkeep froze in place, obviously itching to reach under that counter for the weapon there. The tinhorn froze, too.

"You," Betjeman said to the dealer. "Pull out your piece. Slow."

The sloe-eyed gambler eyed Flint's shotgun, Cutlip's revolver, and the sheriff's sawed-off riot gun, and slowly slid a small blue revolver from its armpit nest and lowered it to the green oilcloth of the faro table.

"All right. All of you outside," the sheriff said softly. "Stay out. If you step back in, you'll walk into lead."

The tinhorn and the barman walked out, their gazes unblinking and alert. They didn't seem much afraid of an old sheriff and two armed citizens. The customers followed. The creaking quietness of the place frayed Cutlip's nerves. Upstairs somewhere, the dollies slept. To the rear was a doorway to Odie Racine's private apartment. Scattered through the big building, no doubt, a dozen other tinhorns, bartenders, muscle men, and flunkies lurked, all of them armed and dangerous.

Betjeman grunted, his usual call to action, and led Cutlip and Flint across the plank floor toward that rear apartment. A silvery worm of light oozed from under Odie Racine's door. Cutlip had never been in there and wondered what he would see.

"Have to watch our rear," Betjeman whispered. "But first—" He nodded toward the door. "Judge, you aim left. I'll aim center. Flint, you aim right. Shoot if anyone resists."

Cutlip nodded, wondering what he—a financier, real estate seller, capitalist, and judge—was doing in a situation like this. But he knew the answer. This wasn't for himself. His pulse lifted madly, and he thought it possible he would die of heart failure.

The sheriff softly clasped the doorknob, found that it turned, and then threw the door open upon a world of blinding light.

52

No one. Odie Racine's parlor contained nothing but the lingering fragrance of the attar of roses she used. Sam Flint had never been beyond the parlor and didn't know what lay ahead. A curtained passage led somewhere. They followed it, walking softly. Beyond the curtains, a hallway led into gloom, but light poured from a doorway on the left.

Then the light faded and a huge shape filled the door. Danny Drinker. One glance was all he needed. He roared, swung into the hallway, and bulled straight toward the three intruders. Flint had the sense of being tied to the rails while a locomotive bore down on him. He could not even level the barrel of his shotgun. But he didn't have to. A deafening crash from Betjeman's scattergun blew buckshot into Drinker. The man staggered backward, looking astonished, and slowly sat down, staring at the bubbles of blood across his middle. Flint's ears rang; smoke choked him, and he coughed.

Arnold Betjeman leapt over Drinker and hurled himself through the doorway. Flint followed. Judge Cutlip brought up the rear. They found themselves staring at Odie Racine's office. She sat primly in a swivel chair decorated with rose-colored needle-point, behind a glossy desk. An open safe with cherubs painted on it stood to the left. To the right, a worktable with ledger books filled the corner. A window revealed an unnamed alley. A gauzy curtain passed light, but an iron grille made the window impenetrable to all else.

Odie Racine smiled slightly.

"I've been expecting you," she said. "But I hoped you'd be smarter. It doesn't need to come to this, you know. I'm perfectly flexible—an ordinary businesswoman."

Arnold Betjeman grunted, ejected the spent shotgun shell and inserted a new one, biting off the end of the paper cartridge and then capping the nipple. Flint eyed the door nervously. That deafening shot would have awakened the entire building, if not the whole sporting district.

"We've a warrant for you, Odie," the sheriff said. "And the rest. Where's the other goon? Fauntleroy."

She smiled pleasantly. "Out of town on an errand," she said. "Do you mind if I look at the warrant?"

"Certainly not," said Judge Cutlip, extracting the sheaf of papers from his breast pocket.

"I'll need my spectacles," she said, reaching for her little black handbag.

"Don't move," snarled Betjeman.

Softly, with a small sigh, Racine pulled her hands away from the bag. Betjeman snagged it and handed it to Flint. He found the gold-rimmed spectacles all right, and also a five-shot, lady-sized revolver. He extracted both items, glad he was in the company of a real lawman, not a pack of deputized merchants.

Cutlip sighed gratefully.

Flint eyed the doorway nervously. He studied Drinker, who sat stupidly in the corridor, almost blocking it, watching blood ooze from a score of buckshot wounds. "They can pin us in here, Sheriff," he said.

Betjeman grunted.

"What did you do to Danny?" she asked.

"There's a warrant for him, too. Where's that gunman?" the sheriff asked.

"What gunman?" she countered.

Betjeman sighed. "All right. We're getting out of here. If we run into trouble, you're likely to get shot. We'll come back for Drinker, if he's alive."

"Why, Arnold, that doesn't make sense. We can come to an agreement."

"I don't bribe," he said sourly.

She turned to her cherubic safe, drew out a flat, black sheet-metal box and unlatched it. All those hundred-dollar greenbacks made Flint dizzy. She smiled gently, saying nothing. Without a word, she pushed the box across her desk.

"That's a crime, too, Odie," Judge Cutlip said.

"Whatever are you talking about? Have I said a word to you?"

Flint heard movement upstairs. The silent building had come alive. The tread of feet reached his ears.

"Let's go, Odie," the sheriff said.

"Why, dear, you'll have to carry me. I hurt my foot."

"Drag you, then," he said. He sprang around the desk, collared her, pulled her right out of that soft chair. She hissed like a rabid cat. All the softness and whiteness drained out of her, and Flint beheld a vicious little catamount. Betjeman unceremoniously marched her around the desk, ripping the neckline of her black-velvet dress as he did so.

She said nothing, breathing raggedly.

"Judge, take the cashbox," Betjeman said. "Get the ledgers later."

Two tinhorns, each armed with a small revolver, materialized in the curtained passageway from the parlor. Betjeman pushed Odie Racine in front of him.

"Lift your arms," Betjeman ordered them, his aimed shotgun speaking as loudly as he. The tinhorns eyed Drinker leaking life into the hallway runner, surveyed the muzzle of Flint's shotgun and Cutlip's revolver, and slowly lifted their arms.

"Drop the guns," the sheriff said.

Both did. One gun went off when it hit the floor, startling Flint. Behind him, Drinker made a harsh sound. Flint glanced backward. A new hole appeared in Drinker's left cheek. The brute slowly toppled backward. Flint felt sick. They all gaped at Drinker for a moment.

Betjeman herded Odie Racine before him, and they pushed into the parlor, where a dozen of her employees milled. Among them were three doxies, one a pasty-faced scarecrow who looked like an elderly widow, another a poor child with a moronic, empty stare, and a buxom black woman in a silvery wrapper. The rest seemed to be squinty tinhorns and tough-looking bartenders.

Betjeman surveyed them. "Don't try. Your boss lady's likely to get hurt," he said.

They worked through, toward the saloon. Betjeman turned to Flint. "Guard our rear," he said.

Flint twisted, walking backward into the saloon while the toughs and tarts watched. A moment later, they reached sunlight. He had scarcely ever seen Odie Racine in the white light of day. She seemed oddly spectral.

"Where's Fauntleroy?" Betjeman asked her as they hiked toward the courthouse.

She smiled.

"Where's your gunman?"

"Looking through his gunsights, dearie," she said.

Flint glanced sharply around the empty street, seeing nothing startling. But that didn't mean the man wasn't watching them, and waiting for the right moment. It made Flint's skin prickle. Two of her most dangerous lieutenants were at large.

They reached the courthouse square, where they could look down Prescott Street, and Flint saw only a deserted business district. It was as if nothing had happened that terrible morning.

They crossed the lawn, entering from the court side, and walked the corridor to the sheriff's office. The building seemed mournful, as if Payday had lost the county seat and this was only a relic of a brief heyday.

Betjeman steered Odie Racine through the door into his deserted office. The sheriff's desk hulked in the corner. They crowded in, not noticing the cell until too late.

The Hired Man lounged there, a pair of revolvers leveled at them, while Fauntleroy pressed into the near wall, holding a leveled shotgun.

Betjeman whirled.

Flint felt ice congeal in his belly, and knew he was dead.

"Don't try it," said the gunman silkily.

"Hello, dearies," Odie said. She freed herself from Betjeman's grip and walked through the opened door into the cell, out of the line of fire.

"Betjeman, put the shotgun on the floor. *Now!*"

Angrily, the sheriff did.

The gunman turned to Flint. "You, too."

Flint thought wildly about pulling the trigger, but knew he lacked that kind of courage. He lowered the shotgun.

"Cutlip, put that cashbox on the desk," said the gunman.

Flint noticed that the judge trembled with every step.

"And leave your revolver there," the gunman added.

"You're talking to a magistrate," Cutlip said.

That evoked mirth in the gunman.

But Basil Cutlip didn't enjoy the humor. He stood more erect, formidable and bulky and stern. "You are talking to a magistrate," he said again, with a voice that brooked no rebuttal.

"Judges croak," the man said easily. And then he snarled, "Put that box down."

Flint's heart hammered. There was something here he dreaded. It wasn't the death or the beating he expected, it was something in Judge Cutlip's demeanor.

Slowly, the judge lowered the heavy box to the desk. The revolver was still in his free hand. He turned and faced the gunman. "You cannot for long terrorize the officials of this county. If you try to, the Territory will rise up and run you to the ground. You may have the upper hand for the moment, but you're doomed. Harm a one of us and you'll sign your own warrant to hell. Lower your weapons. They will only get you in worse trouble."

A deafening crack hurt Flint's ears. He saw the judge stagger backward a step, and then draw himself up. His shirtfront turned red. A cloud of acrid powder smoke filled the cell.

The judge coughed, steadied himself, lifted his hand, cocked the revolver, aimed and fired. The killer died with astonishment plastering his face. The bullet caught him in the heart. Fauntleroy stared at the skinny gunman, who slowly slid onto the bench in the cell. The judge turned slightly, cocked the revolver again, and slowly aimed at Fauntleroy, who hulked at the office wall, frozen. Another deafening shot shattered Flint's ears. Fauntleroy stared stupidly at the judge and sat down on the cell bench, next to the killer, watching himself bleed.

Basil Cutlip walked slowly around the sheriff's desk, eased himself into the sheriff's swivel chair, and died.

53

Sam Flint slouched numbly at his battered desk, unable to work. For the first time in his life, he could not compose stories or set type, or even break down the old issue. Stories cried to be written, but for two days, paralysis had beset him.

Odie Racine's jackal had indeed visited Flint's plant after burning most of the issue in the middle of Prescott Street. But he didn't know much about newspapers. He had collected the rest of the copies and burned them behind the plant, but he had left the type intact in its page forms. It didn't matter. A lot of copies had escaped, passing from hand to hand until nearly everyone in the county had read the issue.

There were times when Flint felt so burdened that he could barely scrape through the hour. If he had not begun his newspaper crusade, good men might still live. He grieved both of his friends, Jerusalem Cobb and Basil Cutlip, sorrowing that he would never see them again, that their lives had been cruelly shortened. But their sacrifice had driven the serpent from Eden.

In less emotional moments, he understood that he was not responsible for either death. He had not pulled the triggers. Each had chosen to fight and to risk death. Jerusalem especially, feeling the nettle of his conscience, had redeemed himself with an act of awesome courage. Oddly enough, Flint sensed that Basil Cutlip had also been redeeming himself, although he had no exact idea of what had been in the judge's mind. The judge's slow, dying act of execution had been so astonishing to the hired killer that it had caught him off guard for the several seconds it took for Basil Cutlip to lift the revolver, cock it, and pull the trigger. It was as if the Magistrate Basil Cutlip had pronounced the death sentence from his bench after all.

Everything that followed the mayhem in Sheriff Betjeman's office had whirled by in a blur. Flint and Betjeman had pulled the still-alive Fauntleroy out of the cell, along with the body of the person who called himself The Hired Man, and had locked Odie Racine within. Fauntleroy still lived, his legs paralyzed by the judge's bullet, his days as a bullyboy over.

Betjeman could never put a name to the wiry, lethal killer who did Odie Racine's dirty work, and eventually the sheriff buried the man in an unmarked grave, not bothering to build him a coffin. No one knew how to reach Drinker's relatives, if any, and so Betjeman buried him beside the skinny gunman. The sheriff carted the groaning Fauntleroy back to the Golden Calf and put him in Racine's dusky-rose bed. He wasn't going anywhere, and if he did, it didn't matter.

Odie Racine languished in the cell. That first night, some of the merchants Betjeman had deputized guarded her to keep the remaining tinhorns and bullyboys from busting her out. But her lieutenants didn't try. Instead, they fled the town, cramming the Tucson stage, or leaving on foot or horseback. Two tinhorns jointly purchased a rig from the livery barn and departed with two of the doxies on board.

The dance-hall girls were still around and the hall stayed open. Flint didn't mind them so much. Some of the less mercenary ones could give the cowboys a whirl without robbing them, and a few would end up getting married. The deserted Golden Calf had been pillaged. The tinhorns had swiped the gaming equipment, and not a bottle of rotgut remained at the bar. Flint had walked through, finding only sinister shadows. Someone had stripped Racine's apartment of every luxury, leaving Fauntleroy on the floor. Flint and Betjeman moved the paralyzed man to one of the old rooms at the back of the Drover's Rest and arranged for his care.

Abel Greene and a young clerk, Nels Gulick's boy, were operating Cobb's mercantile. The town couldn't get along without the grocery and the general merchandise. Each night Greene was recording the day's transactions in Cobb's ledger. Half the town was eager to protect the estate of the young hero, the man they supposed had won the Congressional Medal of Honor, and then proven his courage once again. Via the military wire at Fort Whipple, they had notified Cobb's relatives in Indiana, and had sent word to Cutlip's sons in Illinois, too. Only Flint knew that Jerusalem Cobb had died trying to fill his heroic brother's boots. That story would never be written—at least not until Flint was far away and a lot older. Maybe someday he'd scribble down all the stories he had never published.

County Attorney Culbertson had suddenly gathered courage, once his life was no longer in danger, and had developed a ferocious bill of indictment against Odie Racine. He wanted to keep the confiscated cash as evidence for her trial, and then give it to the county. But that triggered an immediate uproar from each of the merchants who had paid the extortions upon threats to their businesses and lives. In the end, after Greene, Gulick, Short, Wiley, and eleven others had ganged up on him, he grumpily agreed to return the extorted cash to the merchants, in exchange for affidavits declaring each merchant's loss to the extortionists. The affidavits would be evidence enough in court.

But Culbertson insisted on keeping the cash extorted from Zeppel, Cobb, and Cutlip, saying the county needed it for the trial and burial expenses. No one argued very hard against that. He reported that there was a lot of cash left over, the loot earned more or less legitimately from Racine's many businesses. It came to over twenty-seven thousand dollars, a huge sum to milk from a small frontier county. A court would have to settle the ownership of that.

A flurry of wires to Territorial officials had finally won the assurance that the governor would appoint a new magistrate until a special election could be held. There had been talk of appointing Clayton Buell, but Flint knew that the former Reb colonel would never make the grade. The county was pretty much in the hands of Supervisors Jackson and Pollack, as it always had been, and things were running smoothly enough. Both of them had been threatened and extorted by Racine and seemed glad to get their cash back when the furious merchants insisted on it, although Pollack wanted some of the money withheld for more fire and police protection. Flint thought that neither supervisor had shown courage or leadership during the crisis. The *Pioneer* would have something to say about that before the next election.

All these were stories, and Flint knew he had to write them, had to bestir himself out of his slough of despond. He thought that maybe he could start after tomorrow's twin funerals. One of the biggest stories would not begin for a few weeks. The trial of Odie Racine would be the most sensational event in Payday's brief life, and one of the most important stories Flint would ever cover. Betjeman told him that when Alpine County was done with Racine, she would be taken to Denver on warrants, and maybe to El Paso also. Flint doubted that the woman would see much sunlight without bars in between for the rest of her life.

Culbertson had told Flint it would be easy to prove the extortion in court, tougher to demonstrate that she had had anything to do with any murder or beating. The evidence that she had ordered them done just wasn't there. Flint found himself disliking the county attorney, who had been particularly pusillanimous during the worst of it, only to become a bragging blowhard once the danger had receded. Flint suspected that the man had abusively questioned and harassed Racine these past two days, and he made a note to endorse someone else at the next election.

It was odd how things fell out. Cobb had shown unexpected mettle. Cutlip, more entrepreneur than judge, had stunned Flint with his rush of courage. Betjeman, who drifted into the whole affair so inertly, had transformed himself into a tough lawman. But all too many others—merchants, county supervisors, and Culbertson—had crawled into their shells and done nothing.

Flint meant to interview Odie Racine himself if she would consent to it. She just might, he thought, if she could think of something to say in public that might mitigate her sentence. He had started toward the jail the day before, intent on getting a story, but when he stepped into Betjeman's office, his spirit left him. She sat there behind the bars, puffy and arrogant and dead silent. She was speaking to no one but the Prescott attorney she'd hired. Flint stared at her: the source of so much of Payday's grief, the serpent in Eden who had taken away the innocence of the Tonto Basin evermore. And he didn't feel like interviewing her. So he had left the jail, still trapped in a lethargy he couldn't overcome.

That afternoon he summoned up enough energy to begin breaking down the special issue. He trucked the heavy front-page chase over to the bench where his caseboxes rested, intending to break it down. But as he gazed at the momentous page, he loved it. That page, with its "Anarchy" headline, had stirred the town into throwing off its oppressors. That page had saved a community. That page had been composed and set under the eye of cyclops, distributed under the counter, handed out furtively by the town's merchants. He wanted to frame it. He would never write another issue like it.

He remembered that he had stashed a few copies in his outhouse, and went back there to find them. If they weren't there, he intended to run a few issues off, two for his permanent file, and at least one to frame. This proud issue was going to look down from his shop wall, framed and under glass, for as long as he owned the *Pioneer*. But the hidden papers were there, stuffed into a corner of the little privy, and he brought them in. He'd have Tony Stapleton build a handsome frame for each page of that memorable issue.

He thought to himself that this was why he had become a newsman. Yes, a paper's principal purpose was to report the news and earn a profit. But once in a while, a paper could become a beacon, a lantern, a bonfire for the good.

Inspired by his triumph over melancholia, he swiftly broke down the pages, tossing Caslon type back into its cases, removing the wooden "furniture" that yielded white space on a page, and shelving his small, precious supply of large display type that had produced the bold headline.

No one would thank him for that issue. The public never saw it that way. Most men on the street would tell him that he was simply trying to sell copies or jack up the advertising revenue. That was an odd thing about a newspaper. Let it do a public service, risk its plant and its people for a public good, and most of its readers would never suppose there was anything but commercial interest in it.

But Flint didn't mind. He had healed a community, and that was reward enough.

54

Flint thought the double funeral was impressive. Payday's Baptist minister officiated. Flint estimated the throng at over a thousand. They sat on the grass or stood, absorbing the mild December-afternoon sun. The minister got it right: Cobb had made a heroic try to rescue his community; Judge Cutlip, even while dying, had somehow delivered the fatal blow to the "Powers of Darkness," the phrase the cleric used to describe the madam who had almost bled Payday and Alpine County to death.

It seemed an odd funeral to Flint because no grieving relatives were present. Abel Greene had organized the affair, appointed the pallbearers, and selected the sites in the growing cemetery south of Payday. They buried Cutlip beside his beloved Violet, and Cobb alone. There would be stones for each, given by a grateful community.

No one mentioned Flint, or the role the *Pioneer* had played in all this, and he was grateful. He never had sought public acclaim. People tended to be matter-of-fact about newspapers, which suited him fine. In the three days since the liberation of Payday, no one had stopped in to congratulate him, or to admire that crusading issue, or even to thank him. That was all right, too. A paper could be more effective if it didn't seek the limelight. And anyway, it really had been Cobb and Cutlip and Betjeman who'd rescued Payday, and to them the credit would always belong.

He took notes. The minister gave Flint a draft of the eulogies. Most everyone Flint knew in Payday had come. He knew so many in the community now. It had always been wondrous to him the way a newsman got to know most everybody. He sensed a change in mood. For months, fear and anger had coiled through the soul of the town, an unspoken darkness that hung over it. That had vanished. Now Payday could grow, breathe, progress. Now it would be safe. There wouldn't be much of a tenderloin, just a few solid saloons where drovers off the ranches could have a good time and blow their monthly salary.

He had a new campaign in mind. It was time for Payday to incorporate, elect a mayor and a council. Then Payday would be less a creature of the county courthouse. Meanwhile, the county would have Odie Racine's loot to pay for a volunteer fire department, some deputy sheriffs, and a county school system.

When it was over, and they laid hothouse flowers on the graves, and the crowd broke up, he wandered back to his office, intending to begin the work he had listlessly avoided for so long. But he was waylaid.

Merry-Grace Rakoczy beelined toward him, with old Clayton Buell beside her. Her arm was in his, and she looked radiant in her perpetual white.

"Sam!" she cried, breaking loose to hug him. "Oh, Sam." She stopped suddenly, a flush of confusion crossing her lovely face.

Flint found himself shaking hands with his tormentor, and then they fell into silence. The colonel straightened himself and broke it. "Mistah Flint, Ah want to introduce you to Mrs. Buell. Ah don't care what you print, as long as you call her Mrs. Buell."

So they had done it. Flint saw the blush in Merry-Grace's cheeks, and the wordless embarrassment that said worlds of things to him.

"Congratulations to you both," Flint said gravely. "Colonel Buell, I believe a newspaper should stick to public matters. Whatever private arrangements you've made are your own business. From now on, you are Mr. and Mrs. Buell. It'll be as simple as that."

Buell nodded stiffly.

"Oh, Sam . . ." she said tenderly, and he felt lovesick again, wishing life had taken a different turn. His itchy feet had doomed that dream. But he couldn't throttle his hunger for her, which flooded like lava through him as he peered into her soft, warm face and saw the brightness of her spirit and the fond, knowing look she gave him. Without saying a word, she was telling him that the rivers of their lives had come close, but had never mingled.

He wanted to ask her if she was happy, but he realized he didn't need to. She was aglow. She had that bridal bloom about her, shining in her warm eyes, radiating from her golden complexion, lifting her soft lips into smiles. He had lost her. It pierced him. The strange couple in the strange circumstance had made a blessed union. He ached to know everything: how they lived, what her sons thought, what arrangements they had made. How he was treating Nicholas's property. And especially, whether he was good to her. But he could not intrude. A veil lay across their lives. Neither Flint the newsman nor Flint the man who loved Merry-Grace would ever know.

He excused himself and hastened toward his shop, passing along Prescott Street, where small signs on the doors announced that the stores would be closed this afternoon. He hurried past somberly dressed people who were smiling, enjoying the release and relief of a new regime in Payday.

In his sanctum at last, he shed his only dark suitcoat, donned his printer's smock, and pulled out his type stick. He would begin with the funerals. He knew he would be setting type deep into the night. This issue, in its way, would herald a town's victory, just as the previous one had heralded its subjugation and doom.

But the door opened and the Thimble family filed in, each dressed for the funeral. He had missed them in the throng. Horatio looked splendid, and so did Gertrude and the boys.

"Well, Horatio, it's been a long time," Flint said, setting aside his work.

"Yes, and a pity it took a funeral to bring us here," Thimble said. "I want to thank you, not just on behalf of my family, but for everyone in Alpine County."

"I'm touched."

"I have the sense that people don't quite know what you did, or the risks you took. But I know. I worked here long enough to grasp it."

"It really was Judge Cutlip who freed us, Horatio."

"No, Sam. Without your inspiration, he would have done nothing."

Flint didn't argue. That was probably true. Cutlip's final moments had seemed out of character for an entrepreneur bent on repairing his fortunes.

"We read your issue, and it put goose bumps on my arms," Gertrude said. "I thought you wouldn't live to see the sunrise."

"Well, I wasn't sure I would either."

"I suppose I always knew the power of a truthful newspaper, at least in some abstract way," she said. "But this . . . this brought it home to me. You might consider yourself simply a businessman, seeking profit. But an editor is anointed by fate. You can make a place better, or you can let it slide into vice and uncaring."

Flint was beginning to feel uncomfortable with all this. "Horatio, how goes the battle? I mean, on your homestead."

"Well, I want to tell you about that. We put our sheep on, and Buell hasn't threatened us."

"He has other things on his mind."

"Mrs. Rakoczy, yes. They've taken up with each other. I don't know what to make of it."

"Bless them," Flint said. "No matter what the world may think, they did an honorable thing."

"It'll take some pondering," Thimble said uneasily. "I do not think any mortal should lightly toss aside the laws of God and man."

"I know how you feel, Horatio. But it's for the best, I think. I only hope it'll make life easier for you."

"Well, it already has. A while ago, we discovered that our small flock had suddenly multiplied. It had grown overnight to about two hundred fifty animals. We did a count and found that our flock had increased by a hundred eighty. Almost all of them pregnant ewes. A few rams."

Flint grinned. "Buell paid you back."

"Well, now there's a strange case. We thought so, too. I rode over there to thank him, and they told me he was now at the Rakoczy ranch. So I rode there to thank him, and he denied it. Not only that, but he got mad. He told me he'd burn us out one of these days if we didn't leave. But he doesn't. The days fly by. The herd fattens. The ewes'll lamb in a few weeks." He smiled. "I thanked him anyway, and he glared at me as if I were mad."

"That's Clayton Buell's way, I guess."

Thimble nodded. "I know you're busy, Sam. We'll be off now. Hate to leave the flock alone, even with two good herd dogs."

Flint nodded. "Horatio, I could use you here."

"I know, I know," he said.

Flint saw them out and returned to his work, pleased that the Thimbles had recovered their losses. There was so much to write. Sunlight burst through the windows, turning his sanctum golden. It was almost like being in a church. He found himself composing and setting a story, even while his mind wandered far away.

This was truly Eden, he thought. Now these people would be all right. They would be protected in their persons and their homes. They would tax themselves lightly to ensure that. This was a free land, and people would succeed or fail on their own merits. Opportunity sprang from the very earth here, and good men and women would prosper and pass along their achievements to future generations.

But Flint knew he would leave soon. The restlessness ate at him again. If he stayed, he would only look back to this moment of triumph, and pretty soon grow cantankerous and hostile to change. But there was a larger reason: he could not live here, near Merry-Grace, and yearn his life away, or pine whenever she came to Payday. He could not ever have her. No matter where his home might be in the decades ahead, he would always live east of Eden.

Someday soon, he would sell the *Pioneer,* harness up Sherman and Grant, and go on down the road. Maybe he would sell the paper to Thimble. He thought it possible that the old veteran and his wife would prefer town life soon, and see their sons marry and develop the family freeholding. That notion pleased him. Thimble would be a great editor, connected to the next generation and able to hold up the torch.

He thought he knew what his future held. He would drift from town to town, breeding little papers as if they were children. It would not be as good a life as one with Merry-Grace, but it would be good.

He began to think about New Mexico.